D1362560

Published in this format 2015 by Victrix Books

Copyright - S.J.A. Turney

First Edition

Marius' Mules VIII

Sons of Taranis

by S. J. A. Turney

1st Edition

"Marius' Mules: nickname acquired by the legions after the general Marius made it standard practice for the soldier to carry all of his kit about his person."

*For all my loyal readers, still
with me after eight years of
Fronto's troubles. Thank you all
from the bottom of my heart*

I would like to thank those people who helped bring Marius' Mules 8 to completion and make it a readable tome. That's Jenny and Lilian for their initial editing, my beautiful wife Tracey for her support and love, my two wonderful kids for endless procrastinating interruptions. My top cadre Leni, Barry, Paul, Robin, Alun & Stu for beta reading and catching the really dubious typos and issues.

Thanks also to Garry and Dave for the cover work and innumerable other fab folk for their support (you all know who you are, and so do I.)

Cover photos by Hannah Haynes, courtesy of Paul and Garry of the Deva Victrix Legio XX. Visit http://www.romantoursuk.com/ to see their excellent work.

Cover design by Dave Slaney.

Many thanks to the above for their skill and generosity.

Also by S. J. A. Turney:

Continuing the Marius' Mules Series

Marius' Mules I: The Invasion of Gaul (2009)
Marius' Mules II: The Belgae (2010)
Marius' Mules III: Gallia Invicta (2011)
Marius' Mules IV: Conspiracy of Eagles (2012)
Marius' Mules V: Hades' Gate (2013)
Marius' Mules VI: Caesar's Vow (2014)
Marius' Mules: Prelude to War (2014)
Marius' Mules VII: The Great Revolt (2014)

The Praetorian Series

The Great Game (2015)

The Ottoman Cycle

The Thief's Tale (2013)
The Priest's Tale (2013)
The Assassin's Tale (2014)
The Pasha's Tale (2015)

Tales of the Empire

Interregnum (2009)
Ironroot (2010)
Dark Empress (2011)

Short story compilations & contributions:

Tales of Ancient Rome vol. 1 - S.J.A. Turney (2011)
Tortured Hearts vol 1 - Various (2012)
Tortured Hearts vol 2 - Various (2012)
Temporal Tales - Various (2013)
A Year of Ravens - Various (Nov 2015)

For more information visit http://www.sjaturney.co.uk/
or http://www.facebook.com/SJATurney
or follow Simon on Twitter @SJATurney

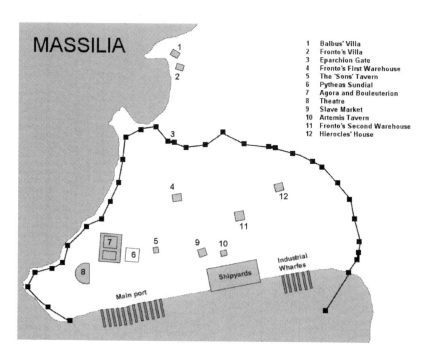

MASSILIA

1 Balbus' Villa
2 Fronto's Villa
3 Eparchion Gate
4 Fronto's First Warehouse
5 The 'Sons' Tavern
6 Pytheas Sundial
7 Agora and Bouleuterion
8 Theatre
9 Slave Market
10 Artemis Tavern
11 Fronto's Second Warehouse
12 Hierocles' House

Industrial Wharfes

Shipyards

Main port

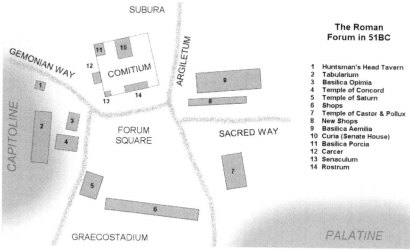

SUBURA

GEMONIAN WAY

COMITIUM

ARGILETUM

CAPITOLINE

FORUM SQUARE

SACRED WAY

GRAECOSTADIUM

PALATINE

The Roman Forum in 51BC

1 Huntsman's Head Tavern
2 Tabularium
3 Basilica Opimia
4 Temple of Concord
5 Temple of Saturn
6 Shops
7 Temple of Castor & Pollux
8 New Shops
9 Basilica Aemilia
10 Curia (Senate House)
11 Basilica Porcia
12 Carcer
13 Senaculum
14 Rostrum

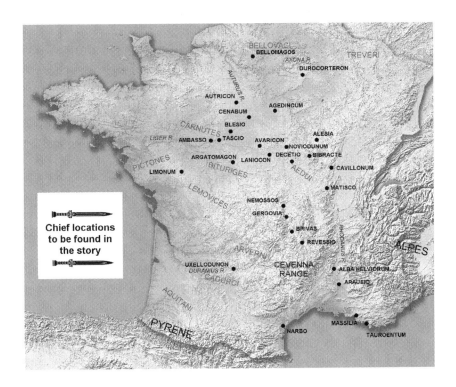

Chief locations to be found in the story

Prologue

AULUS Vincentius stamped his feet in the cold morning air and blew into his frozen hands, his eyes playing across his meagre domain while the adjutant rattled on and on about supply routes and wagon capacities, traders' fees and endless excruciating mundanities. The young, pink faced clerk seemed oblivious to his commander's waning interest as he trotted out figures and facts that went unheard.

Beyond the eager fellow, the depot that had been Vincentius' home and command – and prison – for most of the winter languished under a frost that had killed off all forms of optimistic life, as well as the commander's spirit. As a decurion, he had led a turma of cavalry in the heroic actions at the foot of Alesia's slopes mere months ago, when the Gauls were making their last great bid for freedom. And now? Now the only time he drew his blade was to check it for the inevitable rust, which he would then have the young clerk polish out for him while he rotted away in a sullen mood in his unpleasant quarters. His eyes drifted to that building which, even though he hated it with every fibre of his being, still looked inviting when compared to the cold outdoors and the monotonous reports of the adjutant.

Home. A simple round structure with a stone base as high as the windowsill and timber walls above, topped with a conical thatched roof that was home to a million dreadful spiders and which let in more weather than it kept out. And next to that: a small shed which was young Plautus' accommodation. Other than those two structures, the entire complex consisted of six large supply sheds, one granary, a well, and a stockade that would have trouble holding out against an onslaught of octogenarians. And the goat. Mustn't forget the goat. The stinking, noisy, over-affectionate goat. He wondered maliciously whether he should take pity on the goat and quarter it with Plautus?

Since the collapse of the great rebellion, things had calmed down considerably in Gaul. There were still troubles here and there, and there were endless rumours of new revolts that would be raised in various quarters of the country. But Vincentius had seen the slave trains at the end of last year, heading for Massilia and the *Graecostadia* slave market in Rome. They had looked like hopeless, dishevelled legions marching to war, there were so many of them. And the burial pits after Alesia had been *vast*. After eight years of war, more than half the population of this entire benighted region

1

had been either killed or enslaved. A new rebellion? By whom... the cows? Because there were more of *them* now than men – or there would have been had they not also been butchered and commandeered by Rome. No, there might be a few small troubles to deal with, but the considered opinion of all the senior officers was that Gaul's resistance had collapsed.

Why anyone actually wanted this land in the first place rather baffled Aulus Vincentius.

'Sir?'

He looked ahead once more, focusing on young Plautus. Young? The lad was probably the same age as him in truth, but his eagerness for this dismal supply depot duty made him seem so much younger.

'What?'

'Do we hire four new men, sir, or do we wait for instructions from command?' the man repeated with exaggerated patience.

Vincentius huffed and blew angrily into his hands again. It had both surprised and irritated him when he'd been given this command that he'd had no Roman troops assigned to him. Legionaries would pass through regularly of course, with the supply wagons, but his grand command had consisted of four surly, ill-spoken, hairy, stinking locals who resented his very existence. They had been paid monthly – more than Vincentius thought they could ever be worth, but apparently they were Aedui tribesmen and therefore the commanders seemed to think they needed to be looked after. At least they spoke Latin, even if only as well as a three year old. But then two days ago the four men had gone off-duty, leaving the two Roman officers alone and rather defenceless in the depot, and had gone to carouse in Decetio across the hill. And they'd not come back.

Personally, Vincentius couldn't care less what happened to them, but for two reasons. Firstly, a huge caravan was due in from Massilia heading north to the winter quarters of the legions, which would require a full complement of workers. And secondly, while he hated the locals, and trusted them about as far as he could kick the goat, it felt a lot less safe with only Plautus keeping him company.

'Take the coins from the pay chest and head into Decetio. There'll be a few likely lads that will jump at the chance of steady payment to ride out the winter. See if you can cut the pay offer and still get strong men, though, Plautus. Might as well skim a few coins from the top and make this awful place worthwhile.'

2

As the young cavalryman saluted and wandered off about his business, Vincentius pulled his cloak – an item of apparel that made about as much difference as a gossamer tunic in this weather – tight around him and scurried off back to his hovel. As he approached, he noted with some relief that at least his adjutant had got a fire going while he'd been out for a shit and a wash. A grey column drifted up from the smoke-hole in the centre of the roof.

With immense gratitude, Vincentius pushed open the door of his accommodation, pausing just inside for a moment to let his eyes adjust as the door clunked shut behind him. The difference in comfort of the interior's fire-lit warmth – even if it did still smell of the goat which had clearly lived here before him – was palpable, and he dropped the ice-cold cloak onto the chest near the door and strode over towards the small central hearth, rubbing his hands and anticipating the warm orange glow.

He barely noticed the movement in the periphery of his vision, but some sense made him look up away from the fire, the lights still dancing wild in his retinas, just as the figures emerged from the shadows at the edge of the room. Three thoughts ran through his mind in quick succession.

Where is my sword?

Are these my missing workers?

Where is Plautus?

The answers were clear, and not encouraging. His sword was by his bed at the far side of the room, along with anything else of use. There were more than four men here, and they did not have the same churlish air that he'd come to recognise from his Aedui workers, radiating more menace than irritation. And Plautus would be somewhere out in the compound going about the endless tasks that kept him busy.

He tried to shout out in alarm, but a huge hand clamped across his mouth and stifled the noise. How many figures there were, he couldn't tell, but he could see half a dozen before him, and felt the presence of more behind. They moved like hunting cats, with grace and silence – so eerily, in fact, that he wondered for a moment if they were lemures – the restless dead – come to claim a living victim.

But these were no spirits, for all the terror with which they filled him. Each wore a dark wool cloak that had blended with the shadows at the room's edge, rendering them almost invisible, and beneath the hoods as they looked upon the Roman commander, emotionless,

3

staring cold faces peered out. Identical ones, too. Masks, he realised with what might have been relief had he not been quite so terrified. All of them wore masks much like the cult ones he'd seen the natives using at their religious ceremonies.

Gauls then?

He felt his bowels and bladder fighting him for independence, and struggled to free himself, but the man who held him had a grip like iron and was enormous, his shoulders at Vincentius' head level and his arms like sides of beef.

Who are you? he wanted to ask.

Please don't hurt me was what he wanted to say most.

The very idea that they might be here for anything other than violence was ridiculous. Especially as the man before him stepped forward and his cloak billowed out to reveal a heavy Gallic sword at one side of his belt and a sickle – *a sickle!* – tucked into the other.

'You and I, Roman,' gurgled a voice like boiling pitch bubbling up from Tartarus, 'are going to have a talk. And if your words please me, you will die quickly.'

Plautus sighed as he shouldered his saddle, buffed to a gleaming state of which even his father would have approved. It was not that he hated his lot in life. After the carnage he'd taken part in at Alesia, this duty was a pleasant rest, really. It was just Decurion Vincentius' attitude and bad temper that got him down. No matter what Plautus did to try and improve matters, the officer just didn't seem to care. Or even to notice.

Still, despite the man's attitude, Plautus had managed to strike up a reasonable rapport with a few of the locals, who, he had discovered, if you treated them as equals, returned the favour. He knew an inn at Decetio where the owner kept a stock of not-unpleasant wine, and was even happy to extend him credit if Vincentius was slow with the pay. And there was a very friendly girl in Decetio, too. He decided that the decurion had pissed him off enough already today that he would be inconveniently late back from the city, giving him plenty of time to enjoy the local comforts. He could spin out any old tale of delays to Vincentius. The man never listened to him anyway.

Taking a deep breath and preparing for more scorn, boredom and insults, he rapped on the decurion's door and walked inside.

4

His saddle hit the floor, raising a cloud of dust and goat-hair as he stared at the tableau before him.

Decurion Aulus Vincentius sat before him next to the fire. All around was a pool of gleaming dark liquid in which he sat, unmoving. His feet and hands had been removed – Plautus realised suddenly what was causing the smell of roasting pork, and vomited copiously – and the officer's torso had been opened up with a razor-sharp implement and ravaged, so that his innards were strewn before him on the floor.

Plautus shivered and stared, panicked and sickened, and barely even registered the dark shapes detaching themselves from the shadows at the room's edge and converging on him.

* * * * *

Fronto shuffled in his seat, the cold marble surface barely improved by the single threadbare cushion the brusque attendant had sold him, at a price that had made him mutter and chunter all the way through the corridors and stairwells until he arrived in the stands and at his assigned seat. He glanced left and right. Lucilia seemed perfectly happy, riveted to this performance and with a small smile of satisfaction playing about her lips. Balbus, his father-in-law, ageing and with more white hair on his eyebrows than his head, seemed quiet and content. But then he'd been asleep for the past ten minutes, so he had every right to look relaxed.

Down in the circular orchestra area a man with a ridiculously over-balancing fake bosom tottered around on huge wooden-heeled shoes shrieking out in a 'feminine voice' that sounded like a cat being punctured. The chorus hovered at the edge of the stage, their masks permanent frowns of dismay.

'From the mountains I brought this tendril of freshly cut ivy,' honked and warbled the excruciatingly unfeminine actor. 'Our hunt was blessed!'

The chorus thrummed their response, which Fronto missed, submerged beneath his unstoppable yawn which raised a flash of anger from his wife. It wasn't *his* fault. Well, it was *partially* his fault, admittedly. He never did like tragedies. Miserable, bloodthirsty tales that whiled away a few hours in pointless tedium. Not like a good ribald Roman comedy full of bouncing breasts and humorous misunderstandings and slaves who kept falling over things. But the

Greeks really did love their tragedy. In fact, Greek *comedy* was usually more depressing than Roman tragedies. There was always someone who didn't deserve it getting their eyes put out or being hacked to pieces. Only a few moments ago in this dire rubbish, some messenger in a smiley mask (he'd obviously picked up the wrong prop!) had wandered onto the stage to tell the chorus and the crowd how old Pentheus had been torn limb from limb by ravaging maenads.

Lucilia was always telling him off for relating true stories of the campaign across Gaul that had been so much a part of his life for the last decade, telling him to watch what he said in front of the boys and that he could try and tone down the blood and guts in his stories. Yet while his leisure pursuits tended towards the humorously hedonistic, Lucilia was more than content to sit through hours of Greeks with bad fake boobs ripping pieces off each other and tearing out tongues. If he lived to be a hundred, Fronto swore he would never understand women.

He was aware that his attention had now entirely drifted from the play.

He'd have loved to see some good Roman comedy, but that was one problem with living on the edge of Massilia. Though the land his villa stood on had been claimed as part of the province by Rome, the *boule* – the council – of Massilia still claimed it as theirs. And Massilia was Greek. It may be surrounded by the republic, and there were a number of Roman business concerns in the city, along with a large number of Roman citizens, but the place was still an independent Greek city, and proud of the fact. Consequently there were no uplifting Roman plays to be seen here – just the endless soul destroying tragedies of Greece. There were no bouts in the arena… there *was* no arena. And even the narrow defile that served as a stadium was only used for horse racing at best, far too narrow and tight-cornered for chariots.

Thank Fortuna that the city was seething with *thermopolia*. The small bars and eateries that lurked in most of the city's central streets served a very cosmopolitan array of food and drink and Lucilia had been surprisingly lax in terms of keeping him under control all winter. He kept waiting for the noose to tighten, and had begun to suspect that she was allowing him his one solid bad habit in an attempt to limit the number of lesser habits in which he *could* have been indulging.

6

And perhaps she *was* just being kind, in fairness. Since Alesia, his sleep pattern had been erratic at best. Something deep inside had been triggered during that nightmare of blood and bodies, and he could count on one hand the number of full, uninterrupted nights' sleep he'd had over the winter. In fact it had now gone far enough that he'd begun working on the principle that three to four hours a night was his norm. He knew it wasn't doing him good, too. The black smudges beneath his eyes were evidence of that, as was the fact that some time last week he had dozed off with so little warning that he'd fallen face first into his stew. Only Lucilia's quick reactions had stopped him drowning in mutton gravy.

'*Aaaaaahhhhhhhhhh!*'

Fronto flinched. What was it with these Greeks? The 'woman' was shrieking again now, his/her awful voice given terrible reach and strength by the excellent acoustics of this Greek-style theatre that formed a horseshoe shape around a circular performance area. He blinked as he realised that she was actually screaming now, not singing some drivel about Pentheus and perverts hiding in trees. And he could see why. The white front of her dress was soaking through with a blooming circle of dark red as blood gushed out into the fabric. The screeching shifted up a tone as something happened and a steel point, gleaming with the crimson of fresh blood, emerged from the front between the fake breasts. The actor shuddered and gurgled as the strange cloaked figure behind rammed in the sword point and twisted for a confirmed and most agonising kill.

Fronto stared in horror and turned to Lucilia, who was applauding slowly, her face sombre but pleased. What in the name of...?

Fronto woke with a start and almost fell forward off his seat into the audience members in front. Lucilia gave him a disapproving shake of the head and rolled her eyes. 'You need to see another herbalist. There are some very highly recommended ones in the town.'

Fronto shuddered at the memory of that last imagined scene as below, in the orchestra, the man/woman on the tottering heels was swinging a head made from a tragic mask wrapped in a wig. Tendrils of red and brown rags hung from the fake severed neck in a surprisingly effective imitation of ravaged flesh and blood. He shuddered again as the woman warbled in her cracked masculine voice to her father, waffling on about animals.

'Why does she have a head?'

Lucilia blinked and frowned at him. 'How long have you been asleep?'

'I don't know. Since November, I think.'

'The head is her son's. She and her maenad sisters tore him apart in the tree top.'

'Ah yes. I remember that. And what's this about the lion?'

'She thinks it's a lion she's carrying. Not her son.'

'She needs to study her wildlife a little more, then.'

Lucilia's glare could have outstripped Medusa's gaze, and Fronto quailed.

'Sorry. Look, I'm not enjoying this.'

'It's almost over.'

'Even your father's gone to sleep, and he was looking forward to it.'

'My father is past his sixtieth summer, Marcus. You have not the excuse of age.'

'I have the excuse of exhaustion and boredom. I'll see you out by the exit in half an hour. I need to find some refreshment.'

'Try not to have so much 'refreshment' that you can't walk home this time.'

Fronto sighed. 'I'm not debauching myself, Lucilia. It's just that the more I douse myself, the better chance there is that I might sleep through until at least past midnight.'

He realised that his voice had become gradually louder as he talked and that other spectators nearby were glaring at him. Shrugging at them apologetically, he patted Lucilia on the shoulder, gave her a quick kiss on the cheek and scurried out from the seats, making for the exit.

It wasn't just the bad dreams since Alesia that were killing his healthy nights. There was business, too. Four months into his new career as an importer of wine he was finding out just how hard it was to make a profit in the mercantile world. Especially in a thriving Greek port where Romans had no special advantage. Balbus had helped subsidise his business from the start, but even the unconventional old man had been slightly disapproving of Fronto, with all his rank and position, lowering himself to the world of commerce. The gods alone knew what his sister and mother would say when they found out. His hope had been to fund it himself, or at least with Balbus' aid, and not to have to dip into the family's coffers. That way he could keep his dealings from the family until his business was thriving and he could simply put a factor in charge of it and sit back to reap the profits. *That* was a good old Roman way. But the longer the winter dragged on, the less it looked like the wine import trade would thrive. In fact, if he didn't find another source of income soon to help support it, he might have to give up and try something else.

And that didn't bear thinking about...

His mother, sister, wife and father-in-law had all expected him to either take up some important provincial posting, perhaps when the Gallic war was a memory and the newly-conquered lands had been defined as a province in itself, or at least to take a leading role in Massilia's own government.

And although he would prefer to sit and debate with the democratic council of the Greek city than to idle in the curia of Rome and listen to senators trying to outdo one another, still it held little interest for him. Perhaps, if the wine trade failed, he could persuade the boule of Massilia to take a step into the world of gladiators or chariot racing. Then he could start up a faction of chariots or build a *ludus* to train fighters. He'd even considered going back to the army, when the markets had first almost broken him. Balbus had bailed him out, but not before he'd already half-written the letter to Caesar.

It wasn't even the dreams that were stopping him from going back. It was the knowledge that there was no place for him there. Soon the great army that Caesar had led around Gaul for eight years would disband. Caesar would return to Rome to take up a consulship, those legions that had come with his proconsular position would be assigned to his replacement. The ones granted to him by the senate would be returned and probably disbanded, as would be all those Caesar had levied himself. Without the great spectre of Gallic revolt, there would be no need for the army. So there was no point returning to an army that would be split up and disbanded within the year.

He sighed and reached up instinctively for the thousandth time to fondle the twin figurines at his throat, and once again sighed that they weren't there – one broken and the other given to the Arvernian noble at Alesia. He was convinced that the absence of Fortuna from his person was at least partially responsible for his business' failure, if not for his poor sleep. He'd tried replacing them at the markets of Massilia, but to no avail. The Greeks did not recognise Fortuna. Oh, they sort of did. But they called her Tyche, and in the few usable figurines he'd found of Tyche, she was wearing a flouncy Greek-style *himation* dress and holding up what appeared to be a misshapen club. Not at all like his very sober Fortuna in a stola and palla holding the cornucopia with a wheel of fortune at her knee. Somehow he felt his patron goddess might be a little insulted by the oddness of the shift. But he would have to do *something* about it. And the Greeks recognised Nemesis the same as the Romans, but even in Rome she was rarely actively worshipped outside of gladiator circles, and so no Nemesis pendant had shown up across the months.

He huffed his despondency into the cold afternoon air and his heart sank slightly again as he spotted Aurelius making for him across the square. The former legionary had a face like Jupiter's arse after too much Greek food, which boded badly. And he was carrying a ledger, so it was something to do with the business again.

He looked up at the leaden-grey sky and wondered whether the sky looked any better at Samarobriva four or five hundred miles to the north, where the army wintered. As he stared into the clouds, trying to ignore Aurelius' clamour, the first drop of rain hit him in the eye.

* * * * *

Quintus Atius Varus sat at the small table, an uneaten platter of pork and bread going cold before him as he watched the parade of misery trudge past.

'That's the third one this month,' Brutus noted from the far side of the table.

Varus nodded as he watched the column of slaves shuffling forward, roped at the neck, legionaries hurrying back and forth along the lines, keeping them moving. Behind them, carts were rolling along, loaded with supplies for the arduous, interminable journey – over four hundred miles to Massilia, and then a sea-voyage to Ostia and Rome, where they would further deluge the already flooded slave market. Reports of slave prices plummeting were rife in missives from home, and the nobles of Rome apparently did little but mutter about Caesar devaluing their own stocks and of the potential for yet another slave uprising, given that they now outnumbered the free folk in the city.

10

'This one's not as big. Seems to be the last, too. Look: they're sickly and weak. These are the ones who were too weak to travel during the snows last month. They've been fattened up a bit and now they'll march to the sea, but I'd wager you twenty denarii that more than a third of them die before they get there.'

Brutus sighed and stole a piece of bread from Varus' platter, dipping it in the rich brown stock and savouring the taste in this cold, grey world of northern Gaul as the cavalry officer continued.

'That particular train, you might notice, has Caesar's mark. The profit from those slaves is not going to the army and the province, you know? It's filling the general's personal coffers alone.'

'Who can blame him, Varus? In a year or so he'll have to lay down his command and return to Rome. He'll want to take a profit with him.'

Varus grunted noncommittally. 'Very wise men are saying that more than a third of the population of Gaul has been sent to Rome in chains.'

Brutus swallowed noisily, winced at a twinge of indigestion, and replied, 'and other wise men say another third are dead. Gallic corpses will be feeding the plants of this land for years. That's probably why the whole place is so green and fertile.'

'That and the rain.'

'You're in a cheerful mood today, Varus.'

'I'm sick of winter.' He grunted again and slapped a palm on the table. 'And I'm sick of war, and I'm sick of Gaul. We should have followed Fronto's lead and become civilians. Sunning ourselves on the southern coast with nothing to worry about other than whether our jars of wine have gone bad.'

'That time is coming soon enough, Varus. As soon as Caesar returns to Rome we'll all be going with him. I'm bound for a praetorship, I think, though if Caesar has enough pull in the senate when he's made consul, I might even secure a provincial governorship early. Somewhere warm like Cilicia or Crete sounds like a damn dream after soggy Gaul, eh? And what of you, Varus? Back to Rome for good, or will you try to secure a province with your newfound riches and the general's goodwill?'

'Let's try and make it through Gaul first.'

'Gods, but you're fun today.'

Varus sighed yet again and turned to his companion. 'Don't kid yourself into thinking this is all over, Decimus Brutus. We broke

11

them at Alesia, but we've got plenty of fights ahead of us yet before this place can be safely left and settled. How long have you been watching the Gauls? Do you think the people we fought at Gergovia and Alesia are going to just lie down and accept defeat?'

'You don't think they'll try again, surely?' Brutus replied incredulously. 'After their land's been stripped of two thirds of its population? They're going to find it hard with this few people just making it through the next few harvests. They couldn't *possibly* consider fighting on.'

. Varus coughed in the cold air and watched the resulting cloud of frosted breath dissipate. 'The farmers and craftsmen? No. Nor the women, the children and those who still have a family to protect. But remember how many leaders and warriors there were on that hill where the reserves waited opposite Alesia? They left bitter and angry. That's never a good combination in anyone, but to the Gauls it's fuel. The land will never rise again like it did under that Arverni son of a war-dog Vercingetorix, but there are plenty of lesser chieftains who'll fight on just through sheer bloody-mindedness, determined to make us pay for every foot of land we control. Mark my words, Decimus: before the spring thaw we'll be putting out small fires of revolution all over the bloody place.'

Brutus paused, clearly seeing the truth in his friend's words, the cavalry officer's gloomy mood beginning to infect him too. 'And Caesar can't afford to leave Gaul restless when he goes back to Rome. All those fires will have to be out within the year.'

'See what I mean? Caesar's preparing for his consulship. He'll have the position and the money, and he's always had the plebs behind him, especially when he wins something big. But if he goes home to the adoration of the Roman people claiming to have brought them Gaul as a province, he can't afford to have rebellion flare up in his wake. Then even the plebs might turn against him.'

'So what do you plan to do?'

Varus shrugged. 'I plan to eat my cold pork, drink some sour wine, then go and brush down my horse, and make sure my slave's got my saddle polished and all my kit in good order. I'm going to need it soon enough, I reckon.'

Brutus nodded wearily and watched his friend chew on a piece of poor quality meat before turning back to the slave column. At a conservative estimate of thirty denarii, even for these poor quality specimens, the column just leaving camp represented perhaps thirty or forty thousand denarii. If Caesar's factor in Rome was worth his salt, the net gain could even go up to hundred thousand denarii. And this was the meagrest of the slave columns so far.

By the gods, Caesar really *was* feathering his nest…

Chapter One

CAVARINOS, nobleman of the Arverni, former chieftain and general in the great war against Rome, perked up at the familiar voice and rose from his chair, taking the mug of frothing ale with him to the window, where he peered out.

The central square of Uxellodunon was suddenly thriving after an hour of near-emptiness. Perhaps two dozen nobles from a number of different tribes were striding resolutely across the packed earth towards the large inn where Cavarinos had lodged this past week. He could see men of the Cadurci, his own Arverni and the Ruteni, whose lands bordered these to the south. There were others too. He couldn't precisely identify them, but would have been willing to bet they were Carnutes, Bituriges and Aedui. Their warriors trooped along in an unruly bunch behind them all, eyeing each other as suspiciously as they would had the men next to them been wearing a toga. But even the sight of a gathering of nobles from different tribes was not what made Cavarinos shake his head sadly. That was the sight of Lucterius of the Cadurci – avid anti-Roman, habitual rebel and former close friend of the great king Vercingetorix – leading them all, with great purpose in his step.

That boded badly for all concerned.

Cavarinos stepped back slightly as the group approached. Since the disaster – the wake-up call? – of Alesia, the Arvernian noble had moved around almost continuously, only pausing for a few weeks here and there. The simple fact was that he knew not what to do with himself. He was no longer truly Arverni. He had continued shaving off his moustaches in an effort to remove himself from his brother and the past, and had cast his serpent arm-ring into a wide river on his travels. The Arverni were not what they had been, and they would never be proud again. And if he stopped thinking in tribal terms, and started to think like a Roman, which sooner or later all the people would have to do, then he was not really a 'Gaul' any more either. Because what the Romans called 'Gauls' had ceased to exist as a people after Alesia. Now they were slaves or Roman provincials who just didn't yet recognise the fact. Consequently, there was no home for him in this land, whether inside his tribe's territory or without.

Yet the idea of leaving somehow seemed impossible. Even if he could endure the wrench of breaking those bonds with his ancestral

14

lands, where would he go? To the northern island, where the tribes were all cousins of the Belgae, hard and bloodthirsty, and the land was inhospitable and swampy? Across the river to the lands of the Cherusci or the Suebi, who the Romans called Germani, where life was cheap and death a daily occurrence? To the tribes south of the mountains, in that parched, brown land of bronze and blood, where a war with Rome had been ongoing for more than a century now? To Rome itself, the enemy who had vanquished his people?

And so he had wandered, and he had observed, and he had learned. And most of what he had observed was a dying culture that knew it was about to be eclipsed and eradicated. And most of what he had learned was that he no longer really cared.

The vast majority of people he had seen had been hopeless and dead-eyed, trying to eke out an existence in the impoverished, war-ravaged fields that they were too weak and too few to make work for them. And here and there he had come across small pockets of anger, where a noble who claimed to have been on that hill at Alesia – and they were invariably lying – stirred up trouble among the disenchanted, dispossessed warriors who were truly too few to make any difference now. Even had Vercingetorix remained free and spoken to the masses, there was no longer any hope of success.

The former king had disappeared after the surrender of the oppidum last autumn. Some said he had been quietly murdered in the aftermath, though Cavarinos doubted that. Not only did it not seem to be the Roman way, but also the Arverni king would be too valuable as a symbol to merely kill without pomp and show. But what had happened to him was still a mystery as far as the people of his former army knew.

The familiar voice of Lucterius was closing on the door now, and Cavarinos retreated to the corner of the room and slumped into his seat with his beer. There was nowhere to hide from the gathering of nobles, and he couldn't really see any reason to hide anyway. He was no more their enemy than he was their friend.

The door clicked open and the four other occupants looked up in passing interest before going back to their drinks and food. Lucterius was finely arrayed, though not in armour. His sword, however, remained at his side, as did those of the other nobles accompanying him.

'It is all a matter of time and location,' Lucterius was saying to his cronies. 'If only we could trust Commius and bring him in to our plans, he could prove extremely useful, but after his flight and cowardice at Alesia, we simply cannot rely on him.'

'What use is Commius anyway?' snorted one of the nobles in an accent that was either Carnute or Senone. 'He has ever been but a lap-dog of Caesar. One summer of riding in Vercingetorix's shadow does not make him a hero.'

Lucterius nodded his agreement. 'He is weak and untrustworthy. But he has influence and power. While he languishes up among the Belgae, it is said he already begins to put together an army to lead against Rome's ally, the Remi.'

'There are not enough Belgae left to fight in a tavern brawl let alone a war!'

Nor are there enough of you, thought Cavarinos silently.

'But,' Lucterius countered, 'Commius, as I said, has influence. There is talk that he will cross the narrow sea and bring his cousins from the northern isles to war against Rome. And his people are related to several of the tribes across the eastern river.'

And you think our lands would still be ours if an alliance of the Britannics and the Germanics pushed Rome from it? You fools.

'Then perhaps we should approach him anyway?' an Arvenian noble hazarded.

'No. But perhaps we can use him. Our friends among the Carnutes and the Bituriges will bash their shields and light their fires to draw the Roman gaze, but we cannot afford to lose those lands.' He turned to the outspoken Carnute noble. 'As soon as the Romans are engaged in trying to quench your flames, we need to draw his attention to Commius. Between the two regions the Romans will be kept busy, and we will have time to build our army in the south.'

Cavarinos flashed a glance to the Carnute and Biturige leaders in the crowd and was not surprised to see misgivings written on their features. It sounded an awful lot like Lucterius was sacrificing them to give himself time to raise a force unnoticed. The idiot. As if he could find the manpower to fight off two or three legions, let alone ten!

'Be reassured, my friends,' Lucterius continued, apparently also reading the nervousness of his sacrificial animals. 'We will not lose you. Make much noise. Rebel and shout, but when the Romans come, run to the swamps and the forests and keep your people safe. The time will come when we need them.'

They did not look altogether reassured, but the men at least nodded their acceptance and understanding. Cavarinos took another swig of his beer, shaking his head at the idiocy of it all. The man was so arrogant in his self-belief that he didn't even hold such plotting in private, but spoke of rebellion aloud in an inn. Of course, Uxellodunon was Lucterius' home town and he was lord here, but only a foolish lord believed his domain impregnable and secure from spies. Cavarinos would not be at all surprised if one of the shady fellows in this bar ran off to tell the Romans in hope of a reward. For a moment, he considered it himself. His personal war was over and, while he still felt the base pride of his tribe somewhere down in the pit of his stomach, he now recognised that the good of his people lay in capitulation and peace. Further struggle would only end in worse conditions and more dead. The only hope for the tribes now was to embrace their fate and make it work for them. Become more Roman than the Romans and thereby keep both their pride and their control.

But despite that, he would not run to the Romans and tell them. *Someone* should, but it would not be him. Not now, anyway. The time was coming to leave Uxellodunon and Cadurci territory. He would travel back east for now, to his own Arverni lands. He had not been there since the autumn, directly after Alesia. Perhaps things had improved there over the winter. Probably not, he decided.

His attention was drawn again by the word 'prisoner', and he looked up at the gathering of nobles.

'If they are of no use, why do you not simply dispose of them?'

Lucterius frowned at the speaker – an unknown man with a western accent. 'Only a fool disposes of an asset, even if it is seemingly of no current use. They have already been tortured for anything they know. There are less than thirty of them and they are starving and broken. They are no threat and require very little guarding or maintenance, so we will keep them until we have won or lost. When Esus rises once more we will ride high on a mound of Roman bodies, my friends.'

Cavarinos closed his eyes and took another pull of his drink. Did Lucterius really think he could be an 'Esus' raising the tribes to war once more? He could only ever be a pale imitation of the great Vercingetorix. And his army would be but an echo of that which had held the ground at Alesia.

The issue of prisoners was interesting though. They could not have been taken at Alesia, for the Romans controlled the field at the end of that fight. And while there was every possibility that they had been taken from some supply depot or roving patrol in recent months, Cavarinos doubted it. If Lucterius was trying to hide his army-building from the Romans, taking prisoners would be stupid and dangerous, and would almost certainly attract unwanted attention. And the Romans had not fought down into Cadurci lands in recent campaigns. But Gergovia was a mere two days to the northeast, and the Cadurci under Lucterius had played a large part in that victory. Cavarinos would be willing to put money on the prisoners being survivors of Gergovia.

Paying no heed to the inn's other occupants, Lucterius approached the bar and collected a drink, leaving the others to deal with their own refreshments as he launched off into a tirade over Roman cowardice compared to the cowardice of treacherous tribesmen who should know better.

Cavarinos quickly became aware that although the nobles had paid no attention to who might be overhearing their plotting, the warriors in their retinue as they entered were beginning to look around the interior and focus on the occupants. Cavarinos was clean-shaven – a state so rare as to be noteworthy – and clearly not Cadurci, and trouble could very well be looming on the horizon. These warriors were the best their tribes still had to offer, and any one of them would be a tough proposition in a fight. Standing, he picked up his bag, nodded his thanks to the innkeeper, and made his way as nonchalantly as possible to the door. There he waited for the warriors to enter, and once the entire bunch were inside, packing the sizeable interior, he slipped past them and out into the chilly late afternoon air. Time to move on. Sooner or later someone would mention his presence to Lucterius, and it was faintly possible that this new self-professed 'Esus' would remember the Arverni noble who had shaved off his moustaches before the final capitulation at Alesia.

The oppidum of Uxellodunon sat rigid and unlovely in the winter cold, with rime coating every surface and the muddy furrows hardened to the consistency of iron, threatening twisted ankles and falls at every turn. As high and powerfully defensive as a smaller Alesia or Gergovia, Uxellodunon was far less advanced within, its organisation owing little to the influence of foreign design, and more resembling the settlements of the tribes centuries ago. Houses were mostly of mud-daub and timber-frame, built upon a bed of two or three stone courses. Farmland covered much of the interior and animals roved the plateau arbitrarily, mixing with the few people about on such an unforgiving day. Grass and mud. No paved streets here.

The beauty of such a basic layout was that anything unusual stood out, and Cavarinos was quite surprised he hadn't spotted the stockade when he'd first arrived, let alone during the days he had wandered around the oppidum. Down towards the south-western gate, which stood at a sharp point in the defences on a spur of rock, a timber ring had been installed in recent months, the tips of the posts still sharp and pale.

Wandering across the rutted track, Cavarinos untied the reins of his horse from the hitching post and threw his bag across its back, then began to walk the beast down towards the southwest gate. It was not a natural way to leave the oppidum when heading east, but it would serve two purposes. Firstly, he could have a glance at the prisoners on the way, and secondly, if Lucterius realised he had overheard the conversation and decided that that was a bad thing, a false trail might be of some help.

Slowly, apparently unconcerned, he descended the slope, sticking to the rutted frozen mud and making for that gate. Before he reached it, however, he pulled his scarf up over his nose – a mode not uncommon in this sort of weather, but with the added benefit of hiding his shaven features. Veering off the path, he made for the stockade. The gate to the prison was a simple timber affair held shut with a bar and presenting no hole large enough for a man to pass through. The two locals who were apparently set to guard it looked cold and bored, and neither even bothered to challenge him as he stepped towards the gate, motioning a greeting at them.

Slowing his horse, he bent and peered through the wooden posts of the entrance. The locking bar was clearly unnecessary, which partially accounted for the lax attitude of the pair outside. He could count twenty three Romans in the circular stockade, each filthy and most freezing and naked, a few clinging to the rags of their russet coloured tunics for warmth if not modesty. Each man within was tethered by the wrists to an iron ring driven into the heavy timber posts of the stockade. None of them would be able to move more than a few feet, and they clearly had no hope of escape. Many of them had clearly been beaten, burned and tortured, but his eyes fell specifically on a bull-shouldered bald man sitting opposite. His attire

19

was no different from the rest, but one look at his defiant, solid posture and the strength and complete lack of fear and surrender in his eyes told Cavarinos what he was: he was a centurion. The Arverni noblemen had seen enough of them in his time. The hardest bastards in the Roman world, bar none, gladiators included. They bent their knee to no one except their commander and the gods. The man had clearly been beaten and torn to within an inch of his life, but his eyes remained clear and defiant as he locked them on the visitor at the gate.

Cavarinos sighed, heaved in a deep, cold breath, and turned to his horse.

Poor bastards.

Not his problem, though. He had enough of *them* without adopting more. With a last glance up at the oppidum's centre, he turned to the gate and left Uxellodunon and Cadurci lands. Cavarinos was going home.

Chapter Two

VARUS squinted into the grey blurry morning, the world lit by a watery, inefficient sun. This oppidum of the Bituriges – the latest in a long list – had a name, but he'd long since stopped bothering to commit such names to valuable memory, given that they flew by in a steady stream of campaigning. The low, elongated hill sat between two narrow stream valleys, its northern and southern edges protected by a wide ditch below the walls, the eastern and western by the valleys themselves.

On the Kalends of Januarius, Caesar had responded to a plea from the loyal factions of the Bituriges who had been ousted by rebels of their own tribe, and he had led out Varus' cavalry wing, collecting the Thirteenth from Avaricon and the Eleventh from their own camp, heading west. The column of ten thousand men and horses had waded into Bituriges territory with, in Varus' private opinion, a less-than-discriminate manner, and in the ten days since the army had marched, eleven such settlements had fallen. The rebellious nature of their early targets had been somewhat uncertain as far as the cavalry commander was concerned, for few men raised any kind of resistance to their attacks.

The enemy had been suicidally optimistic, attempting revolution in lands this close to Roman winter quarters. They had so few warriors among them anymore that a Roman action against them was like pitting hungry bears against condemned criminals in Rome's entertainment pits. The two legions had barely broken a sweat, which was something to be grateful for, given that winter still had Gaul firmly in its icy grip and that none of the men were thrilled at leaving comfortable winter quarters and marching out into the wilds before the campaigning season had even appeared on the horizon.

But here they were.

Laniocon – that was the place's name, he seemed to remember – stood defiant and proud on its turf mound with its strong Gallic walls surrounded by ditches and narrow defiles. And yet that defiance was mere show at best, if that. For atop those ramparts a spear point gleamed every few hundred paces. Five years ago, when Gaul had still been a wild and unexplored land for the legions, this place would have blinded onlookers with the number of shining bronze weapons and helms visible above the parapet. Now, after eight years of exhaustive war, most of its defenders were old men and children,

21

and even they would be too few to hold back a scout party, let alone two legions and a wing of cavalry. It was almost laughable that one rider in twenty in this mounted force had been drawn *from* these very Biturige settlements over the years, though now their allegiance was tied strongly to Caesar, who had made them wealthier men than many of their former leaders could ever hope to be.

Laniocon was ripe for the picking.

A cavalry prefect rode towards him from the southern fields, freezing dew settling on his helmet and mail and giving him a strangely ethereal sparkle in the misty grey. Beside the prefect, three of the Gallic princes who commanded the native levies waited hungrily. And well they might, for each oppidum that fell made those men richer and more influential. Even the native auxiliaries knew that Caesar's time as proconsul was almost up and that soon he would return to Rome. When he did, Gaul would become the command of some fat politician and things would settle into status quo, so every man who sought advancement in the land was currently jostling for position and gain in order to secure a better future in what would clearly soon be a Roman province. And those who weren't thinking like that – the few who still laboured under the impression that Gaul would return to being a tribal land – would be disappointed, disenfranchised and poor when the inevitable happened.

The Bituriges in the last oppidum they had advanced on had seen their future clearly enough, and had delivered to Caesar the half dozen men they claimed had taken control in defiance of Rome. The six rebel leaders had sneered at their Roman captors and spat at the countrymen who had sold them out, but in response Caesar had been generous, and that oppidum had suffered no ill effect other than the expense of feeding the legions for a night before they moved on west towards Laniocon.

Here, though, at least Varus was more sure of the need for castigation, for the gates had closed with a resilient thud at the sight of the Roman forces marching against them. Despite the fact that their doom hung over them like a dark cloud among the endless grey, they had seemingly decided to hold out.

'What are your orders, sir?' the prefect asked, reining in his steed.

Varus squinted at the hill again, shrouded in a world of soul-crushing grey.

'There's little for the cavalry to do here, Prefect. Have the force split down into standard alae and assign them sectors of the circuit beyond the ditches and streams. We'll form an outer cordon and watch, just in case this land has managed to muster up a few hundred reinforcements to send them. Remember Alesia, eh?'

The prefect nodded and sighed. 'Why do they persist, sir? Surely they can see they're beaten?'

Varus rubbed his forehead and wiped away the fine film of dew that had settled on it. 'The Gauls are just as proud of their history as we are, Prefect. Can you imagine in the same situation a Roman city just handing their heritage over to an invader?'

'I suppose not, sir. It just seems so bloody futile, pardon the language.'

Varus sucked in air through his teeth. 'Just a little longer, Prefect. The general thinks that the main stronghold of rebellion is at Argatomagon perhaps thirty miles west. Beyond that it's mostly forests and farms until you're in Pictone lands, so there's no point in marching legions out there to round up a few cows and the odd toothless farmer. We'll be back in quarters in a week.'

The prefect's spirits rose a little at that thought as he saluted, turned and began to distribute orders among the princes with him before returning to the decurions of his own command.

The Eleventh had played the active role in the last fight while the Thirteenth had formed the defensive cordon, so this time the Eleventh under Rufio had split into cohorts and formed a ring around the oppidum, within Varus' planned outer cavalry cordon, while the Thirteenth had formed up for the assault. Some few hundred paces south of the Gallic outer ditch, Sextius' legion shuffled into tighter ranks as their centurions moved up and down the lines, jabbing mail-shirted chests and bellowing at occasional lax men. An opportunistic archer somewhere up on the rampart loosed a single arrow, which arced up gracefully past the defensive ditch and then plummeted into the thick grass between there and the waiting legion. Sextius had been careful to muster his force well beyond arrow range, but Varus acknowledged the fact that, standing on that wall and watching the army form ready, he'd have been tempted at least to try, too.

As the whistles and shouts of the officers continued in preparation, a horse broke from the command unit where Caesar in his red cloak murmured into the cupped ear of Aulus Hirtius, his secretary and confidante. Varus frowned as the rider made straight for him and hauled on the reins, pulling up his sweating mount and saluting.

'Complements of the general, sir. He would like yourself along with a few turmae of regulars to follow on the heels of the Thirteenth and make sure the oppidum remains untouched. Caesar wants no repetition of Sidia.'

Varus rolled his shoulders. 'I heartily agree.' Sidia had been a notable fight four days ago, and the rebels there had managed to actually do some real damage to the Eleventh's vanguard. In response, despite Caesar's standing orders, the soldiers had gone in like Nemesis herself, taking out their avenging fury on the inhabitants, raping and burning freely. They had left Sidia a shadow of its former self, half the town a charred and smoking ruin.

This was not a campaign of occupation or suppression. These towns were nominally loyal to Rome now, and had simply been taken control of by a few bad elements. Consequently, Rome could not afford to have the settlements destroyed. The legions were here to liberate, not to violate.

Varus waved over one of his messengers. 'Go and find decurions Oculatius, Granius and Annius. Tell them to muster their turmae to the rear of the Thirteenth in battle order.' The courier saluted and rode off, and Varus continued to watch for long moments until he noted the three cavalry units forming and the Thirteenth settle ready for the advance. In that eerie silence that filled the field of battle while the army awaited the order to move, the commander turned his horse and trotted off across the wet, springy turf to join his men.

Barely had he reached the cavalry contingent when the general's call went up by buccina and the various officers blew their whistles and yelled their commands, the men falling easily into their mile-eating step. Varus watched from his mounted position as the lead elements approached the oppidum's defensive ditch, and he marvelled once again at the hardened professionalism of those men at the front. He had been in a few life-and-death fights himself, but it was different for a horseman, especially one in a position of command. It could never be compared to being given a shield and a sword and told to march straight at a wall into a hail of arrows, probably over agonising obstacles. It took a special kind of guts to do that and not falter.

Slowly the rear ranks of the Thirteenth began to move, following on with no less valour than their mates at the front, and Varus set his riders off at a stately pace in response. They advanced, the oppidum beginning to loom despite the low angle of the slope, and he found himself willing the centurions in the van to give the order. He'd seen where that opportunistic arrow had fallen. The front men must be in range now?

Despite waiting for it, Varus felt his heart flutter at the sudden call for *testudo* given by the lead centurion just as they closed on the ditch. In near-perfect timing, the front ranks shifted into their individual centuries, and several hundred shields clonked into position forming a defensive shell around and above the men. Not even a pause or a missed step. The Gauls up on the ramparts reacted almost instantly, sending out a cloud of missiles at the advancing army. Again, Varus could not help but compare the five or six dozen arrows whispering through the air towards them with the arrow storms of thousands of shafts that had hailed out over oppidum walls earlier in the campaign. It was pitiful by comparison, but in reality they still represented a very real danger, as the odd blood-curdling scream attested. No matter how well-trained or efficient a century might be at forming the testudo, there would inevitably be a few gaps, especially when terrain dictated a change in elevation, and on occasion stray arrows found those gaps.

As the testudo centuries reached the lip of the defensive ditch and began to descend, the formations broke up a little, and the falling missiles found more and more targets. Varus couldn't see the action from his position at the rear, even on horseback, but he could picture it after so many other sieges and counter-sieges over the years. Those men who fell would probably take down one or two others with them, and here and there the formation would collapse, but as soon as things fell apart, the centurions and their optios would be there, calling out and blowing their whistles, sending men to plug gaps. Indeed, a moment later he saw the first men cresting the far side of the ditch and beginning the march up the slope, their formations quickly put back together and once more largely impervious to missiles.

The arrow storm, now joined by sling stones, continued to thud down on the shields as the legion approached the south rampart, and Varus was afforded a good view of the action up the slope as he continued his sedate advance with his riders at the rear. The walls here looked to be a little higher than they had at Sidia, and Varus found himself worrying that the new tactics the two legions had adopted would be insufficient to gain the rampart. His fears were allayed as the whistles of the leading centurions sent out the orders and the lead testudo broke into a run as though they intended to barge the oppidum's wall aside.

As they had practised many times this past week, the lead centuries reached the walls and came to a halt still in solid testudo formation, with their shield-roof up and interlocked, and the rear men in the units dropped to a kneeling position, their raised shields forming a lower step. At that same command, the second centuries following on behind broke into a run, their own testudos unfolding as they charged, using the lower shields as the step they formed and leaping up onto the precarious roof of shields.

Here and there a man slipped, his hob-nailed boots raking the painted surfaces of the shields, and plummeted off to the grassy slope at the side. But the majority of the men, now well-practised, ran up the roof of the testudo and at the Gallic walls, with which they were now more or less of a height.

The defenders panicked, suddenly faced with the presence of Romans right under their noses instead of at the base of a high wall. A few of the braver or smarter ones fought off the attackers for a few moments before succumbing, but many simply stepped back in consternation, uncertain of what to do now that their defences apparently counted for nothing.

What happened next was a matter of conjecture for Varus, as the cavalry officer and his riders at the rear of the legion reached the defensive ditch and had to carefully manoeuvre their beasts down the slope and then back up the far side, losing track completely of the struggle at the front. By the time the riders were back up onto the gentle slope and making for the oppidum's defences, the ramparts were already swarming with legionaries and a mix of alarmed Gallic cries and victorious Latin shouts announced that the southern gate had fallen.

The legion surged forward up the slope with renewed energy, the missiles now falling only occasionally, and even then loosed wild and in panic. Varus held his men back as the centuries swarmed over the walls and through the gate into the city, and as soon as the gatehouse stood open, he pushed his way in behind them, leading his riders.

It seemed that the rebels still had some fight in them since the battle continued to rage in the streets as the doomed enemy fell back through the narrow streets of the oppidum, trying to hold back the Roman tide while seeking somewhere to either hide or make a stand. Varus looked this way and that, painfully aware of the fact that once an army got its blood up and was in the mood to pillage and burn it would take more than an officer with a loud voice to pull them back into line.

Fortunately, it seemed that most of the centurions had their men under tight control, and those units who had lost a centurion in the advance were continuing under the able command of their optios. Here and there a man would run into a clearly empty house with the intent to pillage, and Varus would send two of his men to bring the man back out.

Things were becoming more complicated as the local loyalists, who had been languishing in a town under the control of violent rebels, came rushing out into the streets, waving their arms and trying to explain desperately to the attacking force that they were not the enemy. Fortunately, after so many days of such actions the legionaries were experienced in this type of fight and avoided combat with women and children and anyone before them who was clearly unarmed.

To aid the swift return to control, Varus was pleased to see a few of the more enterprising loyal townsfolk pushing the fleeing rebels back out into the street before the Romans where they could be cut down without a chance to hide, and more than once he spotted locals busily kicking a captured rebel to death. After all, these men had brought a legion to their doorstep, and the loyalists blamed their revolting kinsmen for this much more than they did the Roman officers.

As the horsemen reached the central square of the oppidum with some sort of temple facing them, Varus sent his decurions and their units off in various directions with a remit to keep the peace and make sure the legion was behaving itself. Oddly, as the legionaries continued to push the few remaining rebels back through the streets and the loyal inhabitants largely stayed safely out of the way, Varus watched his horsemen melt away into the oppidum and found himself more or less alone in the packed earth square, just his standard bearer and tuba-player and a small honour guard of regular cavalrymen in attendance. The sounds of battle now seemed strangely distant and muted, though no birdlife yet filled the cold, damp, grey air. He leaned his head to one side, listening carefully to see if he could pick out any area of trouble where he might have to take a more personal command to ensure Caesar's orders were complied with.

The sound had almost been a scream, but had then dropped to what sounded like a muffled whimper. Varus' eyes narrowed as he peered around the square, still listening intently. A scraping noise could have been entirely innocent, though something was troubling the cavalry officer and he dropped from his horse, handing his reins to a trooper as he strode towards the temple from where he was sure the noises were coming.

A two-storey building perhaps twenty feet square and constructed of timber and daub with thatched roof, the temple was dusty, unsophisticated and wet. The door facing the square was closed and its iron hinges were rusty. Varus approached and slowed as he neared the door. His hand went to the pommel of his sword and he momentarily wished he wore a shield, but he had not been part of the attack and had not bothered arming properly for combat. There was no noise issuing from the temple, but he was now absolutely sure something was amiss. The air had that leaden silence that tells of people deliberately holding their breath. His fingers slid down to the carved bone grip of his sword and closed into a fist. Slowly, carefully, he drew the blade. Perhaps he should shout for his men?

No.

Knowing that despite the grey dullness of the January weather, the interior of the temple would be extremely dim, he closed his eyes for a count of twenty, allowing them to acclimatise to the darkness, and then reached up with his free hand and unlatched the door, pushing it open even as he stepped forward.

He opened his eyes as he entered, cutting down the exposure to the outside light to a minimum. His nostrils were assaulted with a smell of mixed ordure, sweat and old blood. The temple consisted of a single room, the second storey more of a small tower with roof lights that illuminated the ground floor. A fire pit occupied the very centre, full of blackened wood, soot and ash, and the walls were daubed with crude designs and figures. At the far side, two tall stones, each higher than Varus, stood close to the wall, each carved with lumpen, misshapen figures, and a statue of a moustachioed man, highly stylised, with bulbous limbs and bulging eyes, stood between the stones.

On the floor, beneath the statue, a legionary knelt, his tunic hoisted up and his pale buttocks exposed in the light. His shield lay off to one side with his helmet and sheathed sword. As Varus' eyes picked out every last detail, he registered the girl's legs beneath the legionary, the heels thumping the packed earth of the floor desperately. At the sudden intrusion, the legionary looked around and Varus caught sight of the soldier's terrified victim, struggling to fight off her attacker even with the legionary's knife at her throat.

'Get off her.'

'Piss off.'

Varus blinked. Common soldiers did not speak to senior officers in that sort of manner, and it took him a moment to remember that he wasn't wearing a helmet or cloak, and that silhouetted in a doorway he could be anyone.

'Get off that woman, soldier. Now!'

He was rewarded with a response this time as the soldier rose, leaving the half-naked girl on the ground, pinned down with a nailed boot as he turned to look at the new arrival.

'I don't answer to donkey boys. Piss off and find your own girl.'

Varus felt the anger bubbling up inside him. 'This girl is no rebel. Rape of the loyal subjects of Rome is a serious offence, legionary.'

He felt his nerves twang for just a moment as he registered just how big the soldier was. He was a bruiser and a veteran, going by his well-used but well-maintained equipment.

'You threatening me, donkey boy?'

Varus cleared his throat. If the man had recognised him as cavalry, then he had probably also noted the apparent rank and seemed not to care. Moreover, Varus realised that now he had threatened the man with serious punishment, the legionary had less to lose.

He hefted his sword as the towering legionary stepped towards him. Freed, the girl curled in pain and shame, sobbing around her nakedness and the rents in her belly the nails of the legionary's boot had caused. Varus snarled.

'Name, century and cohort, legionary!'

'Last chance, horseman. Leave the room and go hump your mare again.'

Varus raised his sword so that the tip hovered around the man's neck height. He was no stranger to combat, though usually from horseback and in the open field. '*Name*, soldier.'

'Ampelius,' barked the legionary as, with lightning speed for such a big man, he jumped two paces forward, ducking left. Varus felt a moment of panic as he tried to bring his sword to bear. The legionary had recognised the long cavalry blade for what it was and had leapt in too close to allow for its effective use. Varus tried to step back, but the door had swung shut behind him and he was trapped. He angled his arm, trying to bring his sword close in defence, even if it might be useless as a weapon.

The legionary raised his dagger, an evil light in his eye, and only by some miracle did Varus manage to jam his sword in the way. He couldn't possibly use it to fight from this distance, but the flat of the blade caught the legionary's wrist, holding the plunging knife away from his neck. The man was strong and Varus' sword awkward and heavy at this angle, and he could feel the blade being pushed downwards by the legionary.

The pressure on his sword was relieved so suddenly that he almost fell backwards with the movement. He stared in surprise at the legionary's face as the man's eyes widened in shock and pain and, as the brute stepped stiffly backwards, Varus caught a glimpse of the Biturige girl gripping Ampelius' gladius in shaking hands, the tip still jammed in the soldier's shoulder. With a grunt, the legionary stepped back again and the girl wrenched out the gladius, the sound of cracking bone accompanying the move as she retreated across the room. The enraged legionary, seemingly forgetting the presence of Varus entirely, spun painfully round, a low growl rising in his throat.

Varus smiled, calculating effective distance as the man took a third and then fourth step away from him, bearing down on the girl. Quietly, the cavalry officer raised his long sword, pulled it out to one side, and then delivered a hefty strike with the flat of the blade on the side of the legionary's head. Ampelius jerked to one side with the blow, and he tottered and fell to the ground, shaking. Varus stood for a moment with his sword lowered, the tip pointed at the prone legionary, then raised his gaze to the girl. She was clutching her torn tunic around herself with one hand and wielding the gladius defensively with the other. Waving his flattened palm at her in a gesture for calm, Varus crouched carefully and rolled the legionary over, plucking the knife from his fingers. Ampelius was out cold but breathing, and the wound in his shoulder had been agonising and had actually chipped the bone, but was far from fatal and leaked blood only slowly. Varus rose once more and focused on the girl.

'Do you speak Latin?'

'Bit.'

'I am sorry for the conduct of this man. He should not have done this. He will be sentenced to a flogging with the barbed whip for this.'

The girl stared at him in incomprehension. '*Bit*' had clearly been a correct appraisal. Varus tried to give her a reassuring smile. She would have no idea what would happen to her attacker, but it would not be enough. Not for the man who had so brutally raped her. Varus found his own sensibilities a little unaccepting of the result too, and a nasty smile replaced the reassuring one.

'Him?' he tried, and the girl nodded. 'Yours,' Varus added, trying to mime giving her the prone soldier. The girl frowned in confusion and when Varus took a step towards her she held up the gladius in defence. The officer nodded and pointed at the sword. 'Sword.' Then at her: 'you'. Then at the legionary on the floor. For another moment, the girl's confusion reigned, but then it cleared as understanding dawned. From the violent, vengeful look in her eye, Varus decided that Ampelius' future looked less than rosy. In fact, the man might shortly be *dreaming* of mere barbed whips. With a nod of approval, Varus cast one last spiteful look at the disobedient legionary and turned, opening the door and leaving the building. His small honour guard was still waiting in the square, and Varus gestured to two of them.

'I'm going to report to the general. You two stay here and guard that door. Whatever you hear from inside, leave the door shut. No one goes in until the girl comes out. Then take her gently to a medicus and have her fed and looked over.'

The two men looked at one another in incomprehension, but saluted and took up position. Varus crossed to his steed and pulled himself up into his saddle. If things were going to settle into the *Pax Romana* in Gaul, it was time someone started to take steps in that direction.

* * * * *

Two days later, Caesar's army marched forth to repeat their success at the oppidum of Argatomagon on the south-western fringe of Biturige lands. The weather had turned less clement, and the sky intermittently spat down rain, sleet and hail depending upon Jupiter Pluvius' mood. Yet despite the depressing wintry climate, the attitude of the legions remained optimistic and strong, partially through the ease of the campaign and partially the regular donatives Caesar paid them from captured goods.

Varus sat astride his mount, watching the Eleventh climb the gentle slope towards heavy ramparts which sat on a low ridge enclosing a tired-looking settlement that was sizeable, if sparsely inhabited. The warriors lined up on the parapet watching the might of Rome roll inexorably towards them were also few and far between, more like frightened mice than the heart of any rebellion.

Varus couldn't help wonder how the general's information had been so far off this time. With each and every action through these weeks of campaigning, the intelligence drawn from the Biturige loyalists had been accurate and had led to success time after time. Yet those same sources had apparently noted this very oppidum as the centre of the rebellion, the home of the revolt's leaders.

Had the real enemy flown the coop before the Romans arrived?

A pitiful smattering of arrows and sling stones fell from the rampart, rattling off the painted surfaces of hundreds of red and black shields. Varus had seen stauncher resistance put up by wandering warbands than by this supposed nest of vipers.

The cavalry officer sat and watched patiently as the last ranks of the legions moved on, the riders starting out at a walk behind them. Once more, the regular squadrons had been given the task of keeping the legions from rapine and pillage, though for some reason Caesar had stuck his confidante, Aulus Hirtius, in with them. And Varus knew the general well enough to know that there would be a very specific reason for such a decision.

He looked across at the spindly figure in the polished bronze cuirass in time to catch Hirtius giving him an appraising look. He tried not to glower in reply. He failed. Urging his steed forward, Varus blinked irritably as his face was spattered with a fresh dose of wind-borne sleet.

Unlike Laniocon, this fortress exhibited no strong defensive ditch and consequently Varus had a continuous view of the action ahead at the crest of the hill, over the serried ranks of the Eleventh. It was clearly a truly one-sided engagement, the legions reaching the ramparts with few casualties, most of their difficulties coming in the form of churned mud underfoot rather than sharpened iron and bronze ahead. Soldiers slid and slipped, struggling to remain upright, but beyond that the siege was very much a foregone conclusion. As Varus watched, the ladders went up among the front ranks. For all the poor defence of this place, the walls were considerably higher than the previous settlement, and the testudo trick would be inadequate to reach the top. Consequently, rather than spend days on end constructing vineae and siege towers, the commanders had had their men cut and construct siege ladders. Looking at the pitiful resistance, the decision had been a good one. Nothing else would be needed. The missiles stopped coming as the few men on the walls were forced to concentrate on the myriad ladders clunking against the stonework instead. Warriors pushed them back with forked sticks, sending the climbing legionaries tumbling back down among their own ranks, and for a moment it seemed the advance might falter.

But there were simply too few defenders, and the Romans were well-prepared and determined. More and more ladders clunked against stone, while the men on the walls had to run ever more desperately to keep them back. Finally the first legionary reached the parapet with glee, vaulting over the top and laying into the men running at him with their forked sticks. The unfortunate victorious legionary went down under a pile of four natives, stabbing and jabbing with their sharpened staves, but by that time another three legionaries were over the top, many more following close on their heels. The fight was over before it began, and within half a dozen heartbeats the only figures visible on the walls were Roman, forcing the few remaining defenders back down into the town. Barely one cohort of the legion had seen any action when the call went up and the oppidum's gate opened, admitting the Eleventh en-masse.

The gap between the rear ranks of the Eleventh and the following alae of horse opened up as the legion surged forward, pushing through the gate and into the heart of Argatomagon. Tapping his heels on his horse's flanks, Varus moved forth at an increased rate, the rest of the cavalry with him, as well as Hirtius on his pale grey, ghostlike steed.

In moments the horsemen had reached the top of the slope and slowed as legionaries funnelled through the gate in the ramparts while their compatriots continued to swarm up the ladders and over the top. Varus watched Hirtius with interest as the general's secretary sat ·impatient, clearly itching to get through the gate and into the oppidum. What was going on? Quietly, Varus called over one of his decurions.

'Sir?'

'I don't expect much trouble from the Eleventh. They've had the speech enough times, but take the other two units and split up, keep things under control, anyway. I'm going to stay with commander Hirtius.'

The decurion slipped away, disseminating the orders, and Varus manoeuvred his steed closer to the staff officer who was almost riding into the rear ranks of the infantry in his impatience to be in. Half a hundred heartbeats later the cavalry were pouring through the gate in the wake of the soldiers who disappeared among the houses, securing every part of the oppidum. Hirtius rode into the centre of the open space, clearly taken by surprise by the lack of surrendering Gauls. The gathering area behind the gate was empty barring a few corpses and a legionary groaning as he clutched a broken leg.

Varus cleared his throat. 'What now?'

Hirtius either heard nothing or feigned such, ignoring him, since he wheeled his horse and set his sights on an old native, who stood by the door of a hovel, his hands raised in surrender.

'You!' the staff officer shouted, causing the old man to jump nervously and rush out a response in his own tongue. 'Do you have no Latin?' Hirtius demanded, which simply raised a look of utter bafflement from the man. Varus was about to chime in when a younger Gaul appeared from the doorway, hobbling and using a crutch.

'I talk bit Roman,' the new arrival said.

'Where are the rebel leaders?' Hirtius demanded of the younger man.

'Not know, sir. Some rebel in town. Some dead. Other gone.'

The staff officer bridled. 'This town is the centre of the Biturige rebels. I want to know where those rebels' leaders *are*.'

'Hirtius,' Varus said quietly, 'I don't think they're here. Maybe they *were*, but they're certainly not now. Look how easy it was to overrun the place.'

Hirtius flashed him a look that only deepened his concern, for in that gaze was a determination, but also a faintly sickened look, as though the officer was fighting his own spirit.

'By direct order of Gaius Julius Caesar, Proconsul of Gaul, I demand that the rebel leaders be delivered to us, and if they are not located and brought forth, every man of property and of fighting age in this settlement will be roped and chained and taken forth in recompense for the rebellious nature of this tribe.'

Varus narrowed his eyes. That was clearly Caesar speaking through Hirtius, and the general never did anything offhand. What could be gained by such an action? There were no rebel leaders here, just a few last desperate warriors and a city full of ordinary folk. The younger Gaul was explaining this in a desperate tone to the old man, who looked stunned. He then turned back to the two Roman officers.

'Sir, my father and I are simply merchants, plying our trade in good Biturige metalwork. We are not rebels. We are loyal to the proconsul.'

Again, Varus caught the slightly sickened look in Hirtius' eyes, and his own widened.

'Is *that* what this is about, Hirtius?'

The staff officer turned to him.

'Keep your nose out of this, Varus. The horse are your concern, not the general's strategy.'

Varus slapped his head. 'I *thought* the name of this place was familiar. Never misses a trick, our general, does he? I wonder if there were *ever* any rebel leaders here.'

Hirtius gave him that mixed, unpleasant glare again, and Varus issued a snarl and wheeled his horse, trotting out of the gate and back down the slope. It took him only a short while to locate Brutus, who was sitting under a shade that was already starting to sag from the weight of the tiny hailstones gathered atop it. The young officer was poring over a map of the territory while swigging water from a canteen. Varus reined in and dismounted, tying his horse to one of the posts.

'You spend more time in staff briefings than me, Brutus. Did you know about this?'

Brutus frowned in incomprehension, and Varus indicated the oppidum of Argatomagon with a sweep of his arm. 'This whole charade. Heart of the rebellion my arse. I'd say there were fewer rebels here than in any other place we've put down this month.'

Brutus shrugged. 'Perhaps they fled the oppidum? They have to have had plenty of warning of our approach, and the rest of their territory fell so easily. Maybe they were just sensible and ran into the wilds to preserve themselves. Doesn't matter now anyway. The Biturige lands are back in loyalist hands, and there'll be no further rebellion here.'

'Brutus, there were never any rebel leaders here, I'd wager my family name on that. This is all about Caesar feathering his nest.'

Brutus frowned and gestured for him to go on, so Varus took the other campaign chair and unclasped his wet cloak, shaking it out and folding it.

'Caesar's enslaving the bulk of the populace, claiming that they've withheld the details of the rebel leaders. Another thousand slaves or two will be heading for Massilia and Rome in the morning.'

Again Brutus shrugged. 'That's the way of war. The beaten are enslaved. And those slaves till the fields and mine the stone for Rome. Don't get too sentimental, Varus. This is still a war until the last rebel surrenders.'

'But these are not rebels, Brutus. These are loyalists – just merchants and farmers and metalworkers. These are the same people as sought our help against the rebels in the first place. Enslaving them actually endangers the peace rather than securing it. If news of this reaches other allied tribes, we could find them turning against us. So we'll have to maintain Caesar's fiction if we want to keep the Pax Romana. Hirtius was not happy about doing it; I could see that in his eyes.'

Brutus offered the cavalryman his flask and when declined, stoppered it and put it away. 'Why would Caesar do that just for a few thousand slaves, given how many he's already taken?'

Varus leaned forward and examined the map closely. After a moment he sat back and tapped with his finger in a small cluster of places around their current location.

'What are those?'

'Mining settlements,' Brutus replied with a frown.

'And they belong to this oppidum.'

'There are plenty of iron and copper mining communities in easier places.'

'Brutus, these are silver mines, I reckon. Or if not, this is a place where silver is worked. Took me a while to realise it, but I wondered why I recognised the name of the place. Argatomagon. Argat is a regional corruption. I've heard it as Argad and Argant and even Arganto. It means *silver*. Argatomagon – 'silver market.' Damn it, it's surprisingly close to the Latin, and the soldiers are already calling the place Argentomagus in our own tongue. The place has made its name through silver.'

'Seems a little...' Brutus paused. 'You're right, though, aren't you? This place was identified as the centre of the rebellion because that's where Caesar wanted it to be. Then we can secure silver and worked metals. There'll be a small fortune at stake here. By raising rebellion, the idiot Bituriges have enriched the general by a heavy margin.'

Varus sagged. 'If I were a cynical man, I might even be given to wonder whether this entire rebellion was fostered as an excuse to wrest the mines from the Bituriges.'

'Don't even think of saying that again, even here and to me. Men with those kind of opinions have a very short career expectancy in the proconsul's command. I see what you're saying, and it all smacks very heavily of the same kind of manoeuvring that led Caesar to drive the Helvetii into Gaul eight years ago and start this whole thing in the first place. But the fact remains that it's done and no good at all will come of speculating in public.'

He sighed. 'Besides, you know the score here. Caesar has to completely pacify the place within the year before he returns for his consulship. He will need to take every sestertius he can out of this place if he wants to stand a chance of power against Pompey back in Rome. Caesar has plenty of friends in the city, but Pompey currently has all the real influence. The general will need to buy the goodwill of half the senators in Rome to get anywhere.'

'And he will have to pay the honesta missio for his disbanding legions,' Varus added.

'Precisely. Settling the men in southern Gaul will cost a lot of money.'

'Well,' Varus stretched and rolled his head, listening to the clicks in his neck, 'the Bituriges are back under Rome's wing now. But there are more rebellious tribes than them. We need to keep our eyes open for trouble in the north, I reckon. The Belgae are overdue a grumble.'

Brutus chuckled. 'You are such an optimist, Varus. It's almost like having Fronto back in camp. You'll be grumbling about women and getting soaked in wine next.'

'Now that's the best idea I've heard all week. Come on. Let's go open an amphora and toast the Bituriges, unwitting bankers of Caesar's career.'

Chapter Three

FRONTO staggered from the doorway of the bath suite, his bare toes knuckling at the feel of the cold marble now he had moved out of the balneum with its heated floors. Massilia was still in the cold grip of winter and although it was more temperate down here on the southern coast than far to the north where the legions huddled in their camps, it still made for a damn cold floor in the mornings. For just a moment he reeled and had to lean on the doorframe for support. It was odd, really. He was feeling as weak and old as he had done five years ago, before his wife and the burly Masgava had helped him return to a level of health and fitness that belied his age. In truth he still was as fit as ever, despite home life having replaced the routine of the legion. But the endless nights of broken sleep were taking a heavy toll, beset by the most appalling dreams, and occasionally by the flailing feet of either Marcus or Lucius, who oft-times yelled in the night until Fronto relented and brought them into bed.

The former officer rubbed his tired, sore, red eyes and wandered over to the large bronze mirror, which had cost half a legionary's yearly pay, but which Lucilia had pronounced a basic requirement of the villa, for it was unblemished and returned an almost perfect likeness of the viewer. Fronto's hand strayed to his purse every time he walked past it.

A corpse looked back out of the mirror, and he almost shied away from the sight. The old man in the reflective surface had turned rather grey-haired since he last remembered and, though some of the reason was the fact that it was still wet from the bath, those once shiny dark locks were now unfashionably long and looking rather limp, like a Greek philosopher gone to seed. Though his eyes were dark pink, they were nicely offset by a pale waxy face and deep grey rings beneath each orbit. His chin was clean-shaven from the session in the baths, but rather than removing age-enhancing grey whiskers, the razor had merely revealed a lot more folds and wrinkles than he remembered having.

For the love of Aesculapius, he was looking old. And he knew that while some of it *was* age – he was approaching his fortieth summer – a lot more of it was his current lifestyle.

Lucilia had spent the winter concerned, but in her usual way she masked her worry by treating him like some sort of petulant in-patient. After these last few years, Fronto had become so used to her ways that he could decode her moods, for even when she seemed snippy, it was almost always a method of self-defence, protecting her heart from that which she feared. And he knew that generally the more crabby she got with him, the more concerned she was. But in recent weeks she had become disconcertingly caring and supportive, and that had almost chilled Fronto to the bone.

At her instigation, he had visited two of the best physicians in Massilia, and Greek physicians were the best in the world. Neither had managed to alleviate his troubles, but both had lightened his purse and had expressed their concerns over the effects that his many old healed wounds might still be having beneath the skin; and also at his 'trick knee'. He had left both practices grumbling over the kind of people that failed to provide a solution to your problem but tried to raise more complications instead. When the second of the two had suggested that he might want to have a check-up in a rather personal area, Fronto had been grateful he wasn't wearing his sword, else the physician might have been busy stitching up a hole in himself. The man had been busy warming his hands in preparation when Fronto left in a hurry.

Then there had been the apothecaries, two Greeks and one Jew, all of whom had once more emptied his purse in return for a small bag of what looked, smelled, and tasted like forest floor. Each of the three had done nothing to bring untroubled sleep. Indeed, the last of the three had added a fairly severe case of the '*Saguntian Squits*' to the night-time upheaval.

Finally there had been the religious angle. Fronto had been reluctant to visit the temples for so many reasons he'd run out of fingers on which to count them. While he acknowledged the existence of the gods in the same way he acknowledge the existence of paving slabs, he generally paid them about the same level of devotion, barring his personal deities. His history with temples was not good. Almost every visit he had ever made to a temple had ended in disaster, carnage or embarrassment. Given the choice, he would take carnage any time. But on top of his general distrust of those men who felt so pious as to take up the priesthood as a career and a general wariness of gods themselves, the temples in Massilia were to the gods of the Greeks. It felt wrong to stroll up to the three great temples on their rocky heights and pray to Athena and Artemis instead of Minerva and Diana, although at least golden Apollo looked and sounded the same in this strangely hairy Greek world. In the end, he had foregone the three great temples of the city and, in the absence of any house of worship for his patron goddesses, had ended up in the small temple of Asklepios.

The temple was jammed in between residential blocks and stores on the slope of the hill to the north of the harbour, by necessity. Rather than choose a lofty perch like the three great edifices that lorded it over the city, the Asklepion had been located where a natural 'healing' spring gurgled from the rock. About that spring had been constructed a modest sacred bath complex, with a small connecting courtyard and precinct, at the heart of which stood the temple itself. He had been greeted at the entrance by a young boy wearing far too much kohl around his eyes so that he looked faintly demonic. The boy had waffled on at him in Greek until Fronto had given him a coin to shut up, and had then escorted him into the temple, where an old man waited – an *asklepiad* – with a white robe, a staff wound round with a carved serpent and a beard he could have lost a young bear in. The ageing priest had listened earnestly to Fronto's problem and given him a list of appropriate devotions, offerings and libations. Another empty purse, a jar of good wine, a small stack of gold coins and a rather unfortunate chicken later, the bad dreams were still there, and Fronto had crossed another god from his diminishing list of deities to give a flying fornication about.

And so, weeks on and a small fortune lighter, this sallow ghoul stared back from the mirror.

Enough was enough. He'd not mentioned as much to Lucilia, but Fronto personally knew what was at the heart of his troubles: he was missing his lucky charms. Nemesis had been broken and Fortuna had gone with Cavarinos of the Arverni. He could only hope that the luck that he himself was sadly lacking was bearing up his Gallic friend. His troubles had started almost immediately following the absence of Fortuna and Nemesis, and until he replaced the figurines around his neck with appropriate quality work, he would not sleep well.

It was too disheartening to lay the blame for the nightmares upon the multitude of deaths he had left in his wake. He was a soldier born and tried, and to think like that would be to deny all that he was.

Of course, he was no longer a soldier. He was a wine merchant now, even if not a particularly successful one.

He would take the blow on the chin and, without a word to his wife, go to the best artisans in town and commission a replacement for each charm in the best materials and at the highest quality. He would have done so months ago, had the money been available. It still wasn't, of course, but he would work it out somehow. He couldn't go on like this.

Of course, the financial side of the business was probably almost as much to blame for his state of exhaustion as the nightmares. He had come to Massilia with grand plans. There were a few Greek wine merchants in town already, of course, but no one with good access to the heart of Roman viticulture down in Campania. And quite apart from the Romans in Gaul who, he knew from years of watching Cita complaining over his stores, created an almost insatiable demand for wine, there was a growing sector of the upper Gaulish society that was starting to turn from their own beer to good southern wine. The trade *should* be lucrative. He'd *felt* that it would be. Even Balbus, who had been initially sceptical and rather disapproving of a Roman noble involving himself too closely in commerce, had nodded his agreement of the workability of the scheme. He would use those local merchant vessels who shipped Gallic goods to Neapolis and came back largely empty. He would fill them with wine from the estates of friends and connections in Campania, which he would be able to acquire considerably cheaper than most others could, and would then sell it on to either local Greek merchants, Gallic traders heading into tribal lands, or to the Roman supply system that fed the army in the north.

He hadn't been able to tell his mother or sister, of course. His letters to them at Puteoli were carefully worded to avoid all mercantile mention, despite being conveyed there by the same factors who were organising his deliveries. His mother would implode from a hefty dose of patrician-ness if she thought her son had become a common salesman, and his sister would be scathing to say the least. After all, even Lucilia and Balbus had been fairly disapproving, but had lived with his decision because at least it had brought him home from the army.

But not telling the family had added the complication of not being able to rely on family finances. He had not touched the vaults of the Falerii and had funded the initial concern entirely from his own capital following his resignation of commission from Caesar's army. Every last denarius he could lay his hands on had gone into acquiring the warehouse in the city, the cart and two oxen, a small staff, and the first stock of wine from Campania. Then he had realised that he could hardly afford to pay the ship captains to transport it, let alone the many sundry expenses that seemed to mount daily.

By the week before Saturnalia he had pored over the figures and gloomily labelled himself more or less bankrupt. He still had the assets, of course – the warehouse and a consignment of Falernian on the dock at Puteoli, but he was unable to pay the staff, animal feed, and shipping. In the most humbling moment of his entire life, he had gone to visit Balbus without his wife knowing, and had begged for a hand-out. The old man had been generous to a fault, which had made the need for begging in the first place all the more embarrassing, but at least now he had enough of a float to see him through hopefully 'til spring. Yet unless business picked up, he would be in trouble again by Aprilis.

His former singulares were helping out. Despite being signed on as household security, they had willingly stepped in to fill roles in the business, but to be honest, they were often more trouble than help. Aurelius had set profits back one evening when he had encountered a bat in the warehouse and dropped a very brittle amphora of very expensive wine as he ran screaming.

The three locals he'd hired were considerably more competent at the actual work – when such work was forthcoming, at least – and yet even they were troubling in their own right. The brothers, Pamphilus with the beak nose and close-set eyes and Clearchus with the tic in one eye and the unsettlingly white hair, were good enough at lifting and carrying and driving the cart. But after weeks in their company there was no escaping the conclusion that they were as thick as two short planks and could be mentally outmanoeuvred by a bowl of beef broth. And they seemed to be dangerously impulsive, too. A horrible combination, but at least a reasonably cheap one. Aurelius hated the pair, and tried to keep away from them, having told Fronto that there was a distinct possibility that he would flatten that beak nose someday. When the brothers had almost run him down in the yard with a cart-load of jars and barrels, Aurelius had had to be dragged away from them screaming imprecations.

And the other hireling… well, Glykon seemed perfectly friendly and helpful and excellently competent at his work. There was absolutely nothing wrong with him, other than the fact that Fronto could feel in his bones that there was something wrong with the man, even if he couldn't quite put his finger on it.

Of course, if he could only get rid of Hierocles, things might be different. But this was a lawful city and not subject to Rome, so Fronto had no real rights here, especially against a Greek who was a citizen of the town. The greasy arse-faced rat of a wine merchant had made Fronto's life hell since his return to Massilia. The former legate of the Tenth had expected healthy competition, and was ready to have to push hard to carve himself a niche in the market. He had not been prepared for Hierocles. The old bastard had taken Fronto's dip into the wine trade very personally and had publically decried him as a foreign agent trying to infiltrate free Massilia and bind her to the republic with ties of trade. When Fronto had responded calmly to the contrary, the man had taken his calm for weakness and had stepped up his campaign of defamation to actively accuse him of crooked dealings and various small criminal acts.

Though Fronto had argued his corner in the city's agora like a good Roman orator and had managed to clear himself of any charge levelled, the stigma of a blackened name seemed to have stayed with him and nothing he could do had rebuilt his reputation. Moreover, being thwarted had simply set Hierocles off on a new path. Unable to remove Fronto through law, he had instead turned to his fellow Greek merchants in the town, further denigrating Fronto and gathering an informal cartel against the new Roman competitor.

Consequently, for the last month, Fronto had found himself repeatedly undercut for deals, passed over by ship captains and the target of seemingly accidental damage to his wares. Business was bad, but even that bad business was dwindling. Soon...

He looked deep into his own eyes in the mirror and was not surprised to see an unhealthy dose of defeat in them. He'd had such high hopes for this business. It was something strategic and real in which to immerse himself without diving into the political cesspools of Rome or the bloodbaths of the army. The military was out of the picture anyway. Even if he felt like going back, which in his current physical state would be truly dreadful, Caesar's time in Gaul was coming to an end shortly and those legions would be stood down as their general returned to Rome to take up higher office. By the time he arrived in Caesar's tent, there probably wouldn't be a legion there to command. And that left Rome as an option. To take up a role in the government and be gradually ground down to sand between the rough edges of Caesar and Pompey. Lucilia had broached the idea once that perhaps he could grease a few palms in the senate and try to secure himself a governorship. Fronto had laughed at that until wine came out of his nose.

He wasn't laughing now.

Who *was* that old man in the mirror?

'Marcus?'

He turned and riveted a beaming smile on his face.

'Don't give me that,' Lucilia snorted.

He let the forced smile slide from his visage and sighed.

'You thrashed around like a windmill in a storm last night,' she said quietly. 'Worse than usual?'

Fronto shrugged. 'Same as usual. I was just finally actually settling and hoping to squeeze in another hour of slumber when Amelgo woke me. Got to get going early today, you see? Irenaeus is due in port this morning and he's one of few Greek captains who'll still give me the time of day. I need to get down to the port and get his mark on my contract before that po-faced bastard Hierocles gets to him and turns him from me.'

'Marcus, you should have a man to do this for you.'

'Who? Aurelius? The brothers? Masgava maybe? No. All our lads are workers, not spokesmen. This is a job for glib tongue and I'm the nearest thing here. Unless you want to take a turn at the steering oars of this enterprise?'

Lucilia gave him a look that startled him, as though she were actually considering it. Hurriedly, wanting to draw the argument to a close before it began, he waved concerns aside. 'Do you know where my best chiton is? The blue one with the white edging.'

'Must you dress as a Greek?'

'When dealing with these people it is better not to over-publicise my Romanness. Irenaeus is a good man, but even he might be better disposed to a man in a chiton than in the red tunica of a Roman officer. Do you know where it is?'

Lucilia nodded. 'Amelgo laid it out in our room, along with your best sandals and the white cloak. You will look quite the Hellenic gentleman.'

'Thank you, my love. Are the boys up?'

'And crawling about like a pair of rodents. Lucius is up on his feet, holding onto table edges and pulling himself round. Marcus, as usual, cannot be bothered to try and walk, and simply sits there drinking. I'm beginning to wonder if the very name is cursed?' The harsh words were delivered with a sly upturn of the mouth to remind

Fronto that she was as dry a joker as her father, and he chuckled. 'He'll stand up in his own good time. Never fret about him walking. Children always learn in the end. You don't see many forty year olds still crawling about on the floor, do you?'

'Only you and your friends on market day after a session in the Ox.'

Again the upturn, and Fronto laughed aloud. Gods, but it felt good to laugh.

His mood slumped again at the all-too familiar sound of a shattering amphora outside in the gardens. The distressing noise was followed by a verbal altercation between the recognisable Greek slur of Pamphilus and Clearchus and the angry Latin of Aurelius and Masgava. Odd though it was to hear a polyglot argument like that, the novelty had long since worn off.

'Why did I put idiots and jugglers in charge of the best stock?'

And it *was* his best stock. The very finest of wines he'd managed to import into the city before Hierocles' cartel of hate had interfered and soured the deal with the trader who had been set to buy it. After another 'accident' at the warehouse, Fronto had had the best stock moved to the villa, and had finally managed to line up another buyer, though for considerably less profit. And now it sounded like he'd have to speak to the buyer and apologise for being at least one amphora short.

'You need more men,' Lucilia said quietly. 'And not ex-soldiers or surly Greeks. You need to get down to the slave market and get some bargains. Go early on the morning three days after market day, when the leftover stock has gone but the new slaves have come in.'

'I don't like buying slaves. I don't really like owning slaves. Father always said a man who works for a wage you can trust, but a man you have to keep at the end of a stick will beat you with it the moment you turn your back.'

'Your father, gods forgive me for saying it, was a hopeless drunk with less sense than a Scythian.'

'Lucilia...'

'Don't snap at me. I'm quoting your sister. I've noted your aversion to owning them, and I know that there are those who won't do it for fear of another slave war. I didn't even argue when you emancipated Amelgo after only a week of being back. But those slaves who are treated well are happy with their lot, Marcus. Slaves are the *norm*. Good grief, even the Greeks keep slaves, and *they*

46

consider themselves the masters of equality. Daddy has slaves. *Everyone* has slaves. And slaves will be careful with your stock out of respect, or at least fear.'

'Listen Lucilia…'

He was interrupted by another muffled crash of pottery and further bellowing in two languages.

'Alright,' he sighed. 'I take your point. I don't like spending money we haven't really got, but I suppose I could maybe buy three or four, if I can find them cheap enough.'

'And another two for the house, Marcus. We're woefully undermanned here.'

He winced, but nodded.

'If money's too much of an issue, talk to Father. I'm sure he would happily lend you a few sesterces.'

Fronto winced again and coughed to cover his nerves. 'That won't be necessary. I'll take your advice on timing though. Five more days until the old stock's gone and the new are in.'

Lucilia smiled reassuringly. 'If it makes you feel better, just keep the slaves long enough to know that they're good at the job and trustworthy, then give them their freedom along with room and board. But at least then they'll be bound to you and more careful than those hirelings out there.'

'I tell you what: five days, and you can come with me and help me choose.'

As the shouting intensified outside, he sighed, kissed his wife on the cheek and strolled off to find his fine Greek clothes to face the day as best he could.

* * * * *

Fronto lurched to the side as a burly Greek with a two-week beard, reeking of sour wine, pushed past him into the throng of the agora and on into the crowd, muttering something angrily. His grumbling was soon lost in the general chaos and din of arguing amateur philosophers, fishmongers, salesmen, beggars and madmen, though Masgava turned and shot the man the darkest of looks on principle.

The entrance and solid, otherwise-featureless rear wall of the theatre loomed on their right, seated at the foot of the green, rocky hill upon which sat one of the city's three great temples. To the left, the narrow, disorganised tangle of streets cobwebbed off into the heart of the city, for Massilia's agora was oddly offset at one end of the wide bay. Behind them the pandemonium of that public space raged and surged like a stormy sea of humanity, but the way ahead was little better. The wide thoroughfare from the agora to the northernmost jetties of the port was packed with life as merchants and teamsters hurried this way and that, carts bouncing and jolting on the cobbled ground, stray dogs winding in and out of the unheeding legs. Men haggled and argued, and the masts of ships were visible over their heads a tantalisingly short distance away. All this, and the sun was still barely over the horizon. On a busy day and with a clear sea, even in winter Massilia made Rome look sedate, calm and organised.

It had taken Fronto some time to get used to the utter bedlam that was the last free Greek city in the west. It had seemed to him that the place had no rules and no order, but long-term exposure was teaching him otherwise. Massilia *had* its rules and its order, but they were a far cry from the Pax Romana, and a foreigner could never hope to understand the workings of the city-state or the Hellene mind behind it in a year of market days.

Slowly, though, he was unburdening his soul of Roman canker. If only Massilia would stop resisting his acclimatisation...

'If you would let us come with you armed and in force, you would not have to fight your way through the crowd,' the huge ex-gladiator grunted.

'And my almost non-existent popularity would disappear into the cracks between the cobbles, Masgava. It's all a game.'

'Other merchants have bodyguards.' The Numidian threw out a finger and pointed at a man in a yellow chiton, dripping with gold and jewels, surrounded by a gang of burly Gauls in mail shirts, their fingers dancing on the pommels of their swords as they eyed the crowd suspiciously.

'He's a Greek. He can afford to stand out because people don't hate him for what he is.'

Masgava eyed the ostentatious jewellery and snorted. '*I* hate him.'

'But here and now, sadly, your opinion counts for about the same as mine, which is to say: not at all. Today is about trying to foster good relations with our Greek neighbours, not asserting our

Roman-ness with red tunics and blades. Come on, that looks like Irenaeus' ship.'

As the two men moved on through the crowd, pushing towards the port, Fronto kept his gaze intermittently on the tall mast, which he felt sure would be the friendly Greek's ship. Very few of the port's sailors would contemplate a black sail, for the ill luck associated with the colour, though Irenaeus allowed himself this little foible, since at the sail's centre Apollo's white raven theoretically overrode all misfortune.

Fronto's heart sank as he emerged from the crowd with Masgava at his shoulder to see the ship's owner busily haggling with a Levantine merchant with a beard like the ancient Cypriots or Sumerians, tightly curled, oiled and falling to twin points at his collar bones. Gods, but the sailor was early. It had been said that Irenaeus would be in Tauroentum, a little way along the coast, and would not arrive in Massilia until the middle of the morning. He was, instead, already part unloaded as the height of the ship riding in the water confirmed. He must have arrived before dawn and, since no sailor in their right mind would try the rocky coast of southern Gaul in the dark, he must have actually put in at Massilia late last night.

The Roman's hopes of getting Irenaeus' mark before any opposition got to him were almost shattered in that realisation. The only chance was that Hierocles and his fellow arseholes were equally unaware of the new arrival. And that the squint-eyed Levantine currently sealing a deal had not filled the hold with a proposed cargo already.

'Make sure we're not interrupted as soon as that Phoenician leaves, alright?'

Masgava nodded and flexed his muscles. A moment later, Fronto was standing a disrespectful three feet behind the intricately-bearded merchant, hovering and trying to catch the eye of Irenaeus. The Levantine had clearly finished his actual business and was now passing the time of day with the Greek captain, and Fronto's impatience was rising at a dangerous rate. His business was urgent and, while he had no intention of further alienating himself from the city's Greek populace, he had no trouble arguing with another foreigner who got in his way.

Noisily, he cleared his throat and the Levantine looked around in surprise. As he turned, his face creased into an angry scowl ready to unleash his feelings on Fronto, but the sight of Masgava, looming a foot taller than Fronto and more than a foot wider at the shoulders, all muscles and teeth gleaming in the sun, seemed to rip the invective from his tongue and leave him with a weak apologetic smile.

'I shall be moving on, sirs. Good day to you captain, and to you, sir.'

Fronto nodded impatiently and waited for the man to be out of the way by only the narrowest of margins before stepping into his place.

'Irenaeus, you're early.'

'Good winds for this time of year, my Roman friend. And your motherland has been almost as kind to me as Poseidon these past weeks.'

His tone was affable, but Fronto was enough of a student of humanity to spot the underlying tension. Something unsaid. Something disquieting. There was a faint troubled look to the man's eyes, which kept flicking downward.

'What's the matter, Irenaeus? You've sold off the last of your hold space?'

The Greek's eyelid twitched as he shook his head.

'Good, 'cause I have a shipment of Falernian costing me warehouse fees in Puteoli, and I need to get it here as soon as possible. Your next trip, yes?'

Again, there was a shifty discomfort in the Greek's expression. 'How big a shipment?'

'Forty amphorae, roughly eighty talents in weight, all well-sealed and stamped by the producer. A good shipment, but small enough still to leave room in your hold.'

'Can we agree on twenty deka?'

Fronto actually stepped back with a blink. Irenaeus had the decency to look rather embarrassed.

'Two *hundred* drachma?' Fronto gasped. 'For a shipment of *forty amphorae*? Gods, man. That's five drachma per jar. I could buy slaves to carry them back from Puteoli for about the same! That's *ridiculous*.' The Roman's eyes narrowed suspiciously. 'Has Hierocles been sniffing around? Did he put you up to this?'

'It's the best I can do, Fronto.'

The former legate, seething, glanced down at the document still open on the rickety wooden desk. 'Bet you can do better for Levantines, eh?' But his roving eyes picked out what looked like an unreasonably high price on that agreement too and the fire died in the furnace of his anger. Irenaeus looked genuinely unhappy, and the same unreasonable terms had apparently been directed at the unknown easterner who had just left. 'What's this all about, Irenaeus? You and I are friends, aren't we?'

The Greek sighed. 'It's the new tax, Fronto.'

'New tax?'

'It went up this morning. A thirty percent tax on all import and export matters involving non-citizen merchant concerns.'

'*Thirty percent?*'

'It seems some influential group of local businessmen managed to persuade the city's *boule* that traders such as yourself are bringing in and taking out goods without a single obol going into the city treasury throughout. Massilia runs on trade, Fronto. The boule will have listened very intently and jumped on the idea.'

'Irenaeus, twenty dekadrachm will make the entire trade worthless. I might even *lose* on the deal.'

The Greek sighed. 'I feel for you, Fronto. You know it's not me, and this is going to hit a lot of Roman, Judean, Gallic and Hispanic merchants. If there was a way I could waive the tax, you know I would. But I have to pass on the tax to the city, so if I help you, *I'll* lose on the deal instead, and I'm a businessman too. You have to understand.'

Fronto sucked on his teeth. 'Can you not grant me even the tiniest bit of leeway? If I promise to try and find a more lucrative deal for you next time?'

'Fronto, there will *be* no more lucrative deal. You'll not get anything better if you continue to operate through Massilia. If you want to make a niche, you'd be better heading down the coast to Narbo and setting up there.'

'Can't do that. Family all live here. Besides, Narbo already has Roman wine merchants galore serving the provincial communities down there. Massilia is the only largely-untapped port, and one of the biggest on the whole Hispanic-Gallic-Roman coast.'

Irenaeus scratched his head. 'Look,' he said, glancing around furtively. 'I'll help you this once. It'll have to be the last time, though. Mark your manifest down on here.' He proffered the vellum document beneath the one just completed by the Levantine. Fronto frowned in suspicion, but filled the spaces with his cargo details, including supplier, warehouse number, weight and quantity. The Greek then turned the vellum around and scribbled his section in spidery Greek text before handing it back, tapping his finger on the price.

'One hundred and thirty drachma?'

Irenaeus nodded.

'That would lift my nuts back out of the fire. Might even keep me going for a while. How can you do it? Will you get into trouble?'

The Greek tapped the top of the sheet. 'No.' Fronto followed the finger and spotted the date that had been freshly added. *Yesterday's* date. 'We sealed the deal late last night at the *Dancing Ox*, mere hours before the tax came in. Do you understand? If you gainsay that in any way at any time, I will be penalised and therefore so will you. You with me?'

Fronto stepped forward and wrapped his arms around the Greek. 'Thank you, my friend. You just saved me.'

'I'm not going to make a habit of it, Fronto. You're going to have to find a solution to your trouble, 'cause next time I'll have to add the full weight of the tax.'

'I understand.'

'Now get out of here. Since we made the deal last night, it would be better if you're not seen here this morning.'

Fronto nodded, squeezed the man in an uncharacteristically grateful hug and then stepped back. With a last nod, he turned and slipped back among the crowd, Masgava following. Even as he stepped away he caught sight of Hierocles and his small cadre of rodents making straight for the jetty that held Irenaeus' black-sailed ship.

'Too late, you slimy bastard,' he snapped with a malicious grin. For a moment he was tempted to stay close enough to watch the Greek wine merchant fume and rant when he learned that Fronto's deal had not gone sour, but the ship captain was right. Better not to be seen anywhere near.

'You were lucky today,' Masgava noted, somewhat redundantly.

'Thanks. I noticed.'

The big Numidian blew out a tired breath. 'I was trying to draw your attention to the fact that even without your little Fortuna doll...'

'*Doll?*'

'Without Fortuna around your neck, you still managed on the strength of friendship.'

'I don't think I can land the credit of that with Fortuna. Just a little desperate begging. The longer I stay in this trade the better I'm getting at begging. Handy, really, since that's probably going to be my sole source of income by high summer!'

'The Greek was right, Fronto. You're going to have to find a solution to this, else you're just going to slide into poverty, and then you won't be able to pay me!'

Fronto looked aside at the gleaming white grin of his friend and rolled his eyes. 'Thank you for your heartfelt support, you big Numidian ox.'

'Speaking of *ox*, shall we go for a jar?' the former gladiator chuckled. 'My treat.'

'Thanks. That sounds good. You've got more money than me at the moment anyway! Then, this afternoon I'm off to the street of the goldsmiths. Time Fortuna was appropriately honoured again. It's a start, eh?'

* * * * *

The squeaking drew Fronto's eyes upwards again and he squinted into the dark rafters until he picked out the two bats wheeling and flittering in the shadows, playing their odd nocturnal games. He smiled to himself, remembering Aurelius' first encounter with the warehouse's resident chiroptera when the superstitious ex-legionary had been busy attaching ropes to the rafter pulleys, had suddenly exploded into a shrieking mass of flapping black hairy beasts, and had ended up hanging from his own ropes by one foot, screaming, while the rest of the former singulares howled with laughter.

That had been a good day.

Fronto had still been positive then.

His gaze dropped once more to the ledgers on the table before him. The numbers added up alright. They added up to one huge steaming turd of a business future. He'd seen criminals being led bound into the arena where angry bears waited, who had longer life expectancies than his business. He really couldn't face looking at those lists any more. In fact he'd not really needed to in the first place. There were servants at the villa who could easily have totted up lists and run inventories without the need for Fronto to get personally involved. But the sad fact was that although the task was as depressing as the year was long, at least it kept his mind busy. While he was fretting about lines of unpleasant numbers, he was not writing around in his sleep, soaking the sheets with sweat and dreaming of faceless *lemures* coming to tear him apart.

And there was the added bonus of being alone. Although Masgava would be irritated with him for going off on his own, the big Numidian would almost certainly guess where he'd gone. And here, the twins were not crying. Here, Lucilia was not trying to be helpful. Here, Aurelius was not arguing with the other staff and the former singulares were not dropping amphorae and blaming each other. Here, Balbus was not being supportive with an air of quiet concern. Here he could be alone with his headache.

'Piss,' he announced with feeling, sweeping the ledger across the table. With a deep sigh, he slumped forwards across the cluttered surface, his arms out and hands drooping at the far side.

'Blargh!' he added, trying to load one sound with every ounce of feeling in his tortured body. His mind began to fill with images of dead legionaries clawing up at him from a sea of smashed wine amphorae and he shook his head to dislodge the unwanted visions.

He had no idea how long he'd been asleep, but he awoke with a start to discover that his drool had formed a huge damp patch on the vellum below him. He could feel it, though not see it, since the oil lamp that had lit his work area had long since expired. Some time, then. Best sleep he'd had in ages. Shame it couldn't continue. What had woken him again?

The gong rang with nine deep booms over in the temple of Apollo, announcing the ninth hour of the night across the dark cityscape. So the gong must have disturbed him. He'd been asleep five hours. Amazing that Masgava hadn't come for him yet. Lucilia would be *livid* when he got back. He decided it might be a good idea now to cut his losses and spend the rest of the night in the warehouse.

He frowned.

Wait a moment. He'd heard the nine gongs for the hour. If he'd been woken by an earlier clang, that would make it the tenth hour at least, if not the eleventh. And he'd spent enough nights in this warehouse over the winter to know that by the tenth hour, the first faint stain of morning light was starting to show through the upper window, highlighting some of the beams in the roof.

Above was just as dark as below.

Logic began to tug at his tired brain. It was still dark, so from experience it could not be later than the ninth hour. And he had heard nine clangs, so that confirmed the precise time. Which meant that there had been no earlier gong. And that meant that something else had woken him.

Fronto the soldier was suddenly in charge again, pushing down the tired, miserable *Fronto the Merchant* and taking his place, alert and concerned. The hairs stood proud on the back of his neck.

The warehouse was pitch black and utterly silent. So silent he could hear the padding paws of that mangy animal *Trojan*, who belonged to a family across the road but had taken to the habit of urinating on the warehouse doors at every opportunity.

And something else.

He was not alone in the warehouse.

Thoughts ran through his head swiftly. Intruders. Clearly, it was intruders. Anyone official or friendly would have opened the door and called out, bearing a lamp or torch. Anyone skulking around in the darkness was up to no good. He listened carefully and was sure he could pick out more than three distinct footsteps at the far end of the warehouse. They were creeping around, but they seemed to be wearing heavy leather boots, and so even creeping they made plenty of noise. Fronto carefully, silently, reached down to his sandals, which had been unfastened for comfort, and slipped them off. With a nimbleness which he still owed to Masgava's ongoing training and exercise program, he slipped out from the seat without nudging the table or the chair. He'd not made a single noise as he rose in the darkness. On the balls of his feet, he padded over to roof support, where he knew Masgava kept a handy length of ash for poking stuck pulleys in the ceiling. His fingers closed on the reassuringly seasoned wood.

Despite the near-complete darkness, his eyes were starting to pick out the faintest shapes of things. He heard a whisper of muttering in Greek across the warehouse, and then a crescent of golden light bloomed behind the racks of amphorae. He could see the shadows of two people thrown onto the wall in that warm glow. There were at least two more, still.

He hefted the staff, wishing he could twirl it to get the measure of its weight and balance, but that would be risking clattering it on a shelf or the floor or ceiling and giving the game away. Masgava had insisted that he learn as many different weapons as possible over the past three years, and it was moments like this he found himself once again grateful to the former gladiator for his enforced lessons.

Almost silently, he padded three shelf-bays towards the glow, ducking sideways into the gloom and protection of the aisle just as the golden glow filled the main hall of the warehouse, right to the table and chair where he'd so recently been in repose.

Thank you, decades of military instinct.

Damn it. At least five of them, he now reckoned as they moved in. The intruders seemed to have decided that the place was empty, and now they began to speak and a second lamp bloomed into life. Fronto was no past master at the Greek language. He couldn't have written poetry or translated the great Gortyn codes, or suchlike. But his basic written and spoken Greek was as good as any high-born Roman with years of tuition under his belt.

'Three each side,' a hushed voice commanded, and Fronto felt his heart lurch. Six! No… seven. Even in an indistinct whisper, that was not a voice used to including himself in the action. That was a man giving orders to six others. He could hear faint muttering among the others. Some of them had strange accents, telling him that they were not native Massiliot, but probably Sicilians or Cretans or some such, come to Massilia for work. They were thugs or hirelings. Nothing more.

His deductions proved slightly askew as he heard a second strong voice telling the others to shut up. So… at least one other proper fighter. They would be the two to take down first, given the chance.

'Check every aisle. Make sure we're alone. Then get to work, but make sure you take only the valuable stuff. This has to look like a genuine theft.'

Fronto felt his blood surging and boiling. No name had been mentioned, but given that little slip, there was absolutely no doubt in his mind who was behind this 'incident'.

He pressed himself back against the roof support, the ash pole vertical and pulled in tight. He watched the first two men pass, peering in half-heartedly, making only a cursory check for lurking figures and completely missing the Roman hidden behind the thick wooden pillar. On the assumption the three at the other side were moving at roughly the same speed, that would leave three men at the rear still to come. It was tempting to wait until everyone passed and then strike, but that was too dangerous. While moving now risked landing himself with enemies on both sides, if he waited, the more experienced men might well see him and he'd lose the element of surprise, ending up trapped in this aisle.

It was fifty-fifty whether that second authoritative speaker would be on this side of the warehouse or the other. He counted under his breath and heard the footfalls of the third man behind the pillar. Taking a silent breath, he stepped out from the support, levelling the staff as he moved. As the figure of the third man came into view, the iron-hard butt of the staff hit the man in the stomach, hard enough to burst organs. There was an explosive rush of air from the man's mouth, almost masking the grunt of pain as the figure fell away with a clatter to the darkened floor.

He knew that the thug in charge would not be so foolish as to walk into the same position – that commanding voice belonged to a man who knew his business. And so, keeping as much of the initiative on his side as he could, he stepped around the corner into the main hall of the warehouse. The leader turned out to be too far away to attack, since he had stayed close to the entrance.

Fronto momentarily weighed up the value of running over and taking down the leader anyway, against the likelihood that the result would be him being brought low by the other five interlopers in short order and then beaten to death. Instead, he decided upon a path of creating as much chaos and confusion as possible. When a legion lost cohesion, men stopped listening to the calls of their cornicen and to their centurions' whistles, and there was a true danger of complete failure. Such was all the worse when a force did not have the discipline of a legion to begin with. If he could keep them off-balance, the leader could not control them and Fronto would have a chance.

'Over by the door!' he shouted in a passable Massiliot Greek. Two of the hired morons turned to look at the second warehouse door, past the empty table, while one was already running back towards his boss. Fronto lashed out with the spinning staff and swept the running man's feet from under him. As the lad fell with a squawk, his legs flailing up in the air, Fronto spun on his heel, allowing the staff to build up momentum as it circled until it struck the flailing legs with the crack of breaking bone.

'What in the name...' came the second commanding voice from nearby, and Fronto reappraised. Two men down but only injured.

Four men still intact, and the leader by the rear exit. Soon they would pull together and he would be in trouble.

Leaping towards the two at the head of the group, who had initially passed him while he hid, he smacked one of them in the centre of the back with the staff, hearing ribs break. The second man jumped lithely out of the way, and two others were now closing on him. Three down, but three well-prepared men now tightening in an arc around him. All three had clubs a good two feet long. He had the reach, of course, but the moment those men got inside the span of his staff, his weapon would be rendered ineffective and he would have to fight off clubs with his fists. The situation was beginning to look rather dire.

Buying himself time to think, Fronto began to twirl his staff around him in a very showy fashion, passing it from hand to hand behind his back with each rotation, making sure to keep himself far enough from walls and shelves to avoid catching the sweep of the weapon. He could almost have laughed. Masgava and he had argued for several hours over why the big man had bothered teaching him such a clearly decorative move. He'd not been able to see any circumstance in which being able to do this would be of benefit.

Yet here he was, spinning the thing like an acrobat and holding off three thugs in the process.

Time. He had a moment to think. Could he get out of the nearer of the doors?

But that would leave these men with free rein in his warehouse. An escape, but hardly a win.

His spin faltered for a moment as the staff caught the hand of one of the men who'd tried tentatively edging closer. It hadn't been his weapon hand, sadly, but certainly *that* appendage would not be useful for some time, if ever.

A cry of dismay at the far end of the warehouse changed everything. The second sound, which followed quickly on the first, was a familiar voice.

'Fronto?'

Not Masgava, after all. In fact, it was the slightly pinched tone of Glykon, the local recruit to his business. He'd found early on that there was something that unsettled him about Glykon, but right now he had to admit that he'd rarely been more grateful to hear his name called.

'Here!' he replied, noting the sudden sounds of a scuffle at the warehouse's far end. He heard the distinctive rasp of a sword leaving a scabbard's collar and flinched for a moment. His spinning staff went slightly astray and he lost his spin-rhythm. Fortunately, the three men facing him had turned their attention away from their prey, focusing on the new activity at the far end.

'Fronto! I'm coming,' Glykon yelled, and then: 'get out of my way you greasy anus!'

There was a sound that Fronto recognised as sharpened iron being turned aside by hard wood, and the interlopers' leader yelled 'pull out!'

Fronto watched the three men turn and run, happy to get out of the range of his staff. The one with the broken ribs was on his feet now, arms huddled round his aching midriff, but running for his life with the rest. One of them was helping up the last man – the one Fronto had first winded. The Roman winced as the escaping troublemakers paused long enough to smash a few amphorae and grab a couple of the smaller, more portable, vases, and then they were gone.

Fronto leaned on his staff for a moment, heaving in grateful breaths. One of the now-fled thugs had helpfully placed their small lamp on the table while they'd faced him and had left it there when they ran, the light continuing to throw the room into golden visibility. As he stumped towards the table and then slid his feet into his sandals, he turned to see Glykon limping down the warehouse towards him. The local employee's stubbled face and close-shorn black hair gleamed in the lamplight. He was holding one arm tight across his chest, blood from some small wound soaking into his chiton, and he'd clearly taken a blow to the leg that had caused the limp but not drawn blood. A lucky man, or else Glykon was more martially-skilled than Fronto had thought. The Greek had held only a short club and had survived a run in with a veteran criminal armed with a blade.

'You alright, Domine?'

The Roman mode of address formed within a Greek sentence seemed extremely odd, but the tone was respectful and concerned, and Fronto found himself warming to the odd man.

'Remarkably, I seem to be entirely unharmed,' he glowered at a mass of pot sherds further along the warehouse and a growing pool of dark red around them. 'My stock does not seem to have borne up quite so well. I think that's the Chian busy running out into the gutters.' He shook his head, turning to more immediate concerns. 'And you? I see you're bleeding. Is it just a flesh wound? We'd best get you seen to. It's a bit early for the physicians to be open in town, but Balbus' major domo is a former field medic, and he knows a thing or two about wounds.'

Glykon smiled. 'Your wife is beside herself with worry, sir. I can walk on to master Balbus' house, or even stitch the wound myself. First thing's first: let's get you home, sir.'

Fronto nodded slowly. 'If you're really alright. I cannot thank you enough for your timely arrival. My business concerns would have been the last of my worries in another quarter of an hour.'

Glykon gestured to the door. 'I've brought the spare keys, sir. Go ahead and sluice down in the fountain outside and I'll lock up and meet you there. You could do without being spattered with other people's blood when the domina sees you. It would raise difficult questions, sir.'

Fronto nodded. 'Quite right. Sage advice, there, my friend. I'll see you outside when I've cleaned up. And when we get home I want to set a two-man armed guard in the warehouse each night. Hierocles has just shifted his game up a notch. I'm going to make him sorry for this.'

* * * * *

'I still don't like this.'

Lucilia nodded patiently. 'I know dear. You're startlingly un-Roman in your outlook sometimes, you know, my love? But bear in mind that these people will soon have a roof over their head, a warm home, good meals and even a few coins. Better than the free but poor of Rome. And every slave you buy is someone you save from fieldwork or the mines, if you're feeling philanthropic again. They won't understand their good fortune after spending their youth living in mud huts and washing in streams.'

Fronto snorted. 'Sorry, Lucilia, but that's the sort of blinkered *Romanitas* that only afflicts those who haven't fought alongside the Gauls. Don't forget that many of them served in Caesar's army. They have their own world that's in some strange ways more civilised than ours. And they don't live in mud huts. They have stone- and timber-built houses with windows and doors and rugs and furniture.'

60

'And there's little chance of another servile war,' Lucilia went on as though he hadn't spoken. 'The Spartacus debacle taught people a lesson.'

'Balls! It taught people a lesson for a couple of years. A few people have shunned slaves, but the rest stopped treating them so badly for a few months until the horrors were forgotten, then they went straight back to beating the boys and humping the girls like a good Roman *pater familias*.'

'Then you be an exception to the rule.'

'You don't understand, Lucilia. The majority of the slaves at the market will be Gauls of one tribe or another. It's possible I was even commanding the fight when some of them were taken. And even if not, they were once free men with a sense of nobility and they're hardly likely to view a new Roman master with any level of acceptance. If you buy a Gaul and speak Latin, watch for a makeshift knife in the night.'

'Then just be choosy about who we buy. I am quite capable of selecting good house slaves. You can steer us right in terms of Gauls, and Glykon knows the trade world, so he can advise us well on who to take on for your business.'

Fronto turned and looked at the dark-haired Greek who followed at a respectful distance. Behind him, Masgava and Aurelius watched the crowd carefully. Masgava had decided that following the 'incident' at the warehouse, Fronto would have an armed guard whenever possible, and the former officer had not the strength to argue. Consequently, while Biorix and Arcadios watched over the warehouse, the big ex-Gladiator and the superstitious former legionary accompanied he and Lucilia, both wearing nondescript local-style clothing but with a long dagger and a short one at their belt beneath the cloaks they all wore against the Januarius chill. The temperature had finally risen last month and the skies had been blue for weeks. At least it never snowed or froze down here like it did in the north, but there was still a chilling wind from the sea.

Glykon was clearly doing his best for the business. He had managed to secure a few small deals, to help alleviate the pressure, with the contacts he had in the city. And he worked all hours, despite a lack of bonus in pay. And, of course, he had saved Fronto's skin in the warehouse. Lucilia had wanted to give him a gift for his timely interruption there, but Glykon had refused, labelling it his duty. He was a good man. But…

61

Far from the agora, close to the huge pottery warehouses and the kiln buildings pouring their pungent smoke into the sky, the slave market was strangely – given the general chaos of the Greek city-state – a much more ordered and solid affair than the sprawling mass of the graecostadium in Rome. Enclosed by a wide boundary wall, the place consisted largely of three large blocks of pens, each subdivided into rooms labelled with the traders' signs, the central yard with a block for the display of wares, a set of wooden seating stands that could easily double as a theatre, and a separate building that housed the market's staff and guards.

The small group approached the gate to the complex, Lucilia almost buzzing with the anticipation of the trade, Masgava and Aurelius watching their surroundings carefully, and Fronto gazing longingly at the *Artemis* tavern across the road. As they neared the pair of guards, Glykon stepped ahead and opened the purse of business funds he carried on behalf of his employer.

'We're here for a private visit.'

The two men looked at the purse and watched as Glykon counted out two small coins apiece, before nodding and gesturing inside. It was the way of things. Those with influence or money or both could arrange such a visit instead of having to sit in the crowd at the public sale in an hour or so and argue with the rest of the buyers. For a small gratuity to the gate guard and a small donation to the market funds, they would be permitted to peruse the indoor pens, select any goods they wished to purchase, and then speak to the merchants who would be here gearing up for the main event. If a deal could be reached early, that slave would be withdrawn from the lists for a private transaction.

Passing through the gate, Glykon deposited a few more obols with a minor functionary, who led them to the first of the three buildings. 'Apologies, *Kupios*, but only the one building is available. We are awaiting a large shipment, but winter is a thin time for supplies, and the other two buildings remain empty at this time.'

'Maybe we should come back another day?' Fronto murmured, but Lucilia smiled at the man. 'I have confidence we will find what we need, sir.'

The man bowed and opened the door so they could enter. The interior was sweaty and warm even from the entrance, and Fronto passed his cloak to the functionary along with the others, to hang on the pegs and await their return.

The next quarter of an hour ranked highly on Fronto's list of experiences not to repeat. The conditions of the slave quarters naturally led to the entire building reeking of faeces, urine, vomit and filth. The inhabitants, familiar with the routine, rushed over to the bars and clamoured to be purchased, desperate to get out of this place. As Lucilia perused them, staying carefully out of reach of the flailing arms, Glykon checked them over. Masgava looked positively ill, and Fronto found himself wondering how long the big Numidian had lived in a place like this before he'd been given a blade and sent out onto the sands. Aurelius looked nervous but then, for such a big fellow, Aurelius always looked nervous.

Fronto watched as Lucilia selected a short, narrow-hipped Spaniard with a face like a fighting dog and the build of a wrestler. Glykon quizzed the man and discovered that the strange figure spoke not only his own tongue, but Latin and Greek, and knew his numbers and letters too. The company in that particular cell suggested that his owner was not aware of his talents, having naturally lumped him in with the other muscle. Lucilia was ever sharp. A bargain had been found already.

He'd tried to argue against her choosing a Gaul at all, though the vast majority of the stock seemed to be Gauls. In the end, he'd had to back down and let her have the delicate red-haired Parisi girl who had been so nervous that Lucilia had had to coax her to the bars. Fronto had his own suspicions as to how reticent the girl might be when she was up at the villa and made a mental note to have her kept well away from blades or other pointy things.

Lucilia and Glykon together then began to set upon the task of finding Fronto some new workers. As they discussed the property on offer, moving from cell to cell, Fronto started to look at the markers on the walls. The script was in a particularly jagged form of Greek and he had to concentrate to translate the words. The names of the various traders were universally Greek: *Anatolios. Nikomachos. Tychon.* His eyes widened as he read the text on the signs below the merchants' names. The traders themselves may be Greek, but the supplier name was also given for transparency of business, and *Kaísaras* appeared on four of every five cells. It seemed too much of a coincidence for there to be more than one man of that name supplying slaves.

'Lucilia, these slaves are almost all from Caesar. They've come down from the fights last year. I probably saw a bunch of these faces at Alesia.'

'Do stop worrying, Marcus. It is only natural that many of Caesar's slaves would end up here. He has to spread the captives about. Sending them all to Rome would simply ruin the market altogether. You're supposed to have a head for business now.'

'I don't like it.'

He peered into Tychon's pen at the denizens and his helpful imagination dressed them in bronze and mail and put blades in their hands. Suddenly he was right back at the desperate fight for the gate at Mons Rea. In fact, he could swear that the one currently glaring at him with wide blue eyes actually threw a spear at him back there. He shuddered and turned away from the pen, opening his mouth to speak. But as he stepped away, a stray desperate hand caught the edge of his pale green chiton and the darker green *himation* worn above it, and he felt his clothes ripped away as he moved. He was jerked to a halt as the material held tight around his middle, leaving him naked to the waist. Turning, he yanked on his clothing, jerking it out of the slave's hands. The functionary, who had been following them around at a respectful distance, rushed over with a thin wand of wood, smacking the errant slave on the hands and eliciting a howl.

'Many apologies, Kupios, but I must really advise you not to get too close to the goods. If you wish a closer viewing, we have guards to keep things under control.'

Fronto grunted as he struggled to separate the two tangled garments.

'Roman!'

The five of them turned at the call and Fronto frowned.

'Roman officer,' added the husky female voice. 'From Bellovaci war, yes?'

'What in the name of Juno...?'

A solitary figure stood in an otherwise empty cell, gripping the bars. She was dirty, but her stance was not one of a broken slave. Straight-backed, she laughed.

'Naked again, Roman. But not so small this time, eh?'

Fronto's blood chilled and he turned to Lucilia to see that her own questioning look had fallen upon him.

'Gods, it cannot be.'

'Marcus, who is this woman who seems to know you?'

'She... err. She was a Bellovaci woman who almost gutted me in a river in Belgae lands – what? – six years ago now? Seven? How in the name of Fortuna did she end up here?'

He gave up trying to disentangle the clothes and simply wrapped them round himself and over his shoulder as he strode over to the cell. She was older, perhaps thirty summers now, and wearing rags, and his memory was not what it once was, but there could be no mistaking those eyes. It *was* the woman who had grabbed his blade while he bathed in a cold river and who had latched on to him like a puppy seeking a home until he'd managed to palm her off on Crispus.

'Why is she in her own cell?' he asked the functionary.

'She's trouble, that one, Kupios. She looks good, but she keeps going out and coming back. No one wants to keep her. Some have beaten her, but they say it makes her all the more defiant. She seems impervious to pain. Sethos the trader loves her. He keeps selling her for a good profit, and she comes back to him cheap to sell again.'

Fronto felt Lucilia's interrogative gaze on his back and shivered. 'This girl was not taken as a slave. She was in the care of an officer.' His helpful memory chose to remind him that Crispus had died years back on a Gallic spear. What would have happened to a girl in his care? His family in Rome would probably not want such a rough *barbaroi* in their house.

'I should have checked up on you when Crispus died.' He turned to Lucilia. 'She was, I think, a girl of good family among her tribe. She was under our protection, but the Fates seem to have been unkind to her.'

'We should get her out of here then, Marcus.'

Fronto stared into Lucilia's gaze and tried to separate the strands of emotion therein. His wife was intrigued, suspicious, perhaps even jealous? But there was a healthy dose of compassion there too.

'Lucilia, you heard the man. She's trouble.' He turned to the functionary. 'How much does she stand to make at auction?'

'Between one hundred and one hundred and fifty drachma, Kupios.'

Fronto sighed. 'We can't go doling out that kind of money, Lucilia. Not for someone we don't desperately need.'

'You said the other day that Captain Irenaeus had saved you quite a bit of money. Marcus, you said she was under your protection. You can't leave her in this place.'

'Lucilia…' he peered into his wife's eyes, but he knew that look all too well. 'If you want her, then we can't get that little redhead you liked the look of.' It was a long-shot, but worth a try.

'Fine.'

He sighed, and strolled over to the cell. 'I never did learn your name?'

'They call me Annia.'

'I'm sure. What do *you* call you?'

'My name was Andala.'

'Then it still is,' Lucilia said firmly. 'Glykon, find this Sethos and haggle him down as low as you can. For every two drachma you save on the hundred and fifty, you can have one of them.'

Glykon smiled and Fronto looked at the straight-backed, pretty young woman who had once held him at knife-point. He could hardly wait for Helladios the goldsmith to finish his new Fortuna pendant. He needed a bit of good luck for a change, and this, while extremely coincidental, did not smack of *good* luck.

Quarter of an hour later the small party of five left the slave markets, Fronto grasping a sadly very thin purse, Lucilia with a satisfied smile. She'd come away with the redhead too, after all. 'I think I would like to spend an hour in the markets, Marcus. Our new staff will need clothing and bedding.'

Fronto sighed. He could really do without spending yet more money he didn't really have on material, but there would be no arguing with Lucilia when she was in this mood. Besides – his gaze strayed across the road – the Artemis tavern was still calling him. 'Alright, dear. But this place is not safe at the moment. My opposition are not above taking those things I love, even in public, so Masgava and Aurelius can go with you.' The two former bodyguards nodded their approval and understanding.

He smiled. 'And I'll…'

'I know, dear. I'll look for you in the tavern when I'm done. Try to be able to talk when I get back. The new slaves are being delivered this afternoon and it would look bad if you can't address them clearly.'

Fronto smiled and kissed his wife, watching her stroll off towards the busy market area, Aurelius and Masgava hovering around her protectively. He was confident that nothing would happen to her. There were no two men in the world he would trust more to protect her.

Turning, he gestured for Glykon to follow and strode into the doorway of the Artemis. It was a tavern he rarely got to – he never seemed to be in the south of the city, where there was no connection to his business or his private life. He'd been in a couple of times over the past year or more, though, and had found the place to be largely patronised by workmen, teamsters and sailors from the port buildings and shipyards that loomed on the far side of the potters' quarter. It had a curious smell, derived from the various industries that surrounded it and from the smoked meats hanging behind the bar.

Fronto heard a strangled noise and turned to see Glykon with a look of haughty disapproval.

'You don't like this place?'

'It is not a place for man of quality, Domine.'

'Despite appearances, I'm not a man of quality,' grinned Fronto, indicating his ruffled and badly-settled chiton and himation.

'Perhaps I should return to the villa and prepare for the new staff?'

Fronto frowned, then shrugged easily. 'If you want.'

'Then I shall see you upon your return, Domine.'

He watched the odd Greek bow, turn and leave, making his way northeast, through the heart of town towards the gate that gave access to the hills upon which the villa sat. With a chuckle, Fronto turned to the tavern. Strangely, it seemed already quite full of life, and no table was entirely unoccupied. In the end, he strolled to the bar, bought himself a cup of medium quality Lemnian, and then made for a table near the door where a man sat alone with his cup. A man, Fronto had noted, who had been watching him with interest as he and Glykon had conversed in the doorway.

The fellow was tall, broad-shouldered and had the build of a manual worker but the face of a thinker. He was clean-shaven, but his dark hair was odd, cut short at the front but long at the rear with braids behind each ear, keeping strands from his face when he leaned forward. His chiton was cut from strong, functional material, and the green and blue container that sat beside his chair had the look of a traveller's kit bag. His features were strange; hard to place. If he had to, Fronto would put him as a northern Gaul, or perhaps a German.

'Mind if I sit?' he asked politely in good Greek.

'By all means,' the man replied in a curious accent that did nothing to help clarify his oddness.

Fronto slumped into the chair with a grateful sigh and threw down a mouthful of wine. 'My name is Fronto. Marcus Falerius Fronto.'

'Yes,' the man smiled. 'Fronto the wine merchant.'

'You know me?'

'*Everyone* in the port knows Fronto the wine merchant. You're rapidly becoming infamous, my Roman friend. Besides, I've watched you and your lot at the jetties many a time.'

Fronto suddenly felt very uncomfortable again. Today seemed to be catching him on the back-foot rather a lot. 'So who are you?'

'My name is Catháin. Well, the bit you'll pronounce is, anyway.'

'You're in the wine trade?'

'Not quite. I was foreman of Eugenios' olive oil business, though he and I had a little disagreement over wages. It seems foreigners are starting to work at something of a disadvantage in Massilia.'

'I hear you there, brother.'

Catháin leaned forward, a questioning look on his face. 'If you are the Fronto who is currently in the sights of Hierocles' artillery, then what are you doing with his man?'

It was Fronto's turn to frown now. 'What?'

'Glykon, the little shit weasel. What are you doing with him?'

Fronto felt as though a trapdoor had opened beneath him. 'Glykon?'

'Of course. He's been Hierocles' man since the dawn of the wine trade. I believe they're distant cousins.'

Fronto blinked and took another slug of wine. Suddenly the reason for his employee's presence in the warehouse the other night became startlingly clear. In fact, he'd be willing to bet that the commanding voice he'd heard from the leader with the sword *was* Glykon. And the man had switched sides and saved Fronto when he realised their 'theft' had gone wrong and the gang had been spotted. Damn it, how had he missed all this?

'Shit. Why has no one told me before?'

'Because you're a Roman, Fronto. You're about as popular as a turd in a bath to most of these people. I'll bet the new taxes are squeezing you tight, eh?'

'You have no idea,' Fronto sighed.

'You want my advice?'

'Given the evidence so far, I'd be a fool to turn it down.'

Catháin grinned. 'Have someone you trust check into all your employees. Hierocles is a devious bastard and he'll get under your skin. Get rid of Glykon and vet the rest carefully. I've seen your workers down on the docks, too. Half of them are soldiers with no idea what they're doing. Separate your guards, your household, and your workforce completely. The guards might think they're being helpful, but your workers would actually be more efficient if the others stayed out of things altogether.'

'Can't really argue with you on any of that.'

'Then, the only way you're going to be able to beat the high tax legally is by improving your business. Secure cheaper sources, markets and transport and seek out buyers as yet untouched by Hierocles so you can carve out a niche from which to expand your influence.'

Fronto blew out a heavy breath and leaned back in his seat. 'Are you for hire?'

'That, my Roman friend, depends upon how much you're paying.'

Fronto snorted. 'My wife is busy spending a small fortune on rubbish at the moment. I'll give you a standard teamster's wage and Glykon's pay on top as soon as I fire him. That should be about right for a foreman, I reckon?'

Catháin chuckled. 'On one condition. When I start to make you money, I take an extra five percent cut of all profits.'

'Done.'

Fronto grinned as he drained the last of his cup. 'Now I shall go to the bar, buy a small amphora of Rhodian to seal the deal, and you can tell me about where you come from, since I cannot for the life of me place your accent.'

Chapter Four

TITUS Mittius rubbed his hands together and blew into them to warm them. Irritatingly, he'd thrown dice with a fellow prefect over duty assignments two months ago and the other officer – the lucky bastard – had secured the supply depot at Arausio in the Rhodanus valley. Apart from the occasional strong wind, that area was a good Roman one, and close enough to the southern coast that the temperature was noticeably warmer. Here at Brivas, in the lands of the Arverni, the great Cevenna mountains kept any warmth at bay and locked the land in cold winter. Frost had formed on his saddle.

'How many more do we have unhomed?'

'Unhomed, sir? None. But many of the houses are near-ruinous. A winter of neglect, you see, sir.'

A winter of neglect.

Because a large portion of the former inhabitants of this Arverni town were now either in the burial pits at Alesia or the slave markets of Massilia and Rome. His job as 'resettlement officer' for the Arverni sounded extremely grand, and it certainly involved plenty of variety, travelling around the tribe's lands and allocating property and trade from the dead to the living poor. Trying to build workable communities from the war-ravaged survivors, so that by spring there would be enough inhabitants to allow the town to live on. It sounded like the very best side of Rome. One might be tempted to consider the seedier side of it, of course. Because when the settlement had the best population manageable and everyone had a home, land and whatever else they needed to live, all those goods that went unclaimed were requisitioned by Rome and sent back to the quartermasters to sell or reassign. But on a practical level it worked for everyone. The Arverni benefitted from Roman organisation helping them rebuild, and Rome gleaned a little profit from the endeavour.

'Very well, Aulus. Once the assignments and musters are complete, send the foraging parties out to the local area and gather stone and timber. Most of these places should be repairable and anywhere you find that isn't, pull it down and reuse the materials. I want Brivas to be self-supporting by the end of Januarius. Then we move on to Revessio.'

The centurion saluted and marched away to his men.

Mittius sighed and looked about the oppidum of Brivas. It was not a defensive place, particularly. More of a civil settlement by the river. It had potential, mind. Reminded him rather of Falerii Novi, his hometown thirty miles north of Rome. In a time of peace, when the summer sun burned the moisture from the land, Brivas might even be described as pleasant.

He shivered in the icy breeze and led his horse around the shattered, ruinous remnant of a building. Not pleasant at the moment, mind.

Time to write a letter to Marcia. The couriers would be coming through tomorrow on their way east. He would receive any new orders from the proconsul's staff, and the riders would take any missives on for Cisalpine Gaul and for Rome. He tried to think what he would say. He missed her. He was pleased with what he was doing and proud to be bringing civilisation and the Pax Romana to the world. He hoped the girls were being good and that young Sciavus had stopped sniffing around after them. Gaul was cold, and he was looking forward to...

Titus Mittius gasped as the cord slipped round his neck and tightened. He was no stranger to combat and his fingers immediately reached down to the sword at his side, but were smashed numb with something heavy and his sword was drawn from its sheath and confiscated. He tried to cry out. Aulus could only be on the other side of this damn building! But the cord around his neck was choking him. Powerless, he gave in and stopped struggling as each movement brought a slight tightening of the cord.

His assailants moved into view, and he felt a supernatural shiver run through him. Several of them, wearing voluminous, heavy, black cloaks with deep hoods, and each sporting a mask with a chillingly friendly expression. Identical masks. Somehow the slight smile in the visage made the figures all the more menacing. Two of them took his horse's reins and moved the beast on. They were being so brazen in full daylight. Most of the populace and the soldiers were across the river, running through allocations and ledgers, of course, but there would still be occasional legionaries, and centurion Aulus Critus, up here in the settlement, while they catalogued and gathered everything for redistribution.

Knowing that he was helpless, Mittius allowed himself to be moved forward towards the house that served as his home and headquarters as long as he was in Brivas. In the most amazingly professional manner, given his predicament, he began to take mental notes. They were wearing trousers and leg wrappings that clearly labelled them Gauls, and probably locals. Either Arverni or other tribes nearby. They included women among their number, for one of the two leading the horse moved with the sway of hips that made her gender obvious. Their masks looked like the cult masks the Gauls used at some of their religious ceremonies. That last thought panicked him, for like every Roman in the army he had heard the horror stories of what druids did to Roman prisoners in their crazed, dangerous cults.

No one came to his aid, despite his hopes, and a few moments later he was being shoved roughly through the door to his house. In the rear, a spring that rose from the ground in the back garden flowed through the house along a wide stone trough and then out to the settlement again. He'd wondered about this curious little piece of hydro-engineering when he arrived, and one of the locals had explained that this house had belonged to a butcher, who used the water in his work. Indeed, many hooks hung from the rafters and he tried not to think too much about them right now.

His hands were jerked round behind his back and tied tightly together, and the pressure of the cord on his throat loosened slightly, allowing him to heave in a deep breath of life-giving air.

'I don't know who you are, but we are here for the good of the people of Brivas,' he hazarded, hoping to shatter their prejudices with a little well-placed explanation.

'Quiet!' snapped the woman in horribly-accented Latin, and a big man who had been just out of sight behind him stepped forward.

'Hardly quiet, Belisama. I want him talking. I want him talking a lot.' This voice was like clotted blood in a wound, like pitch bubbling from a swamp. It made the Roman shudder.

The big figure turned to Mittius.

'I am going to ask you three questions, Prefect. Be aware from the start that you are already a dead man. But how that happens is up to you. You will either die of drowning, or a cut throat, or strangulation, or simple beating. If you are truly unhelpful, it may be more than one. Are you prepared?'

Mittius straightened. He was terrified. The warm, wet feeling down his leg made that absolutely clear. But he was also a soldier of Rome and whatever it was these people wanted, they were clearly enemies of the republic.

'You'll learn nothing from me, when you burst into a peaceful settlement and interrupt the process of trying to restore the land after the war, you *animals*!'

The big man shook off his hood and reached up, peeling the mask away from his features. The raw, torn, ravaged thing that sat behind the mask sent a shockwave of dread and revulsion through Mittius.

'The next half hour is, for you, going to be a time of woe, I think,' the monster said, smiling through a torn face.

* * * * *

Molacos of the Cadurci washed his hands in the spring water until the last of the pink tinge ran off out through the hole in the wall and off through the garden. Rising from a crouch, he dried them on his trousers and looked down at the remains of the Roman, whose throat had suffered periodic, agonising restriction so many times that the red rings around his neck formed a striped collar. The top of his head was matted with blood where the skull had cracked and all four limbs were at unpleasant angles from the body slumped over the trough. Despite the beatings and the strangulations the man had been surprisingly strong-willed, and in the end he had been allowed to drown only until his lungs were full and burning and then, while still conscious and panicked, he'd been pulled back from the stream and his throat hacked from side to side with a serrated knife.

Oh, the prefect of the Arverni resettlement had died badly.

Molacos hated Romans more than any living thing in the world, and he would tear the heart from a Roman girl-child without flinching. But he respected strength. And even while he had hated this prefect as much as any other man of the legions, he had to acknowledge grudgingly that the soldier had remained a man to the end, despite everything.

He turned. Ten other figures stood in the shadowy interior, only a couple of them still disguised.

'Still nothing, then,' old Cernunnos rasped, one of the few still donning the mask.

'No. But someone will answer me in time. And while they resist, we get to kill Roman officers. There can be no goal more true than ours and no path more just. Every one of these vermin that graces his afterlife alleviates the Roman blight on the world of men.'

'Where next?' asked Rudianos, his flame red hair framing a pale, serious face.

'There is a supply depot at Segeta. That is on a major Roman route, and officers there will be well-informed.' Molacos frowned. 'Where is Catubodua?'

'Out stalking some legionary she saw from the window.'

The nightmare-faced warrior snarled. 'Idiot woman. Go bring her back. We must move on before our actions are noted and we bring two centuries down upon us. She knows better than that.'

'You know the widow. If she has two heartbeats to put together she will use them to kill a Roman.'

Molacos grinned, the effect something demonic and horrible. 'Give me an army of Catuboduas and I would eradicate Rome altogether. Still, her vengeance must wait, or our task will fail. Go fetch her while we ready the horses. Segeta awaits us.'

Chapter Five

'THE legions look positively eager,' Brutus noted, wiping a hand across his face and flicking the excess rain away. With a sour look he reached up and pulled back the hood of his cloak, which was now so sodden that the hair beneath it was soaked.

'Of course they look eager,' Varus replied in an acid tone. 'They've all heard of Caesar's largesse with the Eleventh and the Thirteenth. Now every man in the Sixth and the Fourteenth is anticipating a similar donative. Let's hope the Carnutes have a few silver mines as well, or the general might end up out of pocket on this trip.'

Brutus gave a humourless chuckle. Upon their return to winter quarters, following the restoration of the Bituriges, Caesar had codified the payouts to the legions involved so that those men who had received less of the spoils had been topped up from the general's own funds. The legionaries and cavalrymen had been granted two hundred sesterces – a bonus worth two months' pay. The centurions had received two *thousand* apiece. Now, those two legions were back at their bases, living a wild and comfortable life and still managing to put away a little towards their retirement.

The general, his staff and the cavalry had returned to Bibracte, where the general opened proceedings for his assizes and patronage as though Gaul were already a province and the Aedui capital a provincial city in the manner of Aquileia or Salona.

Then, mere weeks after the resettling of the legions, deputations had arrived once more from the Bituriges. Having again taken control of their own cities following the rising of the rebel elements within their own tribe, it seemed that their ever-difficult northern neighbours, the Carnutes, had taken advantage of their weakness and unpreparedness and begun to campaign in Bituriges lands, capturing their settlements and taking slaves and booty wherever possible.

It beggared belief that the army had barely had time to take an evening meal after aiding the Bituriges and there they were again, asking for more help. In other times, Varus might have suspected a trap or some other foul play, or at least some deep, subtle manoeuvring. But the simple fact was that the Bituriges were in trouble and, having lost more than two thirds of their warrior class against Rome, they were in no position to defend themselves. And the Carnutes were a troublesome bunch, for certain. Two years ago,

75

it had been that tribe who had triggered the great revolt with the savage destruction of Cenabum.

So the general had nodded seriously and reassured the Biturige loyalists that he would not allow them to suffer while Rome was here to protect them. Varus had felt just an inkling of suspicion at the general's reaction. Caesar had not been remotely surprised. It was quite possible, of course, given the man's legendary agile mind, that he had already thought through this possibility. Or perhaps, Varus thought maliciously, the general had been stirring something up in order to provide another excuse to march out from camp. The war was essentially over, and the only plunder to be had now would be against the few remaining rebels. It was an unworthy thought for a Roman officer to have about a peer, but Varus couldn't help remembering all the talk back at the start of the campaign that Caesar had managed to manipulate the Helvetii into fleeing into Gaul purely as an excuse to invade the fertile and rich land that had so long been anathema to Rome.

And so in early Februarius the general had agreed to let the Thirteenth and Eleventh rest and recuperate, and had sent for the Sixth and the Fourteenth legions from Cavillonum, a day's march southeast, where they had been in charge of grain storage, gathering and distribution. As soon as the legions had reached Bibracte and mustered, Varus and the cavalry had joined them once more and the army had begun the all-too-familiar journey west into Biturige lands.

In addition to the trouble from the Carnutes, Februarius had also brought rain and a daily blanket of morning fog, and the journey through the oft-marshy lands of the Bituriges was an eerie, white and wet trek, full of nerve-wracking shadowy shapes and muffled noises.

The first few days had been a tiring and dispiriting slog through dismal and sparsely-populated lands. Those settlements the Biturige envoys had announced to be under Carnute attack had been cold and deserted when the legions reached them. The enemy had clearly been there and had stripped the poorly-defended oppida of humanity, livestock and all valuable goods. All that remained was a land of ghosts and the skeletons of towns mouldering in the landscape, picked clean by the Carnute crows.

On one particularly soul destroying morning the cavalry had ridden out ahead to check another silent, lifeless oppidum, and Varus had recognised with a heavy heart one of the fortresses they had been forced to besiege the previous month. A settlement which had been saved from rapine on Caesar's orders and which had thereafter been returned to its legal rulers. The Roman move to save the city's goods and populace from their own traitors had been worthless – they had simply preserved the Bituriges' value to make them a valid target for the marauding Carnutes instead.

As soon as it became clear that the armies were too late to do anything about the raids, the nature of the campaign changed. Disregarding the last few westernmost Biturige towns, Caesar had turned his army north and the legions had marched from ravaged Bituriges territory into that of the Carnutes who had so recently raided them.

Half a day into those lands now, the army had passed four former Carnute settlements, all now long-destroyed, their charred timbers testament to punitive campaigns under Plancus, Marcus Antonius and Caesar himself, as well as the effects of having had legions wintered here over several years. It appeared that few of the Carnute towns remained habitable, and the army found traces more than once of gigantic nomadic sites where large numbers of people had camped for months in a huddle of makeshift temporary shelters.

Varus had been grudgingly opened to the possibility that the very reason the Carnutes were now preying upon their ravaged neighbours might be because the once troublesome tribe now had nothing but the clothes on their backs. If the Carnutes had been forced to change to a temporary nomadic lifestyle with no personal wealth, then raiding the weak would become a natural move for survival. Had Rome's seemingly endless war in Gaul been so ruinous? How could the land ever hope to recover from this? It simply accentuated the folly of continued rebellion.

And now, in the mid-afternoon of the first day among the Carnutes, finally there were signs of life.

Blesio was not one of the tribe's largest or most powerful oppida, yet it had the distinction of being one of few that apparently remained intact. Settled on the north bank of the Liger on a low rise, its walls remained intact and, though they were few and far between, there were occasional columns of smoke wavering up into the wet, grey sky.

The near bank was a glorious wide field of green grass sloping gently to the river. Yet even here, so close to a surviving oppidum, there were signs that a shanty-town of a thousand or more had spent some time in residence opposite the walled settlement. Ahead of the legions, Caesar and a small group of senior officers walked their horses between the areas of dead grass that had been beneath tent leather mere days earlier.

'Looks to me like this lot moved on recently,' Brutus murmured.

'Do you think they were the ones who destroyed the Bituriges cities?' asked the quiet figure of Lucius Caesar, cousin of the general and legate of the Sixth.

The proconsul pursed his lips and shook the rain from his thinning hair. 'This could well have been a warband of some sort, Lucius. There is little sign of civilian life here. It would certainly explain their recent disappearance, with the legions approaching.'

Varus nodded and pointed down to the nearest of the patches of dead grass.

'Look there. Twisted rope. Part of a slave's bindings, I'd say. Looks like the Carnutes came back this way with a column of captives.'

'But why camp here when there is a perfectly serviceable oppidum across the river?' the general's cousin frowned.

Varus sighed. The stick-like Lucius Julius Caesar was a perfectly acceptable commander, and he seemed to know his work, but despite serving last year during the height of the troubles, he was yet to become familiar with Gaul and its workings.

'Likely not all the Carnutes are ravaging their neighbours. Those who still have a town and a population are probably content to simply try and survive the winter long enough to rebuild their lives. I would be willing to wager that the raiders who camped here were refused admittance to the oppidum. Any Carnute leader with his mind on the future will weigh up his options and come down on any side that doesn't bring the legions to his hearth.'

Caesar nodded. 'Let us not tar the whole tribe with the deeds of a vicious few. Come. There is a ferry ahead. We will speak to the locals.'

At the general's order, Varus and Brutus rode forth, along with Lucius Caesar and Glabrio, the two legates in the force. Behind them, close and protective as always, rode Aulus Ingenuus and a dozen of his best Praetorian cavalrymen. The ferry across the Liger that served the Carnute oppidum was little more than an oversized raft with a tethering rail and two burly natives with oars. Varus eyed the vessel suspiciously as they approached. It might feasibly carry four men and their horses across the river, on the assumption that the horses stood perfectly still, the raft was entirely sturdy, and the two men were trustworthy. He would not put money on it. The men looked extremely fidgety and nervous, and well they might, with roughly twelve thousand Romans descending upon them.

'General, you can't go on that.'

Caesar turned with a curious smile. 'I most certainly can, Varus, and I most certainly will. How can I expect my legions to perform the unthinkable with heart and aplomb if I am not willing to risk a rickety ferry ride? Besides, I am labouring under no misapprehension that Aulus here would let me go without the continued presence of a guardsman. Would you care to make up a third passenger, Varus?'

The cavalry commander sighed. The general was ever one to play up to the troops and show off, and now his unnecessary bravado had placed Varus in the position of either appearing cowardly or trusting to the raft. 'Of course, General.' He watched Caesar's eyes sparkle as the man laughed with carefree ease. There was a growing group among the officers who worried that Caesar was beginning to believe in the rumours that he was indestructible. The way he acted sometimes suggested as much.

'Come.'

The Proconsul of Gaul and Illyricum swung from his mount and slid to the ground, walking his horse down to the riverside where the two ferrymen waited beneath the eaves of their small hut.

'Good day, gentlemen. Do either of you speak Latin?'

The two men frowned in incomprehension, and Caesar smiled. 'Ingenuus, you can come over on the second trip. I want your man with the local dialect with me on this journey.'

Varus caught Ingenuus' expression and was under no illusion as to what the bodyguard officer thought of the idea, but they had all been around Caesar long enough to know how little chance there was of changing his mind. The only man who'd ever had that kind of influence was Fronto, and *he* was probably busy now swimming in a pool of the money he'd made in Massilia.

The Praetorian trooper in question, one Sidonius, rode forward at his commander's signal and, at a nod from Caesar, rattled out a question in the local language. The ferrymen looked at one another and stuttered out a reply.

'They have not a word of Latin, general. They claim loyalty to Rome and to be men of Blesio across the river, which they say is also loyal to its Roman vows.'

Caesar nodded and favoured the two men with an easy smile. 'Ask them how much they charge for a man with his horse?'

The trooper did so, and cleared his throat before replying 'One copper coin apiece, general, but they say there will be no charge for the Roman commander and his officers.'

Caesar laughed lightly. 'Nonsense. With the current state of Gaul, every denarius counts for these people. Tell him that we have eighteen riders to ferry across in six trips. If he can do it without incident, he will receive one good Roman silver sestertius for each man from my own purse. Brutus? Have word sent to the legions to make camp on the south bank tonight, pending a decision on our course tomorrow.'

As Brutus nodded and turned, the news was relayed to the ferry owners and the two locals' eyes widened as they bowed sycophantically. Without waiting, Caesar gestured to Varus and Sidonius, who dismounted and followed the general to the raft. As the two ferrymen readied for the journey – the Liger was a wide river here, and fast-flowing – Caesar and the other Romans tied their nervous horses' reins to the bar and held on tight while the raft shook and juddered off the mud and slowly out into the current. Varus couldn't help but note the look of anxious disapproval on Ingenuus' face as he watched from the bank, where he prepared to come across next with Brutus and another of the praetorians.

The raft was sturdy, and despite the size and speed of the river its surface was remarkably calm, and soon Varus found his fears of capsizing or destruction fading. The general gestured to Sidonius.

'Would you ask them if a large band of rebels recently passed through here, perhaps with loot and captives?'

The trooper relayed the question and the two men, their faces revealing their nervous state, nodded and rushed out a reply.

'Several hundred Carnute warriors, general. And many dozens of captives with them, as well as three carts of booty.'

Caesar smiled. 'At least they know enough not to lie on such a blatant fact. Ask them how they crossed and where they went? I cannot imagine they brought wagons of supplies across on this ferry.'

A brief exchange followed, with lots of nodding from Sidonius, who translated the reply.

'According to the ferrymen, a few leaders and warriors crossed the river, but were refused entry to Blesio. They made off north afterwards. The rest of the force with the loot and slaves set off downstream two days ago, making for the ford at Ambasso, where they will cross and head north to join with the leaders.'

Caesar nodded. 'I know of Ambasso. A vexillation of ours camped beside the oppidum there following the siege of Avaricon last year. The ford is supposed to be easy in the summer season, but often submerged in the winter. Still, it has been a mild, if cold, winter, and obviously the locals consider it passable. Once we have spoken to the nobles in Blesio, we will return to camp and the legions can work their way west to cross at Ambasso.'

'We will pursue them, then, Caesar?' Varus presumed.

'If there is any hope of us catching them, yes. They could be fast-moving, compared with our baggage train speed. But they are heading north, and north is Cenabum, which has always been the heart of both Carnute pride and their druids' religion. If the enemy will ever stand to face us, they will do so at Cenabum.'

Varus nodded, though somewhere deep down he remembered hearing that Autricon was their true seat of political power. It had not escaped Varus' notice, though, that Cenabum, while not their true heart, was their great trade centre, and the richest settlement in Carnute lands.

* * * * *

Varus eyed Hirtius suspiciously. The addition of Caesar's secretary on any detached duty was cause for unease as far as the cavalry commander was concerned. The last time it had happened, Hirtius had been instrumental in seizing the mines of the Bituriges on the flimsiest of pretences. And now the bird-like figure was once more riding alongside the cavalry as the force neared the Carnute oppidum of Tascio.

'If the rebels did flee here, it looks to me like they went on running,' the cavalry commander murmured.

'Our intelligence says that this is the location of one of four sightings of the Carnute warbands,' Hirtius replied primly. 'Are you suggesting we ignore the matter?'

Varus glared at the man, who he was beginning to see as little more than an extension of Caesar's grip. In his personal opinion, the Carnute raids had been just that: raids. They were not a campaign of invasion as the Biturige envoys had put it to the general in their panic

81

and desperation. The Carnutes, like most other of the more belligerent tribes, had lost so many fighting men in these last few years that they could hardly hope to mount an invasion. The warlords had simply seen an opportunity and begun to raid their weaker neighbours. It was going to be hard to survive the coming year, and easing the tribe's suffering by taking from weaker groups would make a noticeable difference.

Something in his subconscious suggested that there might be more to it than that, of course. It was tempting to see conspiracies and strategy in everything these days, after what had happened over the past two years. Could it be that some new Vercingetorix was setting fires in the hearts of the more aggressive tribes to keep the Romans off-balance? It had happened a year or so before Alesia, after all. And in more than a month, the general and his armies had spent their time rushing around solving small problems rather than resting and preparing for the season ahead. Coincidence?

He shook his head. Logic suggested the former.

Having failed to catch up with the enemy at Ambasso, Caesar had taken the entire force to Cenabum, where he had found traces in both memory and physicality of the recent passage of warbands with slave chains. Helpful 'loyal' Carnutes – could there be such a thing? – had given Caesar details of four such groups that had passed through Cenabum heading northeast and southwest, doubling back past the pursuing army. While the general had settled the two legions in the oppidum that had so recently been the site of a massacre and a brutal punitive siege, he had sent out the cavalry.

The men of the Sixth and Fourteenth now sheltered in the half-ruined houses of Cenabum, the shells of the town's residences providing some protection and ease from the winter winds, though each eight man contubernium had erected their own tent inside the houses, since few boasted a surviving roof.

And Varus, accompanied by the humourless Hirtius, had been tasked with visiting the towns named by the informants and tracking down these rebels. As far as Varus was concerned it was a pointless task. The Carnutes would melt into the landscape, sell their slaves and separate, taking their gains with them. None of these warbands were going to be stupid enough to hole up together in an oppidum and face off against Caesar's army. None of them were near strong enough.

If these raiders were simple opportunists, they had no need and no desire to confront Rome. And if, despite having brushed the idea aside, they were part of a campaign of distraction, they would do everything they could to evade capture and keep the Romans busy. Either way, Tascio would be unlikely to deliver up Caesar's enemies.

Experience over the past few days, however, had taught Varus how futile it was to try and argue the logic of matters with his solemn companion. Hirtius was an orator, and a good one. A friend and confidante of Caesar's and a man famed for his addresses in the city. No matter how much logic and sense Varus had on his side, Hirtius would talk him in a spiral until he was arguing into his own face. Besides, even if Hirtius agreed, which he had done on occasion, he was bound by his duty to Caesar to an extent Varus had rarely seen in an officer. He seriously wondered if Hirtius might physically explode if he tried to disobey an order.

'There's no one in Tascio, Hirtius.'

'Oh?' The accompanying officer looked across at him with an arched eyebrow. 'How so?'

'It's winter. It's as cold as *Trivia*'s tit. The ground's damp and freezing and the air is grey and filled with icy mist. And how many fires can you see burning in Tascio?'

'None, clearly.'

The air above the oppidum was empty and clear, if depressing and colourless.

'Precisely. No columns of smoke. Therefore no fires. No fires in this kind of weather means no people.'

'Or people with something to hide from an approaching column of Romans.'

Varus snorted. 'Do you really believe anything you say, Hirtius, or is it all disruptive discombobulation?'

'Unless you are about to try and wrest command of the army from the Proconsul of Gaul, Varus, your duty is to follow the general's instructions. And the general's instructions are to search the oppidum of Tascio and harry the enemy if we find them there.'

Varus sighed and turned back to the settlement ahead. Even given the speed of mounted informants among the Carnutes and of the cavalry wing, the trail of the warband had to be even colder than the chilling ground by now. If the rebels had ever been at Tascio, even their footprints would be gone by now.

The oppidum was not one of the great walled defensive sites the army had become so used to in these lands, but a second type with which they were rapidly becoming familiar: a civil settlement with low walls, by a river and surrounded by agriculture and industry. A commercial and residential centre more than an ancient fortress. It seemed that in recent decades, before Rome's interference, a subtle shift had begun in the Gallic nature, away from a state of near-perpetual warfare towards a cooperative commercial drive.

What might have happened to this land if the legions had not slammed down their nailed boots upon it?

Varus slowed his horse slightly, allowing Hirtius to ride ahead a little, then turned and gestured to the leader of his *speculatores* – his scout riders. Cacumattos was of the Aedui, but from nearby Decetio and therefore not too far removed from this area. The Gallic scout, dressed and armed so similarly to his Roman counterparts that he could have blended in but for the long, braided hair and the trousers beneath his tunic, geed up his horse and trotted forward.

'Cacumattos, what do we know of Tascio?'

The scout frowned and rubbed his chin.

'Merchant town, commander. It is Carnute town, but across river is Bituriges, and that hill,' he gestured to a slight rise perhaps a quarter of a mile away, 'is Turone lands. Tascio marketplace for all three tribes. Big trade for pottery and salt. Also iron from upriver.'

Varus nodded. 'Big fishing industry too, I'd wager. I see extra channels cut from the river here leading to catchment areas. Tascio might be small, but I'd wager it's a place of some importance to the Carnutes, as well as the other tribes.'

The scout nodded and Varus, suspicions creeping into his thoughts once more, tapped his lip. 'They're more distant from your home, but what do you know of Durocason and Salio in the north-east and, more locally, Gabrio, just upriver?'

Cacumattos sniffed and rubbed his eyes as he plumbed the depths of his memory. 'Gabrio another crossroads market. Big for cheese and food. Trade with Bituriges and Aedui.'

Varus nodded, a sour realisation forming deep inside as the man went on.

'No sure of Durocason. Small tribe within Carnutes. Think Durocason controls trade on Autura river. Salio centre for druids. Very powerful.'

'Thank you, Cacumattos.'

As the scout bowed from the waist and then trotted his horse back into position among the other scouts, Varus locked his eyes on Hirtius up ahead. He would not be able to prove Caesar's intent, of course, but Varus was now fairly sure as to why he and his horse had been sent to trace the movements of these elusive warbands. Four settlements targeted. Three major trading posts, all secondary to the great port of Cenabum, but each a place of thriving commerce with a speciality, and all likely rich pickings. The last a centre for the druids. These days, with the Romans so regularly camped nearby there would be little physical power there, but the druids were as much the leaders of Gaul as were the nobles, so there would almost certainly be a great deal of wealth there at one time. He had no doubt whatsoever that Caesar had engineered these specific targets. But had he taken the intelligence of the passage of rebel warbands and selected the wealthiest towns en route, or had the warbands also been fictional and this entire endeavour simply yet another excuse to rape the civil settlements of a beaten tribe for the furtherment of Rome. And of Caesar?

With a sense of irritation, the cavalry commander caught up with Hirtius, turned and started issuing orders to his prefects and native leaders.

'When we reach the settlement, I want each ala moving into a different area of the place. Check the whole oppidum. Once you have scoured the streets on horseback, dismount and check out the buildings, but make sure to leave a defensive force as you do it. Anyone you come across, bring back to the gate and we will question them, though I doubt you'll find a single Gaul here.'

Hirtius turned to join him. 'And while searching the town, take note of all livestock, any potential pack animals and any carts, wagons or other vehicles. Once we confirm the place is deserted, I want those items rounded up and brought to the central square.'

'So brazen?' Varus asked tartly.

'I beg your pardon, commander?'

'You're already organising the systematic looting of the place before we've even confirmed it's empty?'

'No, Varus. I specifically stated "once we confirm the place is deserted." Please try to listen.'

Varus ground his teeth as the other senior officer went on to detail what was to be impounded upon confirmation of desertion. Of course, the major trade goods of the area were listed: pottery, salt and iron. Any coinage, armour, jewellery and so on was to be gathered and pooled. While the main trade goods would be loaded for return to the proconsul's headquarters, the small booty would be divided up among the men.'

Varus could almost feel the avarice flowing out from the riders – *his* riders! Not only was the process of looting already defined before they reached the place, but the motivation of the looting parties had just increased tenfold.

'This is beneath us, Hirtius.'

'Commander?'

'These people were beaten. I don't care if there are a few small rebel groups causing trouble – that is no excuse for raping the lands of the tribe for the proconsul's gain. The Carnutes are barely going to make it through the year as it is. If we relieve them of what little they still have, we likely relieve them of the chance of survival.'

'If you are feeling guilty at exercising the just and gods-sent rights of the victor over the vanquished, Varus, then perhaps you should take the Carnutes on as your clients. Your family has no small place in Roman society, and a sizeable vault of money, I should say.'

'You are contemptible, Hirtius.'

'And you are living in a world of dreams, commander.'

Varus watched the crane-like figure of the other officer ride ahead with his personal guard. It occurred to him that possibly Caesar had lost those men from his command who had tried to guide or curb the general when required. Gone were Cicero – back to Rome and politics, Fronto and Balbus – both off to retirement in Massilia, Sabinus – killed by Ambiorix, Crassus – dead on the Parthian sands. Indeed, the only man remaining in the army who still had the influence to change Caesar's mind was Titus Labienus, and the hugely successful lieutenant had spent most of the recent seasons on detached duty in the east of Gaul, away from the main army.

These days it seemed that Caesar's officer corps was filled with young hopefuls from Rome seeking glory, sycophants who saw the victorious general purely as a source of wealth, and old worn-out nobles who cared little for anything other than getting through this last year and securing a lucrative position when Caesar was made consul.

Brutus might be the only man left who could argue Caesar away from a course of mass pillage at the expense of Gaul's future. But

Brutus was tied to Caesar by blood, and consequently had made no move to do so.

Would Gaul even be worth turning into a province by the time Caesar had returned to Rome?

Varus set his sights on the approaching oppidum, grinding his teeth. There would be at least a week yet of Hirtius' company as they systematically stripped the four richest Carnute settlements before returning to the army where, the commander was sure, Caesar would pronounce the rebels beaten and fled, and the campaign another victory, and would then return to winter quarters richer than ever.

Gods help any other tribe who might come to his attention…

* * * * *

'Is it true?'

Brutus looked up from his mouthful of warm bread and butter. 'Hmm?'

'Is it true?' Varus repeated. 'Are the Bellovaci really rising against us?'

'That's the information we have. You heard the details at the briefing. And the news came from the Remi, who are – as you rightly know – the only tribe in the entire land who have been staunchly allied to Rome since the day we met.'

Varus stared sourly down into his cup of well-watered wine. The cavalry had been back from their *glorious victory* over the Carnutes for three days now and still the spoils were being logged and secured for transport to Massilia and beyond. Varus had been so irked at being used as a sanctioned thief that he had rarely crawled out from the amphora since returning to camp. He thought briefly of Fronto in his early days here and began to understand how his friend's prodigious drinking had started. Perhaps long-term exposure to Caesar did that to a moral man?

Once again, at the command meeting this morning, word of another minor rebellion had been received. The Bellovaci, up among the Belgae, were reported to be raising an army for an invasion of their neighbours, the Suessiones. And with the Suessiones having declared themselves subjects of Rome and loyal to Caesar, of course, the army would march on the Bellovaci to put things right. No doubt, in the process, a few of the richest Bellovaci towns would render unto Caesar that which he most desired.

Consequently, Caesar had decided to exercise another group of legions. The Belgae being generally stronger and more tenacious than these central and western tribes, Caesar would take four legions to maintain the Pax Romana. The Seventh were being sent for, where they currently wintered under Trebonius' command, along with Rufio's Eleventh and the Eighth and Ninth, who were currently under the combined command of Fabius. Trebonius would maintain Cenabum with the Tenth and Twelfth, who were marching here with all speed, while the men who had marched into Carnute lands two weeks ago would return to their winter quarters, wealthy and rested.

Yet the timing was all too convenient. At the projected date for the army to depart – two days from now – the two new garrison legions for Cenabum must already have been on the way, which suggested strongly that Caesar knew beforehand that he was going to be leaving and taking the army with him.

'It just seems too coincidental that the Bituriges have a little rebellion, and a matter of days after the legions return to quarters, the Carnutes have their rebellion. We don't even get to chastise them, since they just evaporate into the wilds. Then the legions have a little rest before the Bellovaci rise up and we have to march again. And each time we return with wagon loads of spoils. Doesn't it strike you as a little convenient?'

Brutus shrugged. 'There is the possibility that someone is actively stirring up trouble? It seems the most likely to me.'

'I'll admit that the notion had occurred to me too, Brutus. But isn't the general fortunate that those tribes who are rising up and who we have to go quash are ones who have made it through these years of war with a few solid resources remaining, and we're now capturing those resources. The Carnutes are an important tribe and both they and the Bituriges, despite having been at the heart of the warfare, are so involved in inter-tribal river trade that their economy has survived. And the Bellovaci have been largely untouched for six years now, so I'll wager they're a ripe fruit hanging tantalisingly low now too. But poor tribes like the Menapii and the Cadurci, the Arverni and the Mediomatrici, who have given up everything they could to Rome and lost anything else to war itself, are peaceful and require no Roman presence. There's logic there, yes, but it's still suspicious.'

'Sounds like you're trying to accuse Caesar of engineering wars for profit.'

'*Juno*, Brutus, keep your damned voice down. That sort of comment gets men in the deepest of shit.'

'True, though. Is that what you believe, Varus?'

'It's not far-fetched, let's put it that way.'

Brutus mused over the matter as he took another bite of his buttered bread. 'It may be as you say. It may not. Either way it makes no difference. If that is what he's doing, it is his prerogative. He has the authority and entitlement to do as he sees fit, and everything he's done has been for the good of the army, and of Rome.'

'And of himself.'

'That's an unworthy comment, Varus. The fact remains that the only people who have suffered are the Gauls, and if they stay loyal they will prosper.'

'Tell that to the Bituriges.'

'If this bothers you, Varus, try to turn a blind eye to it for a few more months. Soon the general will be heading back to Rome, the army will disband, and this new province will become the command of some fat, selfish senatorial governor. If Caesar left Gaul a rich and prosperous land, his successor would only rake off all the profit into his coffers anyway.'

'I still don't like it.'

Brutus washed down his bread and coughed in the cold air. 'Then here's a little rumour to help put your fears at ease, Varus. Nothing has been confirmed yet, but I spoke to one of the scouts this morning who had, in turn, been speaking to the Remi riders that brought us the news. The man told me that the name behind the rising that is being spoken up in the Belgae lands is "Commius".'

'Commius?' Varus cast his mind back. The king of the Atrebates had been an ally of Rome since the early days, immediately after that near disaster at the Sabis River, but had turned from Rome and thrown his lot in with Vercingetorix last year, only to leave Alesia unharmed and return to the north. How odd it was that Caesar had never expressed the need to locate and punish the man. Uncharacteristic, in fact. Still, the linking of Commius with the new troubles gave it more legitimacy than the two previous risings.

'Yes,' Brutus replied, sipping from his cup. 'They say that Commius has been stirring up the Bellovaci. And clearly we cannot leave that treacherous scum to his own devices. Two days and we ride north-east. I understand that Caesar is intending to march from

89

depot to depot and station to station and supply as we go. That way we could make Bellovaci lands in four days, maybe even three, not tied to the speed of the wagons.'

'Alright. I'll grant that this sounds a little more serious, but watch what happens when we get there. I'll give you my villa at Antium if we deal with the Bellovaci and don't come out of it with a train of loot-wagons.'

Brutus chuckled. 'I'll remember that. Antium's lovely in the autumn.'

* * * * *

Five days later Varus found himself deep in Bellovaci lands with three alae of cavalry a day ahead of the army, sweeping through deserted oppida and small settlements, trying to ascertain anything concrete concerning Commius and this army of his. Further information from the Remi had added another name to the list of conspirators – one Correus, a Bellovaci noble – and also the names of several smaller surrounding tribes who had thrown in their lot with the rebels.

So the cavalry had been sent ahead to discover what they could of the enemy, and Varus had consequently split his force into large scout parties that passed through the region seeking news.

But in five hours of passing through Bellovaci oppida, Varus had yet to see a human face. The settlements were deserted, all the livestock and goods removed from them. They were mere empty shells, devoid of life and value. Not simply abandoned like the ruined towns of the Bituriges and the Carnutes, but methodically emptied by its own populace, its entire contents moved elsewhere. It was almost a shame that he didn't have Hirtius hovering over him like a vulture this time, since the man would be twitching at the lack of plunder to be had.

He tried not to imagine himself handing over the deeds to his favourite summer villa to Brutus.

In perhaps half an hour the force would have to turn back and meet up with the rest of the cavalry before returning to Bellomagos, where they would encamp and await the arrival of the legions. Varus slammed his fist on the horn of his saddle in irritation. Surely the Bellovaci, if they were building so large an army, would not have melted away into hiding like the Carnutes? So where were they?

His eyes strayed to the northern horizon, wondering where the next major oppidum was and whether they would have time to reach it before turning back.

He blinked, and gestured to a decurion he knew well.

'Avelius? You have better eyes than me. Sweep your gaze around the area and concentrate on the small stand of trees on the hillside. Don't look straight at it, but just catch it in passing and tell me what you see.'

The decurion did so and returned his gaze to his commander. 'Two men on horseback in the shade of the trees.'

'Good. I'd only seen one. But not an army, anyway. We'd have spotted traces of that kind of force. They're watching us, keeping tabs on us. If we want to know anything, those are our men up on the hill.'

'What do we do, sir?'

'We make a show of looking around for a moment longer, then we turn and ride back for Bellomagos. As soon as we drop down into the narrow valley we passed on the way here, you and I, along with your turma of men, peel off and hide there, waiting for them.'

'What if they don't follow us, sir?'

'Then we lose them, but I think we'll be fine. I've felt uneasy all day, and I think they've been watching us since we crossed into Bellovaci lands. They're just good enough that we hadn't seen them 'til now.'

The decurion nodded and went back to inform his men, and Varus called over his officers, explaining what they were about to do. Then, while the cavalry commander sat visibly fuming, gesturing at the empty houses of this small settlement, the men went about searching everywhere thoroughly for the look of the thing. Then, another quarter hour having passed, the alae formed up and moved out in formation, making for the rendezvous to the southwest. Varus felt his nerves twanging as his force dropped down into the defile and then rose to crest the far side of the narrow stream valley, riding on away from the enemy. But the retreating force was not quite complete, for in the bottom of that narrow way, clogged with undergrowth and ancient trees, thirty men paused, listening to the thundering hooves of their compatriots riding away.

Using gestures only, Varus gave out his orders and the unit split into three groups. Ten men, led by Avelius, moved behind a knot of trees out of sight. Another ten, led by the man's second, followed suit behind another makeshift screen. Varus took the remaining ten and they dismounted, tying their horses behind trees and undergrowth, away from the churned earth that marked the cavalry's passage. They then drew their blades and moved into hiding places to either side of the track along which the enemy would have to come if they hoped to track the Romans.

A quarter of an hour passed, tense and silent, but finally, just as Varus was beginning to worry that the decurion had been correct and that the enemy were not coming, he discerned the sound of horses above the rustle of wind-whipped leaves and scrambling wildlife and the gurgle of slow-flowing water around stones.

The riders neared the stream gulley and, though still out of sight, Varus counted what he believed to be three horses. Sure enough, a moment later, as he pondered on how far afield his thundering heart could be heard, three mounted shapes appeared at the lip and descended quickly to the stream bed, following the beaten earth and the prints of hundreds of Roman horses.

He opened his mouth to give the order and almost exploded as one of the cavalrymen leapt from behind a tree and shouted for the men to stop. The moron! Ambushes fail with over-excitement.

Entirely predictably, the three riders reacted instantly, their own alertness heightened by the danger of their task and driving them to action without the customary moments of dither and panic an ambush usually creates. However *alert* they might be, though, they were not *prepared*.

One man with long blond hair and a helmet bearing a boar at the crest burst forward, racing up the slope ahead, away from danger and on in pursuit of the retreating cavalry force. Another, a bare-headed and bald man with a face like a pomegranate, wheeled and raced back up the slope from whence he came, presumably thinking to carry warning to the army. The third, his horse bucking, swept down with his blade and cleaved the stupid cavalry trooper through the shoulder. As the thrashing, agonised form of the dismounted rider fell to the frosty, churned ground, his arm flopping uselessly and crimson pumping into the cold air from the chasm in his flesh, Varus raced from cover. Gritting his teeth, he threw himself at the mounted Gaul in a dive, using his slightly elevated position to his advantage, hitting him in the midriff and knocking him from his horse. The commander landed with his target in the mud and, while Varus had the wind knocked from him, the man on the ground had clearly broken something from the bony cracks as they hit.

For a moment he worried that the man might be dead, but a groan answered that question.

As the commander rose painfully, three of his men rushed over and hauled the pained Gaul to his feet, stripping him of anything he might use to fight back. Varus turned this way and that to check the situation and was relieved to see that his strategy had worked. The men who had fled the ambush had not been prepared for a second surprise. Neither escapee had made it to the top of the bank before those two other hidden units had caught them. One had twisted to fight and had fallen and snapped his neck on the hard earth. The other, though, was in custody, the men busy demanding his blade from him.

Varus looked at the wounded man by the stream.

'You're coming back to our camp now, my friend, where we are going to have a little chat about your tribe and their allies, where they are, and what their intentions are.'

'He will tell you nothing,' spat the disarmed one at the hill crest, 'and neither will I.'

'Well you just told me that you speak excellent Latin,' smiled Varus. 'I wonder if you understand the word *scourged*?'

The enemy scout paled, and Varus gave an unpleasant chuckle. 'Take him to the cavalry. We'll pry a little on the journey back.'

* * * * *

Caesar stood on the wet, cold grass, the latest fine mizzle falling about him like a downward-drifting fog. Behind him, the men of the Eleventh legion worked to get his command tent erected so that he could shelter from the weather. Two of his praetorians had hurried over to raise a cloak above him and keep off the fine rain, but the general had waved them away. What harm could the weather do other than make his helmet plume hang limp?

It had been decided to make camp on the hill of Bellomagos and, though the term *hill* might be over-exaggerating the rather feeble rise in the centre of this unbelievably flat region, Caesar had campaigned through the territory a few times before and recognised the rarity here of any kind of rise. A mole's spoil heap in this land could be labelled a hill.

The four legions were still pulling into position, and the last would still be arriving just before nightfall. The Bellovaci oppidum, a squat site with heavy, low walls surrounding a collection of stone and timber buildings, was deserted and had been emptied of all life and goods, and brooded from its position by the river. The Roman camp was already taking shape, the basic markers in place, and soon the initial base for the new campaign would be complete and inhabited – seemingly the *only* inhabited place in these lands. The army had passed through Veliocassi territory, witnessing no sign of the tribe whose land it was, and into Bellovaci territory with still no human being to greet them. It was, even to a practical old soldier like Caesar, strange and eerie.

He was, however, under no illusion as to what it meant. Commius' rebel sentiments had clearly had a lot more effect here than those poor disillusioned revolutionaries and bandits to the south-west. The Belgae had not suffered as deeply as many others in the last brutal year of the war, and they were the only people in the whole region who might still be able to raise a force large enough to make a spirited attempt to resist Rome. And these consistently empty oppida pointed as clear as any signpost to a single force of the enemy marshalled in one location. If only they also held directions…

A legionary scurried up through the drizzle and saluted as he came to a stop, his breathing laboured.

'Sir. Large force of allied cavalry spotted to the north. They'll be here shortly, general.'

Caesar nodded. 'Once they arrive, have the commander report to me here.'

The soldier saluted again and ran off, and the general used the flat of his hand to wipe the excess moisture from his face. The men of the Tenth were being as efficient as ever, but he still wished they would hurry in their task. He'd had another 'episode' this morning – luckily just after his morning address and before he had emerged from his tent for the journey – and what he had initially thought to be weakness and trembling following his fall had taken quite some time to dissipate. In fact, he'd still had to hide the shakiness of his hands as he mounted his horse and led the column out. And he knew from bitter experience that the prolonged after-effects of his attack presaged another one all too soon. He would fall and shake again before he slept tonight. *If* he slept tonight. Sleep had always been a rare and sporadic thing for Caesar, but it seemed to be becoming more and more elusive with each passing year.

Once again he mused on what it was that had contributed heavily to last night's loss of sleep. A missive had arrived in camp from Gaius Servilius Casca back in Rome, and it had brought troubling news. The new consuls seemed Hades-bent on defying him. Sulpicius Rufus and Claudius Marcellus were supposed to be *supporting* him. Rufus had been a friend at times, and Marcellus had aided him in his struggles against the excesses of Crassus. And yet now that they had achieved the consulship, neither man seemed to have remembered the effort Caesar had put into supporting their bid for the position. Rufus had withdrawn, apparently having nothing to say either for or against Caesar, but his reticence had allowed Marcellus free rein to object to everything Caesar did.

The last time he had been back in Cisalpine Gaul, he had enfranchised the largely-native town of Comum, adding settled veterans to its population and moving the whole city to a new location, draining swamps and reordering the place along traditional Roman lines, and all largely at his own expense. After all, the people of Comum had been among his most loyal and avid supporters in his time as their governor, and had supplied good men for his legions. And in return, last year he had granted citizenship to the place, renaming it Novum Comum and making it a Roman city.

Theoretically, of course, only the senate had the right to make such a grant, but it was common practice for proconsuls, powerful governors and victorious generals to make such grants and then have them ratified by the old fools in Rome. And so he had sent his grant in to the senate and they had approved it as per usual, only for the arrogant Marcellus to overturn it, arguing that his grants had been invalid and illegal.

Such opposition was bad enough, but Casca, who sat in the senate and regularly fed back useful gossip, had also intimated that Marcellus was pushing to have Caesar recalled, and *that* smacked of a plot. As proconsul he was immune from prosecutions, and he would be again, once he became consul. But if the yapping dog Marcellus could manage to drag him back early, before he could achieve consulship, the many enemies awaiting him in Rome would make merry sport of dragging him through the courts for anything their little corroded hearts desired.

He had been sending back increased funds of late, securing the support of the more important politicians and jurors, but the net that would prevent his fall was only half woven so far. He had to have time to complete it – which meant also more money, of course – and he needed the process of his return and elevation to consul to run smoothly, so that he would have the year of his consulship to put down his enemies and clear himself of any potential prosecutions. Years in the planning, and a treacherous former friend with a power complex was trying to undo everything.

His bitter, angry musings were swept aside by a cough. The chief centurion of the Eleventh and veteran of many campaigns, Titus Pullo, stepped before him, and over the man's shoulder Caesar could see the vanguard of the cavalry riding up to meet him – half a dozen men on horseback.

'Piss on Marcellus,' he muttered under his breath.

'Sir?' Pullo frowned.

'Nothing, centurion. What did you want?'

'Your tent is up, general. The furniture is being installed now, but you may want to shelter from the weather.'

'Thank you, centurion.'

'Pleasure sir.' The big officer flashed him a rather impertinent grin. 'Just give the word, general, and I'll piss on this Marcellus myself.'

Despite the forwardness and insolence of the comment, Caesar couldn't help himself and threw back his head with his first genuine laugh in days. 'Why, I do believe you would, centurion. I'll keep your offer in mind, though I'd rather prefer to do it myself.'

Again the centurion grinned, saluted, and then hurried off to shout at some legionary for dropping a brazier and spilling its contents in the tent doorway. Caesar repeated his gesture, wiping the water from his face and focusing on Varus as he rode in and then dismounted almost before his horse stopped, saluting and blinking away the rain. Behind the cavalry commander rode four regular troopers, and between them two natives huddled, bound tight and roped to the saddle. One of them was sitting at an odd angle, the slope of his shoulders suggesting a broken scapula or at least collar bone, and ribs.

'Varus, it is heartening to see you. I had begun to fear for you and your men, since I had rather expected you to be here when we arrived.'

'And we would have been, general, but we happened across these two sorry specimens at our furthest extent and, after a few exchanges with them, I thought it worth checking out their information while we were there.'

At last. Caesar smiled. Good news?

'They were very talkative, after the first few moments. I have a small contingent of Remi and Suessione riders and, since it is their lands that are under threat from these rebels, I thought it appropriate to give them the job of initial interrogation. I watched for the first part, but when they started using the splinters from a broken spear shaft, I must admit I had to leave the scene. Yet whatever they did, they extracted a lot of information as we travelled, and all of it useful. I doubt the best interrogators here will get anything more from them, though you will want to try, of course, sir.'

Caesar, still smiling, nodded. 'And their information?'

'It is no good seeking Commius here, sir. The traitor has left, crossing the Rhenus in an attempt to raise the Germans to their cause.'

Caesar sucked on his lip for a moment. 'He will not be so successful, I think. The tribes across the Rhenus have tangled with us several times and have always lost. Their own lands are under no threat, so they will be unwilling, I suspect, to enter battle with us to help people who have nothing to offer in return. We can ignore Commius. If he crosses back in the north we will have him, and if he tries it further south, he will find himself facing Labienus. I will send a message to the commander to warn him of the possibility. What then of the rebel force and this Correus who leads them?'

'He seems to have put together a sizeable army, sir. Looks like we face not just the Bellovaci, but the Velocassi, the Caletes, the Atrebates, the Aulerci and even the Ambiani. Estimates of their numbers seem vague. Neither of these two is particularly high in their chain of command, but they both seem to think it will be the match of four legions.'

Caesar's brow furrowed in surprise. 'I had not anticipated such a strength. Even with the Belgae having largely escaped last year's horrors, I had anticipated more or less half that number.'

Varus huffed in the cold air. 'We approached the position of the enemy force as revealed by these two, general. I couldn't estimate their numbers myself without getting too close and alerting their sentries. But judging from the smoke columns rising from their camp there are many thousand.'

'And where are they?'

'They took every member of every tribe and all their belongings, so that there would be nothing left for us to take. Their civilian population have been secreted somewhere in the endless woods in the heart of the region, but every man of the tribes who can bear arms has encamped on a high place, surrounded by a filthy and dangerous quagmire. Winkling them out is going to be a mighty tricky proposition, sir.'

'Then we must draw them out to us; make them fight us on ground of our choosing.'

'Might be trouble there, sir. Apparently the enemy are labouring under the impression that only three legions march on them – fortunately their intelligence on us seems to be poorer than ours on them. They are watching out to make sure none of the other regional forces are joining us, hence these living shadows that followed my cavalry around. If there are no other Roman forces imminent, and Correus believes he is facing three legions, then he thinks he outnumbers us and will probably come out to take us. But if he sees we are more numerous than that he will likely just sit in his camp and taunt us.'

Caesar nodded. 'Definitely troubling. Either we face superior numbers and they will come to assail us, or we match their numbers but end up laying siege to what sounds like a perfect fortress.'

Varus huffed again and rubbed his hands. 'And with the weather like this and no real baggage train with us, general, we can't maintain a siege. They would only have to disrupt our foraging and we'd collapse.'

The general was still nodding, but now his eyes narrowed and sparkled with fierce intelligence. 'Then let us play a ruse. We may not have a full baggage train, but we have the various carts and wagons we picked up at the last supply depot. We send the most experienced veterans – the Seventh, Eighth and Ninth in front in our usual formation, with one ala of your old-timers. The Eleventh will arm light and travel behind the baggage, out of sight until the last minute, along with the bulk of your cavalry. Then, with luck, the enemy will commit on sight of the three legions and they will be too late to pull back when the fast-moving, light-armed Eleventh and your other cavalry rush to take the field in support.'

Varus rubbed his forehead. 'It's a workable plan, general. Better than I could come up with.'

'Best get your boys in and rested then, commander. Tomorrow might be a busy day.'

The general straightened and felt a familiar throb in the temple. 'And now I must retire to my tent.' He turned to the ever-present praetorians of Aulus Ingenuus, and gestured to the nearest. 'Be a good chap and send for my body slave. I find I might have need of him.'

* * * * *

The vanguard of the main force followed the scouts, who waved them on from the trees ahead. Caesar's army had moved at its maximum maintainable speed since leaving the camp that morning, but for the last hour the pace had been by necessity considerably slower. The terrain had become more rolling with occasional higher domes of greenery, though it was hard to tell from the soldiers' point of view, since the entire area was so thickly wooded. The rain, which seemed endemic of the darkness at this time of year, had at least held off during the day, improving morale noticeably.

The scouts, who had accompanied Varus the previous day and had carried out a very tentative reconnaissance excursion to this location, roved ahead, finding the best avenues through the trees where the legions could march relatively uninhibited. In the process, they also kept a close watch on the forests through which the legions moved, wary of the potential for ambushes. None had come. It seemed that the approach of the Roman army had remained blessedly unnoticed by the enemy. Perhaps those scouts they'd captured had been the only ones in this area and had not yet been missed? Whatever the reason, the enemy's ignorance was a blessing.

Then, as they'd closed on the location, the scouts had started coming across the enemy pickets. Prepared as they were from the previous visit, they began to move stealthily forward, very quiet and effective, removing the enemy sentries with brutal speed before any warning could be given. Varus wished the Suessione scouts would stop bringing their heads to show him, but he'd not the heart to argue. Their victims were, after all, an army mustered ostensibly to invade Suessione lands.

'Seems we'll have the advantage of surprise,' Brutus muttered as he pulled alongside.

'Indeed. Not that we'll be rushing them,' Varus reminded him. 'After all, we want them to come out and meet us. We just want it to be enough of a surprise that they will react quickly without too much thought.'

'This terrain is going to be dreadful for the legions.'

'And render my cavalry more or less ineffective. But the scouts say the trees thin out as we near the enemy camp. I never got that close yesterday for fear of alerting sentries too soon, but it seems reasonable. You couldn't encamp a force of thousands of Gauls in the middle of a forest. They're on a hill that's more or less surrounded by marsh, so trees shouldn't be an issue. Sinking into a *mire* might be, of course.'

'Fewer negative comments made in front of the men might be preferable, gentlemen,' Caesar muttered quietly as he appeared on Varus' other side, the rest of the staff officers in a knot close behind. 'We're not entirely sure what we're up against, but the men are in high spirits and, since such minutiae can make or break an engagement, I'd like to keep it that way.'

Varus nodded his understanding and the van rode on in silence until Grattius, the primus pilus of the Ninth, cleared his throat and opened up in a song that was off-key and distinctly off-colour.

'The Ninth knew a girl from Palmyra...'

By the time he had sung out the name of that great, mysterious, exotic eastern city most of the First century of the Ninth had joined in, and as the volume rose throughout the refrain, the rest of the legion began to participate.

'Whose owner would not let us near her...'

Varus turned a questioning look on the general as the song went on, rising in volume.

'She liked to demean us, when we whipped out our...'

'Let them sing,' Caesar smiled. 'We're close enough now to have all the advantage we need, and after all, we want them to come to us. Besides, I'm intrigued by the song. You see, *I* once knew a girl from Palmyra too...'

Brutus snorted with laughter as the general grinned.

Ahead, three of the scouts reappeared from the wide avenue, a severed head swinging from one of their hands by the hair like some sort of gruesome censer. 'Look alive, gentlemen,' Caesar said, pointing at them.

'Enemy sighted, sir,' the Suessione scout announced, and Varus narrowed his eyes at the man's tone. He sounded unsure. Nervous?

The army continued on along the avenue, the scouts now riding close to the vanguard, no longer concerned about ambushes or pickets. Varus watched as the trees thinned around them, and suddenly they emerged onto a wide grassy hillside with a magnificent view of the enemy.

'*Minerva*,' Varus breathed in astonishment. Behind him the marching song, which had reached a colourful moment of genitalic description, stopped suddenly as Grattius issued his own exclamation.

'Hercules' bollocks!'

The general silently held up his hand, signalling the army to halt. The cavalry ala, which had been moving in two narrow columns alongside the Ninth, began to pull ahead to form up in the open. Varus stared.

The hillside upon which they stood was wide and gentle, grassy and clear. It sloped down to a valley perhaps half a mile wide and clogged with swampy murk, through which ran what might be considered a river, if only because it was slightly more liquid than the terrain through which it flowed. On the far side of the morass, which curved off to north and south and effectively enclosed the enemy, a similar slope arose to a hill almost half as high again as this one and with a steeper gradient. It was a natural fortress that even without walls was twice as defensive as any oppidum they had faced this winter.

But that unforgiving position was not what had stilled the breath in the Roman officers.

'How can there be so *many*?'

Caesar turned to Brutus in answer. '*Many thousands* was a very vague description, Brutus. We thought them to be a match for us based on information from those captured scouts. And they are certainly a match for us. And I cannot deny that there are many thousands of them.'

Varus coughed in the cold air. 'General, with all the good will in the world, it doesn't matter how enthusiastic our men are, if they come for us, there is a very good chance that we will all be under a turf mound by tomorrow morning.'

101

Caesar simply nodded. The enemy force was enormous. The throng filled the crest of the hill opposite, and was beginning to move, emerging from their camp and pressing forward towards the nearest edge of the slope.

'I reckon they have us at two to one,' Varus said quietly.

'And they're ready for battle,' Brutus added.

'Why have they stopped?' the cavalry commander murmured. 'Because they can't be sure of our numbers yet?' The legions were still emerging from the trees onto the grassy slope behind them, filtering into position and falling into centuries efficiently.

Caesar sighed. 'Partially. Also because they have no need to come for us, after all. Regard their situation. They are well-provisioned, in a strong position, and numerically superior. They are in no hurry to meet us. After all, they are waiting for Commius and a potential influx of Germanic tribesmen.'

'So what do we do?'

The general scratched his chin. 'We dig in while we consider our next move.' He turned to the small number of staff officers who sat slightly apart in conversation and gestured to the older of them, his armour less decorative and considerably more practical than his fellows. The man rode over, saluting as he approached.

Varus smiled. Appius Coruncanius Mamurra was one of the veteran officers of the campaign now. Not a field officer – the man had not commanded a legion or vexillation at any point since his arrival in Gaul six years ago – but his expertise as an engineer had been the backbone of some of the army's greatest feats in that time, and his knowledge and practical sense had made him as popular with the veteran soldiers as his lineage and rank did with the staff officers.

'General?'

'Your thoughts on terrain and fortification, if you will, Appius?'

The old engineer swept his helmet from his head, shaking out the limp crest, and rubbed the sweaty curls that surrounded the gleaming crown of his cranium. He frowned into the cold damp air, thumped a foot down half a dozen times in various places, then turned and examined the trees behind them.

'Good ground for digging. Hard-wearing, but giving turf, with deep earth below. Not too rocky, but with some local bluffs if we need to quarry. Plenty of timber and willow to hand for palisades and fences. We could hardly be in a better position for fortifying, if you ask me. As long as the enemy make no attempt to rush us while we work, we could have a solid fort up by dusk, large enough to shelter all four legions and with room for stabling. It will take another day to add the embellishments, of course, but we'd at least be protected by dark. I would propose a higher rampart than usual, with tall towers. They will give archers and our meagre artillery a great range and allow them to drop missiles on any enemy trying to cross that marsh. With high enough defences you could litter that valley with dead before they managed to cross to dry ground.'

Caesar nodded. 'And willow, you say?'

'Yes. For extra defences close up.'

'With high enough towers, could we perhaps land a missile on the hill opposite?'

Mamurra shook his head. 'If we had the heavy artillery, yes. Perhaps an onager at maximum strain could do it. But we came at speed and only brought scorpions and the like with us. Still, give me a day and I'll make this hill impregnable for you.'

Caesar nodded. 'Do it, Appius. Consult with the unit engineers and the centurions and get the basics up quick enough for us to settle in.'

The engineer nodded and wheeled his horse to locate the engineers in the column. Varus watched the enemy, who were now all gathered on the brow watching the Romans, then turned to view their own army, the rear of which was now arriving, the few wagons rolling out onto the turf and the Eleventh appearing behind them.

* * * * *

The cavalry commander patted his steed on the neck and stroked her forelock gently, holding a small apple in his flattened palm until she took it gently and began to crunch. With a smile, Varus turned and strode from the horse pens. He had asked that the engineers erect some sort of roof over the pens, as the horses needed dry stabling as much as the men tonight. The pens were roofed now with a variety of leather, wool and woven covers all held up by rough-hewn posts. He was not sure whether this was supposed to be a temporary measure or the end product, but at least it kept the worst of the winter weather from the beasts. They might be required for battle in the morning, and would be far more active and manoeuvrable if their joints were not frozen stiff from the cold rains that seemed to fall every night at the moment. The equisio who controlled the pens wandered past, nodding a respectful greeting to Varus, the man's arms too full of animal feed to salute.

Bidding his horse good night, the cavalry commander wandered out into the gloomy dusk, marvelling at the sight of the camp around them. Already a rampart some ten to twelve feet high in places enclosed a vast camp, that embankment itself surrounded by twin ditches each fifteen feet wide and ten deep. Even as the light failed, sections of the army were still at work, hacking the small projecting branches from timbers that would tomorrow be used to construct a covered gallery atop the mound throughout the entire circuit to protect the men from stray missile fire. And the entire system would be punctuated with intermittent three-storey towers. Mamurra had launched into his task with the enthusiasm typical of an engineer. The covered timber walkway would be protected by a willow fence formed such that the sharpened points projected defensively outwards, and the natural flexibility of the material turned blades without taking damage far more thoroughly than solid timber. The ditches' outer edges were vertical, threatening to break the limbs of the first men to fall in and hamper any attack, while the inner faces were angled perfectly so as to provide no shelter from missiles cast from the rampart top. The gates were equally powerful and would be defended by high towers of their own.

When Varus had queried the necessity for such a powerful fortification, Caesar had smiled. His twin purpose made sense. Firstly, to intimidate the Gauls; and it must have done that for, though the enemy had initially hovered at the crest of their hill, constantly surging back and forth as if eager to tackle the Romans and only held back by the will of their commanders, once the rising rampart had become evident from a distance, the enemy had retreated within their own camp once more.

And with the distinct possibility that the army might be here for a while, there would be the need to forage for supplies. It provided a little security to note that such a defence protected the camp at any time when up to a quarter of the force might be absent securing food.

A raucous laugh drew his attention as he strode through the camp back towards his own lines, and his eyes were drawn to a tent on the *via decumana*. At the edge of the Eleventh's section, the centurions' and the signifers' tents sat slightly apart, marked by the presence of the century's standards and flags and two soldiers on miserable, cold guard duty.

The centurion's tent bore the insignia of the First cohort. The loud laugh had belonged to the primus pilus, then. As Varus slowed near the tent, he could see through the open door the figures of two men he vaguely recognised deep in laughter and conversation, and deep in their cups too from the sound of it.

'...and the tribune – one of those foppish boys from Rome barely off his mother's tit, mark you – had the audacity to tell me to pull my men in. I had to bite into my lip to stop myself flattening the posh little prick with my staff.'

'Should have done it,' the other man, another senior centurion he recognised, grinned. 'You'd have done the army a favour. Probably his mother too.'

Taking a deep breath, Varus nodded to the guards, hoping they would not intercept a man in the uniform of a senior officer, and made for the doorway. The two legionaries saluted him respectfully, but one cleared his throat noisily to warn the occupants of Varus' approach. As the cavalry commander ducked into the tent's entrance, the two centurions turned and gave weary salutes.

'Evening you two. Pullo, isn't it? And... Vorenus? I might suggest a little less vocality on the subject of men who could legitimately have you broken in the ranks, eh? Just for the sake of decorum?'

Pullo gave him the sort of look he would have expected if he'd asked the man to strip naked and stand on his head.

'Respectfully, sir, *why*?'

'Exactly because of that: respect.'

Pullo snorted. 'That's a bit rich, sir.'

'I beg your pardon.'

'I remember tell of you putting old Longinus in his place years back. And Crassus. And others. You've a bit of a reputation for speaking your mind, sir.'

Varus blinked and chuckled sheepishly. 'Still, where your men might hear...'

Pullo stalked over to the door and looked around at the two men on guard. 'Flavius?'

'Sir?'

'You remember that tribune with the jug ears we had last year? Went back to Rome after Alesia?'

'Yessir.'

'Speaking freely, I'd like you to sum him up in one word, soldier.'

'That word would be 'knob', centurion.'

Pullo grinned. 'Thank you Flavius. You can skip latrine detail tomorrow.' He turned back to Varus. 'The men already have their own opinions, sir, and we all know what they are. It doesn't matter how hard you polish a turd, it still smells like a turd, and every man knows that from the centurionate to the new recruit.'

Again, Varus could only chuckle. 'Very well. Then I'll leave you to your defamation.'

'Care to defame someone with us, sir? I happen to have acquired this fine large amphora in a small wager involving a cavalry trooper and an eating knife.'

Varus gave him a black look, and Pullo rallied well. 'Oh come on, sir. We know your horse boys have their place, and they've done you proud for years, but few of them could stand in the shield wall and not shit himself.'

Varus' eyes turned flinty and he cast a withering look at the centurion. 'I know there's a strained rivalry between my troopers and your legionaries, centurion, but I don't expect to hear such blinkered, idiotic sentiments from an officer who should know better.'

Pullo shrugged, poured a cup of wine and proffered it to Varus. 'Peace offering? No offence meant.'

Varus sighed and took the cup. 'Fair enough. For the record, I've spent my fair share of time stood up to the knees in shit and blood, facing down the howling horde.'

'I know that, sir. Your courage was never in doubt. Come on, let's forget about rivalries and find someone to pull to pieces that we *both* hate. Have you seen Plancus recently?'

* * * * *

Varus straightened from lacing his boot and sat for a moment until the spots disappeared from his vision and the camelopard that was running around inside his head, churning his brains to mush, stopped for a rest. Gripping the chair back for support, he rose and stood for a moment, trying to marshal his thoughts, the uppermost of which involved the apparently endless capacity for wine of the centurionate. By the time he'd left Pullo's tent last night, he felt as though he'd been physically abused. It felt like a night in Fronto's tent used to feel.

Flashes of memory hit him, of that bedraggled trudge through the rain back to his own quarters. He'd been oblivious at the time, but now it seemed obvious that one of the legionaries on duty outside the centurion's tent had shadowed him all the way through the camp, making sure he made it back intact. And while he had been about as compos mentis as a cabbage by the time he struggled out of the tent, Pullo and Vorenus had been going strong, louder than before and even less guarded in their comments, but completely in control of their bodies and minds, if not their mouths.

Varus realised that he'd actually relaxed last night in a manner that he'd not achieved in months. But now, when the courier from the general was standing outside waiting to escort him, and his head was hammering like the anvils of the legion workshops, he considered last night's adventure to be a rather poor bit of decision making. He was also under absolutely no illusion that the centurions from the Eleventh were not already up, bathed, shaved, armoured and busy shouting at their men, dressing them in neat lines. Even thinking about a centurion shouting sent a lance of pain into the matter behind his left eye. He could vaguely hear the sounds of construction muffled by his tent leather. Or was that just in his head?

'Sir?'

'I'm coming, I'm coming.'

Throwing his cloak over his shoulders and fastening it with the bronze pin, Varus stepped out into the cold, white world of northern Gaul. A shiver wracked him from toe to head and back.

'You alright sir?'

'Never better. Just don't shout.'

Trying to ignore the sly smile the legionary flicked him, Varus glowered and followed across the turf and down the camp's Via Praetoria, which led to the gate facing the gathered Gallic army. His head began to take on that extra crushing pain that could only be the result of a hangover exacerbated by the chill wet mist and the sounds of two thousand legionaries already chopping and adzing timber, hammering posts into place and the myriad other agonising noises of the ongoing fortification of the hill.

Mere heartbeats later, he was climbing the earth mound beside the gate to where Caesar stood with the other staff officers and the watch centurion, as well as several dismounted scout riders.

Reaching the top, Varus peered out into the mist following the direction of their gaze.

Eerily, the enemy camp was clearly visible, along with the sea of humanity within, though the combination of the cold and the swampy ground had resulted in a thick mist that became a whiter, denser fog towards the waterways below. The result was that the enemy's hill fortress rose from a blanket of white like an island in a ghostly sea. The effect did little to lift Varus' battered spirits.

The courier had said enemy reinforcements were arriving and that the general had summoned his officers to the gate. Little looked any different from here.

'Reinforcements, general?'

Caesar turned a withering gaze on him. 'Ah, commander.' Amazing how the man could fit so much admonition into two such simple words. Varus flinched as the general breathed slowly. 'A few moments ago the traitor Commius returned with his Germans.'

Varus' spirits sank yet lower. 'How many, general?'

'Therein lies the good news. They appear to be Suebi, from what your scouts tell me, but at the highest estimate he brings only half a thousand with him. Not a great return on his efforts, but then I did not think the Germanic tribes would be enthusiastic about entering into another war with us.'

Brutus rubbed his eye. 'Your scouts rode round the entire circuit at dawn today. The current estimate of enemy numbers is that they amount to perhaps forty five thousand. That includes the newly-arrived Germans, and must account for every fighting man from each tribe involved. This is the enemy army in its entirety, so if we can finish them here, then we'll have done to the Belgae what Alesia did to the southern tribes. There won't be enough able men left to raise a shout, let alone a rebellion.'

'I'm not sure how you hope to achieve that, Caesar?' Varus hazarded quietly.

'Oh?'

'We're hardly in a position to attack them. Their position is too strong and they outnumber us by too high a margin to be confident of victory.' Caesar nodded, listening carefully, so Varus scratched his head and went on. 'Well, if we manage to lure them out now, we're truly in the latrine. If we meet them straight in the field they outnumber us enough that we could easily lose, especially with the surrounding woods and swamps limiting the usefulness of the horse.

And if we let them besiege us, yes we have a strong fortress now, but even if we forage like mad, it's winter and we'll be very unlikely to pull together enough food to see the army through more than a few days. No course of action looks favourable.'

'Agreed,' Caesar murmured quietly. 'And that is why I sent out riders at haste last night.'

'Sir?'

'I have sent for Trebonius to bring the Tenth and the Twelfth, and to pick up Sextius and his Thirteenth on the way. They are the closest legions to our current position. The couriers took changes of horse with them, so I am confident that they will arrive at the camps by nightfall today. Trebonius has orders to march at all haste without a full supply train, in the same manner as we did. If everything works out as I anticipate, in four days we will almost double our force. With seven veteran legions, I could bring down an army of Titans.'

Varus nodded. Seven legions would, at least, be more than a match for the enemy.

'We need to keep the enemy interested in the meantime, though. We must keep their attention riveted on us. We will attempt skirmishes wherever possible and keep them occupied until the reserves join us. I want the enemy too busy concentrating on our minutiae to notice the underlying plan. I anticipate the legions' arrival, as I say, either in the evening four days from now, or the morning after.'

He turned to the small group of officers and singled out Mamurra.

'Appius?'

'General?'

'Are you required for any further work on the camp?'

The engineer shook his head. 'I think things are progressing well enough in the hands of the legion engineers now, sir. I might be consulted from time to time, but otherwise...'

'Good.' The general smiled. 'I want you to turn your talents to a new project. I want you to plan a bridge across the swamps from this hill to that one. I want it to be sturdy and wide enough for a contubernium of men to march abreast. And most importantly I want it to be able to put in place in a matter of hours. Half a day at most.'

Mamurra blinked, peering down into the sea of swirling, ethereal white below. 'That's near impossible, general.'

'That is why I entrust such a task to a man who has a reputation for achieving the impossible. I do not want it in place now. I want to put it up four days from now, finishing by nightfall. I want it in place a matter of hours before Trebonius arrives with the reserves, so that the enemy have no time to plan anything. I want them off-balance and concerned, and then to suddenly find that their fortress is vulnerable and that their enemy have doubled in numbers and are coming for them unexpectedly. Do you understand the strategy?'

Varus did. It was brilliant. It was also extremely risky.

'General, what happens if Trebonius is delayed by days?'

'Then the enemy will rally and probably destroy the bridge – they *do* have vastly superior numbers, after all. And then our entire strategy collapses. Similar issues occur if Trebonius is over-enthusiastic and runs his men into the ground to join us, getting here before the bridge is built. Then the enemy will have knowledge of our full force and time to plan. So we shall just have to rely on my estimates being accurate, shall we not?'

Mamurra sucked on his lower lip as his gaze moved up and down from the sea of white to the hill opposite. 'It's possible, sir. This mist seems to happen every morning as a consequence of the marshes. We could send teams down there the morning before, under cover of darkness. They could ram in the piles for the bridge in the mist, which would help deaden the sound. Then, when the time came, we would already have the supports. We would only have to build the superstructure. And if we have three days, as soon as this camp is finished we could start putting together the bridge in pieces within the camp. Then we can run out the bridge already partially constructed and assemble it swiftly when needed. And we could start with a causeway of timbers at our side of the marsh earlier. The bridge will only be required for the central, wider, section. It is entirely possible, sir.'

Caesar smiled. 'I knew you would come up with something, Mamurra. Start working on your plans. Take any men you need from any legion and get to work.'

Varus peered at the enemy force. It was an audacious plan, and worked on narrow timings. But it would nullify both the enemy's advantage in numbers and their fortified position.

'I think I need a drink,' he croaked, rubbing his thumping head and looking down into the white world of deadly swamps.

110

'Make no mistake, gentlemen,' Caesar said quietly. 'This is not like the Bituriges or the Carnutes. Once more we face a sizeable army of strong warriors. This is serious business, and upon it rests the peace of all Belgae lands. But we have achieved so much in recent years and Gaul is on the cusp of being settled permanently under the law of the republic. I will not allow all our success to backslide at this point. The war will be over this year. Time to finish it.'

Varus nodded to himself. Certainly in four days' time *someone* would be finished.

Chapter Six

FRONTO leaned forward in his seat and peered around the doorway. Andala the Bellovaci woman – slave, he tried to remind himself – turned to look at him with some odd instinctive awareness and he ducked back feeling guilty, although not entirely sure what about. He could hear Lucilia deep in conversation with the Belgic woman – *slave* – and tried not to concentrate on what they were saying, but it kept insisting itself on him, over and above his own business.

'I must apologise to you, Andala...'

No. You don't apologise to slaves, Lucilia. Even if they fascinate you.

'No insult, lady. I know Roman thoughts.'

'I had been led to believe that your people were averse to bathing. There is so much we don't understand, sadly. You are welcome to use the villa's bath house whenever you wish. I would ask that you make sure it is unoccupied first, and if the floors are cold just let Bocco know and he will stoke the furnace for you.'

No, Lucilia. You don't pamper the help.

'Do I take it you're uninterested in business today?' Catháin said with a strange smile. Fronto ripped his attention from the annoying exchange out in the atrium and back to his new employee. The factor of Fronto's business was always giving him odd little knowing smiles. Sometimes they seemed to convey sympathy, sometimes admonition, and sometimes curious humour. Fronto simply couldn't quite get the man straight in his head. He seemed capricious, irreverent, totally disrespectful when in private, inscrutable and downright odd at times. And yet there was something unexpectedly likeable about him. Despite the vast gulf in their backgrounds and careers, the man reminded him in strange ways of Priscus, and each time he felt that familiarity there was a small twinge of guilt and loss.

Catháin was quite the most unusual companion Fronto had worked alongside, including Masgava. In fact, if there could be a direct opposite of Masgava, Catháin was probably it, and yet the pair had quickly formed a solid, if unlikely, friendship. The strange fellow was an inhabitant of the isles of Britannia, though he seemed not to think so. His homeland, which he called Īweriū, seemed to be only describable in terms of mystical beauty and belligerent bloodshed, from what Fronto could gather. Its people sounded a lot like the Belgae – all punch-ups over honour and too much drink.

Indeed, Catháin had been involved in a small scuffle over a woman – a half-sister, Fronto had discovered with fascinated interest – and had beaten a cousin to death with a drinking vessel. Before the brawl erupted into full-scale tribal warfare, which from what Catháin said seemed to be a national pastime, the young man had scurried down to the seafront of his settlement and had stowed away on board a visiting Phoenician trader. That had been almost a decade ago, and since then the man had been to ports in exotic places that Fronto had only heard of.

But despite a decade of maturity and a world-wisdom settled deep into the man's being, nothing seemed to have removed the impulse of violence that clearly ran in his blood.

'Business?' he said with more acid than he intended.

'Yes, business,' smiled Catháin.

'I thought we might talk about yesterday's incident and how it might impact on my trading.'

'Incident?'

Fronto rolled his eyes. 'Gods, but you can be infuriating, man. You punched a Greek trader between the eyes.'

'It was a good punch.'

'I'm not denying that. It was an *excellent* punch. I've never seen someone go down so quick and heavy from one punch. Maybe when Atenos hit someone once, actually. But still – an excellent punch. Though that's not the issue. Business would probably go much smoother if you didn't punch other traders into next year. The man probably hasn't woken up yet.'

'Ah, for the love of bilgewater, the bastard had it coming. He called me a runt. Men have died for less. And the poor fool was a nobody. Just a visitor, else he'd have known me and known not to rile me.'

'You have a very high opinion of yourself, Catháin.'

'I know what I'm worth. And if you stop messing around and listen, so will you.'

Fronto frowned, his attention finally fully committed to his factor. Despite the ongoing fuzziness he felt from months of poor sleep, he felt brighter than usual this morning, perhaps due to the fact that it was today he was due to pick up his replacement Fortuna pendant. 'Go on,' he asked with keen interest.

113

'How much are you paying for that old shed in the Street of the Oil Traders?'

'I don't know. Can't remember exactly. About twenty drachma a month, I think, more or less.'

'Thought so. You know a friend of Hierocles would get it for eight or nine?'

'I'll bet. But there's no chance of that happening for me. A friend of Hierocles would sooner bed the Lernaean hydra than cut me a deal.'

Catháin grinned. 'That's because you don't know the right people or the right things to say, and even when you do speak Greek, you speak it like a Roman. But think on this: there are other people in Massilia who've had their noses bent by that Greek prick in the past, who will happily help put him in his place. Cancel your premises with half a month's notice if you can. I've got you a secure warehouse two streets back from the port in the Street of the Brazen Carters and you'll need half a month to move everything across, get it secured away and clear out your previous premises. The new one's almost twice the size, comes with its own security, as it's part of a conglomerate, and will cost you eleven a month. Twelve if you want to use the conglomerate's own carts and muleteers, which I would recommend. I know you have your own wagon, but you can only ever deal with one shipment at a time like that.'

Fronto boggled.

'That's... I can't... did you really? *Eleven*?'

'Twelve, with the carters.'

'I hardly need a team of carts and muleteers to hand, Catháin. I can only afford to manage one shipment at a time, anyway.'

'In which case, my dear Fronto, you might as well sign your business over to Hierocles now. Grow or go under, my friend. Grow or go under.'

'And how do you suggest I do that?' Fronto rubbed his tired eyes. 'Grow, I mean. Not go under. I seem to be quite adept at that part already.'

Catháin shrugged. 'I know a few people. Let's try and streamline your current process, and then we'll look at alternate sources and routes and customers. You'd be surprised how many people will help an enemy of Hierocles if you know who to ask. And if it's not a Roman doing the asking, too.'

114

Fronto leaned back again. 'You realise this might start a war. And not just a trade war. That bastard's already tried to take me down more than once. If he thinks I'm actually a proper threat to his business, he'll go all out to kill me, let alone ruin me.'

'Let the bastard come, Fronto. I grew up in the ale pits of the black lake and the fighting dens along the banks of the Oboka. I learned to flatten a man's nose and rip out his groin before I had my second teeth.'

Fronto rolled his eyes again. *Where did he pick these people up?* He had only the vaguest idea of even the location of this strange Celtic isle which apparently did a good trade with southern merchants despite having no contact with Rome, but the more he heard about the place from his new employee, the less he wanted ever to go there.

'Can we visit these new premises?'

'Of course. I'll take you there this afternoon. I think you should get some more rest. You look like you last slept during the civil wars. In the meantime, go sort out your family business.'

'What?'

'The girl you keep looking at. It'll do you no good to keep getting distracted from business by a pretty little backside.'

Fronto's eyes widened and he risked a glimpse round the doorframe again before making *shushing* motions at his employee. 'It's not like that, man, and for the love of Minerva will you keep your voice down. You'll have Lucilia down on me like a collapsing vault.'

'Ah, calm yourself and unknot your underwear, man.' Catháin grinned and made a rather suggestive motion before nudging Fronto and cackling.

'Is that it?' Fronto snapped frostily.

'I've got a few other bits and pieces to discuss, but we can do that on the way to the new warehouse this afternoon – nothing urgent. I'll come back after lunch. Now I need to go train Pamphilus and Clearchus in weights and volumes of amphorae. And on how to handle them without sacrificing every third jar to the god of floors, if you get my drift.'

'Good luck with that. If you can train them just to hit the hole when they piss, I'll consider it a win!'

Catháin grinned again as he rose and backed out of the room with a respectful nod in the direction of the ladies. Fronto leaned to look round the door and found both of them looking back at him with inscrutable expressions. Guilt ran through him like a tide for no reason, and he smiled weakly as he rose and moved out to the atrium to join them.

'My dear.'

'Marcus. I have decided that Andala here should be my personal attendant.'

Fronto felt a wave of uncertainty, but even through it he registered that Lucilia had called her a 'personal attendant' and not a 'body slave'. That boded no good in any way.

'Lucilia, she's not trained in...'

'She is perfectly well versed in everything she needs to know, and anything we come across that she doesn't... well, she's bright and will pick it up very quickly, I'm sure.'

'Then why did she keep getting sold back to the slavers.'

'Because she never found the right family.'

'*Owner*, Lucilia. It's called an owner, when you're talking about slaves.' He felt a touch of self-recrimination, considering his own stance on slaves, but there was something extremely unnerving about the apparent growing closeness between the two women. It was like watching two dangerous Gallic war bands combining their strength while he stood on the walls and waited for the inevitable assault.

'On that count, Marcus, I have decided that she will earn two drachma a week. That way within the year she can buy her manumission and decide whether to stay with us as a friend or to go her own way.'

Fronto sighed. '*Two drachma a week*? That's almost half what I was paying for the warehouse, for gods' sake. Bocco only gets three obols a week and he's indispensable.'

'Didn't Catháin just save you half the warehouse costs?'

Again nervous tension wracked Fronto. How had she heard that? He prayed to Fortuna that that was all she'd heard. He swallowed noisily. 'Well, yes, but saving money doesn't just mean we should spend it on something else.'

'Oh don't be so mean, Marcus. You spend plenty on wine and gambling. I only ask for a few overheads here and there.'

It occurred to Fronto momentarily to try and list the innumerable and very expensive overheads to which she was referring, when compared to the relatively small cost of a few nights on the wine.

But experience had long taught him which arguments to avoid, and he capitulated with an air of equal surrender and bad grace.

'Besides,' she added pointedly, as if reading his mind, 'how much are your two new pendants costing? I know you're picking them up this afternoon. Try not to break them or lose them on the way home.'

'Oh I won't. And I'll need them tomorrow when I speak to the council.'

'Try not to lose your temper and alienate yourself further, Marcus.'

'Lucilia…'

'Yes, like that.'

Fronto sighed, registered the slightly knowing smile on Andala's face with sour grace, and turned to go and find Masgava. It was not a scheduled training morning, but suddenly he felt the almost irrepressible urge to hit something.

* * * * *

Fronto adjusted his chiton and himation and tried to look as official and likeable as possible, but no matter how much he played with the two layers of clothing, they just didn't sit in the same oratorical fashion as a toga. Not that he was particularly comfortable in a toga, mind, but at least the traditional Roman garb exuded an air of authority and serenity, while the Greek garments seemed as haphazard and variable as the Greeks themselves. They were garments clearly suited to sitting in the agora and expounding on the virtues and drawbacks of the circular nature of knowledge, not to making a rhetorical plea in a government environment.

He looked across at the shadow cast by the gnomon of Pytheas' sundial. The time had come. The shadow touched the midday point on the wide paved square, and his eyes were drawn up to the agora beyond, with its own central square and numerous administrative offices and buildings. Specifically, the bouleuterion – the council chamber which was to Greek city states what the curia was to Rome.

'You know what you're doing?'

Fronto turned to Catháin and nodded. 'For what they're worth I have all my arguments marshalled.'

'I'm more concerned about you losing your temper and messing it all up.'

'Now you sound like Lucilia.'

'That's because we both know you well and neither of us will lie just to comfort you.'

'Wish me luck.' Fronto reached up and caressed the intricate gold figure of Fortuna hanging on the thong at his neck, feeling slightly more comfortable for her presence. With a last nod at Catháin, he paced off across the radiating lines of the ancient sundial towards the agora. He had not noticed the cold breeze due to his jangling nerves until he passed through the high arched doorway and into the colonnade of the public space, where the wind dropped and the temperature rose noticeably.

The central square of the agora was already filled with people whiling away their time in business deals and trades, argument and counter-proposition, public haranguing, or simply sitting with a loaf of fresh bread and a cup of wine enjoying the sun. Here, at the heart of Massilia's public forum, the square was surrounded on all sides by the colonnaded walk and the buildings radiating off, and so, sheltered from the wintry wind, the sun filled the space and made it seem more like spring. It would have been a pleasant and relaxing place to be in other circumstances.

Fronto's eyes fell upon the portico ahead. The paid guards of the city – a system Fronto couldn't help but think Rome should adopt instead of relying on the private forces of the nobiles – stood to the sides of the grand entrance, not to prevent access, but to ensure there was no trouble. After all, Massilia was a democracy and theoretically more libertarian than Rome, and anyone had the right to attend council. In practice, Fronto had realised after only months in the city, a Greek democracy was about as fair to the people as the Roman republic. Rule was still effectively the province of the rich, no matter how much they espoused the equality of the demos.

And they were not keen on Romans.

Taking a deep breath and casting up a prayer to Fortuna, he stepped up to the columns and nodded a greeting to the guards as he passed. The portico building led through into a smaller colonnaded square, at the heart of which stood a grand altar to Poseidon, beloved of the Phocaeans who had founded this city, and so crucial to the sea-trade that made Massilia wealthy. Fronto nodded his respect to the altar as he passed. They could call him what they like, but at least he still looked like Neptune in the statues. He realised as he approached the unimpressive doorway opposite that his mind had wandered once more and he'd been lost in a mental comparison of divine images when he really needed to be concentrating on the task at hand. Was that due to his general sleep-deprived state, or more to nervousness over what he was doing?

There was no more time to think, which might be a good thing. His hands trembling with anxiety, Fronto stepped through the doorway and into the dim interior of the most important building in the agora of the city.

The bouleuterion of Massilia resembled a small roofed theatre. A semi-circular orchestra was faced by curved seating stands and backed by a plain wall with arches high up to allow light in and illuminate the interior. Despite the cloudless sky, the sun's position and the season meant that little light actually penetrated the gloom and numerous oil lamps in wall niches actually lit the proceedings.

Fronto swallowed nervously. There were twelve rows of seats in the arc facing the speaker's space, and perhaps half of the seats were filled. Most of those present had beards so long they hid the owner's neck, their hair shaggy and long like the statues of the gods throughout the city. The mean of their age was probably a decade older than Fronto, and *he* was no young man. It was disturbingly like standing before the Roman senate, which he'd done a few times in his youth.

The official who kept proceedings in line gestured for him to wait, and Fronto realised that the silence was not the boule of the city waiting for him, but rather a lull in a speech from a preceding plaintiff. The man, a fat, wobbling fellow of middle years with the swarthy skin of an easterner, looked close to panic.

'I… I can think of nothing else to say in my defence, esteemed councillors.'

There was another uncomfortable silence, broken a moment later by the portly man's nervous fart squeaking out in a place built for perfect acoustics. Fronto had to force himself not to laugh.

'May I?' asked an old man in the seats who looked like almost every other old man present. His colleagues nodded and he rose, gesturing to the man at the floor. 'You cannot supply anything in your own defence barring hearsay, assumption and extrapolations from fact. Yet Alkimachos has provided us with details of your offence and witnesses to confirm their validity. I understand that as a foreign visitor, you will have some difficulty in securing witnesses in your defence, but the simple truth is that this boule can only rule on fact, and the fact is that you have been proved at fault, Ahinadab of Tyros. Since you cannot provide any evidence in your defence, this council charges you with a payment of twenty tetradrachm to the city for the necessary repairs of the jetty, five tetradrachm to the owner of the vessel *Electra* and eight drachma to each captain who was inconvenienced by your actions.'

The swarthy man's face fell in defeat and Fronto felt suddenly very sorry for him. The man looked broken, and the fines that had just been levied would cripple even the healthiest of businesses. As Ahinadab shuffled off the stage, mopping his forehead and his fresh tears, Fronto felt his heart lurch. He was next, and things were unlikely to be any easier for him.

'Marcus Falerius Fronto,' the official announced, 'wine merchant, resident of Massilia and citizen of Rome.' The man waved him forward and Fronto stepped into the gaze of more than a hundred eyes. He felt the sudden need to fart and clenched as hard as he could, refusing point blank to show weakness at this early stage. His eyes strayed around the group. Most were hard to distinguish from one another, but his keen gaze soon picked out the two he'd been told to look for. Cathráin had once again proved his usefulness – the strange northerner was a mine of information about the city. Sure enough, Epaenetus was wearing the green chiton and the yellow himation that made him stand out among his dour peers, somewhere near the top on the left. He was the one to watch, Cathráin had said. *Look into his eyes*, he'd added. Fronto did and he shuddered. Even at this distance, he could see the black glossy orbs reflecting the oil lamps' light. They were the dead eyes of a shark, and with no white showing. It was like looking into the abyss.

He tore his gaze to the other figure. In the front row, on the right, sat an old man who would look no different from most of the others were it not for his missing arm. The stump, removed at the elbow, waved gaily at his neighbour as the two men chattered quietly. Poliadas. Once an emissary of Massilia to Rome, he had visited the capital many times and was said to look more kindly on the republic than most of his peers. Cathráin had made the point rather harshly that the one-armed old man was the only member of the boule with whom Fronto might expect to find sympathy.

'Say your piece,' the speaker in the previous case announced, taking his seat again and arranging his himation for comfort.

120

Fronto cleared his throat and felt panic crash down on him. He couldn't remember anything he'd planned on saying! This, of course, was one of the reasons he'd always been adamant that he would not play a role in Rome's government. Forcing down the panic and squeezing back in the fart that was once more threatening to leak out, he cleared his voice and threw out his arms wide.

'Noble and esteemed members of Massilia's boule, I come before you not as a Roman merchant, or a son of the republic. I come before you as a loyal resident of Massilia.' Nods rippled around the multitude of heads, and Fronto breathed carefully. So far, so good. 'The recent tax on foreign merchants in the city has, I'm sure the esteemed councillors will be aware, already ruined a number of trade concerns that have long held a place in the city's economy. Through careful restructuring and simple luck, my wine business has so far managed to stay afloat throughout the changes, though I am also facing ruin in the coming months.'

Silence greeted this news, and Fronto could feel the lack of sympathy flowing from the seating. 'Massilia was founded as a trade colony by explorers from Phocaea centuries ago,' he went on. 'These lands were once the lands of the Gauls, and now the republic borders your city. Massilia relies upon trade for its lifeblood as it has done ever since the Phocaeans, and we are all, to some extent foreigners in this place. To impose ruinous taxes on non-Greeks is to limit the growth and income of the city in a manner of which your forefathers would disapprove. Can you not see this?'

Damn it. Where had all his good, reasoned arguments gone? His head had apparently emptied of prepared lines and left him with only desperate pleas and semi-aggressive arrogance. At least old one-armed Poliadas was smiling at him helpfully. One of the other old men waved for Fronto's attention.

'You seem to be labouring under the impression that the new tax is aimed at non-Greeks, Fronto the wine merchant. In fact, the tax is applied to all non-citizens of Massilia, regardless of their origin. A Greek speaker from Sicilia will pay the taxes just as surely as a Roman. Yet if a Roman were to become a citizen of Massilia, he would become exempt. And remember, this tax does not apply to those who bring in goods to the city, or to those who purchase goods from us. It applies simply to any non-citizen business within the city who brings in and sells on goods. Such concerns are contributing nothing to the city. *That* is the root of the tax.'

121

'And to become a citizen of Massilia, I would need to give up my citizenship of the republic, I presume?'

The general murmur of the crowd made the answer to that clear. Catháin had brought up the possibility in one of their discussions, but Fronto simply could not do such a thing. He liked Massilia and liked living here, and he hoped to make a good place among the Greeks here as time progressed, but he was a citizen of Rome from a very old family, and no trade dispute would make him renounce that. A thought struck him as he pictured his villa on the hill, and he smiled.

'My business is not *within the city*, esteemed councillors. I have warehousing there, but the centre of my business is at my villa which, you may be aware, sits on the hills behind the city, in territory overlooking the lands of the republic.' It was splitting hairs, admittedly, but he was grasping at straws now, with his reasoned arguments fled.

Epaenetus stood in the back rows and threw an arm towards him. Fronto's heart fell at the sight.

'Therein lies another issue, Fronto the wine merchant. The land upon which you reside belongs to Massilia – making you fully liable to the tax, I might add – but which your precious republic marks upon its maps as its own. Your people are like an avaricious wolf, pacing around the borders of our city, searching for a way in. The very legality of your business concerns is disputable at best, due to the dubious legality of your residence and lands. In your position I would be paying the tax and trying not to draw attention to the irregularities of my affairs.'

Fronto bridled.

'*Listen to me!*' he snapped. 'I have no say in what the republic claim to be theirs. I am not an expansionist Roman working to undermine your city. I am a simple merchant trying to make a living.'

Shit. He'd lost his temper. Exactly what he'd promised not to do. He could see from the faces before him that he was losing any hope of swaying them. Even the one-armed former emissary was frowning. Bollocks.

'So,' Epaenetus smarmed, 'Fronto the wine merchant is not the same Fronto who served as one of Caesar's officers in the belligerent and unnecessary conquest of the tribes in the north? You are not *that* expansionist Roman?'

Shit, shit, shit, shit.

'I was a soldier, doing my duty, if that is what you are trying to determine. And now I am retired, and a wine merchant. But while we're on that subject, I would point out that the city's economy has boomed throughout the Gallic campaign. The trade in slaves alone has made your city – *our* city – rich. Its role as one of the main stopping points for supplies going back and forth, along with the trans-Alpine route, has brought you endless trade and bolstered your economy. So much so, in fact, that I note you have waived the new tax in the case of Caesar's forces, despite being adamant that it be applied to all such groups.'

'The tax is applied to merchants only. The proconsul does not buy and sell in the city. He simply uses the city as a port for the transport of his own goods. And in return for such considerations from us, he contributes to the city's coffers on a regular basis. It is only his reasonable and respectful acceptance of our authority here that eases our fears over such a strong Roman military presence so close to us. You have no such gesture of goodwill to speak for your motives.'

Fronto sighed. 'You are decided that the tax is to stay, and without exceptions, then?'

There was a murmur of confirmation around the council chamber, and Fronto ground his teeth. He'd forgotten his best arguments and lost his temper, and with that he'd also lost any hope of winning them over.

'I will say once again, look to the empty warehouses and stores that only a month ago were thriving businesses bringing in money to the city, but which your new tax has destroyed. So many merchants have given up and moved on. And others will go after them.'

It was futile, but he had to try.

'And yet,' Epaenetus snorted, waving his arms, 'even with the departure of some of the more volatile foreign concerns, it is worth noting that our city's coffers are healthier than ever. The tax paid by those loyal traders who stay has more than offset the loss of a few merchants. I cannot say that the city will lose a great deal of sleep when Fronto the wine merchant decides to return to Rome.'

'You sanctimonious, nasty little prick!'

His outburst seemed to have come from somewhere deep inside without having been filtered by his brain, and Fronto knew then that he had lost completely. Epaenetus had goaded him into alienating the rest of the crowd. He snapped his teeth shut over the rest of the invective that was trying to force its way out. Instead, he shook his head, turned, and stalked away from the gaze of the boule and out into the sunlight.

Damn, damn, damn, damn, damn. Why was it so much easier to convince a force of five thousand men to march up a hill into a hail of arrows than it was to convince fifty old farts to waive a tax?

He stomped across the small square and spotted Catháin sitting on the steps of the portico opposite. The northerner rose as he approached and wordlessly proffered a flask of lightly-watered wine. Fronto took it and threw down a hefty dose. 'That's not going to be enough. Let's go to the *Ox*.'

'It went well, then?'

Fronto flashed him an irritable glance. Catháin shrugged. 'I never expected success, but you had to try. Did you lose your temper by any chance?'

'Once or twice. They goaded me into it.'

'Of course they did, Fronto. They're politicians. What did you expect?'

Fronto grunted and took another swig.

'There's part of your trouble,' Catháin murmured, pointing across the square. Fronto turned and squinted into the sunlight, across the altar of Poseidon, to where he could see the boule filtering out of the building for their midday meal break. Epaenetus, easily spottable in his green and yellow, had drifted off to one side of the square, where he now stood beneath the colonnade, deep in conversation with Hierocles the wine merchant.

'The sleazy, slippery bastards.'

'Again... politicians. Always expect the worst, that way you'll rarely be disappointed.'

'Come on. I feel the distinct need to drink until I can't walk.'

* * * * *

Fronto leaned back against the chair in his new warehouse. He had to admit that Catháin had done an astounding job. He'd never have imagined he could get such a place so cheap. The warehouse was twice the size of the old one, and even with all his stock shelved and stored, three quarters of it was empty. And it had two offices built into the side, rather than just a desk and chair in the central aisle. Now, he occupied one such office and Catháin the other. And there was no need for a constant guard since the entire complex, which he shared with the warehouses of four other businesses, was secured within its own walls and guarded at all times. Outside in the shared yard, he could hear the various teamsters sorting out their rotas for the day.

He almost felt like a proper businessman. Except that, try as he might, he simply couldn't find a way to expand the business. He was staying afloat, just, through the clever little machinations of his weird northern employee, but the effects of the tax and the constant undermining by Hierocles and his cronies prevented any hope of growth or expansion. He'd been fuming over the possibilities for days, juggling figures and working through hopeful correspondence. He'd spent every waking hour in the warehouse, and slept there sometimes too.

Though he had to admit, to himself at least, that a large part of the reason for that was the presence of Andala and Lucilia at the villa. Every day saw them grow closer. Every day they were less like mistress and slave and more like two manipulative, giggling girls, watching him carefully and plotting. They had taken to drinking wine together in the evening and discussing things that Fronto had really wished he hadn't walked in on. Even sleeping in the office had started to seem like an attractive proposition.

He picked up the next communique in the seemingly endless pile and scanned it. Then he scanned it again. Then he smiled and, just in case, scanned it again. Somewhere above, a roosting bird shat on the cloak he had left folded up on the table, but then that was supposed to be lucky. He checked the minutiae of the text, but it was all there. He grinned.

The cartel of Mithonbaal the Syrian had agreed terms. They would pay half the foreign trade tax on the condition that Fronto could guarantee them a full hold from Neapolis each month. It would take some wangling and wheedling to arrange such a thing, but with Catháin's help, he was sure he could do that.

Mithonbaal was one of the few sailors whose business was so healthy and his name so respected in the boule that he was guaranteed to be true to his word and able to keep his end of the bargain. He had five Phoenician ships based out of Syria and plying the waters from there to Italy and beyond, and one of his vessels was in Massilia every month. Moreover, Mithonbaal was used as an overflow by the more influential Roman and Hispanic concerns, when they had spare space or too much cargo, so as often as not a Spanish or Roman trader in the harbour had some link to the Syrian. It was a veritable coup. The man charged more for transport than anyone except the Greeks, but his offer to share the tax would bring the price down to a very reasonable level. Fronto would *make* money. Actual *profit*!

He was on his feet doing the private victory jig he only did in absolute private when the door swung open. Trying not to tangle his legs, Fronto stood straight and the moment of panic he'd felt as he'd seen the state of Catháin's face melted away as he saw his easy smile.

'Good news?'

The northerner chuckled, prodding at a split lip with a square of blood-soaked linen. 'Yes. Good news.'

'You challenged the entire boule of Massilia to a fight and beat them all?'

The man pried open his bloodshot, bruised eye and laughed. 'This? Oh this was just three of Hierocles' thugs who happened on me in a back street. It might look a bit rough, but you should see the state of them!' He opened his other hand, where a piece of floppy, rent and bloody flesh flopped flat. Fronto felt the bile rise in his throat.

'What's that?'

'Better you don't ask, but his girlfriend's going to be furious.'

As Fronto blenched, Catháin roared out in laughter, dropped the torn flesh into the urn they kept for disposing of rubbish, and washed his hands in the *labrum* of cold water. 'Got any bread and butter? Nothing makes me hungry like a good barney.'

Fronto shook his head in disbelief and gestured to a platter on the corner table, much of which he'd left untouched.

'So what's the news?'

'I think I've just solved all your problems, Fronto.'

'Me too.'

'Oh?' Catháin rubbed his hands dry on his tunic and frowned as Fronto explained.

'The Syrian's accepted the terms. We need to secure a full ship every month from Neapolis, but the income will be superb.'

'Good. Every little helps.'

Fronto felt slightly crestfallen for a moment at the offhand manner in which the man greeted such a triumph, but then he noticed

126

the glow of success in Catháin's eyes. 'So what have you got for me?'

'The solution. I've just sealed two completely independent deals today. In terms of transport and shipping, prepare to make a killing. I've got a signed agreement from Caesar's logistics officer in the city. Any military or courier vessel with hold space that comes and goes from Massilia is at our disposal free of charge, on the condition that we give the legions a discount on the wine we bring in. The proconsul's ships are not liable to the foreign trade tax and even though you should theoretically pay it even using their vessels, it'll be a cold day in Aegyptus before any councillor in the city tries to argue with Caesar's men over something like that.'

Fronto blinked. 'Free?'

'Yes. And for just a ten percent discount, which will easily be taken care of by the drop in transport costs. And the number of ships going back and forth means we've pretty much unlimited space for goods. You can make as many deals as you like and be fairly sure we can deliver on time.'

'That's bloody astounding. Was the officer not worried about pissing off the boule?'

'It seems not. Apparently the prefect in charge had a penchant for the fish sauce they make down in Hispania Baetica, but the fellow who imported it has stopped trading here because of the new tax. Consequently, Prefect Atticus is not particularly tempted to side with the city. It's always about who and what you know, Fronto.'

'This could mean the start of something big, Catháin.'

'Better still, it's time to start exporting as well as importing. We're missing out on a huge potential profit that, as far as I can see, nobody has yet thought to plumb.'

'Export?' Fronto frowned. 'Export what?'

'Wine, you berk. You're a wine trader.'

Fronto rubbed his furrowed brow. 'But they don't make wine in the province. The law of the republic forbids it. All the old vineyards and producers in Narbonensis were torn up and shut down. What are we supposed to export?'

The northerner chuckled and produced a small flask from inside his tunic.

'What is that?'

'Try it.'

Gingerly, Fronto unsealed the flask and took a sniff. The hairs in his nose felt as though they were corroding. He winced. 'What *is* this?'

'Try it,' Catháin repeated. Fronto shrugged and, still frowning, took a sip.

'That is *horrible*. What is it?' He pushed the flask back to Catháin and scurried over to the labrum, washing out his mouth and spitting into the urn.

'That, Fronto, is wine.'

'That is most certainly *not* wine. I don't know what it is, but I can only assume it came from the anus of some mythical monster.'

'Your patrician tastes are too fine, Fronto. This is wine made by the Ruteni, just beyond the border of the Roman province. Bet you didn't know the Gauls made wine, did you?'

'They don't,' Fronto replied flatly, which drew a chuckle from his employee.

'I know. It's a little rough. There are four or five southern free tribes that have been making wine for the best part of a century outside the republic's border. They're happy to trade, since the Gallic tribes' economies have never been so poor as now, what with the war destroying their production and trade.'

'But who would *want* that muck?'

Catháin laughed again. 'See? Your patrician tastes coming through again. There are misers in Rome and Latium and Campania and everywhere in between who would buy a thousand amphorae of this stuff to feed to their slaves, servants and gladiators instead of expensive Italian wine. They'll not pay much, but then you can buy it for next to nothing and ship it free. Fronto, it's basically money waiting to be earned.'

Fronto stared. 'It actually sounds feasible.'

'It is. Very feasible. In fact, it's a veritable gold-mine. Everybody wins, and you get to heap up profits through it. If you're feeling generous, you can always donate to the city coffers from your new profits, and try and win a few friends among the boule, or you could send extra money to the tribes who supply you and make influential Gallic friends. Or, of course, you could give me a substantial raise. After all, I suspect I've earned it.'

Fronto laughed out loud. 'Catháin, if you can arrange those tribal imports, you can name your own damn wage!'

'Good. And the next time you feel like travelling back to Italia, I would like to tag along and see if I can seal some better deals there too.'

'Agreed,' Fronto smiled. 'I'm planning to head to Puteoli before summer to see my sister and Galronus. Gods, he's going to be astounded to hear I'm importing Gallic wine!' He slapped Catháin on the shoulder, causing the rather bruised factor to wince, and reached up with his other hand to give Fortuna a caress at his neck. 'Things are looking up, my friend. At last. And mostly thanks to you.'

Chapter Seven

MOLACOS of the Cadurci stalked through the burning wreckage of the inn. By morning nothing would remain of this place but a few sad mouldering beams and some charred stones. It was a little more high profile than their previous strikes, but he had reasoned that by now word of the executions of Roman officers would have filtered back to the authorities and there was no longer any real need to sneak around. Of course, he would still be careful, as there were only twelve of them, and though they were each and every one a killer, forged in the crucible of war with Rome and moulded into the vengeance of the peoples by the will of one man, there were still limits to their ability. Taking on a large group of Romans would be stupid and suicidal, and at this stage he could not risk the plan for the simple love of killing Romans.

He could hear the screaming now. Unearthly wailing like a soul beyond the limits of human endurance. Which, of course, was the plain truth of the matter.

Belenos was sitting in the midst of the conflagration, his feet up on a table as he coddled a large mug of beer to which he had helped himself. As Molacos approached, the golden-haired hunter, as handsome as a child's lullaby on a summer evening, removed his expressionless mask and dropped it on the table in order to take a deep swig of the drink. He flashed a smile of perfect, straight white teeth at his leader, and Molacos grunted a greeting in return.

'Pull up a bench and have a drink.'

'Do you not fear falling beams or tongues of fire?'

Belenos grinned. 'Am I not the shining God who pulls the sun? What have I to fear from burning beams?'

'Don't get clever. And I will not drink that swill.'

'This,' Belenos said after another sup, 'is true Arveni beer. A good brew.'

'This inn was given over to the Roman army, and the owner simply served and serviced Rome. Whatever it made and sold is tainted, and I will have nothing from it.'

'Suit yourself.'

'Is Bellisama almost done, d'you think? The other Romans are all burning and their goods taken or destroyed. It is time to move on.'

The handsome hunter shrugged with a quirky smile. You know my sister, Molacos. She will not leave a job half done.'

'The prefect knows nothing. That was clear even before I left the room. Now she dallies for no reason.'

'Oh, she has reason, Molacos. You know her. She will not rest her blades until she has flensed each and every Roman this side of the Alps. And very likely she will then look beyond the mountains. Our quarry is long gone. We should devote ourselves purely to the killing of Romans. It's what we're good at.'

Another blood-curdling shriek ripped through the silence and died slowly, like its owner. Molacos eyed the creaking, charring roof beams above him suspiciously and held up his arm to shield his face from some of the scorching heat of the bar which was burning furiously, aided by strong spirits.

'We have to go before this place collapses.'

'It will see out this beer. I deserve a rest.'

Molacos was about to retort angrily when the door to the rear room swung open to reveal the inferno beyond and Bellisama emerged, soot-streaked and sweating, weapons cleaned and sheathed, her mask in one hand and a necklace of fingers hanging from her other.

'Dear brother, I missed your last naming day. How poor of me.' With a cackle, she threw the finger necklace at Belenos, who caught it and turned it round and over, examining it. 'You could have left his rings on.'

'I put out his eyes with them and filled the sockets. You can go and get them if you like?'

Belenos chuckled again and slugged down the beer. 'Very well. Where next, glorious leader?'

'We head back towards Gergovia,' Molacos sighed. 'There are a few other potential places on the way and I still live in hope that one interrogation will bear true fruit.'

'And if not, at least we get to kill Romans.'

Molacos shook his head and marvelled at the twins. They were like children, but it was hard not to love them.

Chapter Eight

VARUS glanced around at the men of the Ninth hurrying between the farmstead's huts, gathering armfuls of dry hay and other animal fodder. Most of the legionaries were spending more time than they realistically should inside the huts, and throwing their loads into the cart with wild abandon rather than stacking it carefully before rushing for another building. He could hardly blame them. The rain was near torrential, the ground churned into a thick quagmire of mud and animal dung through which the men slopped and squelched, all the while getting colder and wetter, watching their armour and weapons getting soaked and knowing that even after the foraging was done with and they were safe back in camp, the work had only just begun, with hours of cleaning and polishing ahead to prevent rust. Still, he ought to intervene. It was, after all, the fodder for the cavalry they were gathering.

Two days had passed since the fort's completion, and the army sat behind its defences, seething in the rain and watching the Bellovaci and their allies across the swamp sullenly brooding. There would still be two days before Trebonius arrived with the other legions, at the best estimate, and while the army was managing to subsist on the meagre supplies it had brought with it, augmented by forage brought in by raiding parties, more supplies were always needed, especially with such a large relief force marching to join them. The foragers of the four legions had been out every hour the gods sent gathering firewood, barrels of water, supplies of grain, vegetables and animals whenever possible and now, finally, animal fodder. For throughout the continual foraging, the auxiliary cavalry had been out protecting the parties and using up what little supplies they had in the process.

Every farm and village for more than fifteen miles in any direction had been stripped of its stores, and the legions had been forced to become ever more daring, skirting the swamps that surrounded the enemy and moving many miles beyond them into uncertain territory to find the scarce foodstuffs needed to supply an army in the grip of winter.

Today, luckily, the army had discovered a healthy cache of food in the form of a large farmstead hidden in a depression in the woods and kept secret by geography. As with almost everywhere in this benighted land the farmers had gone, joining the enemy civilians secure in the deep forest, and had taken with them whatever they could carry, along with all their animal stocks. Yet even then, what had had to be left behind was worth more than gold to the hungry and poorly-supplied Roman force: a cart that would have to be pulled by cavalry mounts, sheds full of stored hay, grain, veg and more.

Varus watched the men throw another armful of hay into the cart, strands and chaff flying loose even in the rain. He really ought to shout at them. They were wasting forage and space, and would pay for their sloppiness later. But shouting at them was the job of their centurions, who were in one of the huts, and he just didn't have the energy. For while the forage parties had been drawn in rotas from the four legions and their cavalry escort had been drawn in a similar fashion from the various native levy tribes, Varus and his small cadre of regular cavalry and officers had spent most of their waking hours out on patrol with the groups. It was not that the native officers couldn't be trusted, but they had a tendency to run a little wild and to overextend without a Roman officer to remind them of their orders. Regular cavalry officers played the important role of a mediary between the native commanders and the legionary centurions they were protecting.

Today was the turn of the Remi. There was a large group of Lingone cavalry as well, somewhere off to the north with men from the Eighth, but here at this perfect little find the steadfast and long-serving Remi protected the Ninth.

Varus lifted his gaze from the men rushing back and forth with sodden fodder and his eyes played across the water-logged fields to the edge of the woods. The wide, shallow vale was in principle surrounded by forest, but in truth, while both side slopes were thickly wooded, the head of the valley was only thinly dotted with trees and large rock formations, a small river tumbling down to cut through the flat and feed the farm. And downstream the trees closed in again, but left a space some hundred paces wide on each side of the water. A greensward that looked inviting even in the miserable weather.

The Remi had separated into groups, small detachments of thirty men in very Roman formations, each set in position watching an area of surrounding woodland for trouble. Varus had to chuckle. If there was any doubt that the Gallic peoples would one day fully integrate with Rome, he would point the doubter to the Remi auxiliaries who had, over the course of eight years of war under the eagle, adopted Roman formations, training, ranks, and even to some extent equipment. If things kept going the way they were, in half a decade it would be impossible to distinguish between the Remi riders and the Roman regulars.

Perhaps half the Remi contingent that had come out today were split into these small native thirty-man turmae, and the other half remained in a solid force downstream, watching that greensward, knowing as they did that if an enemy came in force, they would have to come along that valley. Unlike the legionaries, who had downed shields and were running independently about their work, the Remi sat astride their horses, still in tight formation down there at the valley end, ready for action.

He understood. For the legions, this was just the latest in a long list of engagements in Gaul. There was nothing special about this conflict. But the Remi, for all their experience with Caesar's army, were of the Belgae. These lands were ancestral Belgae lands, and the Bellovaci were their neighbours. Remi civilians were as much at risk from this enemy rising as the Romans or the Suessiones who had been the rising's initial target. To the Remi, this was personal, and they were prepared for the fight. Even *eager* for it. To that end, the Remi force here was led by not one of their nobles, but two. One – a *prince* of their tribe, no less – officially commanded, though he deferred to the experience of the older commander who accompanied him in the manner of a cavalry general. And both were sitting with that formation, watching for the enemy. *Hoping* for the enemy, Varus suspected.

'Nearly finished here, sir,' announced one of his decurions, trotting over from the sixty-man regular formation Varus had brought. The commander looked back at the men and noted that most were now sheltering from the rain, awaiting the command to form up when their centurions emerged, while odd figures still scurried back and forth, loading the last few things they could find that might be of use.

'Good. Don't know about you, but I'm sick of being wet through.'

His gaze swept back to the end of the valley and the Remi force gathered there. He frowned.

'Is that what I think it is?'

The decurion peered into the rain and paled. 'Enemy, sir.'

The Remi had seen them too. Half a mile, perhaps, down the greensward, an enemy force was approaching. As Varus tried to pick

134

out more detail, he ignored the commotion among the Remi auxiliaries in between. There were quite a few of the enemy. Not a huge army, but enough to pose a threat to the Remi force facing them. And they were clearly prepared for cavalry. The force bristled with long spears. Far more than one would expect among a people who generally preferred the edge of a sword to the tip of a spear. That suggested to Varus that they had armed specifically to take on horsemen. Indeed he realised that they were honking carnyxes as they approached, smashing metal on metal and drumming on wood, making the loudest din they could achieve, the sounds echoing back and forth among the trees, hemmed in and amplified by the valley walls. Noise. Horses – even trained cavalry horses – could get very nervous around too much noise. Not the din of battle, to which they were used, but the rhythmic battering of ritual noise. Most would hold steady, but in a tight formation it only took a few horses rearing and bolting to cause chaos.

Indeed, as Varus watched, the commotion increased and three horses, riderless, raced from the rear of the formation out into the wide fields of the valley.

'Decurion, send riders out to the pickets. Have every other group form up at the farm with us and warn the others that they will need to pull back and join us at a single call as fast as they can.' The decurion nodded and trotted off to relay the orders to his men, and Varus waved to the two legionary officers who had finally emerged from a hut.

'Centurion. Enemy sighted down the valley. Get your men moving with the cart and we'll protect your back. Once we're up the valley head slopes we'll be safe from the bulk threat and we can retreat to camp in good order.'

The centurion saluted and began blowing his whistle, bellowing orders, but Varus' attention had been grabbed by one of his scouts, whose 'oh, shit' under his breath had still been loud enough to hear. He turned back to the action and his heart fell.

'No, no, no, no, no. What are you doing?'

The Remi were moving. And not just moving, they were rising to a charge.

'What are they *doing* sir?'

'They are letting pride and anger rule their heads, trooper.'

'They'll be in the shit when they hit those spears, sir.'

Varus nodded. 'The Remi are nothing if not brave.'

135

'Do you think they might actually win, sir?'

'Not a hope, trooper. They've been goaded into a trap. Look.'

Peering down the valley, he and the soldier could now see the rest of the enemy, filtering down through the trees at the valley sides, moving to flank the Remi. It would be a slaughter. And it was too late to do anything useful about it, even though he had to try. He turned and gestured to the other decurion. The legionaries had formed up quickly and the cart was already moving for the relative safety of the valley head. The way the enemy had set up the ambush they were kitted for a fight in the open, expecting to massacre the forage party and its cavalry in the farmland. He had to hope they would break off pursuit if the party was prepared for them and already on high ground. No war leader would want to fight up the rocky slope and the various small waterfalls against a veteran Roman shieldwall. No. Once the foragers were out of the valley and up the slope they would be safe.

And the stupid, suicidal charge of the Remi would buy them the time they needed.

But he had to *try* and save them, or at least *some* of them. The leaders, if no one else. He realised with mixed relief and sadness that while at least Galronus – the Remi prince and strongest of all their horse commanders – was safe in Italia with Fronto's family, both Prince Vertiscus, who commanded this force, and Atis, his general, were close relations of Galronus – the prince a brother, he thought?

'Decurion, gather all the remaining Remi pickets and half the regulars and help get that cart up the valley head. We'll be along presently.'

As the officer saluted and sent out other riders to form up the scattered Remi, Varus gestured to his musician, standard bearer and the thirty-man turma. 'Come with me.'

Kicking his steed into life he began to race towards the action.

It was already a disaster. Even as the moments passed in a thunder of hooves and the small relief force approached the edge of the farm fields and the riverside grassland, he could see how few of the Remi might possibly make it out of that mess alive.

Damn it. How could they have let this happen? The Bellovaci had changed the whole engagement now. It was no longer a waiting game. If they were prepared to attack the foragers, the Romans would have to do something about it or become very hungry as they waited for Trebonius and his legions.

As they rode, he looked across at his musician. 'Can you remember the Remi recall?'

It was to be hoped. There was a standing fraternal competition among the cavalry units to try and remember and mimic one another's calls. It had begun years ago as a bet over Gallic beer, but Varus and his officers had fostered the wagers and the games, recognising the value in having such disparate groups able to recognise each other's' calls, despite the wide array of melodies.

The musician frowned as he jolted up and down with the horse's gait, trying to dredge his memory. The Remi's calls went out on a horn not dissimilar to the Roman cavalry *tuba*, and the man took a deep breath, bracing himself against the jolting of the horse, and put the tuba to his lips.

The melody of the call sounded at once both familiar and odd to Varus. He had heard the Remi calls so many times over the eight years of war, and now that he heard it again he recognised it, but it sounded somehow lighter and airier on the Roman instrument.

Without waiting for the order, the musician timed his breath with the horse's motion, taking deep breath after deep breath and repeating the call again and again.

They were rewarded with some commotion at the rear of the Remi force. A number of men had responded to the calls and were trying to extricate themselves from the disaster. Four men fell even as they tried to turn, but a few dozen riders had managed to break free of the fight and were racing towards the Romans. Varus held up his hand to halt his men. There was nothing to be gained from riding into the fray. All they could do now was try and save as many Remi as they could. As the horses fell to a walk and then formed up carefully, he gestured to the musician. 'Keep blowing that bloody tune until they're all with us or dead.'

As the Remi recall blared out repeatedly, Varus waved the fleeing auxiliaries into position with them, watching as more and more of the doomed horsemen tried to leave the battle and join the Roman officer.

Spears lunged, lifting men from their saddles and dropping them into the mire to be hacked to pieces and trampled by desperate horses. The more enterprising Bellovaci with the long Celtic blades were swiping them at waist height, severing and breaking horses' legs to bring beast and rider down together, where they could be stabbed again and again. Where were the leaders?

Varus tried to peer past the approaching Remi survivors, and finally caught sight of young Vertiscus, who was still in the heart of the action, bellowing war cries and he brought down his sword to left and right, each rise of the blade sending a shower of crimson into the air to mingle with the falling rain. He was frenzied, killing like a man possessed. But even as Varus watched and somehow hoped that such insane bravery and strength would bring the favour of the gods and turn the tide, Vertiscus stiffened in his saddle and leaned to the left and the commander could see the spear that had taken him in the side being pushed in ever deeper. Astoundingly, the young Remi prince, even with the shaft inside his ribcage shredding organs, managed to swipe down and destroy his killer. Then the prince was gone, pulled from the saddle down into the murk. His heart in his throat, Varus peered desperately into the melee, searching for a sign of their general, Atis. When he saw him all hope of Remi survival was dashed, for Atis wore a snarl of defiance even though his body was long gone and his head, surmounted by a distinctive golden eagle helmet, bobbed around on the tip of a spear.

'Damn it. Alright. Move out... at full speed. Catch up with the forage party and back to the fort. Now.'

'Commander?' gasped one of the fled Remi, frowning and pointing back at the other Remi who were still attempting to leave the chaos and join up with the Romans who had seemingly come to rescue them.

'We've no time to save the others. Come on.'

As the troop burst into life, racing back across the fields towards the legionaries, who were already at the valley head and trying to goad the cart, drawn by two cavalry horses, up the slope, the musician, exhausted, looked across at his commander, noticing the dark scowl on Varus' face.

'We couldn't save them all, sir. You know that.'

'I don't like leaving brave men, however foolhardy, to buy our escape with their lives.'

'You saved a hundred Remi or more, sir. No one could have hoped for better.'

Varus nodded, saving his breath as he rode. When he got back to camp, and once he'd reported this disaster to the general, he'd have to write an unpleasant letter to Fronto in Massilia, bearing news of the deaths of Galronus' family.

Shit on the Bellovaci!

* * * * *

Varus smiled grimly as the Condrusi scout delivered his report. Though Nemesis was a goddess generally reserved for gladiators and the betrayed, Varus would tonight pour a good libation to the lady of vengeance for delivering unto him that for which he had wished.

The Bellovaci were coming again.

Following the disaster that had reaped a heavy toll on the Remi the previous day he had reported wearily to the general and had been surprised at the venom with which Caesar had greeted the news. The proconsul valued the Remi highly, their tribe the only one in the whole of Gaul who had remained loyal throughout the entire eight year campaign. On hearing of the deaths of the nobles and of near half a thousand Remi riders, rather than dismissing the matter, or fuming incoherently, Caesar had snarled and asked Varus what they could do to avenge the fallen. The commander had been so taken aback by the vehemence of the general that it had taken him half an hour of deep thought to come up with the answer.

The general had liked his plan, had approved it immediately, and given him free rein to put together whatever he needed.

It had taken just hours, with enough good local scouts, to locate another untouched farmstead close to the enemy position. And so he had taken out the same men as yesterday – those who had witnessed the demise of the Remi and knew what they were up against.

Those men of the Ninth even now were busy loading a cart in the blessed dry morning, shields and pila stacked ready for collection. Two of the strongest horses were already in the traces ready to take the laden cart to safety. And the centurions were watchful and ready, even while they played the part of the blissfully unaware foragers. No enemy would recognise them for the same people as the previous day, of course, and other forage parties had been out and about since then anyway. But this one had been designed to draw the enemy's gaze through its visibility, slowness, position and proximity to their camp.

Six of the best scouts in the army, all drawn from tribes who knew the area, had ranged around the periphery watching for the enemy, expecting a similar trap. Indeed, the terrain was almost an echo of yesterday, the farm lying in a low valley surrounded by trees. The main difference here was that there was no easy escape up a slope at the head of the valley. A trap sprung here would likely finish the lot of them, and that fact had, fortunately, been enough of a lure to draw the enemy.

Again, small units of pickets surrounded the valley in an oval at watchful positions, and the other half of the Remi force sat at the entrance to the farmstead, where the stream ran on down the valley between wide green banks. It looked almost exactly as it had yesterday. And it had tempted the Bellovaci, whom the scout announced were even now moving up the valley and filtering down through the woods. Varus thanked the man for his efforts and sent him in a circuit giving the nod for the first phase of the action to everyone involved.

Then he sat to wait with his men.

It had to look the same. Tempting. But the Remi would have to hold back this time. He had spent an hour impressing upon them that very thought. Seven hundred Remi had ridden out today instead of the twelve hundred the previous day, and they had been the very same men – the survivors, who had spent the night in rituals to their own vengeance spirits. And now they once again played the picket roles and sat among the group at the foot of the valley.

Varus watched that force carefully as news of the approaching enemy was relayed to them by the scout and he tensed for a moment, then exhaled gratefully as he noted the hundred or so Remi survivors sit restive but still, awaiting the enemy. He'd half expected, despite his lecture, that news of the enemy would send them racing off down the valley in search of bloodshed. But they sat there, surrounding his little surprise like the pastry around a pie. Enticing. Tasty.

What a pie…

As he waited, he finally heard the booing and clattering of the enemy carnyxes and spears. Things were slightly different today, of course. The enemy came openly this time, including those in the woodland. They did not expect the Romans to fall into the same trap twice, but then they had no *need* of a trap this time. They outnumbered the Remi and had beaten them once. And this time there was nowhere for the forage party and the cart to run. They had no need of subtlety, so they came in force and openly jeering their neighbours, the heads of Vertiscus and Atis, identifiable by their helms, bobbing around on spears at the front of the column just to goad the Remi.

It worked. Two or three of the Remi reacted just too predictably, but their new commanders called them back, and reluctantly they fell into position once more. This time, the Roman auxiliary force would play the part of the lure and the surprise, and it would be the Bellovaci who experienced the panic.

The enemy closed.

'Now sir?' asked the musician next to him, who Varus had put on double pay after his service yesterday.

'A few heartbeats more, I think. Let's get them too close to back out. I want them committed before they realise their mistake.'

The musician nodded, but he put the tuba to his lips ready anyway, breathing deep and slow.

Varus watched.

Closer. Closer. Closer.

The Bellovaci force was beginning to ripple and shake in a manner he recognised. The warriors were itching to get to the fight and were starting to move, straining at the leash as it were, while their leaders held them back 'til the last moment. Any time now they would break and charge. And Varus needed to spring his surprise first, for the enemy would be harder to break when they were already at a run.

Now or never.

'Give the first call.'

The tuba rang out immediately and with the precision of acrobats at a festival in the forum, Varus' combined force changed immediately.

The legionaries dropped everything they were doing and grabbed their shields and pila, forming up at the downstream edge of the farmyard. The picket units began to move. Those at the valley head began the landslide, riding to the next group along, who geed up their horses and joined them as they rode to the third, collecting them and riding for the fourth, and so on. In a matter of heartbeats, the strung out picket units were combining and moving towards the field of battle, turning into a formidable unit as they did so.

But they were just the dressing of the dish. The pie was still the heart.

And now the crust cracked.

Those Remi survivors from yesterday peeled away from the force to either side, becoming the anchor point for the assembling pickets, where the combining forces would gather. The Bellovaci faltered, uncertain of whether to charge, unable to comprehend what was happening and why the front ranks of the Remi force had peeled away.

And then it became apparent to the enemy that only those few front ranks had been Remi at all.

At the centre of that unit – the filling of the pie that Varus was about to cram down their desperate gullets – Caesar's infamous German cavalry bellowed their ululating, howling war chants as they moved to charge.

'Second call if you will, Decimus.'

It had to be done quickly. The Germans would hardly wait for the order. Indeed, they were already moving. As the second call went out, the two centuries of the Ninth began to jog at double time to join the fray, their forage forgotten. The gathering pickets were almost in position now. By the time they had gathered in two units to either side of the valley, the legionaries would be there, and so would Varus' regulars. That meant that the third call would signal two hundred legionaries, sixty regular cavalry and five hundred vengeful Remi combining to serve as the rear-guard, taking any surviving Bellovaci on and butchering the lot.

If there *were* any survivors!

The regulars began to trot forward towards the violence.

A thousand German cavalry, already infamous throughout Gaul and Belgae lands as takers of grisly trophies, were now riding hard at the Bellovaci, snarling and whooping. In theory, they stood no more chance than the Remi had yesterday. In practice, Varus knew upon whom he would place his wager. The Remi had been brave but had ridden gleefully, unthinking, into a trap, while the Bellovaci had been prepared and eager.

Not so, today.

Today, the Germans were entirely aware of what they were riding into, and had no fear. Only hunger and anger. And the Bellovaci had been taken completely by surprise. As was so often the case with war, the unexpected had a worse effect than strictly necessary, purely due to the natural propensity for the surprised man to panic.

The Germans hit the Bellovaci like a battering ram, completely heedless of the spears that the few rallying enemy brought to bear. Varus watched as one German took a spear in his shoulder and simply ignored it, riding down the bearer and hacking at two then

142

three then four men even as he shed his own blood with every drum of hooves.

The effect of the charge was impressive. The Bellovaci force shattered like a dropped vase. Those on the periphery fled into the woods, shrieking for their gods to save them. Some even made it. Varus watched as a number of the Germans, despite having been given extra training in Gallic and Roman cavalry manoeuvres, fell naturally back into their native fighting style, slipping from their steeds once they were in the thick of things and laying waste to anyone they found who was not one of their own.

The shrieks Varus could hear were not the cries of the wounded and the dying. The commander had heard such sounds so many times in his career that he knew them well. Nor were they the sounds of panic and fear. They were the shrieks of agony that more often accompanied the work of a master torturer.

Though at this distance he couldn't see what the Germans were up to, he had seen them fight many times now and could picture the scene. Tearing off jaws to use as torcs, hacking off ears, severing fingers for prizes, putting out eyes just for the feel of the wet pop.

The Germanic cavalry were animals. They were *worse* than animals. They were demons given human form. They were simply the most terrifying thing Varus had ever witnessed on the battlefield. And while they were rarely fielded, when they *were* allowed to slip the leash, the effect they had on the enemy was like a hungry fox in a chicken coop.

All cohesion among both armies was gone. The centre of the valley was a mass of struggling man, some still on horseback, others fighting on foot even as the Germanic horses kicked and bit, their own bloodlust every bit as sharp as their riders'.

'Third call, please,' he smiled to his musician, who let the notes soar. Even as the regulars closed on the valley end, along with two centuries of the Ninth and five hundred angry Remi, the battle was already won. He gave the orders and the backup force began to move in. The legionaries slipped into the woodland to either side, clambering up the hill at speed, chasing down those Bellovaci who had fled up there. They had orders to pursue the fleeing enemy until the fourth call, which would signal the end of the fight.

The rest – the regulars and the Remi – moved forth to the rear of the engagement, staying out of the fight initially, for fear of falling foul of the oft-indiscriminate Germans, but then starting to pick their targets and take out those few small groups of Bellovaci who were managing to rally at the periphery in the hope of achieving something.

The floor of the valley was littered with the dead, which belonged overwhelmingly to the Bellovaci. It had been a massacre on a scale far surpassing the loss of the Remi yesterday. At a guess, three times as many enemy lay dead today as allies had been lost yesterday. And the dying was not over, even if the battle had already clearly been won.

The cavalry fought on and Varus, despite having decided to stay out of it, soon found himself in the thick of the action, hewing limbs and hacking into Belgic torsos with the long blade of a Gallic design he had long since adopted as his weapon of choice. He revelled in the kill, picturing what Commius would think if the Romans went back to camp opposite their position parading a thousand Bellovaci heads on spears.

His sword rose and fell, swept and hacked. Twice he took blows to his shield arm which splintered the wood and leather, and once he felt a stray spear tip rake across his ribs, tearing the links of his chain mail and bruising his side while drawing no blood.

And suddenly it was over. He lifted a boot and pushed a gurgling warrior from his blade, freeing it, only to discover that he was alone in a sea of death and mutilation, the ground spread with corpses and the crying wounded – again, almost all enemies. It was a victory of Titanic proportions. And the Remi were revelling in it, taking their time in dispatching the enemy wounded and enjoying every shriek.

The Germans were gone, howling for blood further along the valley, but he cared not. They had been given their briefing and then turned loose. They would harry the Bellovaci all the way back to their camp, and he allowed them to do it. The sight of the Germans slaughtering the fleeing men and the rest drowning in the swamp as they ran trying to find the safety of their hill would destroy the enemy army's morale, almost as surely as the realisation of what they had truly faced had done to the ambush today.

He had no doubt that most of the Germans would come back alive and laughing, wearing parts of their fallen foes as decoration.

He shuddered.

With a nod to his musician, he had the last call blown, which would bring in the pursuing men so that the force could gather up the forage and make it back to camp. Caesar would be pleased tonight.

And so would Nemesis, who would receive more than one libation after dark this eve.

Breathing heavily and allowing his muscles to relax, the cavalry commander walked his horse out into the field again, into open space, and then took in the scene. Again the scale of the victory was brought home with the carpet of dead Belgae who were now being looted by the vengeful Remi.

And the legionaries were reforming ready to leave, after gathering the last few things for the cart.

And the scouts...

One of the scouts was riding towards him fast. His heart skipped a beat and then began to thump fast and heavy. Please, Nemesis, don't let something mar this day. Not now.

He chewed on his cheek as the Suessione rider drew up and halted his horse, nodding his head in salute.

'What news?'

The scout smiled, and Varus felt that sudden surge of tension he'd experienced evaporate again.

'Commander, I have news that legate Trebonius is closing. He and his army are one day away and will be in camp by nightfall tomorrow in line with the general's plans. His forward scouts were just over the hill from here, seeking Caesar's position.' The man gestured with a thumb over his shoulder to where a small group of tired-looking horsemen were making their way towards him.

Varus grinned.

Time to unsettle the enemy all the more.

'There are a few Bellovaci still alive among the fallen. Take my decurion here and go stop the Remi killing them all. Make sure that some poor bastard overhears you revealing this news and then we'll move out. I'd love to see what happens in the enemy camp when that man limps home telling his friends that three more legions are on the way.'

The decurion, sitting next to him, frowned. 'Sir? The general wanted the enemy unaware until the force arrived, I thought.'

'He did. But with this victory things have changed. We've flayed their arse now and the panic will be spreading among their ranks. If we foster it and increase it, we'll keep them off-balance until the time comes to finish things.'

As the decurion saluted and rode off with a few men and the native scout to leak the news of Trebonius to the enemy wounded, Varus stretched and winced at his bruised ribs.

Time to finish Commius and his rebellion and get back to winter quarters.

Thank you, Nemesis.

* * * * *

'They're not moving,' Brutus murmured, staring at the Belgic hill across the sea of mist. 'Why aren't they moving?'

'It seems they are resolved to fight,' Varus replied quietly.

The two men peered across the white blanket that filled the valley and separated the two fortified camps in the damp early evening air. The sounds of the final touches being added to Mamurra's bridge drifted up, slightly muffled by the fleecy fog. The bridge was in place, despite such perfectionist attention, as was simply attested by the vanguard of the Eighth legion who even now spread out on the slope before the enemy camp, falling into position in battle array, ahead of the original schedule, given the enemy's new tactics of harrying the forage parties, which had continued in small measure despite the loss of over a thousand men to Varus' trap and the Germans' bloodlust. The brutal horsemen had pursued the enemy right into the swamp, leaving a river of blood in their wake and butchering the last few under the watching eyes of the Bellovaci camp. Men had died, falling into the sucking muck of the morass rather than succumb to the trophy taking serrated blades of the Germans.

'I'd hoped they would flee at the sight of the bridge and with the knowledge of Trebonius' approach. Perhaps you should not have had word of it leaked to them?'

Varus nodded. 'I had thought it would make them run, but the Belgae are made of stern stuff.'

The news had come in at dawn that the enemy camp had shrunk in size, though not in number of fighting bodies. The Bellovaci and their allies had used the cover of darkness to send their wagons and supplies, and their wounded, through secret safe routes in the swamp and away into the safety of the forest with the women and children. But the warriors had remained, and now they stood before their defences, watching the Romans crossing the bridge.

146

'I fear we miscalculated,' put in Caesar, stepping his white mare forward and falling in on the far side of Brutus. 'I had hoped to surprise them, but I fear that was a doomed enterprise anyway since they had begun forays and actions against our foragers. And Varus here had the ingenuity to attempt to break them with panic. But I suspect that all we have managed to achieve between us is to harden their resolve and force them to dig in. Now we face a difficult fight up a brutal slope against a well-defended position. Even without having to toil through the mire first, that will be a very costly battle, and at this stage in the pacification I am loathe to lose half a legion in what is, in essence, still just a minor rising.'

Varus nodded gloomily.

'So what do we do, general,' Brutus sighed.

'We have no choice. We must bring across the legions and fortify once more, awaiting Trebonius. He should be with us by nightfall tomorrow, according to reports. Once we have all the legions present, we will look at ways of dislodging them from the hill.'

As the general watched the legion forming up on the far side, Varus and Brutus shared a look and the cavalry commander flicked his gaze across the white sea to the assembling legion on the far side, then up the high, steep slope to the watching hordes of the Bellovaci and their fortifications beyond. The fact that Caesar could only suggest they 'look at ways of dislodging them' was telling. The general always had ideas, was always one step ahead of reality in his strategy. If he had nothing at this stage, then there would *be* no stroke of genius. The only option would be a direct assault uphill into the enemy. It would be costly, and it would be brutal, but the enemy were done for and they had to know that. Why didn't they run?

Because, of course, they knew that the moment they turned their backs, the Roman cavalry would cut them down. They had learned the value of Caesar's horse the hard way. Rather than breaking their morale, Varus' victory had hardened their resolve and left them knowing they couldn't run.

He sighed. There would be little use for his cavalry on such a slope anyway. This assault was a job for the infantry, gods protect them.

* * * * *

147

Late that evening, Varus and Brutus leaned on the wattle fence of the hastily thrown-up rampart. The new camp on the Bellovaci hill's lower slopes was little more than a standard ditchless marching camp. The swampy land of the valley and limestone that lay beneath the soil of the hill made any attempt at a defensive ditch impossible, and the rampart was correspondingly unimpressive. Rather than spend half a day ferrying heavy timbers across the bridge, the fences had been stripped from the strong camp across the valley and re-erected here on the low mounds as a cursory defence. If the enemy descended that hill, it would be down to the weight of numbers and the discipline and bravery of the men, and any victory would owe nothing to the fortifications.

But no one believed the enemy would rush them. Even those men on guard at the rampart stood easy watching the smoke rise from the camp atop the hill, the light of the torches bobbing around here and there. The enemy had retired to their camp as the sunset faded, lighting their fires and torches, and all the Romans could now see were the figures of the guards walking back and forth on the enemy rampart.

It was depressing to say the least, watching the secure enemy and knowing the fight that had to come. Varus had wracked his brains throughout the evening for a way to instil panic among the Belgae and cause them to flee. But they were locked in a countdown to an inevitable conflict. Caesar could come up with nothing better than a direct assault and, while the enemy knew that this would mean the end of their rebellion and death for every man on the hill, they could hardly flee, for turning their backs on the legions and Varus' cavalry would mean too many deaths for no gain.

'Maybe we could find the hidden passages through the swamp at the far side that they used to move out their wagons?' Brutus mused.

'Nice thought,' Varus replied, 'but even if we could find them it would take forever to get even a cohort through them and into position behind the enemy. It would take half a day to get our force on that side of the river, and they would see us coming long before we had enough men behind them to make any kind of assault. It would take hours to get the men through the swamp, which we could never manage unobserved. If they are anything other than utterly dim, they will be watching those routes carefully.'

Brutus slumped over the fence. 'We've fallen on our own sword here, then. We've forced them into a corner from which they can't escape, but which is going to cost us the world to take. At least, gods-willing, there's no reserve army coming to help them this time. Last thing we need is another Alesia. The people may praise Caesar for that victory, but we all saw how damn close that was.'

Varus nodded his agreement. If Alesia had turned the way Gergovia had, Caesar and his army would have been back in Cisalpine Gaul now, hanging their heads in defeat. But there was still time for a failure to cripple the general's reputation, so close to his consulate. He could hardly afford a defeat, or even a desperate pyrrhic win, here and now.

'Looks like they're lighting more fires. Must be colder up there than it is down here, I guess.'

Varus nodded, peering up at the defences atop the slope. A golden tongue of flame was rising into the night, sparks flying to the heavens to warm the gods. Even as he watched, another large bonfire burst into life.

'That's odd.'

Brutus frowned. 'What?'

'Those fires are outside the enemy ramparts. They're not camping out front, so why…' He straightened. 'You don't think…?'

Even as they considered the meaning of the new fires, four more began to roar into life across the hillside. Again and again conflagrations exploded into golden light all along the top of the hill, before the enemy defences. By the time a general cry of alert had gone up in the camp, there was a solid line of fire all across the hill.

'They're going to send them down to the camp,' Brutus coughed, staring at the conflagrations. 'These wicker fences won't stop them. Damn it.'

Varus nodded distractedly, but his eyes were narrowed suspiciously. More fires were rising, extending the line of flames down the slope to either side, to meet the morass below.

'I'm not so sure.'

Behind them, the camp burst into life. Men moved back away from the ramparts at the watch centurion's command in case the burning mass rolled down the hill against the Roman defences.

'Come on,' Brutus said, grabbing at Varus' shoulder.

'I don't think that's what's happening,' the cavalry commander breathed as the last few enemy fires ignited, forming a solid line that divided the hill into two sections, uncrossable without passing the furnace between.

'You want to risk it?'

Varus shook his head. 'If they were going to send burning matter down at us, they'd have done it differently. They would have lit all the fires at once in order to give us no warning. And there would be no point to the ones on the low slopes to either side. And the fires would have taken time to grow. They wouldn't have been so instant to bloom from nothing to inferno. They were lit slowly and sporadically, as though by only a few...'

Varus pursed his lips. 'Go tell the general the enemy have abandoned their position.'

'What?'

'Just do it, Brutus.'

Without pause, the cavalry commander ran across to where the small corral stood, two dozen horses restless within at the commotion. A pair of troopers stood on guard there.

'You two. Mount up bareback and follow me.'

Varus slid into the corral, located his steed and threw a blanket over the back before slipping up onto the beast's back. There was no time for saddling. By the time he walked his horse from the corral the other two were similarly mounted, the last trooper leaning down to fasten the gate behind them.

'Come on.'

The fortification was long and narrow, nestled at the base of the slope between the steep rise and the swamp, with only two gates. One entrance led onto the bridge back to the far hill, where part of the large force remained in garrison awaiting the arrival of Trebonius' legions. The other sat facing the enemy at a break in the wicker fence, and was now manned by a single nervous legionary, the rest having pulled back from the defences at the centurion's command. As Varus and his troopers approached, the legionary looked frightened and a little confused.

'Open the gate, soldier.'

The man looked as though he might argue for a moment, but then stepped forth and unbarred the wicker gate, swinging the leaf in to allow the three riders access. Varus nodded his appreciation and led the two troopers out at a trot and then broke into a run, veering left and racing along before the Roman walls, parallel to both lines of defence and the fiery wall.

'Where are we going, sir?'

'To find out how deep the mire really is. Whoever you pray to best, do it now.'

As they raced towards the edge of the hill, where the continuous line of fire met the swamp, Varus took his own advice. His family patron, drawn through a claimed descent from Aeneas and therefore ties to legendary Troy, was Apollo, and so to Apollo he cast a desperate prayer that he and his steed not fall foul of the sucking mire.

Moments later they converged on the spot he sought and the two troopers, unsure of their task and fearful of the terrain fell back slightly in support of their commander. Varus slowed only a little, still riding at perilous speed, hugging the line of conflagration so close that he could feel the blistering heat on his right side, his horse's hooves plunging into the soft, giving mire at the base of the slope.

Though he recognised the danger of riding a horse at speed through the uncertain and horribly dangerous muck, his attention was drawn more to the fire, and what he saw went a long way to confirming his theory. The fire was not one heavy timber that would easily roll down a hill into enemy defences. It was a true bonfire, built up with scrub and then with many timbers at the heart, which would allow the inferno to burn for hours before it died down.

His horse baulked at the heat and veered out dangerously into the swamp, sinking to the knee in the mire for a moment and almost breaking its leg as its speed was torn from it. The two men behind were having similar problems, one fighting with the murk beneath, the other trying to stop his horse rearing at the proximity of the roaring flames.

Varus pressed on, his horse plodding back out of the deeper muck, blessedly unharmed. Behind him, one of the troopers closed the gap between them but the other had fallen, his horse bucking wild in fear and the rider unable to stay seated on just a blanket. The man had slopped into the mire and now rose painfully and staggered this way and that, watching his horse which had turned and bolted back towards the Roman camp away from the fire.

And that, of course, was the purpose of the fire, Varus griped, grinding his teeth as he and his trooper left the dangerous swamp and regained the turf of the lower slope at the far side of the blazing barricade. Without waiting or answering the desperate questions of his man, Varus angled his horse to the right and began the

151

painstaking climb up the hill to the enemy position, once more parallel to the fires, but on the enemy side.

The trooper had drawn his sword, but Varus hadn't bothered. He was certain now what he would find at the top and, as he crested the hill and ploughed on towards the enemy ramparts, his suspicions were confirmed.

The fiery line had exploded so sporadically because it had been the job of the last few people on the hill. Now, the huge camp stood empty, and silent apart from the spit and crackle of flames. He slapped his fist into his palm in irritation, but then sagged with the realisation that this was *no* failure, really. This was, in fact, what he'd somehow *hoped* would happen. Despite being trapped, the enemy had managed to find a way to flee. They had known they didn't have time to move such a large army out without being seen and harried by Caesar's cavalry. And so they had waited for dusk and begun to evacuate across the swamp by their secret paths. They had lit fires in their deserted camp to make it appear inhabited from below, and those brave few who had played rear-guard had wandered back and forth with torches to complete the illusion. Varus remembered that since nightfall the only sight he'd had of the enemy was those few guards on the rampart. And while he and the rest of the Romans had watched those torches bob back and forth, the bulk of the enemy had been filing off through the swamp, escaping the coming conflict.

He laughed, drawing a concerned frown from his trooper.

'Sir?'

'They won't *all* have gone yet, of course. Their army was so large they'll be an hour or more yet getting into the swamp and I doubt the stragglers will be across before dawn starts to break. But the cavalry can't harry them as they flee, because the blazing screens frighten our horses and it'll take too long for the men to ferry water across to douse the fires. They've covered their own retreat and rendered us ineffective, thank the gods.'

At a leisurely pace, he walked his mount out across the enemy camp to the far side where, for the first time, he looked down upon the wide, swampy valley of the Axona behind the enemy's hill. Oddly, he realised, they had fought one of the most brutal battles of the whole campaign against the Belgae by this very river some six years ago, and probably not too far upstream.

His tired eyes quickly found the enemy. In small groups they moved through the swamp, following their guides, and some thousands still waited on the near slope for their turn to enter the mire. He couldn't quite see, but he could easily imagine how the nearest of those figures would be black, sweaty and soot-stained from their tasks atop the hill.

He chuckled again.

'How do we stop them, sir?'

'We don't, soldier. We go back and report this to Caesar, and we watch *him* sag with relief too.'

'Sir?'

'Don't you see? We've been saved from having to assault their camp. Now they move on to some new location and we'll follow at our leisure and bring the war to them somewhere a bit easier.'

'We can't follow them through there, sir?' the man said, pointing at the swampy river valley.

'No, but there are crossings upstream that our foragers have used for days. We'll pick up the enemy's path in the morning. A trail left by so many thousand men is hard to miss. Come on. Let's go back and report.'

As the trooper nodded uncertainly and followed him, Varus smiled. *Thank you, Apollo, Mars and Minerva, for your guiding hand.* Wherever the enemy were now bound, it could hardly be worse than where they'd left, and with the legions snapping at their heels they would have precious little time to fortify again.

It was a relief. It seemed there would not now be another Alesia.

* * * * *

'They seem entirely oblivious,' Decurion Annius murmured from his position in the trees, peering between the greenery. Varus nodded his agreement.

In the day that had passed since the enemy had fled the hilltop under cover of darkness, Caesar had moved his own forces out and followed, just half a day behind them. The scouts had confirmed just an hour ago that Commius' and Correus' rebel force had taken up a defensive position on a hilltop in the woods – a location that would prevent the mass approach of a legion and would bring any fighting down to the level of innumerable clashes between small groups amid

153

the trees, favouring the enemy rather than the grand formations of the Roman army.

Still, there was little to be done about it, and at least Caesar's army was more flexible than most Roman forces. The revolt would be over soon enough, and Trebonius' relief legions were a matter of a few hours behind as was continually established by outriders to the rear.

But the issue of supplies, even on the move, was still a pressing one, and so the Roman forces had constantly sent out foraging groups with heavy cavalry guards, scavenging what could be found in the few farms and settlements they hadn't already ravaged. It was slim pickings. But then almost on the heels of those riders who brought word of the enemy's current location, another scout party brought the best news of all...

A cornucopia, hidden in the cold green of the Bellovaci forest.

Enough supplies to keep Caesar's army in the field for weeks, as well as numerous other sundry spoils for the taking.

The scouts had found the enemy's supplies. Those carts that had departed the hilltop the night before the army fled had been drawn up in a hidden dell in the woods with only a few warriors to guard them and a small force of Belgae civilians dealing with the wagons and sending out supplies to the enemy as required.

And now that Varus had his eyes on that very location, he had to admit that it had been a brilliant move by the enemy – a manoeuvre worthy of Caesar himself. The hilltop the Bellovaci occupied was above a steep escarpment and nicely defensive, rising like a bald man's pate above the forest of his hair. But it was also too steep from all angles for wagons or carts to attempt, not to mention tight on room given the size of the resident army. So Commius – or Correus, whoever was in overall command of the enemy – had located the supplies in a valley that was so perfectly hidden and away from the site of their camp that it should have gone unnoticed. Indeed the Roman scouts had only stumbled on it entirely by accident when they followed an enemy rider. From the valley, a narrow defile ran almost all the way to the enemy hill, which meant that supplies could be ferried to the army without drawing Roman attention.

It had been perfect.

But the Romans had found it now.

Varus counted two hundred and eleven vehicles and three pens of animals, each vast and well populated with fat, well-foddered animals.

'What do we do sir?'

Varus glanced across at Annius, a strange knowing flash in his eye.

'Under normal circumstances, we would return to the army and confirm the location of the enemy supplies. I would then gather our men and put up the defensive cavalry screen while Caesar chose the legionary vexillation that would come to gather the supplies. That would be the normal and sensible order of things.'

The decurion looked confused.

'And we are not doing that?'

'No, we are not, Annius.' Varus shifted slightly in his saddle. 'Are you a subtle man, Annius?'

'Sir?'

'When you play latrunculi on the steps of the basilicae in Rome, do you often win?'

'Yes, sir.'

'Then count to fifty and turn and look at your standard bearer, then briefly, without noticeably doing so, glance up and right from him to the small rock pile in the woods and tell me what you see.'

The cavalry soldier did as he was bade and there was a long pause.

'Rider, sir.'

'Details?'

The decurion looked rather crestfallen. 'A Gaul sir?'

Varus smiled indulgently. 'A single rider. He is likely Bellovaci. He is certainly Belgae from the colours. He watches us watching his own supply caravan. How many of us are there here, Annius?'

'Less than thirty, sir.'

'Indeed. We pose little threat to him. We know that there are more than a hundred Belgae riders down there with the wagons, and their men could swamp us if they wished. They know the terrain better than us and they outnumber us four to one. We are in grave danger. Certainly, that man should have ridden down to the warriors in the valley and by now we should be watching the enemy streaming up at us. Yet he just watches. Why, Annius? Imagine you're playing latrunculi and transpose the positions.'

The decurion frowned.

155

'He's an observer but... he was *expecting* us?'

'Very good. No surprise as he watches us. No panic on behalf of their supplies. He was *expecting* us. Why?'

The decurion peered into the woodland, remembering how the scouts had followed a fortuitous lone rider out here. He coughed. 'Because we were *led* here sir?'

'Top marks, Annius. Take an extra ration tonight. And why were we led here, then?'

.Because... because... it's a trap?'

'Exactly, decurion. Now, what I would like you to do is this: as soon as I gather the men, ride back to camp, but don't report to Caesar until I arrive. I want you to depart with enough visibility that the rider follows you, leaving me free to move unobserved. I will come back to camp and rejoin you shortly.'

The decurion looked less than happy, but nodded nonetheless. 'Be careful, sir.'

'You can buy me a drink when I get back.'

Varus waved over the cavalry, moving to a thicker area of woods nearby. As the riders gathered, he nodded to Annius and, with a last look at the lone Belgic rider, slipped behind a large area of scrub, trees and undergrowth, hiding from sight. A moment later the Roman cavalry moved out, and Varus continued to peer between the greenery as the enemy observer followed the group at a discreet distance. The moment the Belgic rider was out of sight and there was no further sign of Varus' men, the commander moved out into the open, carefully, half expecting another trap.

For that was what this whole thing was.

A trap. Engineered by Commius and Correus, this was just too tempting a target for the Romans, and had been handed to them on a platter.

Once he was satisfied he was alone, Varus walked his horse through the open spaces in the woodland, keeping in sight the rock where the enemy watcher had been. As he reached that spot and peered around, he was unsurprised to find the signs of more than one rider. A number of men had been stationed here. And while it had not rained for two days now, the ground was soft enough from the preceding downpours that the tracks might as well have been painted by a vase painter in red and black. Numerous hoof prints led off towards the north. Slowly, keeping an eye out for other watchers, he followed.

These hoof prints took him two and a half miles into the forest, where finally he rounded a menhir – one of the strange religious stones of the old Gauls – and was afforded an impressive view of what awaited them.

He gave up counting after a hundred and, using that block as a guide, estimated the number of the enemy warriors gathered in the woods ready to fall upon the Romans as they gleefully commandeered the Belgic supply wagons.

'Not today, my friend,' he whispered as he scanned the enemy force.

Six thousand, he reckoned. Based on that initial hundred-count, there were around six thousand men waiting to ambush a Roman forage party. Moreover, among the group he could see a small group of Gallic nobles and an honour guard of tough warriors. The ambush had been laid by either Correus or Commius himself and one of those two rebel leaders was part of the force.

The enemy army had been estimated at roughly forty five thousand warriors. That was drawing on every capable man from numerous tribes. This, then, was perhaps an eighth of the entire enemy force. Its destruction would certainly weaken the enemy, but the true opportunity here was the destruction of morale. Whichever of the two enemy leaders was here, his death or capture would wreak havoc on the spirit of the remaining enemy.

But it would have to be done carefully. If the enemy knew the Romans were aware of the trap they might pull back to their camp, or their leader might depart. The Roman force would have to give the appearance of falling into their trap until the last moment.

Tearing his gaze from the enemy's temporary encampment, he wheeled his horse and picked his way carefully back through the woods, taking a slightly circuitous route to make sure he did not bump into that same rider following his cavalry. Time to report to Caesar and plan a little surprise for the Bellovaci.

* * * * *

Correus of the Bellovaci watched his sister-son Andecamulos riding towards him with a hungry look and smiled. It warmed him to think that his people were so confident and content with their lot. It went some way to allaying his fears over this entire situation.

Months ago, Commius of the Atrebates had come to him, seeking an allegiance in defiance of Rome. At first, Correus had turned him away, labelling him an idiot and a troublemaker. After all, he had received more than one overture during the winter from the Arvernian and Cadurci nobles who had led all the peoples to disaster last year, seeking to begin a new rising, and he had solidly rebuffed *their* proposals. The Belgae were now the only strong people left in the land, and what did they care for the plight of the southern tribes who had already crossed the last river once and were now trying to swim back to life?

But Commius had been persuasive. He had stood before the Bellovaci council and his honeyed words had hooked the interest of so many nobles that Correus could do little to dissuade them. Commius had pointed out how the Bellovaci had suffered under Roman campaigning less than a decade ago, reminding them of a debt of blood still owed. Then he had brought their memory to a moment last year when the Bellovaci had sat on the hill opposite Alesia and watched the revolt fail before leaving and returning to their own land, appealing to their sense of pride in that they had come for war and left without prosecuting it fully.

And as if blood-debt and pride had not been enough, he appealed to their greed.

He had pointed south and east to Suessione lands, who were bound to the Remi, and reminded the listeners that those tribes had surrendered their liberty to Rome, tying themselves to Caesar, and for their betrayal of all the free peoples they had been made rich. The Suessiones lived in comfort and ease, surrounded by the best goods Roman money could buy while the Bellovaci lived a frugal life unfettered by Rome's trappings.

Pride, guilt, debt and greed had turned almost every head among the Bellovaci's nobles, and once Commius had stepped out of the council chamber, Correus had held his moot. Even his son and his nephews had been in favour of throwing in their lot with Commius. The tribe would annex the lands of the Suessiones and take their goods, defying the Remi and their Roman masters.

Correus had had no doubt that such a move would bring him in direct conflict with Rome again, and he had argued with his people, but they had been adamant. And now, he was truly beginning to regret having let the Atrebate king silver-tongue his nobles. Despite the Bellovaci's best laid plans, the Romans had moved in response to

Remi messengers so quickly that Correus' people had had little time even to impose themselves upon the Suessiones, and had instead found themselves under attack by a Roman army that had marched at unbelievable speed from the western lands and into their own.

He had been nervous to find himself and his people trapped on the hill with Caesar's army digging in opposite him. He had waited patiently for Commius to return from across the Rhenus with his new allies and had been scornful and disappointed at the meagre reinforcements the man had succeeded in securing. So as the Romans moved on them, with three more legions close behind, Correus had taken his tribe through the marshes and retreated to his second position of strength, hoping to weaken the Romans through lack of supplies. If he could keep their foragers from securing sufficient food, and in terrain where their armoured ranks could not perform their deadly shield wall manoeuvres, he might be able to hold, and even beat, Caesar's army.

Commius had been all for skirting round the enemy and trying to hit them from the rear, but Correus knew how effective the Roman scouts could be, and had no doubt that they would be aware of such a move before it could be effectively prosecuted. So he had come up with the trap. He had relied on the Roman scouts finding one of his carefully-placed riders and discovering the location of the baggage. In their deprived and ill-supplied state, the Romans could hardly resist the opportunity to take the carts. Correus had put two hundred of his very best warriors, led by his own son, down with the vehicles and had taken personal command of the ambushing force. Six thousand men waited here, camped, with two thousand more, split into two groups close by, as reserves.

The best of the tribe awaited the arrival of the Romans. Almost nine thousand trained and experienced Bellovaci warriors, tempered in the fire of decades of war. He had left the rest with Commius at the camp, the weaker warriors and those who were too influenced by the Atrebate king's honey tongue to comprehend reality. But when they took the Roman scouts and foragers and placed their heads on spear points, then rode back to the camp, even the faintest hearts would remember their strength and see Correus, not Commius, as the leader here.

The time, it appeared, had come.

Andecamulos was not just his sister-son, but was also the leader of the scouts who kept watch on the forest for the Roman soldiers.

And the young man, his braids flying behind him, was clearly coming with news. Correus straightened.

'Nephew.'

The young warrior bowed his head. 'My king. The Romans approach.'

'Their numbers?'

'Perhaps a cohort. No more than half a thousand.'

Correus huffed. 'So few? Do our supplies not merit the attention of a legion? I had hoped to put many thousands to the sword today. Still, at least we will have a victory to bolster our people and they will have a defeat to cripple theirs.' He turned to find his brother, who was sitting close by. 'Give the order quietly.'

The man nodded and rode off, throwing out gestures to the groups of warriors. Pausing only long enough for a cleansing preparatory breath, Correus rode forth to his chosen position. At the edge of the valley in which their supplies sat, he reined in among the trees with an excellent view of the potential field of battle. Even as he waited, he could see signs of the others falling into position. Six thousand men came to a halt in a U shape around the supply valley, ready to fall upon the Roman foragers.

The following wait was interminable. Twice he had to send messages to sections of his army to pull back further into the trees, as they had become visible to the shrewd eye. Finally, he was satisfied that his people were in position.

The warriors down with the carts and wagons were doing an excellent job of looking entirely unprepared for trouble.

And the legion came.

Andecamulos had underestimated by a little. There were nearer a thousand than five hundred, and Correus smiled in relief. Their death would be a horrendous blow to Roman pride and morale and a real boost to his army's. The Roman commander had clearly decided that surprise was the key to overwhelming the meagre defence force in the valley, and his son reacted instantly to the appearance through the edge of the forest of red-garbed, steel-clad legionaries. The civilians moved back through the supplies, to the ravine that ran to the main camp, while the two hundred veteran warriors steadied themselves for the onslaught.

The Romans poured from the trees onto the springy turf, where they began to reform into their regular, organised units without losing any speed of their approach. Probably two cohorts of Romans bore down on the warriors before them, outnumbering the Bellovaci defenders by some four or five to one.

The Romans looked eager, but then *of course* they did. It would be a slaughter. Apart from the eight thousand other warriors waiting in forest, that was.

'Signal Bitucos and Helicon. Once we move out, I want the reserves to close in behind them and cut off their escape. No Roman leaves the valley alive.'

The rider he had addressed nodded and picked his way through the trees out to one of the wider paths where he could thunder across to the reserve commanders with their orders. The horseshoe of Bellovaci would pour from the woods, surrounding the Romans, and the two thousand reserves would close the circle behind them.

A massacre.

He watched, tense, as battle was joined down in the valley, the front ranks of the Romans reaching the veteran warriors while the rear lines were still emerging and forming up. All around him, Correus could feel the tense urgency of his men. They all wanted to move. None of them liked seeing the best of their men in such a dangerous position. But they had to wait. They could not spring the trap until the Romans were fully committed and could be surrounded.

It felt like centuries passing, watching the Romans with their brutal efficiency cutting down the greatest warriors of the Bellovaci, though his son and the men there were making good account of themselves, taking a number of the enemy with them.

Finally, the Romans were all on the grass and formed up, and the woodland behind was devoid of further arrivals. Tense, eager to put an end to these armoured foreigners, Correus held up his hand and with a cutting motion swept it downwards.

A carnyx honked at the signal and its sombre melody was picked up at half a dozen places around the valley. With a sigh of relief to be actually doing something, Correus rode his beast out of the trees and to the top of the slope above the Romans. The valley in which the supply carts sat was surrounded by slopes like this, as well as the narrow river, and even as he began to edge his mount slowly and carefully down the incline, the rest of the ambush emerged, those on horses also picking their way down carefully while the majority of the warriors on foot simply charged headlong, heedless of the danger of falling, turning ankles and breaking necks.

161

It was like a landslide in a horseshoe shape.

Correus listened carefully to the calls. He could hear the Roman centurions putting out their orders, followed by the whistles and the dip and swipe of the standards to relay the commands to any who hadn't heard. He was surprised not to hear the Romans order the retreat, though it bothered him not at all, as the two thousand-strong reserve forces emerged from the woodland behind the Romans and sealed them in.

He heard various commands he recognised and even as he picked his way towards the fight saw them being carried out by the centuries of men.

Contra-equitas!

Centuries were forming themselves into a specialised form of the 'tortoise' formation that was designed to counter cavalry, the entire unit presenting a flat face of shields at two angles, bristling with sharp javelins.

Orbis!

Other centuries of men combined to present a circle some four bodies deep, outward facing and revealing no point of danger to the enemy.

All very good. It would be of no use, of course. They were trapped, and the numbers were simply too uneven. For all their fancy manoeuvres, the Romans would die where they now stood.

At last his horse reached the flat ground of the valley bottom, and Correus joined his warriors in charging the Romans, his bodyguard staying as close to him as they could. The Bellovaci king laughed at the simplicity of it. When it came to this point battle was a joy, for there was nothing to worry about, barring his personal safety. The conclusion was already set. The Romans had lost the moment they entered the valley.

Correus urged his horse forward and made for the large orbis formation, hefting his spear. With a flourish and the practised eye of a seasoned warrior, he selected one of the legionaries whose shield was not quite high enough, and cast the spear, immediately thereafter drawing his long blade. The missile caught the legionary between shoulder and collar bone and threw him back into the formation, but the Romans were quick. Rather that the blow catching the Romans by surprise and leaving an opening in the circle, the man was hauled backwards out of the way and another man was instantly in his place.

Correus had fought the Romans more than once, but this was some of the most efficient manoeuvring he had ever seen.

He frowned as the entire orbis, which had been fighting now for perhaps a hundred heartbeats, made one heavy thrust and swipe that forced their enemies to step back and, in the intervening moments before Correus' men could recover and strike, the entire front line had been replaced by the second. He watched in fascination as the men who had tired at the front gradually filtered to the safest position at the centre where they could rest while their compatriots each moved a line forward.

He couldn't rely on wearing them out, then...

Still, the Romans were dying. Slowly, and with a higher casualty rate among the Bellovaci than he would prefer, but at least they were dying, and soon there would not be enough to form any kind of defence. Then, the remaining exhausted legionaries would fight their own last, desperate, individual duels until swamped by Correus' men.

The king's attention was caught by a booing sound, and he looked up at the reserves, who were not engaging, merely preventing any hope of escape. What were they doing putting out calls? There was no call necessary now until he decided to rein in his men and send them back to the camp.

He frowned, looking for the errant carnyx or horn player, but he couldn't spot him, for the reserves appeared to be in turmoil. What was going on?

Then, like a cracked dam that has reached its point of structural failure, the reserves broke, flowing from the treeline and into the open ground. Correus cursed Bitucos and Helicon for their unnecessary eagerness. Their involvement was not necessary – they should be remaining in position. The force Correus commanded alone would finish the Romans, but it was important that none escaped.

He took an idle swing at a Roman who happened to be close enough, though his attention was really on the reserve forces. He waved to his carnyx player and shouted to be heard over the din of battle. 'Go tell Bitucos and Helicon that they're...'

His voice tailed off as the reserves flooded the valley, flowing like the burst dam around and past the pockets of action. And in that same moment, his eyes caught movement beyond them, and he understood with dreadful clarity.

163

Four columns had begun to emerge from the trees. They were not moving in shield walls, but in what looked like some kind of parade formation. And he knew why. Because at the front of the columns came the standard bearers, the eagle bearers and the musicians, who, now that they had cleared the woods, burst into a deafening triumphant melody. That sight alone would be enough to make a brave man run, but the fact was that each of the four columns was led by an eagle, backed by a man carrying a flag with the legion's number.

Four legions!

Suddenly the eight thousand men he had with him seemed a rather feeble proposition, in the face of probably twenty thousand legionaries. And where Caesar's legions went so went their auxiliary slingers and archers, and – he prayed to Taranis it was not the case, though without any real hope of efficacy – the Remi and other Gallic horse, and even the Germans.

Damn the proconsul. Correus had sprung a trap on the Romans only to find his entire ambush at the centre of their own trap. Staying would mean death for all of them, and if the best of the Bellovaci, and their king, died, then the rest of the force up at the camp would collapse in terror.

'Signal the retreat,' he shouted at the musician, but when the man put the carnyx to his lips, he paused, and no sound emerged.

'Sound the call!' he repeated with urgency. The Roman orbis had now exploded and reformed into a square which was beginning to push outwards, taking the fight back to the Bellovaci. They had fresh heart, knowing that their fellows were here. Correus was momentarily distracted as he was forced to defend himself against a giant of a man. As he put the Roman down with some difficulty, he walked his horse a little further from the fray and over to the musician. Reaching out, he grabbed the man by the tunic and almost pulled him from his saddle.

'Sound... the... retreat!'

But the man was still silent, staring. Correus turned to look at whatever it was that had captured the man's attention and felt his blood chill.

All around the valley, the treeline had burst into life, more Romans appearing in a complete circle, surrounding the Bellovaci. Damn the proconsul – he had split his legions and sent some ahead to surround them. But his keen eyes picked out the eagle and the flag near the defile that led to the camp. No. A *fifth* legion. His heart in his mouth, and already knowing what he would see, he raked the ridge around the valley with his gaze until he found the other two eagles with their flags and standards. The Roman general Trebonius had arrived with his three legions. Now, Correus' eight thousand faced somewhere in the region of forty thousand Romans.

Hope deserted him.

His men were running for the woods, but it was a futile, panicked move. Wherever they fled, there were more Romans waiting for them. Only one small group was free and out of danger, and that very fact gnawed at Correus more even than this unmitigated disaster.

The civilians who had initially fled to the defile had managed to run, and the Romans seemed to be making no effort to pursue them. Sharp of the Roman commander, for those women, children and old men would even now be carrying morale-destroying word of this catastrophe to the camp and the rest of the army.

The revolt of the Bellovaci had failed.

He hoped that when his people back in the camp realised all was lost, they might tear open Commius of the Atrebates and leave his flayed corpse hanging from a tree for the crows. It ate at him that his best men would die here for his error in judgement, but what really burned into his soul was the fact that he would die in this valley without getting a chance to personally gut the silver-tongued Atrebate for what he had done.

'Come, my king.'

He turned and frowned at his bodyguard. 'What?'

'We must get you away from this place.'

'There is no escape,' he replied in the hollow voice of a defeated man.

'Your guards can force a path through the enemy, my king.'

'No they cannot. Even around the valley top, they will be forty lines deep. No. We fight here, and we die here.'

The man continued to plead, but Correus snarled defiance and turned, seeking out the most important man on the field. His eyes fell on a man with a transverse crest, marking him as a centurion. As the combatants parted for a moment, he also saw the man's harness full of medals and the torcs and corona hanging from it. A veteran, heavily decorated. A worthy opponent.

165

He marked the man with a gesture of his sword and started to move towards him, though the Roman had not returned the sign that had been indicative of the desire for a personal duel of heroes. Shrugging as he closed on the man, a legionary swung up at him as he passed, and Correus swept his own blade down, turning the gladius aside and taking the tips from all four knuckles. The man screamed and dropped the sword, staring down at his hand, and Correus took the opportunity of the lowered face to bring his sword down heavily, hacking into the flesh and bone at the back of the man's neck. He felt the spine go and the soldier fell away, curiously at one and the same time limp, yet twitching.

Another legionary came to stop him, but his bodyguard was there and pushed the man out of the way, killing him on the third stroke. Correus once more set his gaze upon the centurion, and suddenly his world exploded into a blurred kaleidoscope. It took a moment after the blow to his head to realise that someone had killed his horse and that he was now on the ground, his head swimming from contact with the hard turf. Desperately he realised he was surrounded by Romans, and none of them were the centurion. One of his bodyguard fought off a legionary, pushing him back into the crowd, and then reached down to help him up.

Correus gripped the man's free hand, but then the guard's fingers stiffened and the pointed tip of a gladius emerged through the side of his neck, showering the king in a torrent of his man's blood. Desperately, he wiped the worst away, rolling to one side so that the body fell not on him, but on open grass.

Trying to recover his wits, he pulled himself painfully upright, realising only as he saw the centurion's crest between two other soldiers that his sword had disappeared somewhere in the fall. Angry beyond reason, he reached down to his belt and drew his fighting knife – a weapon of last resort for a true warrior.

'Come for me, Roman!' he bellowed in thickly-accented Latin.

The centurion actually turned and noticed him, but it was an unseen legionary who answered.

'Gladly, Gaul,' came a voice from off to his left and he felt a horrific pain in his side as a pointed blade punctured his mail shirt end on, driving deep into muscle and then organs.

Hissing, more in shock at the lack of honour in the man than from the pain, he turned. The legionary had already accounted him dead, turning to his friend and laughing at his little moment of humour.

Correus lashed out and caught him in the cheek, driving his knife in, shattering teeth and splintering jaw, slicing through the tongue with its bland jokes. The soldier screamed, though the wound muffled the noise. Correus, king of the Bellovaci, was dead, and he knew it. Apart from the mortal wound in his side, he felt two more blows, one of which ruined his leg and the other slid between his ribs. But none of that stopped him taking out his fury on the laughing legionary.

'Not so... funny... now...'

By the time the fifth wound he took severed Correus spinal cord and he flopped useless onto the ground, his blood and intestines pouring out onto the grass, he knew he had stabbed the legionary many dozens of times. The man was, miraculously, still alive, for he was shrieking in horror at his ruined body, each limb shredded and his torso full of rents and holes.

Correus felt the darkness closing on his senses and with it came an odd feeling of peace. The din of battle seemed to fade away and suddenly the centurion's crest was in front of him, upside down as the man leaned over him.

'Brave. Stupid, but brave.' The Roman officer leaned down, gently pulled open the king's mouth and pushed a small silver coin under his tongue before driving his own blade in deep and speeding up the advance of the blessed darkness.

* * * * *

Varus sat astride his mount, shivering in the cold of the morning, and glanced across at Brutus, who looked equally uncomfortable. Trebonius rode slightly ahead of them alongside Caesar in the place of honour for a victorious commander. Behind them marched the legions – all seven in good array and better spirits, their eagles leading the way. It was an impressive column. One of the largest displays of Roman forces Varus had seen in all his years in Gaul. Seven legions.

And ahead, across the narrow river which ran into that same defile that emerged some miles distant at the baggage valley that now served as a mass grave for eight thousand Bellovaci, stood the camp of the enemy.

And its gate was open.

'Sound the horns,' Caesar commanded. 'Let's see what happens.'

The cornicen blew their instruments, issuing the standard call for parley or recognition. As they fell silent again, there was a long pause. Varus watched intently as occasional figures appeared in the gateway up the slope. It was no oppidum or city, but a simple temporary camp atop a hill, surrounded by a hastily erected fence, and the gate was simply an area where the fence had been removed.

Still, that gate, such as it was, was open, which suggested surrender rather than defiance.

A moment later, half a dozen riders emerged through the gap and began to wend their slow way down to the waiting Romans. Varus watched with interest. They were all nobles, but he could see no sign of Commius of the Atrebates, a man who after years of repeated contact he would recognise quickly. The ambassadors reined in their horses close to Caesar and bowed. It did not escape Varus' notice that the general did not return the gesture, and he knew Caesar well enough to know that that fact presaged no good for the ambassadors.

'Proconsul,' the first man greeted Caesar. He was well turned out and wearing enough gold that he sagged slightly under the weight, like a wet tent. His old, grey braids hung down by his ears and the loose steel-coloured hair at the rear whipped in the breeze.

'Yes.'

The man looked somehow taken aback by the curtness of the general's response.

'I am Orcetrix of the Bellovaci. I speak for the tribe in the absence of Correus.'

'Death,' corrected Caesar.

The man looked confused at the way this was going, and Caesar fixed him with a cold glare. 'Correus is not absent. He is dead. He lies in a field of eight thousand of your tribe who sought to ambush us. Stop attempting to fawn and dissemble. I have terms, but you may speak your piece first.'

Caesar was angry. Varus knew that such coldness was much more indicative of ire in the general than was shouting. Orcetrix seemed to have come to the same conclusion, for he licked his lips nervously and cleared his throat.

'Caesar is famed far and wide for his clemency.'

168

Varus almost burst out laughing. The general didn't *look* particularly clement right now. But the noble was continuing unabated. 'Correus was a troublemaker, rousing our people to war against Rome. We have long lived under the shadow of his fury and his autocracy. Now that your blessed arrival has rid us of his dangerous presence, we are at last free to follow our hearts' desires, which are to hold tight and dear to our alliance with Rome.'

Caesar sniffed in the cold air.

'Is that it?'

'We offer payments of appropriate tribute and the granting of noble hostages against such a dreadful miscalculation ever happening again, in return for an agreement to allow our people to go in peace and settle once more in our villages.'

Varus felt sorry for the man. He could see Caesar's fingertips drumming impatiently on the saddle.

'And what of the other rabble rouser? Commius of the Atrebates?'

The man looked suddenly very nervous.

'We are unable to locate him, Caesar. He was last seen several hours ago. No one seems sure when he slipped away from the camp, but his five hundred Germans are also gone, so we assume he has fled to the far side of the Rhenus.'

Caesar nodded but Varus noted the irritated drumming on the saddle increase in furious pace.

'Clemency, you say?'

'Err... yes, Caesar? For those of us who found ourselves carried to war against you at the whim of those who would guide our movements against our will.'

'My intelligence puts one Orcetrix of the Bellovaci on the hillside opposite Alesia with the Gallic relief force last autumn. Are you about to deny the presence of either yourself or your tribe in a grand revolt against Rome last year?'

'Ah. Well, now...'

'You claim to be pushed into war, and yet we know you rose against us last year, even if you managed to flee the scene largely undiminished. Perhaps we should have chastised those who came to Vercingetorix's aid following our victory over the Arvernian. Then you would have had neither the strength nor the numbers to do such a thing again this winter.'

'Yes, Caesar, but, well... you see, the thing is...'

'Silence.' Caesar's anger was made manifest in his tone of voice and even though it came out as little more than a quiet hiss, the word cut straight through the man's blustering and silenced him.

'You are rebels and enemies of Rome. The only reason I am even remotely tempted towards leniency is that I wish to settle Gaul and put an end to the endless wars. Here are my terms.'

The man looked hopeful at the general's words, but Varus could imagine what Caesar saw as lenient at this point, and he doubted it matched up with Orcetorix's ideas.

'In addition to the noble hostages that you have already offered, it seems an appropriate punishment that perhaps a fifth of your army, and the best of it, from what I can see, already lies as carrion. However, I cannot allow such a large force to remain at arms. You will deliver to us all weapons in this camp, and one man in every four of fighting age will be taken to the slave markets to ensure that you are unable to attempt something like this again.'

The man looked stunned. 'But Caesar...'

'I am not finished. We have impounded your entire baggage train, which I presume, given the fact that we found your settlements stripped clean, contains your winter and spring food stores. I recognise that your people will perish without that grain, and so you are to be given the opportunity to purchase it back at the standard trade rate set by my chief quartermaster, which is six silver denarius per bushel, or whatever your local coinage equivalent makes up.'

'General...'

'The gold on your person alone would probably feed a family for a year. See that you gather enough payment to provide for your people. *That* is what a leader does, rather than attempting to pin the blame for his failures upon the dead. These are my terms, and they apply equally to each tribe involved in this revolt. I presume those others behind you represent your allies? Return to your camp and make the appropriate arrangements. When you have the hostages, the slaves, the weapons and the grain payments for me, return and our transaction will be completed.'

He stopped drumming his fingers and raised his hand, pointing at the quailing man's face.

'The legions will camp here for two days before they are once more distributed appropriately. And when I leave Bellovaci territory, pray to each and every god you recognise, Orcetrix, that I never have to return, for if I find myself brought back here to sort out trouble again, I will have new shield covers for every man in my twelve legions made out of your people's skin. Do you understand me?'

Orcetrix cowered, nodding, and backed away.

Varus watched the dejected party leave. Caesar had been angry. That much was clear. But something deep inside insisted on highlighting the fact that perhaps eight thousand able-bodied slaves, plus the loot from the wagons and the weapon sales, and finally the huge ransom that would be paid for the grain would altogether amount to a sum fit for a king. The proconsul would probably make more from this outcome than he had from the silver mines of the Bituriges or the trade ports of the Carnutes.

Another tribe's riches had become Caesar's.

Chapter Nine

MOLACOS looked at the broken Roman and slowly removed the cult mask from his face. The weeping, agonised soldier looked up in horrified fascination at the ruined face of the thing behind the mask and quailed despite everything that had already been done to him.

'Who will be able to answer my questions? I grow tired of interrogating Romans and my time is precious. Tell me where to go and I will grant you the mercy of a quick death and not give you to Catubodua, the avenging widow, who waits outside the door with her roll of skinning knives.'

The soldier whimpered through a face full of tears, blood and snot, and after a pause, Molacos sighed and rose, making for the door.

'No. Wait,' wailed the man.

'I am listening.'

'My legate from the Fifteenth is on his way back to Rome. Gaius Antistius Reginus. He'll be less than a week behind me, and will be passing through Gergovia on his way. He will be able to answer your questions.'

Molacos nodded. A *legate*. The commander of a legion. A man of senatorial rank and one of Caesar's own circle. A rare opportunity to interrogate such a highly-placed man. Excellent.

'Well done, man.'

Fishing in his pouch, he produced something and dropped it on the floor in front of the ruined soldier. The man stared at it. A snare, made of some sort of sharp cord, knotted to allow it to tighten. He's seen such things used, used them himself when hunting rabbits to supplement the legion's rations on the march. They occasionally killed by strangulation, but more often by biting into the windpipe and blood vessels as the animal struggled.

Molacos was rising.

'What is this?' the soldier gasped. 'You said you would give me a quick death!'

'And I have. You have until I open the door to kill yourself, or Catubodua will come in and do the job for you much more slowly. I suggest you are very quick. She is literally salivating at the thought of peeling you.'

He ambled towards the door, listening to the whimpering behind him. His hand closed on the door handle, pulling it inwards and even

172

as Catubodua, her impassive mask hiding her hungry grin, strode past, he could hear the gagging noises as the soldier tried desperately to strangle himself in time.

Chapter Ten

FRONTO reached down and picked up the exquisite coloured glass containing the expensive Chian and took a sip. Barely watered at all, it warmed as it coated his mouth with a rich, velvety taste. He smiled.

'If you want to just give me money, then give me money. You don't have to muck about with all this.'

'This?' Balbus raised an eyebrow inquisitively and Fronto grinned at his old friend and, more recently, father-in-law.

'You buy the best wines I can import at the standard full price I charge the unwitting and you save them for when Lucilia or myself visit. I've noticed this. Even Pamphilus and Clearchus have commented on it, and neither of them could outthink a milestone. You know I would just bring a good amphora when I visit anyway.'

'You don't think I save all of it for you, do you?' Balbus chuckled. 'My favourite Greek medicus in the city tells me that thick red wine is actually good for my heart, and the less water I add the better. Imagine that? And so, if I'm not watering it down, of course I'm going to choose the very best. I've had trouble with the heart for years, but I'm currently in rude health and I intend to remain that way long enough to watch my grandsons take the toga virilis and get enslaved by some Roman girl with swaying hips and fluttering eyelashes.'

Again, Fronto grinned, though with a touch of sadness at the core of the smile. Balbus was perhaps two decades older than Fronto, and he himself was no glowing youth, long past the age when most Romans fathered their children. He hoped the old man's heart would hold out that long. He made a mental note to take a jar of this very same vintage to the temple of Aesculapius... Asklepios, damn these Greek naming conventions... and use it as a libation in favour of the old man's health.

'Anyway, what were we talking about?'

'You were worrying about your slaves,' Balbus smiled, taking another pull on his wine and smacking his lips appreciatively.

'Lucilia keeps pointing out that you have no issues with keeping slaves.'

'Lucilia looks a lot but sees little.'

Fronto frowned. In his experience it was much the other way around. 'Go on?'

174

'There is not a single slave in this house, Marcus. Many of them were brought here as slaves, but I paid a good weekly stipend and set manumission at an easy target to reach. Of the slaves I have bought since I settled in Massilia, only two did not work hard, do me proud, and buy their own freedom within the year. And both of those two I sold in the end to the fishing concerns. One was lazy and one was greedy and neither had a future with my house, so now they work hard gutting fish, when they could have had an easy life here. I have seven former slaves, now freedmen and –women, working in my household and lands. And they all continue in their former roles, but for a decent wage. You'd be most surprised I expect to hear that the best paid of them all was a totally unbroken Aedui girl, who it turned out has an affinity with horses. She now manages my stable and has three lads working for her. I'll not introduce you to her, given your history with comely Gauls...'

Fronto gave his father-in-law a black look.

'And the other fourteen staff I have here,' Balbus went on, 'are all ex-military, hired after they received their honesta missio, or in one case released early with a missing arm. He turned out to be an excellent cook. He made that fine meal you just ate, in fact. I trust my ex-legionaries, and it saves me having to hire guards like yours. Any pair of hands in my villa could pick up a sword with at least some skill and put the pointy end in an interloper, regardless of their daily duties.'

Fronto nodded at his friend's sense and wondered how Lucilia would take it if he explained that her father didn't really trust slaves in his household either. He sighed.

'Anyway, it's this Andala woman that bothers me. Her and Lucilia are starting to get very close. They act far more like giggling girls together than mistress and slave and it's making me very nervous. It's like living with a crocodile and a bear and finding the pair of them shaking paws and eyeing you up while they lick their lips. It's only a matter of time before Lucilia embarks on another of her 'I have to change Marcus campaigns.'

'Really, Marcus. My daughter can be a handful, but she knows what she's doing running a household. She learned from the best.'

'She gives that Bellovaci girl far too much freedom.'

Balbus chuckled again. 'This from the man who doesn't like keeping slaves.'

'That's not what I mean. Did you know that the day before yesterday I came in late and found that while Lucilia and the boys were fast away in the arms of Morpheus, Andala was sitting in my office polishing my best gladius? I wanted to rant at her, but that would have woken Lucilia and I somehow know that I'd come off at the end as the loser in that encounter. But I took the sword from its customary place on the wall and hid it under my bed with the old campaign tunics and cloaks. And the girl is always in our rooms now. Lucilia seems to have promoted her to looking after the boys. Wouldn't *you* be nervous?'

'I say again, Marcus: she knows exactly what she's doing.'

Fronto sighed and sat back with his glass of Chian, giving it an appreciative sip. 'The only bright side is that one of my former soldiers, Aurelius - you remember him?'

'The one with the bats, yes?'

'That's the one. He seems to have something of a torch burning for her, and I've noticed the odd look when she observes him that reminds me of the German cavalry when they spot a small, poorly-armed patrol. Guarded hunger. I'm going to try and foster the thing from both sides - see if I can pair them off and get her out of my hair, but that in itself is difficult as it means I'll have to spend time at the villa instead of hiding out in the warehouse.'

Balbus snorted.

'Have you had any news from Gaul?'

Fronto tried to fight the all-too-familiar sense of loss as he ran over the list of friends now passed who would have been the ones to send him all the news. Now only Atenos remained in the Tenth, and Atenos was about as likely to write a letter as he was to paint his backside blue and dance on a table asking for a 'Syrian Surprise'. In fact, the only person who had sent Fronto a missive since the day he left Caesar's camp had been Varus, and the cavalry officer had been brief and terse.

'Little. But I hear rumours. I tend to spend time down with Caesar's supply officer in the town, and news leaks through. Sounds like there are numerous small revolts breaking out across the north.'

'Nothing dangerous, though?'

'No,' Fronto shrugged. 'Just last ditch attempts from a defeated people. After Alesia even their best were beaten, and they knew it. Only idiots and lunatics will hold out now.'

'Have you given any thought as to what will happen when the proconsul finishes his term and heads back to Rome?'

Fronto blinked, and Balbus smiled oddly. 'You fool no one, Marcus. You can play the wine merchant for a while. You might even turn out to be good at it. But we all know that one day you'll go running back to the military. You are the oddest imaginable Roman patron, you know? All the others use the military as a stepping stone. Not you. Sooner or later, once he's made consul, Caesar will find a new front upon which to fight, and as soon as he does, you'll go running.'

'Not again.'

Balbus barked out a short laugh. 'Don't be absurd, Marcus. Of course you will. If I hadn't collapsed in action years ago I'd be racing back myself. Hell, despite any arguments I might have with Caesar, I'd be heading to his command tent now if I could. You're not a home body. You never were.'

'Life's full of surprises, Quintus. My acceptance of the quiet life might just be one of them.'

Both men took a quick sip of the exquisite wine and looked up at the sound of the commotion outside. A moment later, as they both sat up, Balbus' doorman, a former legionary of the Eighth, stomped in, bowing and saluting, clearly unsure whether he should be following military or civilian protocol. Balbus nodded encouragingly.

'Beg pardon, sir.'

'Yes?'

'There's a foul-mouthed barbarian at the gate demanding to speak to master Marcus Falerius Fronto. I would have automatically turned him away other than the fact that he has half a dozen of master Fronto's men with him.

Balbus raised an eyebrow, and Fronto turned to the former legionary. 'What did the 'barbarian' call you?'

'I'd rather not say, sir, but it'd make a whore blush and my mother will be spinning in her urn. And he threatened to flatten my face, too.'

'Catháin,' smiled Fronto. 'Might be important.'

Balbus gestured to the legionary. 'Let the man in, Scortius.'

'Yessir.'

Another brief altercation at the villa's door was followed by the slap of soft leather boots on marble as the strange northerner made his way through to the triclinium, Balbus' doorman scurrying along behind, trying to get in front to lead the way and failing dismally.

'Fronto, we've got a problem.'

'And good evening to you, too, Catháin. This is my father-in-law, Quintus Balbus, former legate of the Eighth.'

Catháin gave a brief nod in Balbus' direction and clapped his hands together in a business-like manner. 'You know that Helvian wine that we're shipping to Rome?'

Fronto nodded and noted Balbus' curious expression.

'It's a big deal. Two hundred amphorae of the stuff bound for a gladiator ludus in Rome. The stuff tastes like something that leaked out of a badger's arse, but the lanista is willing to pay good silver for it regardless. It's the deal of the year. Something like a thousand percent profit.'

Balbus nodded appreciatively.

'Well there's a problem, Fronto,' the northerner grunted, slapping his fist into his palm. 'I got a message from Antidorus the teamster and rushed down to the port. The shipment was due to be loaded onto a trireme called the *Demeter*, but the captain's refused to take the load on board and won't tell us why. All he said was I should take it up with the logistics and quartermaster office in the city. I went to see Fabius Ambustus, given that he and I now have something of an understanding, but the guards at the office tell me he's too busy and won't let me see him. Meantime the Helvian wine moulders on the quayside. If it could smell any worse I'd wonder if it was going off. If we can't get it loaded this afternoon, I'm going to have to put it back into storage and hope for the best.'

'Shit.'

'Just that,' agreed Catháin. 'If that shipment doesn't sail in the morning, we'll be late with the delivery. At the very best we'll be looking at a daily-increasing fee for the delay. If we're really unlucky, he'll cancel the deal altogether and we'll be left with undrinkable wine to shift suddenly - enough of it to float a trireme, ironically.'

Fronto nodded. 'And every day's delay will drop our profits enough that a week or so will put us in danger of making a loss.'

'Quite so.'

He turned to Balbus and sighed. 'Sorry to interrupt our afternoon, but this is something I need to take care of urgently. I might be back if I can sort things out fast enough.'

Balbus smiled indulgently.

'Go. Play merchant and play it well. I shall see you in due course.'

Nodding his thanks, Fronto turned and grasped Catháin's hand as the man offered to help him up. 'Come on. I need to quickly change and then we'll head down to the office.'

'Change?' the man asked curiously.

'The uniform of a senior officer still carries a lot of weight in military circles even when you've retired, and I keep everything pressed and clean, just in case. I just hope Andala's not been messing with it all while she's looking for my sword again.'

* * * * *

He'd expected it to feel entirely natural when he donned his Roman military tunic, cloak, belt and so on. He was, after all, a soldier born and forged in decades of war. And yet, as he and his small group of companions bore down on the office, he found he was shrugging his shoulders constantly, uncomfortable in the snug fit after the very giving and light Greek-style chiton and chlamys. The fact that it no longer felt normal disturbed him somehow and reinforced his refusal to consider a return to the martial life - a refusal that Balbus had clearly disbelieved.

He hooked a finger in his bronze-plated belt and turned it slightly so that the fittings for the dagger didn't catch on his cloak as it had so often done, evidenced by all the pulled threads in one small patch of cloth.

The two bored-looking legionaries by the door of the office building that had been granted to Caesar rent free by the city's boule eyed the small party approaching them with interest, but did not straighten to attention.

Behind Fronto, Catháin, Masgava, Aurelius and Arcadios walked, looking as strong and implacable as they could. Fronto himself was prepared for an argument. *Everything* seemed to involve an argument these days, whether at work or at home.

'I need to see Prefect Fabius Ambustus on a matter of the utmost urgency.'

The legionaries shared a look that contained surprisingly little respect, given Fronto's apparel.

179

'The prefect is very busy, sir. There's a waiting list for meetings, but he's not even considering granting an audience until after market day.'

Fronto ground his teeth and tried not to lose his temper. Market was still three days away. What was Ambustus doing? A decade of command coursed through Fronto's veins as he leaned towards the insolent legionary and brought his angry face so close his breath would fog the man's eyeballs.

'I may not be wearing the knotted belt of command, soldier, but you might recognise the stripe on my tunic denoting my former rank. I held, and still do hold, the ear of Gaius Julius Caesar, proconsul of Rome, and your commander's commander. I hold a rank of authority in both Massilia and Rome and served over a decade TRYING TO KEEP RUNTS LIKE YOU FROM GETTING THEIR HEADS TORN OFF BY GERMAN CANNIBALS!' As the soldier leaned back against the wall, away from the blast of fury that had burst from Fronto's maw, the former legate allowed a horrible smile to cross his face. 'Now I am going inside to speak to the *prefect*,' he announced, trying to demonstrate the gulf in rank that separated him from this entire outpost's staff in one stressed word. 'You can try and stop me, though I strongly recommend against it, or you can exercise that fat, blubbery useless arse of yours by running ahead to warn Fabius Ambustus that I'm coming.'

The soldier nodded hastily, clearly not trusting his tongue to words, and slipped in through the doorway. Fronto paused long enough to glare daggers at the other door guard. 'I do not wish to be disturbed, understand?'

The soldier quailed and nodded, and the officer turned from him and stumped into the building, his escort following close on behind.

Fronto had been to visit the man a few times. Like all military bureaucrats, Ambustus considered himself about three ranks more important than his uniform confirmed. He ran the office in Massilia like a despot of ancient times, but it was hard to argue with the efficiency with which he maintained Caesar's supply, transport and courier system through the port. Some of the value of his role had disappeared several years ago when the general had finally opened up the secondary trade route through the Helvetian territory from Vesontio, but during the summer sea and river transport was still by far the fastest way to move anything.

180

Each room in the building was occupied by a different actuarius or librarius, each surrounded by piles of writing tablets, sheaves of vellum and scrolls of parchment, each scribbling furiously or affixing their stamp to an official request or record. For a moment, Fronto was struck by an unusually high level of activity even for this place. On previous visits there had always been one or two rooms at least that lay dormant, their occupant off for the day or at midday meal. Not so, today. In fact, each and every one appeared fraught. Still, he resolved not to weaken his purpose. He would know why the offer of transport had been rescinded without a jot of notice.

Ambustus sat behind his desk, rubbing one hand through his thinning hair as he counted down a list with his other forefinger, his lips moving silently. The legionary who had run ahead was standing to one side of the room looking extremely nervous.

'Prefect?'

The man held forth a hand without looking up, his voice rising to a whisper as he counted over the top of the interruption. When he'd reached the bottom of the page, Ambustus scribbled his figure in a tally column on another sheet and straightened.

'Ah, the inimicable Fronto and Catháin and your small group of heavies. I see you have taken to intimidating my men now. What can I do for you? Nothing trivial, I hope?'

Fronto felt his ire rising again and Catháin's hand clapped down on his shoulder in warning. He allowed the anger to subside. Few bureaucrats reacted well to provocation.

'Prefect Ambustus, my sincere apologies for this intrusion, but the matter is of extreme import to my business. I shall not keep you long.'

The man leaned back in his chair. 'Go on, sir.'

'I have a large cargo of amphorae that are due to be shipped to Rome on the afternoon tide.'

'Poor timing, I'm afraid.'

'So I gather. The captain of the Demeter would not allow the loading of the cargo, despite the fact that my factor here tells me that the ship rides so high in the water she can only be empty, and all her rigging and crew appear ready to set sail. I had believed we had a deal in respect of my shipping cargo in any vessel that has space.'

Ambustus gave an exaggerated sigh. 'Would that such were possible, Fronto. I realise this might seriously damage your business. What vintage is the cargo?'

Fronto narrowed his eyes suspiciously. 'A poor native brew.'

'Ah well. Sadly, I was going to offer to buy a portion of the cargo in recompense, but I cannot stomach the local wines. There is, then, very little I can do. My hands are tied.' He held up his hands open palmed to demonstrate the phrase. Fronto narrowed his eyes further.

'I suppose I could find a small cut to help ease your troubles, Ambustus...'

The prefect frowned and then, realisation dawning, lowered his hands again. 'You misunderstand me, Fronto. I am not seeking a bribe. This is not a matter of sweetening the pot until I relent. I simply cannot give you permission to load the Demeter.'

'Why not?' snapped Fronto.

Ambustus gave Fronto a pointed look, nodding at his companions meaningfully. The former legate pursed his lips in annoyance, but turned to Masgava and Catháin. 'All four of you head back outside and wait for me there. I'll be along presently.'

The big Numidian gave him a disapproving look, but the four men backed out of the room and Fronto waited until he could hear nothing but the rhythmic work of the clerks. 'Alright. What's this about, Ambustus?'

The prefect sighed and gestured for Fronto to sit. When the former legate made it quite clear that sitting was not going to happen, he took a deep breath.

'It is not just the Demeter, Fronto. I cannot allow you to load any cargo on any Roman vessel in port.'

Fronto opened his mouth to shout something, but Ambustus pushed on.

'It is not my decision, before you threaten to have me beaten, Fronto. I am required by order of the proconsul himself to keep every Roman vessel in port empty and prepared to sail at short notice. Every ship that arrives will become subject to that order, and each ship already in port has been forced to empty itself of any cargo and cancel all shore leave for its crew.'

Fronto felt the wind taken from his sails at the realisation that the prefect was, in this case, completely powerless.

'Why?'

Ambustus leaned forward and lowered his voice conspiratorially. 'If I tell you this, it is told in confidence to a member of Caesar's staff, for all your retired status. I will hold you to your military oath and expect you not to breathe a word of it to another living soul. Do you understand?'

Fronto, rather taken aback by the vehemence of the man's words, nodded. 'Agreed.'

'There are small caravans of slaves and booty coming in all the time and being stored under guard in anonymous warehouses in Massilia, but I have been told to await one particularly large convoy, following which all goods in storage are to be combined with the new arrival and shipped to Rome in one fleet with solid military escort.'

'A big convoy, then?'

'The centurion who delivered the orders intimated that I would be able to buy most kingdoms with the proceeds from it. Booty the likes of which you will never have seen. So you understand why I cannot release the ship to you. You could ask the captain, but unless he is willing to defy the proconsul's orders, you will have no better luck there. It simply cannot be done.'

Fronto sagged slightly. The man was right. It mattered not how angry he became or what arguments he could marshal, no captain or officer in Massilia was going to defy Caesar's orders, even for a senior officer. No amount of honey could sweeten the pot enough for that.

'My apologies for wasting your time, Ambustus. I appreciate your candour.'

The prefect gave a troubled smile. 'I'm truly sorry, Fronto. I do hope you can find alternative transport until this matter is resolved, and rest assured that as soon as my hands are no longer tied by the proconsul's needs I will happily release any free space to you. In fact I wish I could help you defy the boule more than I can, given the stink they are raising over our blocking up of the port with so many ships docked without intention to sail.'

'Thank you, Ambustus. I'll take my leave and keep my tongue. Good luck with your task.'

Turning on his heel, he marched from the room and through the corridors until he emerged into the sunlight once more, where his friends had gathered in a small knot and were arguing. They fell silent as they saw him and waited impatiently as he strolled over.

'The prefect cannot help us and it's not his doing. No Roman ship is leaving port for the foreseeable future by order of the proconsul, and nothing will change that, We need to find an alternative transport for the Helvian wine as fast as possible.'

'Why are the ships impounded?' Aurelius asked curiously.

'I cannot relay that information, I'm afraid. I gave my word.'

'Caesar's treasure convoy,' snorted Catháin, and Fronto frowned at him.

'Keep your voice down, man. Where did you hear that?'

'In a bar yesterday. It's only rumour, but it's well-supported by visible evidence. They say a treasure convoy is coming to Massilia on its way to Rome.'

'And it's supposed to be secret,' murmured Fronto. 'I don't think even most of the army know yet by the sounds of it. Keep this to yourself, man. If word leaks to the wrong sectors of Gaul and that convoy is attacked, there could be a hell of a backlash at us.'

Catháin shrugged. 'The news is out there, Fronto. Perhaps you should tell the prefect, so he doesn't blame you?'

Fronto sighed again. 'I suppose it'll be common knowledge soon enough anyway. Since no Roman ships are moving, the Massilian boule are hounding Ambustus. When he's forced to explain why or lose his deal with the city, the council will know, and within a day word will be on every street. I suspect I'm safe. Safer than that convoy, anyway.'

'Regardless, my prime concern has to be finding another ship for the Helvian amphorae.'

Catháin nodded. 'There are two or three fairly friendly Baetican and Lusitanian traders in port today, all down at the shitty end of the docks. They're not popular because they trade almost exclusively with the Iberian ports and those around the Pillars of Hercules, and they have a monopoly there that most Massilian Greeks would eat their own grandmother to find a way into.'

Fronto snorted. 'I'm damn glad I've got your extensive knowledge working for me and not for them, then.'

Catháin gave him a look loaded with hidden messages, and Fronto made a mental note to raise the man's salary and buy him a gift before he decided that Spaniards might pay better.

'Come on. Let's go see these Baeticans, then.'

* * * * *

Fronto slumped against the doorframe as he entered his villa, pausing to kick off the soft leather boots and remove his cloak, tossing it towards the hook near the altar to the household spirits and missing by a wide enough margin to knock over the statues of the penates and scatter incense ash all over the marble floor. Waving a tired hand at it, he staggered into the atrium. It had been a tiring day and a bad one, too. Thankfully, Catháin had managed to pull his backside out of the flames once more with a personal introduction to a Baetican captain who knew the strange northerner well enough to call him 'arse-face'. Still, a potential thousand percent profit had been halved at best. And further trade deals going on looked to be troublesome with the lack of cheap transport.

Still, the Baetican had taken them at a price that Fronto knew to be more than reasonable, given the current situation. The man was making a rare journey to Rome instead of west, delivering cargoes of oysters and red ochre pigment from the Balearics that he'd collected en route. His appearance at Massilia at all was pure chance, since he had a small shipment of tin from Baetica that he'd failed to unload in the Balearics but would sell well in the Greek port.

His spirits flagged again as he heard Andala deep in discussion with Lucilia, both voices raised not in anger but in some sort of concern. That boded ill for Fronto. He edged quietly through the atrium on bare feet and peered around the doorway into the triclinium.

Lucilia lay on one of the couches, her hands weaving fretfully. Irritatingly, Andala reclined on the one next to her like some Roman matron at leisure. He started to move angrily, his mouth opening to shout, even as he registered two more sights that stilled his movement and his tongue both.

One was the fact that, despite his having hidden the fine gladius with the orichalcum hilt, Andala now had one of his more utilitarian military blades in her lap and was cleaning the leather binding on the grip.

The other was the sight of two of his men standing with their hands behind their backs, faces downcast. One was a recent acquisition whose name he couldn't yet remember. The other was Clearchus, one of the brothers who'd worked for him for months. Even a brief glance at distance drew his attention to the bruising on their arms and, as Clearchus raised his face to answer a question, Fronto was stunned at the damage to it. One eye was swollen shut, the nose twisted at an agonising angle and the lip swollen and raw. Both men were liberally spattered with blood.

Before he realised he was doing it, Fronto had stormed across the floor into the room.

'What in Hades happened?'

Lucilia looked up at him, her face grave, and answered before even Clearchus could get his painful mouth to work. 'Your men were set upon by armed thugs as they left the warehouse. Not thieves, either, since they smashed the jars of Alban vintage the pair were conveying and stole nothing. If it hadn't been for the timely interruption of a passing gentlemen and his guards, these two poor fellows would probably be dead now.'

Fronto felt the anger that had been muted and contained all day finally boil to the surface, unhindered. His lip curled up into a snarl that made it hard to speak.

'When was this?'

'Noph more phan an hour ago,' the second victim said through broken teeth. Fronto flexed his fists. 'Hierocles,' he grunted. A statement, rather than a question, but both men nodded painfully anyway. 'Enough is enough. The bastard has to be taught.' He paused, waiting for the warning against unnecessary violence from Lucilia, but she simply nodded her agreement, and he noticed now the bowl of pink water and the pink towel by her feet with which she had tended the men's worst wounds.

Wordlessly, Andala reversed her grip on the plain gladius in her hands and held it out, hilt first, to Fronto. He met her eyes and for the first time felt something akin to understanding pass between them. He nodded and took the sword.

He was a soldier, born and forged in decades of war, and he'd had enough pussy-footing around with petty criminals masquerading as merchants. Hierocles had to come down from his pedestal, no matter what the fallout with the boule of Massilia.

He turned and stormed out of the room purposefully, reaching out to swipe his cloak up from the altar in the vestibule.

'Masgava? Gather the men.'

* * * * *

'What's the plan, sir?'

186

Fronto glanced across at Aurelius. It was an excellent question. He had left the villa with his blood up, determined on a course of brutal action. He was still just as determined, of course, to pay Hierocles back for his actions and to end this trouble once and for all, but as the cold air of a Massilian evening bathed his ruddy face he had started to calm and think a little straighter. He could not *kill* Hierocles, no matter how much he might want to. This was not a Gallic battlefield, and murder was a capital offence in the city. Likewise, then, he would not kill any of Hierocles' men. But he would hurt the man, and badly. Hierocles would hardly drag them through the courts for a beating, given how many counts of the same for which he was responsible. It would be opening a veritable Pandora's Box of litigation that would harm Hierocles every bit as much as Fronto. So as long as he stopped short of actual killing, he felt safe from legal repercussions.

He turned to Masgava.

'You've been training the lads in their spare time, I remember. Did you teach them straight combat, or some of your more subtle methods?'

The big Numidian shrugged. 'I teach a man to fight in any way he can or must with whatever he can find. You know that.'

'Good.' He turned back to Aurelius. 'We're going to drop in on Hierocles. He has a number of tough men, but not as tough as us, with former soldiers and gladiators.' He raised his voice to catch the whole group. 'But the important thing is there must be *no* killing. Preferably no blades, even, though that might be unavoidable. But unless his men draw swords on you, keep your blades sheathed. Punch and kick, bite and thump. No one is to go in too heavy handed, got it?'

The twelve men around him nodded.

'You two are fairly new. I need eyes on the street. The city guards patrol these streets irregularly, and I don't want to suddenly find myself up to the armpits in local law enforcement. When we go in I want you to stay by the entrance. If anyone approaches, step inside, whistle loud and close the door. Got it?'

The two new men nodded, looking rather relieved.

'How do we get in in the first place?' asked Aurelius.

'Leave that to me. As soon as we're in, I need each of you thinking on your feet. We don't touch women, children, slaves or other civilians. Arcadios and Dyrakhes, you two are in charge of

187

rounding up any non-combatants. The first room we come across that's securable, you hustle them all into and keep them safe. Anyone who comes at us with fists or weapons is fair game. Any of his men – and after the last few months, we can recognise most of them – are fair game. If you happen to find Hierocles, shout me.'

'It's not much of a plan.'

'It's good enough. Everyone set?'

The gang rounded the corner of the Street of Golden Arcades which, in typical non-Roman-linear style, wound like a snake up the hill towards the temple of Apollo. Hierocles' house sat slightly back from the road, a narrow path leading to the door between well-tended gardens, the frontage between the next two buildings sectioned off with a high wall and a gate with its own little guard house. Hierocles was wealthy and careful.

As they approached, Fronto gestured to his men to move to the side of the street, keeping only Masgava with him, the rest out of sight of the gate unless the guard stuck his head out into the street. As the others moved up the incline along the fronts of other houses, Fronto and Masgava strolled out ahead, straight for the gate, their cloaks hiding the weapons at their sides, but the hoods down to allow easy recognition.

'Stay there,' snapped a voice in thick Massiliot Greek as they neared the door, and Fronto came to a halt, with the big Numidian at his shoulder. After a moment, a hatch in the gate opened and a pale face emerged, beady, glassy eyes peering out into the evening.

'Fronto. What do you want?'

'I wish to see your master.'

'He won't want to see you, Roman.'

Fronto put on his most humble face, despite the irritation with which that filled him. 'He might. I find I am in difficulty sourcing transport once more and your master can help me.'

The man blinked in surprise. 'Why would he do that?'

'Because I have two deals to conclude, and in return for his help he can have one of them. Both are good deals. Better for me to make Hierocles richer than for my business to fold.'

The man laughed. 'I suspect my master will think differently, but I'm sure he will enjoy laughing at your misfortune. The big dark animal has to stay outside, though.'

Fronto turned to Masgava, who was almost radiating the desire to cause violence. He tried to look undecided and then with exaggerated reluctance, nodded. 'You wait for me here, Masgava.'

The big man nodded, still glaring at the gate guard. The pale face grinned and there was a rattle and click as the gate was opened from within. Fronto stepped forward, making to enter as the gate began to swing inwards. Then, without warning, he took a long step and slammed his shoulder against the gate, which hammered back against the man opening it, knocking him against the wall of his little guard house. Fronto heard with gratification the whoosh of air from the man's lungs as he hit. Entering, Masgava waved the others in and slid through into the dark, tree-shaded garden. As his men moved into the house's grounds, Fronto pulled the winded guard from behind the door.

'Poor decision there, but I'm grateful.'

Even dazed and winded, the man tried to bring up a knife from his belt. In response, Fronto smacked the man's head back against the stone wall of his hut and watched the eyes roll up white accompanying the satisfying clunk. Before the man fell, Masgava was there. With a quick grab and twist, he broke the man's knife arm at the elbow. The forearm hung limp at a horrible angle and the knife fell away. Fronto stared.

'He'll live,' sneered Masgava. 'But he won't use a knife until he retrains with his left.'

'Shit, I'm glad you're on my side.'

The men were already across the grass and path now, closing on the house. Behind Fronto, the two new lads took control of the gate, one standing just inside and one out. A brief squawk caught his attention and he turned back, jogging across the garden to catch up with his men. His gaze fell upon the source of the noise and he boggled. A roving guard in the grounds had appeared from somewhere and tried to shout an alarm, but Catháin had hit him like a rolling boulder, knocking him to the ground. Even as Fronto opened his mouth to hiss a reminder about not killing, he saw the strange northerner deliver three blows to the man's face and then jab down with his fingers, putting out the guard's eyes. The man tried to scream, but Catháin's hand was over his mouth and with simple casual violence, the northerner slammed the man's head back to the gravel of the path, driving the blind guard's wits from him. Before he stood, he took the unconscious man's blade and stood, examining it.

189

A fine, curved *xiphos*, probably of Cypriot manufacture, looking at the colours and shapes. Fronto hurried over.

'Was the blinding strictly necessary'

'Are you wanting to send Hierocles a message, or tickle his arse with a feather, Fronto. Gods in ale, but the blind bastard'll live.'

Fronto shook his head and moved over towards the house's main door, where Masgava had taken control of the small band. Nine men. There would be at least as many inside, but blissfully unaware of what was coming. Fronto felt a moment of shame and fear at what they were doing. Sneaking around and invading people's property was not really his way, and it galled him to be doing so, but he hardened himself. These very arseholes had tried to kill him more than once and had attacked his men numerous times, trying to beat the last two to death. He didn't like this, but it *was* justified. He reached down to the figurines at his neck. Nemesis felt cold and reassuring. Fortuna would have her part to play tonight, for sure, but it was Nemesis' raid beyond doubt.

Masgava gestured a couple of times at Fronto and then took Aurelius and ran off around the side of the building, leaving Fronto frowning and wondering what all the gestures had meant. Still, Masgava knew exactly what he was doing, and Fronto trusted him implicitly, so he ignored the disappearance of two men and reached for the door.

Once they were inside, all hope of subtlety would be lost. Surprise would quickly fade, and something would have to replace it for Fronto's men to retain the upper hand. *Confusion* would be that thing.

Taking a deep breath in preparation and checking that the other six men were still with him, he reached out and threw open the doors to the house, stepping inside. In the short hallway that led to the central courtyard a young woman stopped in her tracks, alarm radiating from her as she dropped the armful of folded laundry she was carrying. She managed a brief muffled squeak before Arcadios wrapped himself around her, one hand across her mouth to cut off the cry. The Greek archer nodded to Dyrakhes and the two dragged her to the left side of the corridor where a doorway led to a darkened room. Fronto couldn't see inside but, given its location, it was likely a storage room for cloaks and boots and the like. Being dark, it was clearly unoccupied, which was perfect to contain the civilians.

The archer and his companion shut the door on the panicked woman and locked it from the outside before moving across to search the room opposite. Fronto knew that the element of surprise was about to disappear, and stepped out of the corridor into the main courtyard, preparing to change the game. He didn't understand Greek housing conventions particularly well, and knew Hierocles' residence not at all. Easier than searching every room was to keep people off-balance and bring them to you.

'Fire!' he bellowed in good local Greek. 'Fire in the *balanea*!'

He didn't know where the bath complex was, of course, but it would probably be at the rear of the residence, which would drive the occupants to the front, where Fronto and his men were waiting for them. Moreover, a fire in the bath house was far from unbelievable. The furnace would be burning hot on such a chilly March night and, if he were to be truthfully uncharitable, the Greeks were considerably less conscious of the safety requirements of such edifices than stolid Roman engineers.

As Fronto moved out into the centre of the courtyard, surrounded by a colonnade that would have looked more at home in Corinth than this far west and containing a central altar to Hermes liberally scattered with offerings, he heard the cry of 'fire' being echoed across the residence. Chaos blossomed.

Fronto found himself moving towards the end of the courtyard, where two doors led off, but also a central passageway that had to lead to the rear sections of the house where the servants' and guards' quarters would be, as well as the kitchens, stores and bathing complex. Hierocles would likely be through one of those doors, since the house had a second storey at the rear side of the courtyard only, and the stairs up would be somewhere there. Hierocles, by his very nature, would automatically site himself higher than anyone else. Behind Fronto, the rest of his men were pushing open doors and either emerging quickly, empty handed, or struggling inside, laying flat those of the Greek's thugs who opposed them. Occasionally Arcadios and Dyrakhes would appear, dragging a screaming slave off to the room where they were being kept out of danger. Even as he watched, Dyrakhes received a vicious bite to the forearm for his pains and, bless the man, he struggled on without taking it out on the girl.

Finally, in response to the fire alarm, people began to emerge from both doors and the passage ahead in a panic. Arcadios was there instantly, shouting in his native Greek, directing the terrified slaves and servants back towards the front door, away from danger. As they moved gratefully into captivity more of the thugs began to appear and Fronto's men set to work, breaking noses and arms, concussing and brutalising with ruthless efficiency. Hierocles' hirelings, still in panic and confusion at the supposed fire in the baths, ran straight into the arms of Fronto's men, unaware that they were under attack until they were on the ground, groaning.

As Fronto stood apart from the fighting, keeping his eyes peeled for a sign of the master of the house, he heard a feral roar and Clearchus, still clutching his side from his earlier beating and with poor depth perception from his swollen-shut eye, charged past Fronto and slammed into a big blond man with a flat nose and a single eyebrow that almost circumnavigated his head.

'Think you're big and clever now, do you, shithead?' the man howled through split lips as the two men hit the floor, the blond brute being winded as he struck the marble with the angered Greek atop him. Clearchus hit the man four or five times with bruised and lacerated knuckles until his former attacker's face was covered with so much blood it was hard to tell which was his and which belonged to Clearchus.

Fronto nodded approvingly. Nemesis was truly at work tonight. Then his eyes caught a stray movement and he leapt forward urgently. His hand locked around Clearchus' wrist just as the wronged man was about to bring down his knife into the blond ruffian's face.

'No!'

Clearchus struggled for a moment, trying to break Fronto's grasp and finally the fight went out of him. He dropped the knife, submitting to Fronto, and instead delivered another half dozen violent blows to the man's head. As the Greek rose unsteadily, his anger still simmering, Fronto paused for a long moment, watching nervously, but finally the big blond mess on the floor took a single breath, and then another. Satisfied that at least Clearchus hadn't killed the man, he looked up.

It was fortuitous timing that he happened to glance around. Another heartbeat and he'd have missed Hierocles. The Greek merchant had emerged from the passage wrapped in a towel and otherwise naked, sweaty and wet. Fronto caught his eye even as the man recognised what was happening in his courtyard and turned, running back into the passage.

Snarling, Fronto gave chase.

In the dark corridor, someone took a swing at the Roman invader and caught him a blow to the side of the head, swinging him around. Then Pamphilus and Clearchus were there, restraining the attacker and laying into him with merry abandon. Fronto reeled for a moment until his head cleared and then ran on. He turned a corner and met two sets of doors both standing open – a store room and a kitchen complex. For a moment he peered into them until he decided they were almost certainly empty and ran on.

The corridor emerged into a small guard chamber and Fronto took in the situation with dismay. Hierocles had reached the house's rear door and three of his thugs occupied the room with small clubs, protecting their master. Fronto pulled himself up short at the door. He was armed with a gladius if he cared to draw it, but this was still three to one, even if their master stayed out of it. And the three men were, if not professional fighters, then at least clearly gifted amateurs.

'Shame for you, Fronto. All this effort. And me untouched. But rest assured that when I report this to the boule, they will know that you broke into my house with intent to kill.' Even as he spoke, Hierocles slipped on his chiton and reached out for his cloak.

'We've killed no one, you idiot. We've been careful.'

Hierocles laughed as he slipped into his light leather shoes and gestured at the three other men in the room. 'When you beat Fronto senseless and toss him out, keep his sword and use it to kill one of the girls.'

Fronto's eyes widened. As a foreigner in the city – and especially one who had already ranted at the city council in session – it would not take much for them to convict him of murder. His blade in a young girl would almost certainly seal his fate. He looked over his shoulder for aid, but the others were all busy back at the heart of the complex. He was alone and seriously outnumbered.

Shit.

'Thank you, Fronto. Thank you from the bottom of my heart. I've been struggling for a way to take you out of the equation, but kept coming up blank. Then you do this and answer my prayers. When you meet the young girl in the next world, give her my apologies, won't you?'

Laughing, Hierocles opened the door and stepped out into the darkness of late evening as the three thugs took a deliberate, menacing pace towards Fronto.

There was a resounding thud and Hierocles reappeared from the dark, spinning. Behind him, Masgava stepped into the room, blowing on sore knuckles, Aurelius at his shoulder, and the two men made their way in to face Fronto's beaming smile. The big Numidian's punch had almost killed the Greek merchant. As Hierocles floundered on the floor, groaning, blood began to leak from his nostrils, ear and mouth simultaneously, and bloody snot-bubbles appeared as he breathed through his shattered nose. The bruise began to come up almost immediately and covered almost a quarter of his head. Despite his long shared history with Masgava, Fronto was impressed with the blow.

The three thugs stopped moving. Leaving them to Aurelius and Masgava, Fronto strode over to the fallen Greek. For each step Masgava took, the three thugs took one back away from him towards the room's corner. One of them dropped his club immediately and held up his hands in surrender, his eyes wide in panic.

Hierocles whimpered. Still dazed, he reached up to touch his bruised head and cried out in pain.

'Yes. I think Masgava cracked your skull in more than one place. He has strong fists and he's very quick.'

The man tried to focus on Fronto but one of his eyes seemed unwilling to move from some spot on the floor. 'Aghhh... I... urgh...'

'This is where our little competition ends, Hierocles.'

The man could do little but whimper in reply.

'Know that I am no longer taking any shit from you. You will never again touch my men or my goods. I cannot stop you using mercantile and political practices against me and, while I consider that low and contemptible, there is no law against it. But any more theft or violence against my business will be visited back upon you tenfold. Take this as a friendly warning. There is nowhere you can go and nothing you can do to stop me getting to you.'

Hierocles groaned.

'I shall take your silence as tacit understanding. The next time one of my men comes home wounded, you will be searching the sewers for your teeth. Final warning. Stay out of my way.'

As the man writhed in pain and panic, Fronto rose and gestured to Masgava and Aurelius. 'Come on. Time to go home.'

He made his way back to the corridor from whence he came, the other two turning away, but the big Numidian sharply snapped back towards the three thugs and flashed them a smile. The one who'd dropped his club wet his chiton.

Moments later Fronto emerged from the house with his men at his back. A quick glance confirmed that they'd taken a few bruises and that Pamphilus had broken two fingers, but they had escaped successful and essentially unscathed.

With a chuckle, Fronto pulled the figurine of Nemesis from his neck, lifted it and kissed her full on the face. 'Thank you, lovely goddess.' Swiftly, he planted a second kiss on Fortuna and then tucked them back in his clothes.

'Home time, lads. I'm in the mood for a small party and I know where there's a good stock of wine.'

Chapter Eleven

CAVARINOS stood in the side street and looked about with a strange mix of sadness and nostalgia. At the lower end of the dusty road he could see the heavy ramparts, and beyond that only bright, cloudless sky and the tips of the blue hazy mountains to the south. Lining the street on both sides were stone and timber buildings that were painfully, hauntingly familiar, and mostly derelict. And to the north, the road met the main street of the oppidum that ran from the west gate to the public square near the eastern end.

For a moment he considered strolling down to the walls and looking over at the slopes and the lesser hills at the foot of the oppidum, but the thought that he would be looking down on the site of the greatest victory the Arverni would ever claim somehow made that unpalatable, and he turned his gaze from the south back to the house where his uncle had lived and where he had spent so many summers as a boy.

Indeed, he had resided in this very house during his time at Gergovia as the great revolt picked up pace and the war progressed. He'd not been back since Alesia and, though some of his personal effects were almost certainly still inside, despite losing the war and his prolonged absence, somehow it felt wrong to open that door – like disturbing a tomb.

Gergovia was very much a tomb.

It stood as a monument to the last great hope of the peoples against Rome. It was a cenotaph – the empty tomb. And yes, the oppidum itself had stood empty for so many months, but a veritable legion of the dead from both sides lay under mounds down past that wall, staring up at the fortress with dead, accusing eyes. And now, despite the tribes' attitude to this strangely hallowed place, life was coming back. A Roman prefect with an auxiliary force of spearmen from Narbonensis, along with a few regular clerks and quartermasters had taken up residence in Gergovia, in the house where Vercingetorix had planned the war against them. The prefect was a 'resettlement officer', tasked with repopulating the oppidum with what was left of the Arverni – which was more than most tribes, given Caesar's galling sparing of the tribe from slavery after Alesia. And so now almost a thousand Arverni were camped on the heights out past the west gate, awaiting the allotment of property for their new life as subjects of Rome. There was even talk that in due course

Rome would relocate the tribe to a Roman style settlement on the plains below, though that would be years away yet, when 'Gaul' had a governor and a garrison and paid taxes and worshipped Roman gods.

Perhaps a hundred people had so far been set up in the better houses – the ones that had not fallen to wrack and ruin since their abandonment. Cavarinos was not one of them, of course. He was merely a visitor to this place that had once been his home – a pilgrim to the site of that last victory. In fact, since the Romans were being their usual officious and immovable selves and not granting access to anyone until they had been assigned a place, Cavarinos had slipped in among a family being escorted to their new home, and had easily peeled off inside and disappeared into the empty streets to find his old house.

He wasn't even really sure what he was doing here, other than that he had felt a curious pull all the time he had been in the region and had, in the end, found himself powerless to resist. And where he would go when he left here was an equal mystery. Soon he would have to leave the lands the Romans called Gaul. He was a spirit from a bygone age, drifting among the wreckage of his world, and every day here tarnished his soul a little more. But where he would go he did not know. To Rome was unthinkable, somehow. To the land of the tribes across the northern sea? Perhaps, but he was a warm-blooded southerner and that island was a cold and rugged place, even less forgiving than Belgae lands, and it did not really appeal. To Iberia perhaps? Though there had ever been a cultural gulf between the peoples of that land and the peoples of this, as though the high, serrated mountains that separated them physically also divided them in their hearts.

And so he continued to wander as a ghost of a war long since lost.

Angry with himself, he turned away from the house and caught movement from the corner of his eye. Frowning at the unaccustomed sight, he stepped back into the shadow at the side of the street, his instincts warning him to remain unobserved. The small group passed along the main thoroughfare at the end of the street, unaccompanied by Romans. Odder still, they were no Arverni family heading for their resettlement. The cloaks they wore bulged at the waist where belted swords ruffled the material, and their hoods were pulled forward, hiding their features.

As the last of the dozen or so figures passed, it paused for a moment and turned to look down the street. The head came up and, as the hood fell back, Cavarinos noted the strange glazed cult mask that covered the face, glinting in the sunlight. The figure studied the alley for some time and Cavarinos remained still, perturbed by the mask and cloak, despite himself. Then, silently, the figure moved on and disappeared from view. Cavarinos paused for a count of ten heartbeats and then began to move quietly up the road towards the main street. At the corner he stopped again, peering cautiously out into the thoroughfare. The main street sloped up, but at a barely visible incline. The public square was visible from here, though it had undergone changes since it had fallen into Roman hands. The open space was now enclosed with a wall that utilised the surrounding buildings and sealed or gated off the streets that met there. It had become the Roman depot, with the houses of the wealthy Arvernian nobles now barracks for the Narbonese spearmen and the few legionaries. Three Romans – regular soldiers in their russet coloured tunics and gleaming bronze helmets – guarded the entrance to the compound. Most of the occupying 'resettlement' force would be busy in various places around the oppidum sorting out housing and repairing buildings and walls, fences and sheds in preparation for their granting to native families. A skeleton guard only would remain in the compound. After all, the only folk in the town were those dejected families that the Romans had rehomed. They had nothing to fear in Gergovia.

But clearly they did.

The dozen – and now he could see them clearly there were precisely twelve of them – cloaked figures were striding up the street as bold as orichalcum, making straight for that guarded gate as though it were they in command here and not the Romans.

Cavarinos turned and looked down the street, willing himself to be able to see the west gate, even though he knew the curvature of the street and the slope would not allow it. Somehow in his mind's eye he could picture the two spearmen who guarded the west gate, riddled with stab wounds and tossed carelessly aside like a child's doll. These dozen people had not entered Gergovia with such care as he. They would have left bodies in their wake, he was certain.

He was equally certain over the coming fate of the three men at the compound gate.

Trying to suppress his natural urge to shout a warning, he slipped from doorway to doorway and alley to alley, shadowing the newcomers at a safe distance – close enough to see what was happening, but safely unnoticed. He was quiet and agile, and he knew it.

It was his duty as Arverni – bred into him over years of rebellion – to aid the fight against Rome in any way he could, and these people *had* to be Rome's enemies. That was plain to see. And yet the longer the war had gone on, the more he had turned in favour of peace. That war was lost now, and despite the deep-seated feeling that he should be with those cloaked figures, he held his tongue and remained in the shadows.

Yet if his goal was truly peace and a harmonious cohabitation with Rome as he'd come to suspect, why was he not prepared to shout a warning to the Romans? It was not a matter of self-preservation, despite the fact that calling out would almost certainly mean death for him as well as the Romans. Twelve against four was poor odds, and somehow he knew these people to be killers despite their hidden nature.

No. Not self-preservation. Somehow, he couldn't bring himself to warn the soldiers that had so long been the enemy of his people.

It was a horrible realisation that he was neither a rebellious Gaul, nor a peaceful Roman subject.

He was a wraith, tied to a world that no longer existed.

As he watched, the Romans turned towards the approaching cloaked figures. With typical Roman arrogance they did not raise an alarm. They assumed all was safe, since they had control of Gergovia. They must be unobservant to miss the bulge of weapons and the sinister aspect of the masks. The leader of the guards was a man with a crest on his helmet, but not a sideways one like a centurion. He was their second-in-command. What did the Romans call them again? Ah yes. Optio – *chosen man*.

Today he had been chosen by death.

The optio challenged the cloaked figures, but made no move to defend himself. Three of the cloaked figures stepped forwards swiftly. At last the optio realised he was in trouble and went to draw his sword. As two of the swiftest warriors Cavarinos had ever witnessed whipped out their blades in a fluid move and put them simultaneously through the necks of the two legionaries, the cloaked figure out front swung a punch at the optio. The Gaul was huge – by

199

a head the tallest of the cloaked group, and with the shoulders of an ox. The optio reeled from the blow, stunned and prevented from crying out a warning as he'd so clearly intended.

As Cavarinos watched, sickened, the huge cloaked figure grabbed the optio by neck and groin and dropped to one knee, bringing the body he held like a weightless toy down onto the raised kneecap and snapping his spine in two. The officer tried to shriek but the big meaty hand slipped up from the neck over his mouth and the big man leaned close, apparently asking a question of his crippled victim. When he removed his hand, the officer desperately stuttered out some whispered reply.

The giant nodded his acceptance of whatever he heard and, as the Roman shuddered and retched in agony, slowly reached up and with disturbing ease turned the man's head to face backwards, accompanied by the tearing of tendons and the cracking of bones.

The big man stood, leaving the lifeless Roman on the ground.

'Come,' said a new figure from within the group in a strange, hoarse voice, and Cavarinos marked that man as the leader, despite the uniform appearance of the entire group. The dozen figures left the dead Romans where they lay and moved into the compound.

In apparent response to whatever information they had received from the officer, the dozen figures separated as they entered the depot. Three cut left and three right, moving methodically to the two other side gates where they no doubt found and dispatched more guards, though Cavarinos could not see the action from his poor vantage point. Then, as the groups of three re-emerged, they moved into selected buildings.

The other six figures made straight across the square to what had once been a luxurious house belonging to Gergovia's resident druid. Now, a red flag adorned with the ubiquitous golden eagle and SPQR sigil hung from the upstairs window, denoting the presence of Rome. With the boldness of the invincible, the six cloaked figures entered the building and closed the door behind them.

Cavarinos held his breath for a long moment, staring into the now-empty compound. Despite not having committed himself to either side in this small engagement, he felt certain he needed to know more about what was happening here. It smacked heavily of all the clandestine manoeuvring that had occurred in the two years leading up to the revolt.

He could move *now*. The square was empty. Six had moved into the largest building and the others were scattered among the other structures, but all were inside. To move could cause him trouble if one of them happened to emerge once more as he crossed the open. Would being Arverni save him from their wrath? Somehow he suspected not, even if he'd looked the part. And he didn't. He was still clean-shaven, his hair pulled back behind him. He wore Gallic clothing, but his serpent arm-ring and noble's torc had gone, and at his neck he wore a figurine of a Roman God. Somehow he knew his appearance would be held against him no matter what he said.

Still, the square was empty and precious time was passing as he deliberated.

His heart in his throat and thumping a speedy tempo, Cavarinos slipped out of the shadows and loped quietly across to the gate, trying not to pay too close attention to the three corpses that lay there. His eyes darting back and forth between the various doors, he settled on the big house ahead. Clearly that was their objective, the rest simply keeping the garrison out of things.

No one emerged, and no faces appeared at the windows as he ran quietly on soft boots, shushing gravel despite his care, and he dived into the shadows at the far side, next to Vercingetorix's house. As he stood in the shade, heaving in silent breaths, two figures stepped out of the side buildings, perhaps having heard movement. Both peered intently around the square, shared a look, and then moved out, searching the area swiftly.

But they were not Arverni, for they moved with unfamiliarity around the square, peering into places where Cavarinos knew a man couldn't hide. Who were they if not Arverni?

Cavarinos *was* a child of this tribe, and he knew Gergovia like he knew the lines on his hand. Staying in the shadows, he moved to the rear of Vercingetorix's house, ducked past the animal shed and turned right, running along the back of the buildings, silent on the turf. The Roman compound perimeter had made use of the boundary wall of the house's rear field, but had left open space behind the buildings themselves, just as he'd assumed. Now easily safe from the prying eyes of the pair in the square, he passed the rear of three houses and arrived at the druid's two-storey residence.

His fears were confirmed by the screaming of a man within, and he could hear curses and angry imprecations in Latin. Who was this man? Not the prefect, for he worked out of Vercingetorix's house and was apparently inspecting the oppidum's granaries this morning. This was another Roman, and important enough to have drawn the attentions of the dozen cloaked killers.

With the ease of a man familiar with every wall and window, Cavarinos closed on the house's rear wall and climbed up to the store shed that was built against it. Quickly he peered round it, aware that anyone looking out of the rear window of the house might see him. Fortunately, no one seemed to be manning that window and on agile toes, Cavarinos crept up to it and crouched, rising to peer through the bottom corner.

He was not shocked by what he saw. Sickened a little, but not shocked. The Roman was clearly a very senior officer. He wore the same uniform – and had similar armour hanging on the wall – to that Cavarinos remembered Fronto wearing and so this, he assumed, was another legion commander. A *legate*, he remembered. The man was already agonised and ruined. In this state most men would already be begging for death, so Cavarinos could only admire the Roman's tenacity, as the haughty face turned on the cloaked figure.

'Gaius Antistius Reginus of the Fifteenth, bound for Rome.'

'Stop saying that,' snarled the leader with the hoarse voice and smashed a shattered exquisite Roman glass into the man's cheek, grinding it into the flesh and lacerating his face. Reginus whimpered, and yet didn't scream.

'I will not tell you anything,' he panted painfully. 'The convoy will not fall into the hands of filthy rebels!'

Convoy? Interesting. Cavarinos frowned as the torturing came to an abrupt halt. The leader paused and despite the mask Cavarinos knew he was frowning. Reaching up, the man pulled back the hood and slowly removed his mask. The face beneath was like chopped meat and even Cavarinos found himself recoiling for a moment. Reginus looked as though he might retch, even in his own current situation.

'Convoy?' the ruin-faced man murmured in confusion.

'Yes,' Reginus answered in equal perplexity. 'Caesar's convoy. That's what you're wanting, yes?'

'I care not for some convoy of Rome,' spat the hideous leader. 'Perhaps I should have made myself clearer at the outset? I am hunting Esus – the saviour of the peoples. It is the Arverni king I seek. Tell me where I can find Vercingetorix.'

Reginus boggled for a moment, and then started to laugh.

'Is that what this is all about? You *should* have been clearer to begin with. His fate is common knowledge.'

The cloaked leader, clearly extremely irritated, smacked the Roman with the back of his hand. 'This is not the case. I have interrogated every Roman officer I can find, and no one knows. The king was taken prisoner by Caesar, but some think he is in Samarobriva. Some in Rome. Others think he is in a secure, hidden place, and others say he is already dead. No one has been able to tell me with any certainty.'

'You have been asking the wrong men, Gaul. I will happily tell you with clarity and certainty where your *former* king is. He is forever beyond your reach, in the carcer of Rome, on the slope of the Capitol. He languishes in the most secure place in the Roman world where he will stay, sleeping in his own waste, until the day his execution is ordered, and then he will be killed.'

Another of the figures – a woman, Cavarinos realised in surprise – cut in. 'When will that be?'

Reginus shrugged. 'Who knows? A year. Two?' He is too valuable to kill offhand. Caesar will have a triumph in Rome once he has returned for his consulship, and Vercingetorix will be dragged around the city in chains for the delight of the crowd before any execution is ordered.'

The woman turned to her leader. 'We still have time, Molacos,' her mask-muffled voice announced.

The meat-faced leader turned angrily on the woman and slapped her, despite the mask covering her face. 'No true names, Catubodua. Are you a fool?'

The woman snarled in reply. 'There is no one to hear but a dead Roman.' Even as Molacos rounded on her again, she lanced out with a sword and drove it through Reginus' eye and deep into his brain, killing him instantly.

'That was foolish,' Molacos muttered.

'He told us what we wanted and now your name is a secret once more.'

The giant of a man who had killed the optio outside leaned down and spoke, the mask making his voice oddly hollow. 'How do we get to Rome?'

Molacos sighed and cleaned his blade on the dead legate's tunic before sheathing it. 'Lucterius has a sympathetic Ruteni trader in Massilia who can arrange passage for us. Come, Mogont. Gather the

203

others from the barracks. We have a destination at last. Massilia, then Rome.'

As the man replaced his mask and hood, Cavarinos noticed a symbol on the cloak's front. A wheel and a thunderbolt. *The signs of Taranis.* So, Molacos was Taranis, was he? The most powerful of the gods. And Catubodua? The crow of war. He would give money to know who it was behind *that* mask. Women warriors were not common. And Mogont, too? Even as the big man turned and left with the others, Cavarinos could see the jagged stylised mountain shape on his cloak identifying him with Mogont – the lord of mountains. Gods. Twelve gods. It would be fascinating to see what other symbols he could identify and what gods they claimed to be.

But more important was what he had learned of their true identity and their goal.

For he knew Molacos...

The hunter that was Lucterius' pet and who Cavarinos had believed to have fallen at Alesia. It seemed he had survived, at least in ruined form. As the men disappeared from the house out into the square, joining up with their fellows, the Arvernian prince rose from his crouch by the window, torn by choices. It should be none of his business. And yet it was. It *really* was.

And, being his business, and the twelve of them having stated an intention to find, and presumably free, his cousin, the great Arverni king, he should by rights be throwing in his lot with them. But the practical man that was Cavarinos, who knew that Gaul was a Roman thing now, and that nothing would halt that tide, could see only extended violence and horror in dragging out the revolution. It would be better if Vercingetorix had been killed at Alesia. Better for him. Better for the tribes. Better for everyone.

Massilia.

Fronto was in Massilia. Now why did *that* leap to mind?

He knew the answer to that question at once. Because despite the fact that Cavarinos was a ghost, drifting in the aether, disconnected from both his own people and the conquerors, Fronto remained the only person whose opinion he felt he could count upon. The Roman had spoken sense throughout the war and had even been one to advocate a peaceful solution to save the tribes. Fronto would know what to do.

Another thought occurred to him, too. Molacos hated Romans more than anyone Cavarinos had ever met. More even than

Vercingetorix. And Fronto had gone to become a wine merchant in Massilia. What were the chances of Molacos and his psychotic, vengeful group passing through that great port without hearing tell of the former companion of Caesar's who lived there. And when that happened, Cavarinos wouldn't give two copper coins for Fronto's chances.

Still undecided about his views on Molacos' end goal, he at least was now resolved on one thing: he had to beat the cloaked 'gods' to Massilia and warn Fronto. Then he could seek Fronto's counsel on other matters, once the former legate had moved to a place of safety and avoided the wrath of 'Taranis'.

Massilia, then. At all speed.

Chapter Twelve

THE officers of Caesar's senior staff sat in a semicircle facing the general across his littered desk. No one here ranked lower than a legate, and Varus wondered at the lack of attendance from the usual bulk of officers - senior tribunes with vexillatory commands, auxiliary prefects, cavalry prefects, and the usual extras such as the engineering genius Mamurra. It seemed that only the most high-ranking had been required to attend.

He turned to see Brutus looking back at him with the same curiosity burning in his eyes, and smiled. These days, with the army generally commanded by serious, career-minded men with little or no sense of humour, Brutus' companionship for the season had been gods-sent. Most of the old hands were gone now one way or another, and that camaraderie from the early days of the campaign was notably absent these days. Still, the war was almost finished with, and soon they would all be adjusting to civilian life, their great patron no longer needing their talents in the field.

The brief campaign against the Bellovaci had felt like proper warfare, of course, but in truth it was a small thing in comparison to the gargantuan field battles and sieges in which the army had been involved in previous years. The death toll against the Bellovaci had been pleasantly low, and the army still felt more relaxed than it had for years, certain that this was the last fight. The Gauls seemed to be suppressed, and the Belgae now had collapsed beneath the Roman boot.

Indeed, in the two weeks that followed the end of that rebellion, Caesar and his army had moved into the Atrebates' land, driven by the seeking of revenge on the traitor Commius, and then on into the territory of the Eburones who had so troubled Rome over the past few years. Both tribes had been cowed and feeble, yet both had been stripped of all remaining assets by the general.

Varus and Brutus had talked long about that in the privacy of his tent.

And now the army was back at the south-western edge of Belgae lands.

The general finished scratching some list on a sheet of vellum and straightened, performing a quick head-count with his piercing gaze. Seemingly happy with the result, he rubbed his temple for a moment and then cleared his throat.

'The time has come to separate the army once more,' the general said. 'The north is, in my opinion - and in that of those others I have consulted - settled. There is almost no chance of a future rising here. The northern Gallic tribes are depopulated and impoverished and in no condition to cause trouble, and now the Belgae are in the same position. Indeed, there are few areas of the land that can still raise a warband, let alone an army, and so the legions can now be reassigned appropriately.'

Peaceful postings? Varus frowned. That was not the way of Rome. Legions were raised for wars and disbanded at their conclusion. Some were occasionally kept on, paid for by their patron, when other areas were looking troublesome or when that patron expected to be assigned to a difficult province, or even if the senate decided they were of continued use, but most were disbanded when they were no longer needed. And certainly an army *this* size - a size rarely fielded in the history of Rome - would not be kept mobilized, considering the fact that Caesar would soon be moving into his consular role and staying in Rome for a while.

'The Treveri are still something of a threat,' the general went on. 'Despite repeated campaigns against them over the years, we have generally granted clemency in the aftermath and the dolts ever take advantage of that to raise trouble again as soon as the opportunity occurs. It is time to drive the fight and the spirit from them for good, to put them in the same position as their fellow Gauls.'

So not all peace, then...

'Labienus, you are my most able vexillatory commander, your skills have been proved time and again. You, I charge with the final pacification of the Treveri. They border the Germanic tribes, who continue to threaten and stir up unrest with people like Commius, and you are also authorised, if information is forthcoming, to deal with that particular traitorous vermin. Take the Seventh legion,' a quick nod there to Plancus, the Seventh's legate, who sat close by, 'who are one of the most experienced and strongest of my legions both in spirit and on parchment. You will have to take a slightly circuitous route and pass by Agedincum, where you will also collect the First. They may only have been with this army for a short time, but they are a consular legion who cut their teeth years ago under Pompey. They will be returning to their former role at the end of the year but until then, with two veteran legions at your disposal, you should encounter no trouble against the Treveri.'

207

Varus peered at Labienus, sitting with his helmet on his lap, his hair so much greyer than he remembered it being when they had first met eight years ago. Labienus was nodding professionally.

'Divide all spoils, including slaves. One half will be sent via the Rhodanus valley to Massilia. The rest will be divided among the men as you deem fit. I shall eagerly await news of your success.'

Labienus nodded again and sat quietly.

'Fabius.'

The legate straightened at the sound of his name.

'My latest reports suggest that the other most troublesome area is in the west and the southwest.'

Fabius frowned. 'Beg your pardon, general, but isn't Caninius already there with the Fifth and the Fifteenth?'

Caesar nodded and steepled his fingers. 'He is, but the scale of that region is rather impressive. There are something in the region of fifteen tribes that occupy the lands between the Pyrene mountains and the Liger River and border the western sea. And many of those tribes were only peripherally involved in the rising last year, so they are more populous than others. Given that Caninius has only two legions, one being freshly-raised last year and still green in many ways, and the other being a legion often kept in reserve, it seems sensible to me to send extra men to make sure the region is stable.'

Fabius nodded his understanding.

'You will take the Eighth and Roscius' Ninth,' another nod to Roscius, 'two of my most veteran legions - and join with Caninius at his base of Noviodunum. By autumn I want to sleep soundly knowing that the west and the south are either happily working towards the goal of a Gallo-Roman future or suppressed enough that they neither would nor could consider rising against us. I am hopeful for a peaceful, positive solution, but with four legions and auxiliary support you will, of course, impose peace and stability at the end of a gladius if it is required.'

Another nod.

'Varus?'

The cavalry commander sat up a little and concentrated.

'You will take a wing of the cavalry and join Fabius in the west. The army will be moving quick and light, resupplying at the various stations on the way, and he may have need of fast-moving, roving cavalry support, particularly given the hilly terrain that I understand is the norm in the southwest.'

Varus nodded.

So that was it. More suppression of tribes. At least the southwest was new territory for Varus, and he would see different terrain and hear different tongues. It was odd that he had become so used to the north and east of Gaul over the years that even with no grasp of the native language and no concerted attempt to learn it, he had begun to recognise words and the roots of names. He could already remember a dozen of their gods and could identify many tribes from their symbols and colours. The Aquitani and their neighbours were - Crassus had once informed him - as far removed from the rest of the Gauls as a Sicilian was from a Roman. And Varus remembered once trying to follow the lyrics of a song sung by a Sicilian in a tavern and fathoming perhaps one word in three through the thick accent and strange idioms.

New lands.

'And Brutus?' Caesar continued.

So Brutus would not be coming, it seemed. The general had another task for him. Fabius and Caninius were good men, but Varus could hardly picture sitting up late at night with a lightly-watered wine and roaring with laughter at humorous reminiscences with either of them. Across the tent, the young officer looked up with interest.

'To you I assign the most important task.'

This phrase captured the attention of every man in the room, and the officers leaned slightly forward as one.

'The spoils from the last few weeks of campaigning are gathered at Durocorteron, where the Remi guard it carefully and have arranged for wagons, beasts and horse escort. You will collect that wagon train and escort it to Agedincum. There you will find that numerous other wagon columns have gathered under the protective gaze of the garrison. There are a few last slave chains with them, but most of the convoy will consist of wagons of spoils. Once the Durocorteron wagons are added to the mass, the entire column will move south via Bibracte and Vienna under your command. Every ship available will be waiting in Massilia harbour - I have already notified the authorities there of your approach. Bear in mind the unprecedented value of the column. It would make a fabulous prize for an enemy of ours and while I cannot see any tribe having the manpower or the guts to try for such a trophy, you must take every precaution.'

Varus glanced across at Brutus, who was calm and quiet, though his fingers were drumming nervously on the chair arm, and well they might. This was an assignment that could make a man's career or see him broken. It did not escape Varus' notice that the task had been entrusted to one of the general's own relations, perhaps the only man Caesar felt he could trust enough?

'Security, Caesar?' Brutus asked quietly.

'In addition to the Remi horse and the various smaller escorts that have accompanied each single convoy to the Agedincum meet, you will take the Twelfth Legion. They will travel the entire journey as dedicated guards for the convoy. Once you arrive at the port in Massilia, the fleet and their marines will take on the responsibility for escort, still under your command, and the Twelfth will move down to Matisco near the Narbonensis border, where they will take up the role of garrison to protect Roman provincial interests from any last throes of Gallic trouble.'

'And the destination of the convoy, Caesar?'

The general pursed his lips and Varus realised that the general had intended to reveal the intimate details of the task only in a quiet post-briefing manner to his cousin. A quick glance around the room seemed to satisfy Caesar that he was safe enough speaking in front of those present, though. After all, that was clearly why the bulk of the officer corps were not present.

'The fleet will convey the wagons to Ostia, where you will oversee the transfer to barges that have also been prepared in advance and should be waiting empty for you. You will take the entire convoy in one trip to the emporium of Rome and then through the city to the Quirinal hill and the house of Gaius Servilius Casca Longus near to the temple of Salus.'

Brutus frowned. 'Casca, general? Might I enquire about...'

'No,' Caesar cut him short with a sharp look. 'You may not. Curiosity is a favoured trait in a student, but it is oft-times a detriment to a good officer. Servilius Casca is expecting the arrival of the column. He will oversee the transfer of the slaves to the graecostadium and has made arrangements for the wagons and their contents.'

He leaned forwards as though speaking to Brutus alone, ignoring every other fascinated face.

'Bear in mind, Decimus Brutus, that this convoy has to reach Rome safe and intact. A great deal rides on its arrival, and if every man in the Remi cavalry, the Twelfth Legion and the fleet has to die to achieve that, then die they will. Do you understand me?'

Brutus nodded his agreement, silent still, chastened by Caesar's sharp words.

'Very well. The rest of you will remain with me and the remaining force. We still have a few tasks to complete in the north before we move south again, but at this point I will take the opportunity to assign specific duties to you all.'

The rest of the briefing went by without incident or interest to Varus, who spent much of the time studying his peers. Labienus, assigned to the Treveri. The only man in this army with a track record to rival Caesar's. It seemed entirely possible that in the absence of old Crassus, Labienus could take on the role of that leg of the tripod that seemed to support the republic these days. If the man had the chance to move out from under Caesar's shadow, he might be every bit as popular and successful as either the general or Pompey. Perhaps that was why his role was so often downplayed. Last autumn, Varus had finally found the time to read Caesar's commentaries on the war that had been circulated among the people of Rome for years. While they were largely accurate, barring some self-congratulation and narcissistic third-person praise, they did at times diminish the accomplishments of men such as Labienus in favour of the general.

His gaze moved on to his friend. Brutus was still young for such a role, his career owed entirely to Caesar's patronage. But his accomplishments spoke for themselves. He had commanded Caesar's fleets several times, including that glorious victory against the Veneti in the west - another likely reason for his selection to command the convoy that would have to take ship at Massilia.

Thoughts of Massilia inevitably brought a mental image of Fronto. Shame Varus was assigned to the western tribes and not the convoy. He would have enjoyed dropping in on the Tenth's former legate and sampling his wares.

Fabius was already looking twitchy, as though ready to be off to Noviodunum with all haste. Perhaps he had realised he was being given the chance to shine like Labienus and was hoping for a challenge in the west. Gods, Varus hoped not. He had had enough challenges in Gaul now. A peaceful transition from tribal land to Roman province seemed a glorious prospect to him. His own family name was known enough in the city and the senate even before

Caesar's repeated references to him in those commentaries that had continued to make him the darling of the Roman people.

Rome.

He found himself considering the destination of the convoy.

The Serviliae Cascae. Long had they been allies of the Julii, and the current crop – the brothers Gaius and Publius – seemed to be holding to the same values. But while the Servilii had old patrician roots, the Casca branch was a dulled bronze to the ancient gold of the line, their crowning achievements being tribunes of the plebs and the occasional aedile. No real power or influence. Of course, there was all that gossip years back in Rome - rumour of Servilia Caepionis, a distant cousin of the Cascae, having been one of Caesar's mistresses, and even that Junius Brutus might be Caesar's secret son. Such things were said quietly, only by the careless, and even then far from the ears of Caesar's people. There were clearly connections there.

But regardless, the Serviliae Cascae were neither influential nor rich when compared to many of Caesar's clients. The fact that he might entrust a king's ransom to them was interesting.

As Caesar continued to ramble to his men on the subject of the suppression of tribes, Varus began to think ahead of what he might require for the coming journey.

The west beckoned.

* * * * *

Noviodunum was not the thriving military hub Varus had expected to find. For the base of two legions and associated support, it languished quiet and still. The Eighth and Ninth legions were still pouring across the plains behind them, the terrain here south of the Liger River flat and uninteresting. The seemingly endless fields lay dormant through lack of attention, full of unharvested crops from the previous year, rotting down into the earth.

The war had ruined this region of Gaul.

Noviodunum had been an oppidum. The army had fought a determined enemy here. Now that enemy was gone. Long gone. The oppidum lay devoid of Gauls, occupied instead by two legions, who had reused the ramparts and what buildings they found a use for. The few locals who remained now lived in makeshift hovels outside the walls, eking out a sad living by meeting the needs of the occupying force.

But even from here it was amply evident that said force was not currently in occupation.

'What do you make of that?' asked Fabius, astride his dappled grey as the two commanders sat ahead of the approaching army, peering at the ramparts beyond the stream.

'Empty. More or less. Certainly Caninius and his legions are not in residence.'

'And yet Caesar's last report places him here.'

Varus shrugged. 'Situations change and it takes time for missives to cross country. I wouldn't even be surprised if we crossed the path of a courier somewhere on the journey without realising it. What worries me is why two legions should have moved out of their base at once. Must be something fairly major, or the man would have sent a vexillation. A cohort or two would be sufficient for anything short of a war.'

Fabius looked less than convinced. 'Sometimes a legion or two is required to make Rome's point.'

'If that's happened, then we're probably looking at another fight anyway. I don't relish the possibility of a repeat of what happened with the Bellovaci.'

The legate nodded silently and took a deep breath. 'Do you think it's safe?'

Varus squinted and could just make out the insignia rising from the gate top. Not the bronze boar, wolf or horse standards of the Gauls, but small red squares flapping in the breeze - too far away to make out anything other than basic colour and shape. 'I can still see the standards of the legions above the walls, and the bridge is intact, so it seems unlikely there's been any trouble. Plus there are a few columns of smoke, so someone is there keeping themselves warm.'

Fabius sucked in air through his teeth and turned to the junior tribune at his shoulder, a young man with an acne-ridden face and more experience of books than battles. 'Have the men encamp outside the near ramparts, this side of the stream. Varus and I and my guards are going to investigate. Once the legions are in position, have the senior centurions report to me in Noviodunum.'

As the tribune saluted and rode off inexpertly, the legate's small bodyguard fell into formation and accompanied the two senior officers towards the garrison. The stream that cut off this side of the former oppidum was narrow. Too wide for a horse to jump, but otherwise no real level of protection, for all its depth and steep banks. Caninius' forces had constructed a solid timber bridge in recent weeks and it was wide enough for three riders abreast. Beyond that, the gate of the oppidum sat open, a wall in the Gallic style disappearing off in either direction atop the rampart. Though the leaves of the gate were tied back, two bored-looking legionaries stood to attention at the sight of the approaching column and the officers out front. Fabius reined in at the walls, Varus and the guards with him.

'Do I assume that Gaius Caninius Rebilus is not currently in residence at Noviodunum, soldier?'

Varus looked up at the banners, bearing the marks of both the Fifth and Fifteenth legions and then back down to the soldiers.

'He is not, sir. Might I ask your name and business?' The man looked nervous, addressing such a senior officer with so curt a question, and well he might. Varus had seen some officers react badly to being questioned over anything so basic. Fabius appeared not to be one of them. Such a question was to be expected of anyone seeking entrance to a fortress, regardless of rank.

'Quintus Fabius Maximus, lieutenant of Caesar, commanding the Eighth and Ninth legion, with orders to link up with your own commander. If he is not present, to whom shall I present myself and my officers?'

The legionary flushed slightly despite himself.

'The most senior officer in camp is Centurion Aurelius Memor, *Hastatus Posterior* of the Sixth Cohort, Fourth Century of the Fifth Legion. He will be in the headquarters building, sir, which is to say the big one with the tile roof off the main square. The legions' flags hang out front, sir, so it's easy to find.'

Fabius turned a raised eyebrow to Varus, who shrugged. The rank of the centurion given identified him as one of the lowest ranking centurions in the most junior legion in the army. For the man to be in charge of Noviodunum, the garrison here must be tiny.

'Thank you, soldier. Keep up the good work.' Fabius gestured for his guards to follow and urged on his horse, trotting into the oppidum, bound for the centre. Varus fell in alongside him. Noviodunum was not large - one of the smaller oppida they had encountered, in fact, but it was well-appointed. Its houses were of good quality and its gardens well-tended. The streets were rough as usual, but the occupying garrison had given them a new surface of gravel to combat the mess winter made of such places.

Here and there they spotted signs of garrison life, though with little current activity. Houses stood empty, but with horse tethering posts outside recently installed by the Roman occupants. Some houses had portable grain querns by the doorstep where the legionaries had ground their flour for bread. Signs of occupation, if not life.

The first soldiers they saw were two streets in from the gate. Two men were busy with a large barrow load of limestone chippings filling pits in the road. The two men were so surprised to see officers that it took them a moment to drop their tools and straighten into a salute, clouds of white dust blooming up around them.

Varus and the others returned the salute and rode on into the heart of Noviodunum.

The 'headquarters building' was notable for three reasons. It bore the flags of the legions. It was the largest and best-appointed structure on the square. And most obvious of all, it was actually occupied.

A legionary by the building's door snapped to startled attention at the sight of the approaching officers. It seemed that even with such an empty base and no immediate threats, the centurion had maintained a guard not only at the oppidum gate, but also on the headquarters. Such a man would likely also have a guard on the granaries and the stores. Despite the man's mediocre rank, it boded well to see such attention to duty. Fabius turned to his men.

'Stay here in the square. You can dismount and relax. We may be some time.'

He gestured to Varus and the two men approached the door.

'Quintus Fabius Maximus and Quintus Atius Varus to see your commander.'

The legionary saluted. 'If you'll follow me, sirs.'

Varus and Fabius exchanged a glance again. That the man had to leave his post to show them in confirmed the small size of the garrison. The two officers strode in through the door. All in the headquarters was in good order, though only one room they passed was occupied, a clerk busy working through piles of tablets, who didn't even look up at the noise of footsteps passing. Centurion Aurelius Memor was a thin, wiry man with skin like teak and a scar from ear to nose that gave his mouth a permanent and unfortunate sneer. He rose hurriedly at the arrival of his visitors and saluted.

'Centurion. Good. I hope you have a few moments for us?'

The officer's surprise was quickly replaced by a professional solemness and he gestured to the seat opposite. 'Please, sir. Take a seat. I shall just fetch another and some refreshment.'

Again the two new arrivals glanced at one another. How short-staffed were they that the garrison commander could not even afford a man to attend him?

Varus gestured at the seat and with a smile of relief Fabius sank into it, rubbing his hips, sore from the long ride. After a few moments, Memor returned with a second chair and placed it beside the first. As Varus thanked him and took his seat, the centurion hurried out and was gone again for a while before returning with a tray, upon which sat a platter of fruit, jars of wine and water and two cups. He placed the tray before the officers and returned to his side of the desk.

'You must excuse all the bustle, sirs.'

'You are truly a man for all roles, centurion. Tell me: how many men are here under your command?'

Memor sighed meaningfully, and then looked embarrassed, remembering the rank of those he was addressing. 'A single undermanned century, sir. We have sixty two on parchment, sir, but only twenty four active soldiers.'

'So few?' Varus murmured.

'Yessir. There's been an outbreak of the flux.' He hurriedly waved his hands before him in a calming gesture, despite the fact that neither of his visitors had reacted. 'It's under control though, sirs. No danger, but most of my men are still too weak to deal with active duty. We only lost three, so I thank Mars and Minerva daily for that.'

'I can imagine. You seem to be doing an excellent job of maintaining the garrison despite your situation, centurion. I will commend you to your commander when I see him and advocate your advancement to a more significant position. And speaking of Caninius...'

The centurion nodded. 'I understand, sir, and thank you. Legate Caninius has both legions with him at Limonum. We were only left here to act as couriers for messages and overseers for supplies.'

'Limonum?' Fabius frowned and glanced across to Varus. The name was familiar to him, but he couldn't quite place it.

'It's the chief oppidum of the Pictones, sir. They're a pretty civilised bunch, and Limonum's about a hundred miles or so south-west from here.'

216

'If they're so civilised,' Varus asked with interest, 'why did Caninius have to take two legions there?'

'He's gone to help their prince, sir, a fellow called Duracius. He apparently voted against their part in Alesia last year and holds to his allegiance. He's holed up in Limonum under siege from the nastier elements of his own tribe and from the Andes from across the Liger River. Soon as he heard, Legate Caninius mobilized the legions. Said we had to look after our allies.'

'Very much so,' Fabius agreed. 'Good man. So he took the legions against these Andes, then. When was this?'

'About two weeks ago, sir. If I'm honest, I'd have normally expected them back a while ago now, sir. About a week ago we had word that the legate had camped close to the siege, but there were more of the bugge... the enemy were considerably more numerous than the legate had expected. I've been starting to get quite jumpy over the whole thing, but even with the best will in the world, I can't spare a man to ride for Limonum for news. We just have to sit tight and hope that the commander is alright.'

Varus looked across at Fabius. 'It's still early.'

The legate thought for a moment, then inclined his head. 'Agreed. Thank you for your briefing, Centurion. As I said, I shall be sure to bring your name to the attention of Caninius when I see him, which will be soon. I cannot imagine that he is in difficulties, or a messenger would have carried word of it. Still, all things being equal, given this news it would be remiss of us to delay in joining him. My legions are settling in to make camp, but we shall change that immediately. There are still three or four hours of good daylight, and we can be well on the way to Limonum by dark. Do you have a map of the region?'

Memor nodded and fished around in his documents for a moment before producing a scroll and passing it over. Varus took it, unrolled it for a moment until he located both Noviodunum and Limonum, and then showed it to Fabius, who nodded.

'Thank you, Memor. We will move immediately, and I promise you that I will send word once we have arrived at the place and every other day thereafter. I shall also leave you a few contubernia of my men to make up your numbers and ease your burden.'

The centurion looked greatly relieved and smiled as he stood. 'Thank you, sir.'

Varus reached out and clasped his hand. 'I shall also leave three of my riders. It might be useful for you to have men who can act as couriers and messengers.'

'Again, thank you, sir.'

Returning Memor's salute, the two men strode from the building and as they emerged into the pale light, Varus looked across at his fellow officer. 'Are you as confident about this as you sounded in there?'

Fabius looked a little uncertain, but he smiled. 'It's a rare occasion when a force that size gets itself in so much trouble it can't even send a messenger for help.'

Varus nodded, though his mind toyed with the memory of what had happened to Sabinus and Cotta and an entire legion up in Eburones lands a few years ago. Rare, yes, but not unknown.

'I think, regardless, we'd better move as fast as we can.'

Fabius hauled himself up into his saddle and gestured across to his guards to mount up. 'Agreed. To Limonum, then, at best speed we can manage.'

* * * * *

Varus reined in alongside Fabius once more. The scouts had been entirely accurate with their description. The land hereabouts was so uniformly flat and sporadically forested that it was difficult to find a vantage point with a view of their objective, but the scouts had found a low hill with an unobstructed view of Limonum and the armies.

The oppidum sat within a wide bend in the river, the far side protected by a ditch and a high rampart, the nearer river-wound side by little more than a ten foot wall of the usual Gallic style. Despite the defences being considerably meaner than some of those fortifications the Romans had encountered and overcome in their time in Gaul, it was still something of a difficult proposition. The far side was strong, and the weak side was protected by the river, reachable feasibly only by a native timber bridge.

The Andes and their allies had encamped in a mass at the near end of the bridge, facing the oppidum. Varus felt relieved to see, just as the scouts had described, Caninius' two-legion force camped only a quarter of a mile from the enemy in a well-constructed turf and timber fort.

'Why has he not engaged them?' Fabius muttered from beside him.

'Numbers, the centurion said. Superior enemy numbers.'

'They look fairly evenly matched to me,' the legate replied. 'And that always means an advantage to Rome.'

Varus nodded. The two forces did indeed look more or less equal, but he squinted into the distance suspiciously. 'Look there.'

'What?'

'Beyond the oppidum.'

Fabius followed his pointing finger and took a moment to see it. A second enemy force roughly the same size as the first was encamped along the treeline on the far side of Limonum, sealing off the settlement from the west, too. Odds of two to one, then, after all. Perhaps Caninius had been right to err towards caution. Caesar would not thank him for losing two legions at this stage in proceedings.

'What to do, then? We could head around to the south in a wide arc, cross the river there and come up on the second enemy force, evening things out?'

Varus tapped his lip thoughtfully.

'The enemy will have scouts out, expecting something. I doubt we would take them by surprise and, gathered at the treeline, we'd never get to meet them in open ground. You know how hampered we are by woodlands. If they retreat into there, my horse are useless and your men lose all the advantage of formation. We'd be better joining up with Caninius and outnumbering the nearer force. At least we could halve their numbers.'

'Sir?'

Varus turned at the scout's voice. There were few riders on this low hillock. Fabius' legions were still a good ten miles away, crossing the flat land and heading for the siege, and the two officers had ridden out ahead two hours ago with the scouts and a small cavalry detachment to confirm the outriders' findings. The scouts were now ranging around the locality, and two were trotting towards them now. Varus gestured to them and the riders slowed and pulled up, saluting.

'Who are you?' Varus frowned, not recognising the colours or insignia of one of riders as belonging to his own force, though the other scout was known to him.

'Tonantius. *Exploratores* unit of the Fifteenth Legion, sir.'

219

Varus' brow rose in surprise. One of Caninius' scouts.

'Well met, man. Tell me: why has your garrison back in Noviodunum heard nothing from your army if you are simply encamped here?'

It was a blunt question, but Varus had been dying to know since he'd encountered the poor understaffed centurion back at the base. The scout's face took on a resigned, yet somehow angry, look.

'Three times couriers have been sent, sir, but none have returned. We have assumed they did not reach the oppidum. After the third, the legate decided to stop wasting good men.'

'Sensible,' murmured Fabius. 'What happened to them then?'

The man of the Fifteenth shrugged. 'The enemy have many scouts like ours, and a far greater number of horse. Their men are all across the countryside and they know the terrain much better. Begging your pardon, sir, but our lot can't even take a shit without the enemy knowing what it weighs half an hour later.'

Varus nodded. Rome placed a great emphasis on the heavy infantry tactics of the legions and often failed to recognise the advantages that proper cavalry could bestow. He frowned. So if the enemy knew everything that was going on…

He turned to the scene before them again and peered off into the distance, his gaze raking the countryside.

'Do you think they're watching us right now?'

The scout nodded. 'I'd wager news of your arrival is already making its way back to the enemy, sir.'

Varus smiled wickedly. 'And what are the chances they know of the two legions following on perhaps ten miles behind us?'

'Very good, I'd say, sir. Certainly they'll know before they're another five miles closer, even if they don't now. And they will have taken note of two new senior officers coming in from the east wearing red cloaks and plumes. That can only mean a relief force. Any local would recognise that.'

'What are you digging at, Varus?' Fabius coughed.

Varus' grin widened and he folded his arms, still addressing the scout. 'And if they hear that two more legions are coming and that Rome's forces will match or exceed theirs?'

'They'll run, sir. No doubt about that.'

'Back to their own lands across the Liger.'

Fabius was shaking his head. 'No, Varus. That's no good. If they run before we can get here, they'll just melt away into their own lands and we'll not get to deal with them. If that happens we'll never be able to leave here, else they'll just come back and do it again. We need to deal with them now and prevent a repeat of this mess.'

Varus was chuckling now.

'You leave that to me. I have an idea.'

* * * * *

Caninius stood on the gate of his camp's ramparts and watched the enemy.

'It never ceases to amaze me how they can hear things before us, given that they're further away.'

Cophus, chief centurion of the Fifth, nodded his agreement as he peered at the scene before them. They had received news from the scouts of Fabius' legions only a quarter of an hour ago, and already the enemy force was decamping on both sides of Limonum, moving off to the north at surprising pace.

'Give the word, sir, and I'll get the lads moving.'

The two men stood silent for a moment. The legions, even at a fast pace, would not match the fleeing Gauls in their lightweight gear, unencumbered and with their feet given wings of fear. But at least they would catch the rear-most of the enemy. They could harry them all the way back to the Liger and maybe even catch a reasonable number of them before they crossed the river and vanished.

'Consider the word given, centurion. Have the Fifth strip down to the essentials and give chase at speed. Try to maintain unit cohesion, though. I'd hate to have the enemy suddenly turn and form up and our boys to be all over the place in chaos. Give chase in good order and kill or capture as many as you can.'

Cophus saluted and turned to give the orders to the signifer beside him. Caninius looked the other way along the wall top. The Fifteenth's primus pilus was elsewhere, busy with his duties, but in case of sudden changes in plan their chief cornicen stood near the commander, his curved horn over his shoulder. He gestured to the musician.

'Have the Fifteenth form up outside the south gate. Once the Fifth have moved off to harry the enemy, have the Fifteenth in full kit sweep around to the west. The enemy have two baggage trains – one for each force – and they will meet at the crossing three miles downstream. While the Fifth are killing the Andes, the task of the Fifteenth will be to seize the enemy's baggage and supplies and bring them back here.'

The cornicen saluted and began to blare out the assembly calls for his legion.

Caninius peered at the enemy, swarming like a kicked-over ant hill, back to their hovels in the north. Most would escape, but at least he could capture the baggage and punish them a little as they ran. Shame the news of Fabius' legions had come so quickly, otherwise they could have won a great battle here. Instead, the Eighth and Ninth would get here too late.

* * * * *

The tribune fussed along behind Caninius, urging him to return to the camp, repeatedly overusing words like 'duty', 'command', 'safety' and 'caution'. Ignoring the man, he felt nothing but gratitude for the wind on his face after three weeks of languishing in camp and watching the enemy starve his ally in the oppidum. He was a good officer but he knew he was no swordsman, and the tribune who hurtled along behind him was correct, in truth, but it felt good to be taking the fight to the enemy anyway.

Night had fallen on the ride, and danger was everywhere, but Caninius felt secure, regardless. His bodyguard were with him as well as the two turmae of horse he'd had attached to his legions. Over seventy men, all told, and the enemy were far ahead.

The Fifteenth had returned to camp with the enemy baggage after an hour-long contest at the crossing, bringing perhaps two hundred captives with them. The Fifth had chased on after the enemy and disappeared to the north. The legion had been gone for an hour when it occurred to Caninius that he had set no limit on their chase, and in the excitement he had not taken into account how far the Liger was from Limonum. Forty miles, the tribune had estimated. As the afternoon wore on, he had considered sending a small courier detachment to halt the legion and have them return to base. But the fact was that he had to kill or capture as many as possible in order to try and prevent the Andes from being able to repeat their belligerent act as soon as Rome's forces moved on, and so he had sent no word, allowing Cophus to pursue the enemy as per instructions, all the way to the Liger.

222

He hoped he hadn't been foolish. All it would take would be for the enemy to realise that they outnumbered the Fifth by such a margin and to pull out of their panicked flight and form up, and half of Caninius' command might be wiped out. His career would never recover from that.

As the sun had begun to descend towards the horizon, he'd finally broken, unable to take another hour twitching at the rampart as he stared into the unchanging north. Giving the Fifteenth orders to leave a cohort with the baggage and the camp and to follow on even through the night as fast as they could, Caninius had gathered his meagre horse and rode out into the dusk in the hope of catching up with the Fifth.

Forty miles.

A loaded army with baggage train would take four days to reach the Liger at best. *Without* baggage, and still in full kit, a good veteran unit in full health could do it in two at a push. Cophus, watching his men move out in simple mail shirts and with swords at their sides and shields slung over their backs, had confidently informed him that by midnight his men would be paddling in the Liger, celebrating their victory.

All along the route from Limonum to the river, they had passed signs of the pursuit. It had been a running battle – quite literally much of the time. Enemy bodies, and a few Roman ones, dotted the ravaged and well-trodden landscape on their journey north, and more than once Caninius had been forced to jump his horse over a hitherto-unnoticed pile of bodies, difficult to discern in the gloom.

And now darkness was here, though in truth with the clear sky and the bright moon, full darkness was actually considerably brighter than dusk had been, and it certainly made riding horses easier.

'Look there, sir,' called a decurion in front, pointing, and Caninius strained to see ahead. The riders were cresting a hill, hemmed in by a copse and a small farm on their left and a cave-ridden chalky rock escarpment to their right. Ahead, the most magnificent sight awaited as he passed across the rise.

The Liger River, here one of the widest and most impressive in Gaul, wound like a silver serpent, gleaming in the moonlight, from left to right. Some five hundred paces wide, it was here and there interrupted by sand banks, and yet it was still a breath-taking sight in the silvery glow. And directly ahead stood the objective of the fleeing Andes. Over the preceding years, having campaigned in the

223

area more than once, the legions had constructed a bridge here to replace what had been a native ferry service, the position such a strategic one, just downstream of the confluence of the Liger and Vinana rivers. It was a strong bridge, built to last. It had been useful at times for the movement of troops and goods, though now it was clear that it had also facilitated an invasion of Pictone lands by their neighbours across the river.

But it was not the silver ribbon of the Liger that drew his breath from him, nor was it the powerful bridge stretched like a blackened arm, reaching across that wide watercourse. What made him rein in sharply was the battle, or rather the lack of it.

The enemy had reached the Liger clearly not long before Caninius and his horse had arrived on the scene, and they had begun to cross, their rear ranks forming up as best they could to hold off the pursuing Romans. As hundreds of Andean warriors fled across the timbers of the bridge, their compatriots bravely held their rear, and did it well. Their sheer numbers and the prevalence of spears meant that they had formed something of a phalanx against the legionaries of the Fifth, who were keeping their distance, unwilling to close.

And well they might not. Cophus had done well forming his men facing the enemy, but only an idiot would have ordered the Fifth to charge that wall of shields and spears. Both sides were exhausted from the flight to the river, but the Romans were armed only with swords and lacked the pila they needed to try and break the shield wall. Indeed, they would be slowly recovering from their run as they watched in irritation their enemy flee to safety. There were simply too many Gauls and they were too well equipped to contemplate launching an attack, and so the Fifth watched them leave.

Caninius hammered his fist on his saddle horn in irritation.

The sons of whores were going to escape.

His gaze rose from the fight to the forests on the far side, in the Andes' own territory. Once the enemy were in among those trees all hope of stopping them was gone. As his sight dropped again to the conflict, he frowned. His eyes had caught some kind of movement, which seemed odd, given the darkness and the depth of the woods across the river.

He peered up intently again.

And then he saw them.

Cavalry pouring along the north bank of the Liger. Roman cavalry, seemingly, and an awful lot of them. Many alae of auxiliary horse and even some regulars, as attested by the standards visible in the bright moonlight, recognisable as Roman despite the distance. How had Roman cavalry appeared on the northern bank?

It mattered not who they were or how they came to be there. The fact was that they were there and that changed matters.

Not for the better, though.

Curse that mysterious cavalry.

The fleeing Andes reaching the far side of the bridge were scattering into smaller groups and vanishing into the forest that lurked above the river bank, but as the Roman cavalry arrived and began to seal off the northern end of the bridge, the whole thing began to choke up. Vicious fighting broke out between the fleeing natives and the horsemen at that far end, and things remained at a tense stand-off at the southern end, but that wouldn't last for long.

While Caninius had no desire to see the enemy get away into the trees, he had only intended to harry them and pick off the rear ranks as they fled, for the enemy still outnumbered him by at least three to one, and were better equipped for the fight. And now that enemy had had their escape route sealed and were left with no choice but to fight. The Fifteenth were coming along behind but it would be many hours yet before they arrived, and there was little doubt in Caninius' mind: unless he ordered a general retreat, the Fifth would be obliterated long before the other legion reached them.

And, of course, if he *did* order the retreat, that mysterious wing of cavalry would be butchered in due course. The idiot horse commander had doomed either himself or the Fifth, or potentially both of them.

'Come on.'

'Sir?' The tribune who had been fussing throughout the journey looked astonished.

'A Roman general doesn't run from a defeat. He falls on his sword in disgrace. If I'm going to lose a legion here, I'm going with them. I'd rather decorate a Gaul's spear tip than face the general and explain this to him. Let's get down there and join the action.'

The tribune was shaking his head. 'Sir, that's insane.'

'Just draw your sword and fall in with the rest, Plautius.'

Resigned to the unpleasant fate that awaited, Caninius formed up his seventy or so horse and gave the order. The slope was long but gentle, the chalk escarpment peeling off to the right and the copse left behind as they descended to the field of battle. Even as the riders moved up to a canter, the fighting ahead had started. The Gauls, now desperate, knowing they were trapped, began to throw spears and loose arrows into the tired Fifth, who sheltered painfully behind their shields, taking whatever punishment the Gauls cared to throw at them.

Gallic carnyxes were sounding their calls now, noises like cattle with terminal flatulence echoing out across the river and the near bank. They were joined by cavalry horn calls from the far side and the blaring cornua of the Fifth, sounding the command to surge forward into hopeless battle. The noise was, frankly, astonishing. It had to be hard for the bulk of the soldiery to pick out their individual calls between the hundred different instruments going and the general noise of battle.

A thousand paces to go. The slope was gradually flattening out as they descended towards the action. What use seventy cavalry might be in the coming nightmare was beyond Caninius, but he was determined that if the Fifth were to go out, they would ruin the Andes forever in the process. All they had to do was kill three men each. With less reach to their weapons. After having travelled near forty miles in twelve hours – about the maximum pace a commander had ever put his men through. With no hope of victory...

He cast up a quick prayer to Mars, his patron god, for his aid in the coming clash.

The musicians of the three forces were truly ruling the air over this battlefield in a war of their own.

His ear picked something up and registered it for long moments before it began to nudge his brain and draw attention to what it had heard. Then ear spoke to eye, and Caninius dragged his attention from the fight across the field and to the east.

He stared in bafflement.

More horns had joined in the cacophony, and there, glittering in the silvery moonlight, trod the ranks of Rome, moving at a standard march and crossing the grass like an inexorable tide, bearing down on the left flank of the enemy.

Eagles glinted in the silver sheen, backed by dark flags that would be red in daytime, but appeared dark grey by the light of the moon. Gleaming standards led what appeared to be two legions in all their glory. Fabius! Somehow he'd not marched on Limonum, but had known to come to the Liger crossing instead. Was the man omniscient?

Even as he boggled, Caninius' mind performed a simple, happy calculation. The numbers were now more or less even and the enemy was trapped. Moreover, the way the new legions were moving, they were reasonably well rested. The tables had just turned on the Andes in the most astounding way. Where a moment earlier the legate had foreseen only brutal death or an ignominious visit to Caesar, suddenly he now saw the end of the Andes and their blasted incursion. Rome would be victorious.

He whooped.

The new arrivals on the field had been seen now. The Andes broke into a panic, many trying to push past their friends onto the crowded bridge, others being hurled or knocked from the bridge to splash into the dark waters where the ones in mail shirts sank without trace and the clothed or naked ones began to swim desperately downstream away from the clash. The unlucky ones hit a mudbank and broke apart before sinking slowly into the sucking murk.

The defensive line facing the Fifth collapsed, and the centurions took advantage of the change to make their move, the legion piling into the enemy and hacking, stabbing and slaying everywhere they could despite their exhaustion. Only the enemy's right flank was open, and even there only a short stretch of it, close to the river bank. Andean warriors were fleeing across the grass or into the comparative safety of the water.

The cavalry on the hill around Caninius were cheering now, all having drawn themselves to a halt around their commander.

'Thank you Mars. Thank you Fabius,' grinned Caninius, and then turned to his small cavalry force. 'Come on, boys. Let's get stuck in and help the tired Fifth.'

Behind him, the tribune was shaking his head again in disbelief. 'They're beaten sir. You don't have to do this now.'

Caninius laughed, and couldn't help but notice a faint edge of hysteria in his own voice. 'You're absolutely right, Plautius, I no longer have to do this. Now I *want* to do it. Come on.'

The tribune stared in horror as his legate drummed his heels into his horse's flanks, urging the beast on into a run towards the chaos below, where the Andes were now in disarray, some fighting a desperate last stand while others threw down their weapons in an attempt to surrender, and yet more waded out into the dangerous waters of the river in the hope of achieving freedom.

The battle had only just begun, but it was already over.

227

* * * * *

Varus wiped the blood and sweat from his brow and sagged in his saddle. 'The timing was lucky. It could have gone horribly wrong, but it was the only way I could think of to defeat the Andes without them fleeing back into their woodlands and vanishing – and that's something interesting. How familiar are you with tribal standards?'

Caninius and Fabius exchanged a blank look and shrugged. Varus rubbed his sore neck and gestured to the far side of the river, where precious few of the enemy had managed to make it into the woods and flee. 'There were a lot of different signs on display down there, but among the boar standards that are symbolic of so many tribes, the few 'twin horses' of the rebel Pictones and the wolves of the Andes, there were quite a few spread-winged eagles.'

'*Roman*?'

'Not quite,' Varus leaned back in his saddle. 'The eagle is also a tribal symbol of the Carnutes.'

'Surely for the love of Jove the Carnutes wouldn't dare raise a sword against Rome again? Not so soon after Caesar stood on their necks this winter?'

'It would certainly appear imprudent,' Varus sighed, 'but I spent plenty of time riding among the Carnute lands in the winter, and I know their standards. There were Carnutes in that army, which helps explain why it was so large. The Andes are a smaller tribe, and the rebel Pictones were few. Being bolstered by the Carnutes would give them both the numbers and the confidence to take on a Roman force. I also note with some interest that no Carnute standards can be found with those taken in the fight. Somehow the Carnute elements managed to melt away. It's possible there are still Carnutes among the prisoners, but they will be all-but impossible to identify.'

'We're going to have to deal with them then.'

The cavalry commander nodded wearily. 'They seem to be a tribe that simply do not learn from their mistakes. They'll need to have this one explained to them rather forcefully.'

'Should we contact Caesar?'

Varus glanced at Fabius with a frown. 'No. You're the senior commander in the field here. Labienus prosecutes wars in the general's name and only apprises Caesar of the situation when he's already won them. It is *your* decision.'

Fabius nodded unhappily, clearly uncertain about making command decisions on that level. 'Then we'll have to send at least a legion into Carnute lands to chastise them.'

Caninius, gore- and mud-spattered, turned to Varus, a weary smile on his face. He looked tired, but then every last man on the field looked exhausted. 'The next question is what to do with the captives. Take hostages of the powerful, ransom others, and take a slave tithe before sending them back to be resettled, I suppose,' he murmured. 'Though sending them back is asking for another rising, especially if they think they can count on the Carnutes for aid.'

Varus looked across at Fabius meaningfully and the legate nodded in return.

'I think we can safely anticipate Caesar here, Caninius. There's been something of a shift in standard policy. Send the weak, the old, the children and the women back to their homes. Anyone who's strong enough to wield a spear should be roped together and sent to Massilia, along with a half share of all spoils. The rest can go to the men.'

Caninius whistled through his teeth. 'You think that's Caesar decision.'

'Trust me.'

'Well it'll prevent future unrest, I suppose. You'll do the same with the Carnutes?'

'I will. Leaving them broke, undermanned and unarmed seems to be the only way to keep them down,' Fabius grumbled. 'For now, let's get things wrapped up here and get to camp. There are plenty of tribunes who sat at the back during the fight who can deal with the clean-up. Those of us who drew a sword and rode with Mars need some sleep. Then after we've had some time to recover we can arrange a march into Carnute lands. How far is your camp from here?'

Caninius gave a humourless laugh. 'Near forty miles. I'd suggest we made camp here, but the whole thing was so much of a rush all our gear is back at Limonum.'

'My horse and I can manage forty miles if there's a bed and a cup of something soothing at the end of it,' Varus murmured. 'Slowly though, the poor beast has had a tiring day.'

Fabius tapped his lip. 'Returning to Limonum would be a waste of time for my men. We've got the essentials with us. We'll make camp here and cross the river in the morning, moving back northeast and dealing with the Carnutes. We can use your old base at Noviodunum as our centre of operations. Your centurion there's a good man and he'll be grateful to see us.'

'I suppose with the fight knocked out of the Andes there's no need for such a large force here,' Caninius replied, and all three men fell silent, watching the legions below herding groups of prisoners to be roped and gathering the dead for burial. The sound of thundering hooves drew their attention, since everything else on the field of battle was now moving at an exhausted pace, very sedate and quiet. The commanders turned to see a small cavalry detachment with scouts ahead riding for their position.

'Who's that?' Fabius asked blandly, almost too tired for curiosity.

Caninius sighed. 'Must be the vanguard for the Fifteenth, who're following on behind. They must be closer than I thought. They must have moved damned fast.'

'They appear to be in a hurry, certainly. They must not know it's over.'

Varus' brow crumpled into a frown to see a senior tribune in among the riders.

'Senior officer riding like Hades has a spear at his back? Odd.'

The three men blinked away their exhaustion, coming alert with the realisation that something else was happening here other than the reserves arriving on the field. As the horsemen reined in, the senior tribune danced his mount out front and saluted his commander and the other officers.

'Tribune. You seem to be in something of a hurry? The legion sprinting is it?'

The man shook his head, rolling aching shoulders. 'We're not with the infantry, sir. I passed the Fifteenth around twenty five miles back. I came from the camp with important news from our friend in Limonum, sir.'

'Spit it out then, man,' Caninius said wearily, yet with a sense of foreboding.

'It seems there is an army on the move towards the Narbonensis province, led by a rogue Senone leader named Drapes.'

'Gods, first the Carnutes and now the Senones,' Fabius grunted. 'A gold coin to the man who can name me a tribe that's not busy rising against us. Don't they realise they're beaten. Who is this Drapes, then?'

'I know the name,' said Varus, drumming his fingers on his saddle horn. 'He was one of those they say was at Alesia with the relief forces. I'm starting to wish we'd pushed to stop them fleeing that hill, despite the state we were in. Every noble who got away had a small army with him and they all seem to be causing trouble now.'

'That's only half the problem, sir. The Cadurci's leader is reputedly leading a second army to link up with him on the way.'

'Luterius, yes?'

'Lucterius, I believe, sir. He's another that was with the relief at Alesia. I couldn't get any solid estimates of numbers, but the Limonum prince seems to think that the two armies together will be strong enough to do serious damage to Narbonensis. Certainly since Lucius Caesar returned to Rome and the legions were reassigned, the Narbo garrison alone will not be strong enough to stop them.'

Varus nodded his agreement and heaved in cold breaths of night air. 'There's a legion on the way to protect that border, but it's travelling slow with a convoy via Massilia and won't arrive until long after any native army reaches the place. What can the tribes hope to achieve with such an act? They must know we'll punish them for it.'

'Could be a revenge attack?' Caninius mused.

Fabius rubbed his hands together. 'You've seen what's happening: the whole land is still rippling with dissent. There are minor rebellions all over the place – more or less every tribe – but we're not in any great danger as a whole, since they're all so disorganised and separate. You know how bloody-minded these Gauls can be. They're beaten and everyone knows it, but they're fighting to the last drop of blood and if they can get some sort of symbol to rally round, we'll be dealing with risings all summer and into the winter. Imagine the morale boost that would wash through the more rebellious hearts if they hear that Narbo and the Roman south has fallen to them. They will call it 'reclaiming their ancestral lands'. Can you picture it?'

In the silence that followed, each of them did so, unhappy with what they were seeing.

'There's another danger,' Varus said quietly. 'Caesar will return to Rome next year for his consulship and the governance of this place will be granted to whoever the senate favours. Imagine what'll happen if a *bad* governor gets the place, or just an ineffective one. Caesar's army will have gone with him and it'd take time for a new commander to raise legions. If the tribes can just keep their spirit of rebellion burning until Caesar's left, there's a faint chance that the general's successor will lose everything we've achieved these past seven years. We can't let these two tribes ravage Narbo and raise new sparks all over the place.'

'South, then,' Varus sighed. 'With little or no rest.'

Fabius and Caninius nodded and the latter turned to the newly-arrived tribune.

'Time to turn round and ride back. Have the Fifteenth stop their advance and return to camp. They can get everything ready to march south, and press the Pictone prince we just saved for additional cavalry. Wait at Limonum for the Fifth and after a short break we'll head on to deal with this southern army.'

The officer saluted and turned his horse.

'And Tribune, see if you can find out anything else about this army, in particular their last known location. We don't want to have to search everywhere between here and Narbo for them.'

'Gods, but I could do with a snooze,' Caninius sighed as he turned to Fabius. 'I take it just the Fifth and Fifteenth will be heading south then? You're bound still for the Carnutes?'

The legate nodded. 'Can't turn south and leave the Carnutes at our back. You know what'll happen. I'll deal with them, settle the Pictones and Andes, and then follow on.' He turned to Varus. 'Caninius will need you more than I.'

'Very well. Two legions and a wing of cavalry. Hopefully it'll be enough to beat Lucterius and Drapes. Good luck with the Carnutes. They're a tricky bunch. They'll be dug in and hidden all over the forests.'

'Good luck in the south,' Fabius countered. 'Don't let them cross the Roman border or we'll all be knee deep in the shit. Best get going.'

The other two nodded their agreement. Roman lands were under threat, and this was no time to dither. 'Get your men mobilized again, Caninius,' Varus breathed. 'We must move immediately.'

* * * * *

'It's another damned Alesia,' Varus snarled, shading his eyes from the morning sunlight and gazing east bitterly.

It was horribly familiar – some two hundred miles southwest of that place of bloody slaughter, and yet a hauntingly recognisable echo of the site of Vercingetorix's last battle. From Varus' viewpoint on the high slope above the river, he could see every element of Alesia reflected in this place.

The river cut through a wide plain so reminiscent of the plain of mud and blood at Alesia. And just like that other place, two small rivers crept east, reaching out like arms around a high oppidum like an upturned boat, topped with a walled settlement and further protected by chalky cliffs that defied scaling for much of its perimeter. Just like Alesia, the scouts said that the eastern end was more of a gentle slope, but that side had been much more heavily fortified in times past. Nowhere was a simple proposition. Any attack on this place would be hell.

Caninius looked equally sour at the sight. The two legions had needed a day's rest before they moved on south, and Varus had chafed at every hour in Limonum, fretting at the delay and knowing that each heartbeat they tarried, vengeful Gauls moved a heartbeat nearer to Narbo. But once they'd begun to move, he had to hand it to Caninius, they'd moved fast. The Fifth and Fifteenth had travelled light – *expedite* – taking only the faster wagons and leading them with strong, speedy horses rather than the usual oxen. The army had covered the hundred and forty miles to this place in three days and, while every man in the army now looked fit to drop and the baggage, speedy as it was, lay strung out over the last ten miles with the rest of the day to catch up, their impressive pace had seemingly wrong-footed the enemy, trapping them here.

The information they had received from the Pictone prince had placed the enemy army at the chief oppidum of the Lemovices, where the two armies were to combine. The Roman force had arrived at the place to discover that the combined forces of the Gallic rebels had moved on south the previous day. Helpful locals there had vouchsafed that the enemy was bound for the Cadurci fortress of Uxellodunon and, cresting the rise this morning, it appeared that the intelligence had been correct.

233

For Uxellodunon – and gods, but it *was* another Alesia – showed every sign of full military occupation. The walls, high above the rocky cliffs, were packed with men. Not just sparsely like the poor bastards Varus had seen in the risings early this year, but *packed*. And with them were standards of many shapes. The initial forays by the scouts to ascertain the precise lie of the land had come under missile attack from the walls and the strength of that scuffle showed that the enemy were not only numerous and belligerent, but were also well supplied. A tough proposition.

Varus found himself almost considering a drastic course of action. It would be easier to face the enemy under almost any other circumstance. If the army retreated ten miles or so, perhaps the Gauls would quit this place and move on Narbonensis. Then perhaps the Romans would catch them in open terrain and could make an easier job of it. But this place was only a hundred and fifty miles from Narbo itself, and a mere fifty or sixty from the border and the first peaceful Roman settlement. To let them go now was to place Roman civilians in grave danger. Besides, the enemy seemed to be quite comfortable here, so there was no guarantee they would move on quickly. After all, if they were desperate to press on south they could have done so ahead of the legions, even if only just. He brushed aside the unpleasant thought that the enemy were simply biding their time. Behind him the cavalry and legions were massing, awaiting their orders.

Caninius looked extremely unimpressed. The poor sod had just come from trying to break a siege against superior numbers, via a battle that had almost gone badly for him and now to an oppidum that looked more or less unassailable.

'What else can we do?' the legate sighed. 'Settle in for a siege. The scouts have identified three suitable strong points. I'll split the legions into three groups with six or seven cohorts apiece and you can assign the cavalry to them appropriately. Then at least we can be sure we have them trapped while we consider the next move.'

Varus chewed his lip. 'There are not enough of us to take that place, Caninius, and if they're as well-stocked as they seem, we could be here for anything up to a year. Our next move might be to send to Caesar for reinforcements.'

Caninius curled a lip at the thought of having to ask for aid. *Labienus* had never had to ask for help, and it appeared that Caesar had already sent Fabius to his aid once, assuming he couldn't cope with just two legions. 'No. Not yet. We have them hemmed in. Fabius will come soon. Maybe you could send a group of riders and urge him to move at speed?'

Varus peered at Alesia's echo and nodded. The last thing he wanted to experience was a repeat of that bloodbath. *Gods, let Fabius be quick.*

Chapter Thirteen

MOLACOS of the Cadurci sat astride his horse and peered down at the wide valley, wondering if there was some other route they could have taken. But he knew there wasn't, and no matter how much time Lucterius thought he could buy, Molacos knew that time was running short. His task had already taken far longer than they'd expected, and it would still take some time to get to Rome, extricate the king and return him to his people. Only then, with Vercingetorix at the head of the new rebellion could they even hope to bind all of the tribes together and achieve what they had failed last year.

Since Alesia the surviving nobles of all the tribes had come to the inevitable conclusion that if they had not argued and dallied, and had simply thrown all their strength behind the Arverni king at the beginning, Caesar's head would now be mouldering on a spike and the land would be free. Well when the next rising came, they *would* fight. Even now many were busy causing just enough trouble to keep Caesar's eyes on the north and away from Lucterius and his gathering forces, or the small select band of hunters and killers tasked with returning the king to his place.

Molacos raked his scalp and punched his palm every time he was alone, knowing that his delays in finding anyone who could reveal Vercingetorix's actual location and situation may well already have caused a failure in the plan. By now they had all been expecting he and his killer gods to be making for Uxellodunon with the king in tow, to combine with the growing army. Gaul was underpopulated and starving, and no one was labouring under the impression that this would be as easy as last year. But it was their last chance. If they gathered the army and put the king at its head everyone, young and old, man and woman, would grab a sickle or spear and throw their every ounce of will and strength into the fight.

But if it went wrong or they lost, there would never be another chance. Rome would have won.

It was a desperate thing.

His gaze raked the occupants of the wide Rhodanus valley.

More carts and wagons than he might have thought existed. It was quite unbelievable, really. The convoy stretched out of sight to both left and right, still filing around a distant bend in the valley to the north and gradually rolling out of view to the south, bound for Massilia. And it was well guarded. At least a legion, by his now expert estimate, lined the convoy as it rumbled on, along with cursed Remi and their allies riding along the sides.

He could see a small group of officers on horses sitting still not far from his position, apparently deep in discussion with a scout. It was imperative that Molacos and his men get to Massilia and board their friendly boat as soon as possible. Waiting for that monstrous column to pass would take forever, and they would then be in the port, blocking things up and making life difficult for Molacos and his people.

The twelve of them had first moved to cross the high ground some forty miles west of here, but it had quickly become apparent that since the legion that had guarded the border had been reassigned, the clever man running the Roman provincial garrison had carefully utilised his small number of soldiers in setting up guard posts and fortlets all along the edge of Roman territory. Until they'd reached the Rhodanus, Molacos had found no place where they could possibly have passed towards Massilia unobserved.

And now, moving into Roman lands, they had to rely on stealth and not violence, lest they fail through their own conspicuousness. The only place they could pass the Roman border unnoticed would be the Rhodanus, since the quantity of traffic up and down the wide valley on any single day was vast and multi-national. Twelve folk of the tribes could easily lose themselves in the endless mercantile traffic.

But not today. Damn the Fates and the gods and the shit-eating Romans for making the day he reached the border the same as Caesar's cursed column. The coming day or two would be a hell of difficulties, or yet more impossible delays.

'What now?' asked a hoarse voice made eerie by mask and hood.

He looked back at the speaker, Cernunnos – one of the few of his group to whom he would consider deferring. Each and every one was a killer and a master of the art, though each was driven by their own goals, from Molacos' own devotion to his master Lucterius, through Catubodua of the Lemovices, fighting here to avenge her husband King Sedullos who had died at Alesia, and to Belisama and Belenos, the crazed twins who had seen their father tortured to death for information. But apart from himself, the only one who was here purely with the goal of returning Vercingetorix to his place was Cernunnos, a respected master druid who had once led the Arverni priests, seers and druids in their devotions. He would do nothing were it not for the greater good.

'We have no time to seek another way, even if there was one. It has to be the Rhodanus. If we wait for this convoy we will be a further day behind, plus any extra days they cost us by blocking up the port on their way to Rome. Unless we can get ahead of them some way...'

'We could kill them all,' interjected Mogont, the giant. 'Take the convoy, free the slaves and then stroll into Massilia?'

Molacos turned on the big man. Mogont was generally less belligerent than some of the others though he had his own score to settle, having been gelded by some arsehole Roman officer after killing his horse. But that kind of talk was plainly stupid. Twelve men and women against a legion?

'Don't be an idiot.'

'I didn't mean alone. I meant with them.'

Confused, Molacos followed the giant's pointing finger and blinked in surprise.

On the hills at the far side of the valley a large force was mobilizing, from here looking like swarming insects. 'Who..?'

'They are the Helvii,' Cernunnos said quietly in his strange, ghostly voice.

'There is no possible way you can see a standard from here,' Molacos growled.

'I see many things far beyond the realm of your eyes. They *are* Helvii.'

Molacos opened his mouth to argue, but he had rarely experienced a druid who was wrong when he made such a pronouncement. They had the ears of the gods and on occasion spoke with their tongues. He felt a faint shudder run up his spine.

'But the Helvii are Rome's allies.'

Cernunnos turned to him slowly. 'Enough gold and slaves to buy a place among the gods can turn the most loyal of heads, Taranis. And these are Helvii lands. See how they have chosen a part of the valley where the river limits their movement, there are no settlements to get in the way, the slopes are shallow enough for a cavalry charge and the wagons have been strung out in single file due to the depth of the undergrowth, stretching the Roman army to its limit. There are no more than two thousand Helvii there at most. Maybe as little as a thousand. They could not hope to destroy a legion in the field, but here they can hit the army quick and hard at a weak point and cut the column in two. Note also how they have waited until the Roman commanders are close so they can cause the maximum chaos by killing the leaders first. They may lose, but they have at least a reasonable chance of success if the Helvian leader can maintain enough control throughout the fight.'

Molacos boggled. It was just as Cernunnos said. And if they joined in, they could take the column. Free the slaves! Retrieve the spoils. Fund and man the army…

He shook his head angrily. He was being tempted and distracted just as the Helvii had been. He could not afford to be side-tracked from his task, even for this. Vercingetorix was his goal, and the king was worth ten of these columns when it came to uniting the tribes.

'It is too dangerous. Roman commanders are often clever beyond reason. There is a chance this column will fall to the Helvii, but you and I, Cernunnos, we know that there is more chance they will be broken by some unexpected Roman manoeuvre. We cannot afford to throw in our lot with these traitorous Roman pets.'

'So what *do* we do, then?' hulking Mogont asked.

'We *use* the Helvii. It is not as though we sell out our own, since the Helvii are a Roman tribe now.'

'You don't mean…'

'That is exactly what I mean.' He straightened, turned and gestured for the other eleven to close around him. 'Cloaks and masks off and stowed. We are loyal Allobroges now, serving Rome and living in their province. I will remain masked and cloaked at the back – my face is too recognisable and memorable. Cernunnos can lead and do the talking in my place. No moves against the Romans, and watch your tongues. If you speak their language make sure not to react poorly to anything they say.'

He turned to Cernunnos as, uncertain and unhappy, his men and women began to remove their god-cloaks and ritual masks. 'You know what to do?'

The druid nodded. 'I have plenty of experience in tricking the Romans and feeding them lies. As soon as we crest the hill, everyone make as much noise as you can as though trying to attract their attention. As we descend, stay a little back. Catubodua, you come out front with me and be my wife. The rest of you keep out of the way and look respectful.'

Without waiting for their comments or agreement, recognising the fact that the Helvian force across the river was almost ready to act, he kicked his horse and broke into a run, racing for the crest and the slope down into the valley. Molacos kept himself safely among the crowd behind as they joined him, dashing down the hill and making directly for the officers.

The group began to shout warnings, those who had no grasp of Latin whooping instead. The reaction from the Romans was immediate and Molacos congratulated himself – they were sharp and quick, these officers. The fight *would* have gone badly for the Helvii. Before the dozen riders were even closing on them, the officers were protected by a shieldwall of legionaries in three files with spears out in their standard anti-cavalry move. Archers appeared as if from nowhere, arrows nocked and strings pulled taut, and Remi riders were gathering in groups, just in case. The wagons rolled on behind them.

'Tribune!' shouted Cernunnos as they rode closer. 'Tribune!'

It was a good guess. Legions usually had a legate or even a more senior officer with them, but even a cohort on the move would have a tribune with them, and so there would be at least one among the officers.

Cernunnos and Catubodua slowed, the former holding up his hands in a gesture of peace. One of the Romans gave a gesture and the shieldwall opened enough to let him step his horse forward. The twelve riders reined in, the 'couple' out front only ten paces from the Roman, the rest gathered in a group further back.

'What is your business?' asked the Roman. Molacos took in his youthful good looks, light and agile physique, sharp, clear eyes, but most of all, the red belt knotted across his cuirass, denoting his position as some sort of general.

'Your column is in grave danger, sir. Helvii gather on the far slope in large numbers.'

Molacos watched with fascination as the Roman seemed to study the druid, his gaze digging deep into Cernunnos' eyes. After a few heartbeats he straightened.

'Tribune? Prefect? Halt the column and have the entire legion form up in strength on the eastern side of the convoy. Have the wagons begin to double up, every other one pulling alongside to tighten the line and give us manoeuvring room. Send word to the rear to bring up the reserves on the far side of the valley and have all the

240

missile troops mount the wagons for extra range. Every sixth wagon contains a scorpion bolt thrower, so have them all loaded and manned ready too.'

An older officer looked at him as if he were mad. 'Sir?'

'Do it.'

'The outriders have found nothing, sir. These Gauls could be lying... leading us into a trap.'

The general turned a hard look on him. 'This man is speaking the truth. Follow my orders or by Juno I will find someone to replace you.' As the tribune trotted off, the officer gestured to another rider – a Remi by the look of it.

'Take three men and get a good look at these Helvii. Confirm what looks to be their intention and come straight back.'

As they moved off and the officer gestured for the shieldwall to disperse to their normal assigned place, he nodded to Cernunnos. 'I must thank you for your timely intervention. I have, I confess, been expecting some sort of attack throughout the length of the Rhodanus valley, though I was beginning to feel safe now, in the shadow of Rome.'

'Will you move against them?'

The officer shook his head. 'If they come, we are now ready and we'll fight them off. But I don't think they *will* come. The Helvii have too much to lose. If they think we are ready for them they will call off their attack and disperse. I will give you nine coins to one that you have saved us a fight altogether today.' He smiled. 'Though I fear you will be in danger from reprisals. They may well be watching you speaking to me. Where are you bound?'

'Massilia, sir,' Cernunnos answered easily. 'My wife and I have property there as well as back in Allobroge lands. I have a modest concern in the city trading in wine.'

The officer brightened. 'How marvellous. You may be acquainted with a friend of mine. Fronto, the former legate of the Tenth also trades in wine in Massilia.' The man chuckled and failed in his jollity to notice a moment of dark recognition in the druid's eyes at the name. 'For your safety you will, surely, allow my column to accompany you to the city? My name is Decimus Junius Brutus Albinus, pro-tem commander of the Twelfth Legion.'

Chapter Fourteen

CAVARINOS felt his spirits sink as he looked ahead through the open gate of Alba. Like all the Romanised settlements of the Roman province, this city of the Helvii was something of an odd mix. Still boasting a traditional wall in the form of the old oppida, the interior had obviously been completely redesigned at some stage following the tribe's inclusion within Rome's ever increasing territory. The grid of streets was a standard Roman form Cavarinos had seen before on visits to Narbo and other large 'Gallo-Roman' towns. And the Helvii there were still wearing trousers as they had centuries ago, but more often than not with a Roman style tunic above. There were as many clean-shaven faces as moustached or bearded.

But it was not the oddness of the cultural clash that had plunged his mood into darkness. That was the fault of the commotion. In the main street leading from the gate, perhaps two dozen locals were arguing in a rather urgent, panicked manner. And among their number, at the centre, sat a cart. Though he could not pick out the detail at this distance, the bundle on the cart was wrapped in a red cloak, and that identified it better than anything. As if that was not bad enough, between the occasional moving of the men's' legs, he could see the dark pool that had formed beneath the cart.

Casting a black look at the sky and mentally cursing Toutatis for bringing him such ill luck, Cavarinos rode on into Alba Helviorum. He was surprised at how quiet the town was, despite the commotion in the street. A place like this normally hummed with life, from the ringing of hammer on anvil to the calls of street hawkers and children playing their games underfoot.

This place felt surprisingly empty. As he neared the arguing crowd one of the Helvii looked around and saw him, shaking his friend to stop the argument. A heartbeat later, the small ruckus had fallen quiet and each of them was looking at the approaching rider, silent and expectant. It occurred to Cavarinos that they might well think him one of their own nobles. For all his Arverni heritage, Cavarinos wore his face clean-shaven and had stopped wearing his serpent arm-ring or any other obvious identifying items. Moreover, despite their rising against Rome last year, the Arverni had been trading across the border with their recent enemies for decades, and the cut and material of their clothing owed much to Roman influence. Likely they thought him a Helvian noble.

242

He sighed. 'What happened to him?'

He gestured at the cart with its morbid burden. The local he had asked frowned in confusion. Cavarinos' accent was most certainly not Helvii. 'He has been killed.'

'I gathered that,' said Cavarinos, rolling his eyes. 'He's an officer. Passing through was he?'

The man shook his head. 'Head of an engineering detail that's designing the aqueduct,' he replied quietly. 'What they did to him...' he shuddered.

Cavarinos nodded grimly and walked his horse over to the cart where he leaned across and lifted the corner of the red cloak. Beneath, the pink of the flayed muscles was crusted with dark red, though the body still leaked through the boards of the cart. Cavarinos tried not to breathe in too heavily as the flies emerged in a small cloud from beneath the cover. It had been quite recent. Within a day. Hours, in fact. His enquiring mind could not help but ask *where the skin had gone*.

'Did you see the killers?'

'No,' the man replied and opened his mouth to say something, but his friends shot him a warning glance and he clamped his mouth shut. Cavarinos sucked his lip in suspicious interest.

'Let me guess. He'd been tortured and left in his room. And any soldiers guarding him had been dispatched quickly and efficiently.' The men nodded.

'I'm not going to enquire as to what's going on here. Your secrets are yours. I'll be on my way.'

'But,' the first man said urgently, 'you know something about this?'

'I know who the killers are. If you value your life, don't press this.'

'But what will we do? The authorities will blame us!'

Cavarinos scratched his neck absently. 'I think you'll find the authorities will have more to worry about. This isn't an isolated incident. In fact, it's happened all over. I was hoping to have outrun it by now, but it seems they're ahead of me. Perhaps their arrival in Roman territory will slow them. They will have to be more careful now.'

The man looked at him oddly, and Cavarinos realised he'd spoken out loud what was essentially an internal monologue. 'Burn him and pot the ashes, then deliver him to the authorities and tell them the truth.' With a last glance at the unfortunate Roman, he trotted on through the town, heading for the Rhodanus River, which would lead him most of the way to Massilia.

They were ahead of him. His mind helpfully superimposed Fronto's face on that ruined body on the cart, and he automatically picked up his pace.

* * * * *

Fronto laughed as young Lucius tottered about on the grass, chasing the red and black butterflies that were a common sight around Massilia in the winter. He chuckled out loud as Lucius fell headlong on the grass and let out a strange shout. It was almost words, but not quite. Lucilia would have run across to him, all concern that he had hurt himself, but Fronto was becoming accustomed to Lucius' noises, and that one was frustration. Indeed, the boy was up again in moments, wobbling a little before ploughing on, laughing, after another butterfly that had crossed his path.

Fronto leaned back on the wall, resting his head against the gatepost. It was nice to live in such a climate again. He'd grown up by the sea at Puteoli and had spent most of his career around Rome and Puteoli or over in Hispania, where the heat was similar though considerably drier. But the last seven years up in Gaul had been rather eye-opening. He'd not believed that so much rain was possible. Parts of northern Gaul couldn't have been much wetter if you submerged them.

He closed his eyes and enjoyed the warmth of the sun on his eyelids.

'Civilian life clearly suits you.'

His eyes snapped open at the comment and he had to look around in confusion for a while before he spotted the figure by the tree at the side of the drive. Recognition was instant, but his mind fought him for a while, insistent that he was wrong and this couldn't be who he thought it was.

The Gaul smiled. 'I have to say that I'm relieved. I was half expecting to get here and find you peeled and pinned to a tree.'

Fronto simply stared. Behind him, Lucius let out a squeak of triumph that quickly turned into a howl of frustration, and then slid back into giggling and the thumping of tiny feet on turf.

244

'I'd not thought to see you again,' he said, recovering from his surprise a little.

'I had never really intended to come,' Cavarinos replied, walking his horse towards the gate. 'However, events in the wide world, as usual, drive the course of my life and despite everything I find myself in Roman lands, seeking out Romans in defiance of my own. It never ceases to amaze me the strange twists and turns our lives take.'

Fronto gave him a sour look. 'Shouldn't you be with the Arverni, planning to rise against us? From the news I catch that seems to be the fashion.'

Cavarinos laughed with not a trace of humour. 'There are visionless lunatics all over the land who are trying to push along a dead horse called freedom and make him run. They only drag out the inevitable and bring upon the tribes yet more woe. And that is partially why I'm here. I hadn't realised it until I found a flayed centurion up in Alba Helviorum. Until then I was coming purely out of respect for a former opponent. But somehow I think it's become bigger than that now. What's happening needs to be stopped, not just to save your sorry hide, but for the future good of the tribes.'

Fronto slid from the wall and opened the gate. 'You are speaking in riddles, Cavarinos. Have you been hanging around with druids?'

'It's been a long and very unpleasant journey, and I had to ride down into town to find out where you lived. If you are, as I seem to remember, a wine merchant, it would be appropriate, I think, to offer some of your wares to a tired guest.'

Fronto snorted and closed the gate behind the Arverni noble. He turned to the house. Aurelius was standing by the door. He'd been there for half an hour now, cleaning his nails with the tip of a knife and other such sundry pastimes. Clearly he had recognised Cavarinos as no enemy, if not a friend, but even then he had his hand on the pommel of his gladius as he watched intently. The former members of his singulares had taken their duties very seriously since the attack on Hierocles' building, fearing reprisals, and one of them was never far from his side, armed and ready.

'We're fine, Aurelius. Would you do me a favour and walk Cavarinos' horse round to the stables and leave it in their hands.'

Aurelius came across, nodding a greeting at the Gaul as he took the reins and walked the horse around the side of the house, his eyes never leaving the new arrival. Fronto paused to pick up Lucius who was struggling to pull up a weed in the lawn and then led his friend to the front door.

'This is no social call then?'

Cavarinos rubbed his arms and hands as they entered and smiled sadly. 'I am some way from enjoying a social life yet, Fronto. But it does make me happy to see you well, if clearly tired.'

'Business is more tiring and more complicated than warfare, Cavarinos.'

'Which is one reason why the tribes make poor traders, but have been fighting each other for centuries. We were never a complex people.'

Fronto stopped in the atrium, casting a prayer across to the altar of the household gods as Lucilia came strolling in at the far side of the small pool, carrying young Marcus, asleep in her arms.

'I see you had luck getting Lucius to sleep, then?' she noted archly. 'Honestly, Marcus, you could at least *try*. He'll be awake all afternoon now, and he'll play merry Hades with us tonight.' She noted for the first time the figure behind him and smiled warmly. 'Are you going to introduce me to your friend?'

Fronto lowered Lucius to the floor and steered him away from the shallow impluvium pool before straightening. 'Lucilia, this is Cavarinos, a prince of the Arverni and formerly one of Vercingetorix's most trusted generals.'

Surprise flashed across her face, but recognition soon replaced it. 'Cavarinos? The one to whom you gave your precious Fortuna?' She chuckled as she crossed the room to them. 'You have no idea how miserable he's been without his precious goddess. In the end he spent a small fortune on a replacement.'

Fronto cast her a withering look. 'I was suffering for want of luck. It was basic common sense to replace it.'

Cavarinos smiled and pulled out the figurine hanging at his neck, worn but recognisable. 'I'm not sure how much luck it's brought me.'

'You're still alive, aren't you?' Fronto sniffed. 'A third of the people of Gaul aren't.'

'And this would be your lovely wife, then, Fronto? I don't believe you ever told me her name?'

Fronto snorted again. 'The only times we've ever talked we were enemy leaders in the middle of a war. I didn't tell you my shoe size or my favourite colour either.'

246

Cavarinos gave him an indulgent smile, and Lucilia glared at him before turning a wide smile back on the Gaul. 'Lucilia, daughter of Quintus Lucilius Balbus and wife of a mannerless brute. Pleased to meet you, Prince Cavarinos.'

'I think the title is rather moot now, my lady. But it is a pleasure to meet you.'

'Shall we retire to the triclinium, then?' Fronto asked, but Cavarinos nodded pointedly at Lucilia.

'Somewhere private, then?'

Cavarinos nodded. 'I don't mean to be rude, my lady, but there is a private matter we must discuss first, before I can afford to relax.'

Lucilia acquiesced and bowed, retreating from the atrium in the wake of the slapping footsteps of Lucius. 'Then I shall have cook rustle up something appropriate for, say half an hour?'

Fronto nodded. 'Thank you, dear. We'll be done shortly.'

Gesturing for Cavarinos to follow, he headed towards his tablinum – the small office that he still occasionally used in his villa. As the two entered, he shut the door behind them, noting the fact that Masgava had appeared silently in the atrium, armed and watchful. As the door closed, he nodded at the big Numidian, trying to convey the message that he was fine. Turning, he strode across to one of the two chairs in the room and sank into it, the cushion expelling a puff of dust beneath him.

Cavarinos looked around at the room with interest. The walls were covered with maps showing major trade routes and wine-growing regions, seasonal tide charts and so on. The desk was piled at one side with writing tablets. And five amphorae of different sizes sat by a wall. The floor was a mosaic that showed Bacchus cavorting. 'This looks just like a Roman headquarters. You make me smile Fronto. Even as a merchant you approach your business as if it were war.'

'You have no idea how close the two can be. Right down to the shedding of blood in fact.'

He reached out and picked up a small jug from a low side table and unstoppered it, filling two fine, painted glasses showing birds in flight. 'Ever had Alban wine?'

Cavarinos frowned. 'Possibly. Years ago we did good trade with Roman merchants. I had excellent Roman wines in those days.'

'Not like this.' Fronto added roughly the same amount of water to his wine and slid the jug across to Cavarinos. 'Now, tell me what it is that brings you to Massilia.'

The Arverni noble took a sip of the wine, tasting it before watering it, and then took a small swig, nodding appreciatively. 'That *is* good. Alban? That's from close to Rome, yes?'

'Just south. Maybe fifteen miles along the Via Appia.' He fell silent, expectant.

'You're in danger, Fronto. Or at least, I think you are.'

'I'm always in damn danger. Who from this time?'

Cavarinos rested his elbows on the table. 'What do you know of our gods, and of the leaders of last year's revolt?'

'To the former, a little. I can name a few and tell you what they do, I suppose. And your commanders? Well I saw a lot of them at the surrender, of course.'

'My people are tenacious,' Cavarinos sighed. 'Even long past the horizon of common sense. It will be years before the tribes resign themselves fully to Roman rule. Some will be quicker than others. But there will still be troubles and arguments. For some, last year's war is not yet over. Those with little vision see our catastrophic defeat as a mere setback.'

Fronto shook his head in disbelief. 'You're not suggesting there'll be another revolt, surely?'

'Smaller ones are already happening, Fronto. And they will gradually combine and escalate, bringing everyone who can grip a spear into the fold. The only reason it hasn't happened yet is that it takes something very special to bind the tribes together. We are permanently in a state of war. It is the nature of the tribes. Vercingetorix, with the help of the druids, managed to do the impossible. Even then, with him in command, there were dissenters and naysayers. If they had all joined in with their whole heart, your general would have lost at Alesia.'

'I can picture that,' Fronto said, remembering the large relief army on the second hill.

'But while a second rising would be bad for Rome, it is my inescapable conclusion that it would be very final for the tribes. A repeat of last year, dragging in every last able body, would still not win the war against Rome, and the main result would be that my entire culture, our people and our world would disappear forever. We would become names in your dusty Roman history books.'

'I tend to agree with you there. Your people never want for heart or courage, but common sense can often be lacking. One day I will introduce you to a special case called Atenos.'

Cavarinos chewed on his lip for a moment.

'There is a group of very, very dangerous men and women in your lands right now, wielding a dual purpose, neither of which is good for you.' Noting Fronto's intent, alert silence, he continued with a sad note in his voice. 'One of Vercingetorix's generals who survived among the relief forces, Lucterius of the Cadurci, is busy trying to rebuild the army of united tribes. He had a trusted man who fought at Gergovia and Alesia and who was horribly wounded – disfigured, in fact – at the latter. He is fanatically loyal to his king and the only thing I fear might drive him more than his loyalty is his utter hatred of Rome.'

'And he is in Massilia?'

'He and eleven others, masked and cloaked, have been rampaging around the land, torturing Roman officers to try and locate the great Arverni king. They have discovered that he has been taken back to Rome, and they are bound for the capital, via this very port.'

Fronto scratched his head. 'A dozen killers in masks are going to Rome to try and rescue Vercingetorix? Is that what you're telling me?'

'In short, yes.'

'They're mad. They'll never succeed.'

'Don't be too sure, Fronto. I don't know what Rome is like, but these dozen are very dangerous indeed. And very secretive. They identify themselves with twelve of the gods of our peoples, and I have seen their handiwork. They butchered a legate.'

Fronto blinked in shock. 'A *legate*? Who?'

'I think his name was Reginus.'

Fronto pictured the legate of the Fifteenth and rubbed his eyes. 'That's unbelievable.'

'As I say, do not underestimate them. I do not know who they all are, but I have seen two or three of them without their masks. They are all deadly. And they all hate Rome with a passion. Moreover they had been moving for months about the land butchering Romans and still no one knows about them.'

'Other than you.'

'Other than me. And while they will be coming through Massilia on their way to Rome, given their activity so far I cannot see them failing to take action when they learn that one of the legates who was responsible for their defeat at Alesia is in the city. And your name is well enough known that it will happen.'

Fronto nodded slowly. 'And you think they're in the city now, then?'

'They may be, though you may have time yet. They were hours ahead of me at Alba, but they will have to move very cautiously through Roman territory, while I simply rode fast and openly. I almost certainly passed them on the way. Besides, there is a huge Roman supply column a day or so north of here. I passed them without too much trouble, but a dozen armed and masked killers will have to be very careful. They will probably have to wait until the column enters the city before they can move south.'

Fronto took a swig of his wine. 'Sounds like Caesar's treasure train is almost here then. Good. The port has been at a standstill for weeks waiting for it. Once that's in Rome and the ships are moving again, my business will heave a sigh of relief.'

'And I will be able to move on.'

In the strange silence that followed, Fronto found himself speculating. 'I…' he paused to rearrange the words in his head. 'Wherever you are headed, might I offer an alternative?'

Cavarinos raised his brow in interest.

'Stay with us. I have good men here. And a prince of the Remi is close to my family. You seem to be a man with no place. Why move again?'

Cavarinos shrugged and drained his glass.

'I have no intention of being tied up in a fresh war, so the north is lost to me. But I am not a Roman, Fronto. I am Arverni. There is somewhere out there for me, but Massilia is not it.' He took a deep breath. 'Yet I have no intention of letting a dozen maniacs rekindle a dead rebellion. These Sons of Taranis need to be stopped, so I will stay for now.'

He smiled. 'Now pour me another glass of that excellent Alban before we go and join your lovely wife while I catch you up on what I know is happening in the north and you fill in the blanks for me.'

* * * * *

Fronto pointed angrily at the slave girl. 'I don't give a hair from Jove's left bollock what her intentions were, I distinctly and very clearly said I did not want her touching my swords!'

Lucilia reached out with a calming hand and patted him on the arm. 'I gave her permission, Marcus. She has been complaining for weeks that you don't take care of them and that there are spots of rust on the blades.'

Fronto glared in exasperation. 'You *do realise* that means that she's been unsheathing them when you aren't looking anyway?'

'You of all people should know better than to let your kit get rusty, Marcus. You may not intend to join Caesar again, but that's no reason to let things go to ruin.'

His glare darkened. 'Don't change the bloody subject!' He turned to Andala who, he noted, did not look remotely cowed and showed not a breath of remorse. In fact, she looked thoroughly defiant and even slightly angry. By gods sometimes she actually reminded him of Lucilia. Could there be shared blood between the Belgae and the Lucilii?

'Masgava, would you be good enough to take all three of my gladii and my daggers and put them in a locked box?'

'They'll be no use there if you get in trouble,' the big man rumbled.

'For the love of Jove is there no one in this household who actually has any intention of doing what I ask?' Fronto bellowed in vexation.

'Not if what you ask is not in your best interests,' Masgava replied calmly.

Fronto glared at the three of them, feeling a little like a retiarius with a torn net and a broken trident facing three armed opponents in the arena. He spun and stomped angrily across the room to where Cavarinos stood peering at a large map of the republic on the wall.

'You see the sort of crap I have to put up with?'

Cavarinos turned with an indulgent smile. 'Roman women, I fear, are not that different from Arverni ones. Accept defeat gracefully, Fronto, and rally your men for future battles.'

Fronto glared at him, and Cavarinos laughed, pointing at the map. 'Your people call our tribes *Gallia*, correct?'

Fronto nodded, still irritated.

'Then I think your map makers have been toying with you. Look at this place.'

Fronto peered at where he was pointing, out to the east, past the border of the Republic in Anatolia. 'Galatia?'

Cavarinos nodded, and Fronto smiled. 'That is another land, ruled by a king called Deiotarus. He's a client king of Rome, and they're strong allies of ours.'

'But the name?'

Fronto nodded. 'I am given to understand that they are related to your tribes, going back a number of centuries. Pompey used to say they have their own Gaulish language. Probably not unlike yours, I imagine.'

Cavarinos frowned and tapped his lip. 'I am interested in Galatia. It is on the other side of the world, yet you say it is a land of my people with its own king? Independent?'

'I believe so.'

Cavarinos nodded. 'I think, then, it is for Galatia that I am bound when this is over.'

The room's five occupants turned in the silence that followed, listening to the sound of several footsteps in the atrium outside. Moments later, Aurelius appeared in the doorway.

'You have another visitor, Domine.'

Fronto frowned. His guards never used such a noble term, mostly calling him by name. As Aurelius backed aside, bowing, three more figures appeared in the doorway. He didn't recognise the men to either side, though they were clearly tribunes. But the man in the middle...

'Brutus!'

A genuine smile spread across his face as he hurried across the room to the tired-looking officer in the doorway. He caught sight of his major domo standing respectfully some distance behind them, waiting for orders, while he held the three officers' cloaks.

'Amelgo? Have a meal prepared and plenty of wine. Could you have extra cushions brought in too? And a bowl of warm water for our guests to give themselves a quick clean up?'

As the servant dashed off, Fronto grinned at the three officers. 'You're welcome to use my baths of course, but from the looks of you you've just dismounted and you'll probably want a seat and a cup of wine first, yes?'

Brutus gave him a tired smile. 'A drink would be most welcome, Marcus. These two, by the way, are Pontius and Gamburio, tribunes

252

of the Twelfth who have come with me all the way from the north.' The two officers bowed.

'Good to meet you. A fine legion, the Twelfth. I remember their formation. Come on. Sit yourselves.'

Brutus sank to a cushioned seat with gratitude.

'I presume this means that Caesar's wagon train has arrived?' Fronto hazarded. 'I guessed someone important would be commanding it. Glad it's a friend. And maybe, since you're a friend' you'll be able to squeeze a little shipment of mine aboard the triremes you're taking to Rome?'

Brutus shook his head. 'Sorry, Marcus. I've been down into town with the wagons and talked to the man in the offices. Sounds to me like we'll fit most of the cargo on board, but there's not even enough room for my full load. I'm going to have to do a deal with the more reputable local captains. Or send the other wagons around the coast and down through Italia, though that will mean having to temporarily reassign a cohort or two from the Twelfth. It's all a bit of a headache, to be honest.'

Fronto was pleased enough to see his friend that he ignored the irritation over the fact that his business would continue to stagnate for a week or more yet.

'Well at least you're here and safe,' Fronto chuckled. 'A target like your column must have been tempting for half the tribes of Gaul.'

Brutus nodded, scrubbing ruffled hair. 'We almost fell foul of one attack, from the good and loyal Helvii of all people! But fortunately we were warned in time and the enemy retreated without an arrow loosed.'

Cavarinos stepped away from the wall now, rubbing his hands together.

'Did you say the Helvii?'

'Yes.' Brutus narrowed his eyes at this strange Romanised Gaul who he didn't recognise.

'When was this?'

'Three days ago now.'

'*That's* where they were, then,' Cavarinos nodded to himself. 'I wondered why Alba was almost empty. The Sons of Taranis must have been right behind them. Hopefully they got bogged down behind your column and delayed.'

Brutus frowned in confusion. 'The who?'

'A cult of killers. There are twelve of them, led by a disfigured man.'

Brutus' brow furrowed further, and he turned and muttered something to the tribunes, who nodded their agreement.

'A dozen, you say? This disfigured man… would he be wearing a mask?'

Cavarinos, coming vividly alert, stepped forward so forcefully that one of the tribunes dropped his hand to his sword hilt, but the Arvernian drew himself up in front of Brutus.

'A cult mask? Gleaming glaze with a straight mouth and small horns?'

Brutus nodded. 'He was a servant, they said, who'd been disfigured by the pox.'

'He was disfigured by a cavalry sword at Alesia,' Cavarinos said quietly, and turned to Fronto. 'They're here. They're in Massilia now, and they had no trouble getting here. They had a Roman escort.'

Brutus looked across at Fronto.

'Who are these people, then? These Sons of Taranis?'

'Rebels, killers and lunatics,' Fronto replied. Damn good job for you that you had the Twelfth around you, then. From what Cavarinos tells me, you'd probably be decorating a tree now if they'd found you on your own.'

Brutus' frown deepened yet again as he turned to the Gaul.

'Cavarinos? Of the Arverni?'

Cavarinos nodded.

'I saw you at the surrender of Alesia. Fronto, you are keeping very odd company.'

'Odd, but good. Brutus, do you know where those twelve will be now?'

The senior officer shook his head. 'We parted ways at the city gate. They could be anywhere by now. Damn it. Something felt off about them all that way, but I just put it down to jumpiness, given what I was transporting. What are they doing here?'

Fronto opened his mouth to speak, but Cavarinos was there first. 'Primarily trying to take ship, but while they're in town I would be astonished if they don't try and send Fronto here to meet his gods in person. And if you are, as you appear to be, Decimus Junius Brutus Albinus, Caesar's cousin, then I would make very sure to keep a large guard of legionaries around you at all times. You will be every bit as tempting a target as Fronto.'

Brutus nodded. 'The legion will be moving off towards Narbo when the ships depart, but after that we'll have the marines to look after us. I think I'll be safe. It'll take a week to load the ships and prepare to sail, I reckon.'

'I doubt the Sons of Taranis will stay in port that long,' Cavarinos noted. 'They will delay departure long enough to try and kill such valuable Roman officers, but their objective requires that they leave as early as possible, and they'll want to get to Rome ahead of the convoy, as that will block up your port and draw a lot of gazes to incoming ships.'

Fronto crossed to stand in front of Brutus.

'Alright, Decimus. You can't take my cargo, but I tell you one thing. Once these bastards have run from Massilia, they're heading for Rome, and I will follow them and put them down. So you'll make space for me and mine on the ships or I will personally cripple enough of your men to make room.'

Brutus chortled. 'Subtle as ever, Fronto. Alright. We'll make sure to keep room for a few passengers. Just make sure you stay alive until we sail.'

Fronto smiled. 'You stay safe with the Twelfth until we're ready to leave, Decimus.' He glanced across at Masgava. 'In the meantime we need to secure the villa completely. No little shopping trips to the agora. No theatre visits or strolls along the coast path. Everyone stays in the villa under guard and everyone is armed. Even Catháin and the workmen. If a mouse farts in this place I want a man with a sword looking up its arse. Understood?'

As Masgava nodded his total agreement, Fronto turned to Cavarinos.

'Meantime, you and I are going to spend a little time in the town and turn over a few rocks, see what crawls out.'

Chapter Fifteen

THE Cadurci oppidum of Uxellodunon rose from the mist like some behemoth of ancient legend, its 'upturned boat' shape inky black against the dusk sky. The fog was chilly, though the evening was far from cold, with spring enfolding the land in its warm blanket. The evenings were warm and the gentle broiling of the land resulted in the huge carpet of mist that rose from the rivers and streams and irrigation channels that surrounded the oppidum.

The bulk of the Romans would be safely tucked away inside their tents, expecting no trouble, but Lucterius knew from long experience that despite such things the Roman sentries and pickets would be far from complacent. And the officer who had chased them to this site seemed to be shrewd enough. He had concentrated his forces in three locations where they could react to any move in force and could concentrate their supplies and organisation, each camp with a solid cavalry element to speedily deal with anything for which the infantry would be too slow. But they had also created a cordon around the place, with men on watch so close that they could speak to one another. A message from the Roman commander could circuit the oppidum in perhaps a quarter of an hour. Worse still, the man had had a wicker fence thrown up around the entire circumference, excepting where features of nature prevented it.

Then they had settled in to lay siege.

There had been arguments in Uxellodunon.

Drapes – damn the man for the only chief who was senior enough to vie for control – had blamed Lucterius for being too slow and getting them trapped here. It mattered not how many times Lucterius explained that he had intended to tarry here anyway, with or without the Romans. Drapes had urged for a breakout in force and to continue their journey south.

But it was too early. Molacos had been insistent that he would retrieve the great king and return him at the appointed place on the Roman border on the first day of the month of *Qutios*. Lucterius was no fool, though, and he knew to add a month to that, for Molacos was being proud and boastful as was right in such a great warrior. Lucterius had agreed to meet Molacos and the king with his new army on the eve of the festival of *Lugnasa*, which marked the start of the harvest season. Thus he had intended to come here, to his hometown, to train this new army and rest and prepare. Then, at the

256

end of Qutios, they would begin to move south. They would meet Molacos and the great king at the edge of Roman lands and would then sweep down and destroy Narbo. He felt sure that the tribes in Narbonensis would rally to the cause of freedom if the local authorities and garrison were destroyed. And when those tribes – the Volcae, the Ruteni, the Tectosages and various others – joined the cause, it would almost certainly bring the taciturn and reluctant Aquitani tribes of the mountain country down to join in.

The northern and the eastern tribes had been smashed – there was no hope of a new rebellion being born there – but the south and east remained strong. They only had to be shown the way, shown that Rome could be beaten and driven out, and then they would rise. The burning of Narbo and the triumph of the once-defeated Arverni king would do that.

Of course, the presence of these two legions under the man Caninius had thrown a stick in the wheel spokes of the plan. But sticks could be removed. And Lucterius still had over a month until he had originally intended to move south anyway. Drapes had worried that the Romans would send for reinforcements, but Lucterius had prepared everything. The north was still rising with every man they could muster. They were little more than a gad fly biting the hide of Rome, but they were keeping Caesar and his other generals busy. It was simply bad luck that this Caninius had run to help the Lemovices while Drapes had been there. Otherwise the plan would be moving forward without Roman interference.

Still, he was confident that they would win. He had as many men as the Romans and as long as he could meet them on favourable terms, he would win the day. There could be no pitched battle in open land, for that was where Rome became ascendant. And attacking the Roman defences was foolish – they had learned that at Alesia.

So there was one way. An army was only as good as its supplies.

Uxellodunon had good stores of grain and a source of water. Half the plateau was given to the cultivation of vegetables and fruit and the husbandry of animals. Uxellodunon could hold out for as long as they wanted it to. And the men would never go hungry during all that time. They would eat well. But the Romans had chased them here without the usual wagon train, and that meant that they were reliant upon forage. They must be running very short now of the meagre supplies they had brought with them, and would be hunting animals and sending forage parties out to locate farms.

They would be unlucky. The war had taken its toll on the tribes and few farms had yielded a healthy harvest for two years now. Unless they found the supply dump at *Serpent Ford*, six or seven miles southwest of the oppidum, that was. It had originally been stored there with the intention of being brought inside the ramparts when the army arrived, but the Romans had been too close and so the supplies remained where they had been left.

If the Romans found it they would be well fed for long enough to ruin the plan. But two more weeks without adequate supplies and the Romans would be forced to quit the siege and move back north to where their own supplies were. Then the Cadurci would move on. Or, if he was one of the more belligerent of the Roman commanders, this Caninius would judge his position untenable and decide to launch a desperate attack. And if he did that, Lucterius would win easily and destroy two legions into the bargain.

It was all dependent upon his men remaining strong and well fed while the Romans starved and weakened.

When he had told Drapes about the cache of food, the man had strained at his leash, wanting to rush the enemy lines and either retrieve or burn the supplies to make sure the Romans did not get them. Lucterius had been calm and organised and had explained that he had a plan.

He would take five hundred men and retrieve the supplies. There could be no *more* than five hundred, lest the Romans notice them sneaking past and bring them to battle. Then he would lose. But five hundred men he could get through the Roman lines. Then they would bring the supplies back to the oppidum, not only weakening the chances of the enemy but strengthening their own.

Drapes had lost his temper and roared his distrust into Lucterius' face. Not only had Lucterius led them into a siege and got them trapped by two legions all because of some faint timeline to which he was working, but now he proposed to sneak out of the oppidum and run, leaving Drapes to his fate.

Lucterius had put on his most patient voice and explained once more that he was simply going to fetch the supplies, but Drapes had the bit between his teeth and accused him repeatedly of trying to flee now that things had gone wrong. And the more Drapes spat and raged, the more the lesser chiefs had nodded and begun to look at Lucterius with distrust.

It was madness. Was he not the architect of this whole plan? Was he not behind the renewed dream of freeing the tribes from the Roman yoke? But in the face of bile and invective, all the idiots could see was that Lucterius planned to leave the oppidum. In the end, he had been forced to acquiesce and agree to Drapes joining him on the mission. They would take the five hundred men – two hundred of his loyal Cadurci and two hundred of Drapes' Senones. And several of the more nervous, distrustful lesser chiefs would come with a dozen or so men each. It was utterly ridiculous. The bulk of the new rebel army remained well fed and rested, training in the oppidum under the command of one of the smallest and least important chiefs in this army. Meanwhile anyone with any influence was busy sneaking out of the place to retrieve stored grain.

All because of Drapes' distrust.

Idiocy.

Carefully, he lifted his foot out of the brackish water and gestured to the tangled root that had almost tripped him so that the men following on behind would not fall foul of it.

This place, which in his childhood they had called the *marsh of dead horses* for some unknown reason, was the only place a breakout could be achieved. To the southwest of the oppidum, towards where the river plunged into a narrow valley, the two tributary streams that fed into that river met in a tangled swampy woodland. The ground was so soft and flat here that the streams flooded the woodland and created a troubling marsh. The Romans might have created a bulge in their cordon to enclose the whole thing, but that would have meant taking it right back towards the river, and the sense of order and neatness that seemed endemic of the Roman mind would not allow for that. Instead, the cordon went to one side of the marsh, where a sentry sat at the driest point he could find, and picked up again with a similar man on the far side.

The marsh was not wide. The pickets might not be able to see each other, but they were close enough to shout to one another, as the escaping warriors had confirmed when they were treated to a shouted ribald story about some Syracusan whore. Fortunately, the flow of the streams through the undergrowth mixed with the vast array of marshy wildlife created a constant murmur of watery movement, and the sound of five hundred men moving very slowly and carefully through the hidden ways between them remained unnoticed by the pickets. And, of course, the mist helped to dampen sound anyway.

Drapes had actually, when he'd heard about this place, suggested that the whole army move through it and escape. He genuinely believed they could get the army past the Roman cordon and be halfway to Narbo before Caninius knew they had gone. Which only went to show that Drapes *was* an idiot. Five hundred men through here was dangerous enough. Many thousands would stand no chance.

Indeed, he would have had no nerves crossing this place with his five hundred Cadurci, all of whom knew Uxellodunon and this marsh and could navigate it with their eyes closed. These various Senone and other allied idiots, though, were making so much noise it was amazing they hadn't already drawn the attention of the sentries.

It was at that moment that Lucterius' new plan formed.

When they got to the supplies, he would suggest that he remain with his men to guard the dump while Drapes began ferrying the grain back to the oppidum. There was not a jot of doubt in his mind as to the idiot's reaction to that. Drapes would narrow his eyes suspiciously and decide that *he* would guard the supplies while *Lucterius* ferried them back, for the Senone chief would worry that Lucterius would flee as soon as his back was turned and leave them in the lurch.

Far from it.

If he could leave Drapes with the last vestiges of the supply dump while he transported the rest into Uxellodunon, he would effectively have removed the stupid thorn from his side. Drapes would be outside with two hundred men or so, while Lucterius had the entire army in the oppidum. He might even then be tempted to alert the Romans and let them deal with Drapes appropriately.

Someone pushed him in the back and his thoughts came back to his present situation as he turned an angry glare on the man behind him. Tarbos, a lesser chief of the Petrocorii, was urging him on, his lip drawn back in a snarl. If he had dared to speak, Lucterius would have pointed out to the turd behind him that the reason he was moving slow was because he was currently traversing an area of slimy stones beneath the surface of the water. He resolved not to point to them and hoped the man would slip under the water in his mail shirt and drown.

If Drapes was the hunter (which was something of a reach for a man with the intellect of a root vegetable), then he had three hounds.

Bimmos of the Santoni would be the one to reach the prey and bring it down without the need for his master. When the war actually began again, Bimmos would be effective, if he could be dragged out from beneath Drapes. Lugurix of the Pictones would be the hound who did exactly what was asked of him; no more and no less. He would bring back the bird Drapes had brought down.

Tarbos of the Petrocorii – the moron currently sloshing along behind Lucterius – was the third hound. He would be the one unaware even of where they were, who simply spent all his time curled into a ball, licking his own arse.

Behind him, Tarbos slipped on the slimy stones and almost cried out, but grabbed hold of Lucterius' back to stop himself falling. Lucterius resisted the urge to turn and knife the man. He was nothing but a liability.

With considerable relief, Lucterius saw the gradient begin to rise and the boles of the trees that came ghosting out of the mist thinned out gradually. They were at the edge of the marsh of dead horses. They were past the Roman sentries. As he climbed out of the water and through a short section of sucking mud to the springy turf of the valley side, he kept low.

The Romans would not be paying a great deal of attention to this area. It was outside their cordon of watchers, but one of the three main Roman camps sat on the gentle slope only a few hundred paces away at the confluence of the watercourses. He could just see the faint flicker of the Roman torches far off in the mist. Turning his glare on Tarbos again he motioned for him and the stream of men following to keep as quiet as possible.

Holding his breath, aware that this was the most dangerous part, he kept low and stalked across the grass until he reached the shelter of a small copse of chestnut trees that marked the end of the perilous journey. From there on, they would have the shelter of trees and hedges until they were around the first bend of the river and out of sight of the Roman lines.

Then to Serpent Ford and the supply dump.

As he waited for the rest of the five hundred to reach the trees and relative safety, he could feel Tarbos' eyes on him and he turned to meet the man's gaze. There was something troubling there. It was not just the distrust and sneering dislike he'd so far experienced from the idiot. This was something else. Why was he continually watching Lucterius? Why were he and his ten men even *with* Lucterius among

261

the Cadurci contingent, instead of back with his huntsman master and the Senone warriors?

Did Drapes really distrust him so much that he'd set this shaved ape to watching him? If so it was a poor choice of spy.

He resolved to make damn sure he did away with Tarbos as soon as Drapes was no longer a factor.

* * * * *

Varus yawned and rubbed his face vigorously. Years of waking early on campaign still never made rising in the pre-dawn hours any easier. Plus, he had to admit in the privacy of his own mind, he was not as young as he once was. His gaze slid up through the endless, soul-sapping mist to the golden sky above, the first mackerel-skin stain of morning having already given way to the early sun that hit the ground and raised the ubiquitous mist. Every dawn and every dusk this place issued a white cloud like the breath of some giant subterranean creature.

Within an hour it would be properly light.

He could have relied on a lesser officer, of course. Doing the rounds was something that most commanders left to their lessers. Caninius certainly wouldn't be strolling around his camp at the moment. He rarely rose from his cot until the sun was above the horizon. But Varus had learned from the best. Caesar knew the value of the personal touch. And Fronto too. A few others. Not like this new breed of officers that seemed too distant to be a part of the army proper.

But the importance of a personal appearance could hardly be measured. Varus' men knew him and valued him already, but it was handy to have the respect of the infantry, too. Often in such situations the two branches of the military would have to work in concert, such as at Alesia last year. And a personal appearance from a senior officer made men feel valued. Especially the poor bastards who had done the last night shift of watch in the cold and the dark and the early morning mist.

'Morning, lad.'

The sentry looked around. Good man. He'd had his gaze locked on the ground ahead of him and left and had not noticed the lone horseman walking up behind him from the Roman side. But then, unlike many of his fellows, this poor sod had a troublesome spot to watch. At the edge of the irritating marsh that spread like a suppurating wound from the twin waterways, the lad had to watch not only the forward ground, but also whatever he could of the tree-covered, mist-soaked marsh.

'Good morning, sir.'

'Nothing doing, I take it?'

The young soldier shook his head. 'About an hour before dawn the fires were stoked and lit up there. Heard the slaughtering of animals for breaking their fast, sir. Not a pleasant noise, but I'll be buggered if it didn't sound damned tasty down here.'

Varus laughed. It was good to hear such light humour being tossed about on such a dark subject. The Roman forces were getting very hungry indeed, living on half bread rations and hard-tack biscuits. Soon, hopefully, Fabius would arrive with extra supplies. Certainly there was nothing to be found in the local farms and settlements. Whatever they had managed to produce in the area – probably not a lot after last year – had clearly already been taken into the oppidum before they arrived.

'I'd certainly not argue with any man who plonked a plate of mutton before me right now,' grinned Varus. 'Gods, I'd eat a dog's arse if it were cooked with enough onions!'

The soldier burst out laughing and Varus' grin widened. This was what men like Caninius missed out on by not consorting with the lower ranks. Oh, it did something to a man. Somehow it cracked the noble outer that coated the patrician class and many of the equites and injected something of the common man. And that created men like Fronto, who were sometimes disapproved of by the higher echelons of the army. But by the gods it made good leaders and fighting men.

He crouched next to the young soldier.

'Do you know what I had when I woke this morning?'

The lad cleared his throat nervously. Varus was well aware that even in times of privation the officers were treated to foods denied the men. The lad would be trying not to imagine what delicious foods Varus had tucked into in his tent. In actual fact, he had eaten only plain bread with a little salty butter. The boy was nervous.

'Go on. Guess what I had when I woke up.'

The lad cleared his throat. 'I... I have no idea, sir.'

'A boner,' Varus announced with a grin.

The young soldier dropped his shield as he exploded with laughter.

The other noise was so quiet that Varus almost missed it, but years of dealing with Gauls and their clever, wily ways made his ear twitch and the hair stand proud on the back of his neck. His spine shivered as though a hundred ants traversed it.

Quietly, he leaned forward and whispered in the lad's ear.

'Tell me a story. A loud one.'

The lad frowned, so Varus urged him with a hand gesture. As the young soldier began to recount some fairly dull tale of training, Varus rose from his crouch and padded as quietly as he could over to the trees nearby.

He somehow thought he knew what he was going to see, but was surprised by one aspect of it. The splash he'd heard could have been any animal in the marsh, but the quiet, almost inaudible curse clearly wasn't. It had been too quiet to identify as non-Latin but, accompanied by a splash, it was no sentry. He'd known even before his eyes picked out the movement in the mist that it was Gauls sneaking through the marsh. What he hadn't been expecting was that they were heading *to* the oppidum, rather than *from* it.

And they were carrying bundles of grain and sacks and bags. They were resupplying the oppidum! And they were moving very slowly.

He did a quick calculation. He had no idea how many men there were in the marsh, but surely they wouldn't try and sneak more than a few hundred through here, else it would be too risky? The sentries were placed in the Roman cordon every two hundred paces. While it would take a while to gather enough men from the sentries to fight the Gauls, he could drag in maybe a dozen quickly enough to hold them off, while the garrison of the camp at the confluence was alerted. In a matter of two or three hundred heartbeats half a legion would be bearing down on this place. That was, after all, the point in sentries and strategically placed camps. He crept back to the young soldier and gestured for him to arm up and stand. As the lad did, clearly aware something was up, Varus took a deep breath and filled his lungs.

'Alarm! Gauls in the marsh!'

Waving for the lad to follow him, he ripped his sword from its sheath and ran towards the tree where he'd seen the Gauls. A quick glance over his shoulder confirmed that away across the grass the next two sentries were already moving, converging on his position.

Good.

Now all he had to do was not die until the rest got here.

Tense and vibrating with that nervous energy that comes at the start of battle, Varus raced into the marsh, the young soldier behind him.

The Gauls had been taken by surprise and seemed to be suffering a lack of command cohesion. Some of them dropped their precious grain in the marshy water where it would be instantly ruined, drawing blades. Others grasped their heavy burdens over their shoulders, drawing a sword with a free hand and preparing to fight while horribly encumbered. Yet more simply shouldered their supplies and ran like hares for the safety of Uxellodunon.

Taking advantage of their disarray, and heedless to the danger, Varus picked a big man who had dropped a sack and drawn a sword and simply ran at him like an enraged bull. The big warrior raised his sword to bring it down on the charging Roman but at the last moment Varus dropped to a running crouch, swiping out with his blade as he passed. He was a cavalryman. The Gauls would be expecting legionary manoeuvres, using the traditional thrusting gladius of the infantry. But Varus' sword was a horseman's blade. Long, honed for slicing, and much more like the Gaul's own blade, the sword sliced into the man's legs at the top of the knees, below his tunic's hem. Though the sword bounced from the bone and came away clean, the man issued a high pitched keening noise and fell into the swampy water on agonised legs.

Varus was already up, slashing at the next man, who was having trouble wielding his long sword while trying to maintain his grip on the heavy sack at his shoulder. The man's extended arm was smashed to pieces by the blow, the wrist and hand that held the blade all-but severed, hanging by a thread as the man screamed and dropped the sack.

Again Varus was off like a demon, low again this time, his sword taking a man in the calf down to the bone, wrenching it back out as the Gaul pitched face first into the brackish swamp. A cut up that took a man in the side before slicing through the sack he carried, releasing a torrent of grain that fell like a pretty cascade into the green murk. A slice high again, bouncing back from a shoulder blade, but effective enough to send the man flying into the water.

265

Varus stopped as he realised there were no more Gauls. He had actually fought his way to the front of the resupply column. With immense satisfaction that penetrated even the fog of war, he turned and looked back through the mist. There were screams and calls. He stood for a moment, shaking slightly and taking stock. Two enemy blows had landed during that frenetic run, though he'd not noticed either at the time. One was a flesh wound in his upper left arm – had he taken a shield from his horse his left arm would not now be coated in sticky red – and the other was a nick in his hip that had touched bone where the flesh was thin, but had actually miraculously done no real damage.

Satisfied that not only would he live, but that he was in fact still in fine fighting condition, he turned and ran back towards the sound of fighting. As he saw the first shapes in the mist, he halted. Better he stop them getting any closer to the oppidum than get too bogged down fighting at the centre. He could hear shouts in Latin and see the shapes of legionaries, so several sentries were clearly now involved and, thankfully, over the top he could hear the whistles of centurions fairly close – evidence that reserves were pouring from the camp.

A desperate shape emerged through the mist, bloodied sword in hand and sheaf of grain over shoulder, and the Gaul's eyes widened as he realised that he'd not achieved freedom as expected, but had, in fact, met the Roman officer who had demolished the front of their column.

Varus snarled and leapt at him, his sword flicking out and taking the stunned man in the throat.

Two more figures appeared behind as the first fell gurgling away, and Varus readied himself. All he had to do was hold the marsh and stop them getting away one at a time. These two were clearly nobles, from the quality of their clothes, weapons and few trinkets. The taller of the two, with a shrewd, instant recognition of the danger, pushed his friend towards the Roman officer and turned, barrelling off through the mist at a tangent towards where Varus and the lad had so recently been discussing food.

He had no chance to follow. The blocky, wide-shouldered noble who had been pushed at him knocked him backwards and he staggered. The noble was unencumbered with food and swiftly drew a sword, brandishing it at Varus and jabbing with it once, twice, thrice.

Varus watched the brute's eyes. He was squat but strong. In a fair fight he would be a difficult proposition to take down. Years of fighting against men like this alongside men like Fronto had taught Varus the value of an *unfair* fight, though. There was no glimmer of intelligence in those flat, dark eyes.

Ripping his pugio dagger from his belt, Varus made sure to brandish it obviously. The bull-necked noble's eyes flicked to the dagger and back twice. Content that he had the man's attention, Varus threw the dagger off to the side a few feet, where it disappeared with a 'plop'.

The thug's gaze followed the arc of the weapon and stared mystified at the ripples in the unpleasant water. He only began to recover his wits as Varus hit him in the chest with his shoulder, knocking him back against the bole of a tree that rose from the gurgling water, driving the breath from him. The cavalry commander gave his stocky opponent no chance to recover, bringing down the sphere at the base of his sword hilt on the big man's wrist with a hard crack.

He heard more than one bone shatter and the thug let out a pained cry as his sword fell away into the water.

Varus was irritated now. His sword came up horizontally, the blade just beneath the man's chin, the keen edge resting on the man's throat apple.

'Don't nod unless you want to die. And swallowing's probably inadvisable, too.' He noted the man's widening eyes and grinned. 'Ah good. You speak Latin. That'll make things easier. Here's how things stand.'

He took a breath and lifted the blade's edge a finger's breadth so that it rested on the flesh below his chin and not on his neck, allowing him to speak without injury. 'Your little resupply mission has failed completely. If you listen carefully you will now note that nearly all the voices you hear are Roman, not your own people. Your own people are mostly under the surface of the water now, mouldering. You, however, appear to be a nobleman. I will give you my word that if you answer all my questions truthfully, you will be ransomed back to your tribe for an appropriate figure. Do you understand?'

The man whispered 'yes,' trying not to move enough to draw blood on the blade beneath his chin.

'Good. How many men are there in this column?'

'Just over two hundred.'

'All your men?'

'No. Mostly Cadurci under that traitor Lucterius!'

Varus pursed his lips. The tone of his voice made it fairly obvious that Lucterius had been the man who'd pushed him and run off. Inwardly, Varus cursed. Lucterius was, seemingly, the man behind all this. If only he'd got the bastard. Still, perhaps one of the others had.

'Where are the supplies from?'

The man's eyes darted left and right but, resigned, he sighed. 'The river bends four times about six miles away. There is a fortified farmstead there. It was a store house.'

'And if we go there now, what will we find?'

The man remained nervously silent.

'Because of you I've lost an expensive dagger. If you don't answer my question, I will carve its weight out of your stinking hide. Talk to me.'

The man growled. 'Another three hundred men under Drapes. Mostly his Senones.'

Varus nodded his satisfaction. The other major leader of this army, then. Even if they'd lost Lucterius, perhaps they could destroy this small force and capture Drapes. He grinned. It had turned out to be a surprisingly good morning so far. He wondered whether Caninius had emerged from his tent yet. A figure barrelled out of the mist, clutching an arm across his front. A legionary, sword in hand but shield missing, blood trickling down that limb. It took him a moment to realise that it was the young lad he'd been talking to at the start of all this. He grinned, genuinely pleased to see the fellow. Other legionaries were coming up behind him. It seemed the fight was over.

'Here you go, lad. This noble's yours to ransom. I suggest you pluck him of valuables before you send him to the stockade.' He then looked across at the next figures. 'There's no more this way. Get word to Legate Caninius. Tell him we need to send a cohort upriver and that I'll attend him when I've gathered my cavalry. We'll find a fortified farm with a few hundred Gauls and perhaps some more supplies.'

The soldiers saluted and turned, running off. Varus looked at the legionary. 'You alright dealing with him?'

The young man looked the stocky Gaul up and down and with virtually no warning, smashed him in the temple with the hilt of his gladius. Varus only just managed to pull his blade away in time and prevent the slicing open of the noble's throat as he slid unconscious to the murk below. The legionary sheathed his sword and reached down, stopping the Gaul from being submerged with his good arm before hauling him up and, with a little difficulty, throwing him over his shoulder. He grinned.

'I'll manage, sir.'

Varus laughed and saluted the young legionary as he staggered away with one broken arm and a stocky prize over his shoulder. The cavalry commander dipped his blade in the water and then wiped it on his tunic before sheathing it.

Now to run off and find his horsemen. There was a small force of Germanic riders attached to his wing who had formerly been part of Caesar's dreaded German horse. Only fifty or so of them, but the evil bastards spent every day around the corrals with their horses ready for action, simply awaiting the opportunity to cause mayhem. It would take time for Caninius to get his men moving, and for Varus to have a cavalry ala ready to join them, but he didn't want word of this reaching the farmstead and the Senones there running away with all the food. They needed to be kept busy until the main Roman force could get there. He pictured their leader's face when he heard he was slipping the leash with free rein to cause bloodshed.

Varus shuddered.

* * * * *

Lucterius staggered past a low hedge and down to the river bank. He was furious. Never in all his years of fighting had he encountered such incompetence. Drapes had insisted that he bring the squat moron Tarbos with him back to the oppidum – yet again, mistrust leading to dangerous incompetence. Lucterius had argued, but the fact remained that Tarbos was coming with him whether he wanted the man or not and it wasn't worth arguing a lost cause.

They had made their slow and irritating way back in his unbearable company, arriving back at the plain below Uxellodunon just before dawn. The mist would allow them to get back even though the darkness had now passed.

269

And then it had happened. As before, Tarbos had been so close to Lucterius that anyone would think they were lovers. And the stunted turd had dropped his sack of salted meat into the water. Even as Lucterius had paused and listened for a moment to make sure they hadn't been discovered through such idiocy, the moron had actually sworn out loud. Lucterius had hit him, hard, with the flat of his sword, but the damage had been done. Moments later a Roman ran into the mist, followed by another, and then all Hades broke loose.

It had been surprisingly satisfying to throw Tarbos at the Roman – the only bright side to this debacle. Then he had run. And not towards the oppidum. Though he couldn't see it, he knew that now the alarm had gone up the Romans would be swarming and the oppidum would be closely watched. And so, despite everything, he was running on his own. Separated from his army by the might of Rome and the idiocy of his peers.

There was only one hope, now. He had to find a relief force and break the Roman siege before they managed to get their own reinforcements from somewhere. If he could break the siege, he could still take the army south.

And he had one last gambit to make. Because there was only one tribe left in this part of Gaul that could provide the manpower to fight a legion. Caesar had left the Arverni unpunished after Alesia, presumably to make them unpopular with the other tribes. But that meant the Arverni could still field an army, unlike most survivors of Alesia. And the Arverni were like brothers to the Cadurci, living beside them and sharing a history and many combined bloodlines. He hadn't wanted to approach them until he had Vercingetorix free again, but this mess had changed that.

Hardening himself as to the fate of Drapes and the others, Lucterius kept his head down and followed the line of the river east, making for Nemossos and the home of the highest ranking Arverni left their freedom.

The Arverni would turn the tide.

* * * * *

Varus drummed his horse's flanks, driving it up the slope. Behind him came Caninius and then scouts, the tribunes of the Fifth and the mounted musician, in case orders needed to be relayed urgently. Since they had marched out of camp at the fastest sensible pace, unencumbered by packs, the river had gradually become more and more snakelike, carving its way southwest through the landscape in great loops this way and that, each loop harbouring an area of rich farmland and a once-thriving farmstead, long since abandoned. And every time Varus crested a rise at the outer bend of the river to see such laid out before him, he drew in a tense breath, expecting it to harbour a few hundred rabid Gauls. Each time he had exhaled calmly.

This time, however, they had clearly reached the correct loop.

The farmstead before them was surrounded by a low palisade and contained a large building at the centre along with perhaps half a dozen other structures scattered about the place. An irrigation ditch in an adjacent field had been extended to loop around the place, forming a minor moat.

The Germans had been at work.

Though unable to form a concerted attack on the three hundred men in the farm behind their defences, the Germanic cavalry had the enemy pinned in that stockade, riding around just outside arrow range. The evidence of earlier clashes lay about the scene: German horses and riders here and there who had come too close to the palisade and had fallen foul of Senone arrows. A small group of six Germanic bodies in a heap at the water-filled ditch, where some kind of assault had obviously been attempted and repelled.

The remaining thirty five or so riders had taken to keeping the enemy contained, waiting for the rest of the army. Varus' gaze swept from there to take in the rest of the landscape.

'Do you see the ford?' Caninius asked, pointing off into the distance. Varus nodded. At the next loop of the river, where the flow curved back this way, the shallow water could easily be made out by the change in colour. The winter meltwaters had gone, and the warming of the world had lessened the depth and flow of such rivers so that seasonal fords were beginning to show again.

'Now look at the farm,' the legate urged him, and Varus squinted into the sunlight. While the German cavalry were riding in circles around the place and a few of the trapped Senones were in defensive positions around the circuit occasionally loosing a desultory arrow at them, the bulk of the enemy were concentrated around a closed gate at the far side of the enclosure.

'They're going to make a run for it,' he said, spotting what Caninius had cleverly picked up on.

'We lost Lucterius in the marsh,' Caninius grumbled. 'I'm damned if I'll lose this Drapes too.'

Varus shot a sidelong glance at the legate, but the comment seemed to have been delivered in a matter-of-fact, objective manner with no blame attached to Varus for being the officer in command of the fight that had lost Lucterius. He nodded his agreement. 'I'll take the horse and seal off that route. You ring them in with infantry.'

Caninius turned to the musician and gave his orders, and Varus simply gestured at his standard bearer who waved the banner and got the cavalry moving. As the cohorts began to cross the hill and move down towards the fertile farmland in the loop of the river, Varus' horsemen raced to catch up with him and then achieved a loose formation as he led them at a safe distance from the farm around the hills at the valley side and to the high ground that rose beside the ford.

As he and his riders thundered their way along the valley, the warning went up in the enemy camp and that gate was thrown open, enemy warriors running for the ford at the base of the hill. Varus urged his men on, noting as he did so two more groups that had peeled off left and were running for the river bank at the furthest extent of the curve. He could see no gleaming of mail on those groups. Sharp buggers they must be, running for the river rather than the ford, hoping to swim to safety and trusting that the Germans behind them would not risk their mounts in the deeper, faster water. Varus had watched those Germans for a year or more and was fairly sure that they would ride off a cliff if it meant taking an extra head.

Still, they were making a run for it and doing well.

It was, however, going to be a race for the ford. The enemy, though on foot, had been considerably closer to the ford and were running for their lives, which always gives a man a turn of speed of which he didn't previously know he was capable. Varus urged his men on, kicking his own steed into an ever faster pace. If the Senones achieved the ford, they might just be able to hold off the cavalry there – where they would be so much less effective – until their leader and his best could get away. It would certainly be a hard fight.

Leaning forward in the saddle, Varus veered his horse slightly to the left, aiming to cut off the fleeing Senones and secure the high ground by the ford. The better horses and horsemen kept pace with him. Others were beginning to string out along behind. The ford was

272

now maybe fifty heartbeats away and Varus was almost close enough to the enemy to smell their sweat. The front man of the fleeing Gauls turned to look back over his shoulder and Varus could see his eyes, bright and desperate, yet defiant and brave. The man gave two quick gestures and a small group of the running Senones suddenly halted and turned, their blades out.

Varus focused on that man giving the orders. If he was not Drapes then he was at least another noble or chief, for he was clearly in charge here and the warriors supported him so blindly that they had turned into their certain death to save him. That group of two dozen or so men holding their ground in the face of the charging cavalry would most certainly die, but they might just delay the cavalry long enough to allow the leader to make it across the ford and into the woods beyond.

Trusting his men to take care of the problem, Varus gestured to the decurion following him – one of his oldest and most trusted riders. While the bulk of the horse – composed in the main part of Remi, Allobroges, Mediomatrici and other allied tribes – rode directly at that small group of defenders in an effort to take that high ground and prevent the rest of the fleeing Gauls from achieving freedom, Varus and his single turma of riders slewed off sharply to the left, arcing around that small defensive group.

He could sense the decurion staring at him as if he were mad, which he would clearly have to be to do this. His face set in the rictus of battle, Varus cut across the line of enemy flight, behind the leaders who were nearing the ford and the line of men trying to prevent pursuit, but ahead of the bulk of the fleeing Senones. Across, and to the river.

With little chance of reaching the ford in time by forcing through the enemy and achieving that spur of high ground, the only option open had been a direct line. Consequently, he cut across the path of the men, straight down the bank and into the river, making for the middle of the ford downstream through the deeper water.

He winced as his horse jumped from the bank and plunged into the cold torrent, which came to midway up its flanks. He had been lucky, he knew. He'd reasoned that upriver of the ford and this close, centuries of sediment and dross would have built up, making the river shallower than it would be downstream, and he'd been borne out. The men around him had probably expected to find themselves in deep water, their horses swimming and panicking, but instead, the

273

beasts would be able to touch the river bed and walk, though the surface of the water was high and the beasts would find it hard going. At least the current was with them, helping propel them towards the ford rather than fighting them every step of the way.

A tremendous splash behind him announced the arrival of the decurion, and he was followed by more as the cavalry jumped, whooping, into the river, racing as best they could for the ford.

The enemy gambit had worked. A quick glance to Varus' right, and he could see over the riverbank that the small wall of enemy warriors had arrested the advance of the horse, Varus' cavalry busy fighting to pass them. They were dying, as were the other Senones fleeing behind them, running foul of the horse who had now achieved the high ground and were denying escape to the rest.

But the leaders were beyond them now, already at the water's edge and ploughing down into the ford. Varus urged his mount on, pushing through the water, targeting the centre of the ford and praying to Fortuna and Mars both that he had calculated correctly.

As he forced his way forward, he watched intently the party of eight warriors, including their noble or chief, wading out into water that reached above their knees. They were strong and fit and were making surprisingly good headway, considering the difficulty. But Varus had been accurate with his estimates. Even as he felt the horse beneath him move faster and easier, he saw the water's surface gradually receding down his legs, past his shins, his feet and then below the horse's belly, freeing the animal up to move more easily. The rise to the ford, formed of years of pebbles, sand and mud carried down by the current and drifting up against the crossing.

Behind him, he could hear the eager shouts of his men, gleeful that his gamble was paying off and that they had survived the deeper water with no trouble and would now reach the mid-point of the ford before the fleeing enemy.

Varus watched the Gauls come to the same conclusion and despite their already surprisingly fast pace across the river, still they managed to pick up speed, slogging through the water like Titans, desperate to get ahead of Varus and his men. The far bank presented only a very short grassy slope before the valley side rose sharply, covered with woodland and undergrowth. If the enemy leaders reached that treeline they were as good as lost. Cavalry were less than useless in forests.

Once again the enemy leader – Drapes he presumed – gave a command and five of the eight refugees turn and sloshed back through the water, drawing their blades and preparing to stop Varus' pursuit.

'Oh no you bloody don't.'

With a gesture of his own, Varus sent his own men against those five while he recalculated, veering slightly left and running along almost parallel with the ford. His horse was faster in the water than the men on foot and he quickly outpaced those five who were trying to stop him, and who instead now concentrated on the bulk of the cavalry riding directly at them.

Varus found himself chasing down three men on his own and threw out joyous thanks to Fortuna as one of the two brutes accompanying the chief lost his footing in the water on some misshapen stone, plunging with a squawk into the current and disappearing underneath, rising with difficulty a few moments later, coughing out water, his sword lost and wits befuddled.

Dropping his reins and using his knees to guide the horse like the well-trained Roman horseman he was, Varus drew his pugio dagger from his belt with his offhand. He carried no shield, being an officer, and now that free hand was of great value.

He was no marksman. He'd used a bow once or twice to no great effect, and he'd practised with the scorpion bolt throwers of the legions with at best moderate success. But throwing… ah well. Throwing was different. A boyhood spent skipping stones across water had given him an eye for range and a shoulder for the throw.

He glanced briefly, regretfully at the dagger. He'd only picked the damn thing up from the supply wagon before they'd set off to replace the one he'd lost in the swamp. To lose two pugios in one day would seem careless. The quartermaster would find a nickname for him when he went again, helm in hand like a beggar, requesting another replacement.

Still…

Biting his lip and concentrating, he drew his arm back high and threw the dagger with all his might.

The weapon was most certainly not designed for throwing and it spun in the air, but his aim was surprisingly true, and the dagger clonked into the back of the other big warrior's head. It hit badly, at the crosspiece below the grip, but with enough force to knock the man forward into the water, where he floundered in panic, trying to rise.

Varus, his sights still upon the leader, simply rode over the struggling warrior, cracking his bones and pulping him under-hoof as he bore down on his man. The second warrior disappeared beneath the surface with a scream.

The leader was at the bank. Varus watched him climbing up onto the grass and preparing to sprint for it. Kicking his horse's flanks, forcing it to run even faster, Varus rose from his saddle, prising himself out from between the four horns that kept him safely settled in even the worst conditions.

The Gaul had his blade out and was running. Varus felt the change in rhythm as his horse moved to dry ground, no longer fighting the water. In a straight race, the man would reach the trees and flee.

This was not a straight race.

His horse was now no longer under his control, his hands busy balancing rather than gripping reins and his feet now on the seat of the saddle as he rose like those Greek acrobats that danced on horses and bulls. The beast beneath him was a trained war horse and stayed on course despite his lack of control.

He tensed, bent his knees, and leapt.

His head clonked into that of his quarry as he hit and the pair went down on the grass in a tangle. He hissed as the pain from this morning's hip wound lanced through him at a particularly bad twist in the fall, but what was filling most of his mind was a ringing sound.

As the pair rolled to a halt, Varus tried to clear his head, his eyes blurred with the shock. Reaching up and only missing twice, he undid the leather thongs that kept the cheek plates of his helmet tied, and ripped the helm off, casting it away, where it rolled across the grass.

He could feel the tender part of his head where they had collided. It felt dangerously soft and even a gentle prod felt like someone driving a tent pole through his brain. *Jove, but that hurt!*

He realised that the man beneath him wasn't moving, and tried to focus. The Gaul's chest was rising and falling, so he was still alive. But as Varus none-too-gently turned him over, the huge lump and welt on the man's head came into view. Of course. Varus was helmeted – the Gaul was not. He examined the man's head briefly,

276

but it didn't appear to have cracked like an egg and there was no blood leaking from nose or ear to betray a serious internal injury.

The man would be seeing three of everything for a while though, and when he awoke it would feel like those same Greek dancers were cavorting inside his skull.

The man wore good bronze and gold torcs and arm-rings, the latter twisted into the shape of an 'S' with intricate design. His middle left finger bore a ring with the shape of a pentagram, and the one next to it a horse, again with an 'S' above it. Tell-tale designs of the Senones. There was little doubt in Varus' mind that this was Drapes, the other important leader of the revolt. Grimly, still shaking his head in a vain attempt to clear it, Varus hauled the unconscious noble up and carried him across to his horse, where he threw him unceremoniously across its back behind the saddle. Gathering his helmet and the fallen swords, he arranged everything and mounted once more, turning to look back across the river.

The high ground near the ford was occupied by his cavalry, herding a few prisoners into a line. The riders in the river had finished off all but one of the fleeing men and were playing some sort of brutal game with him, batting him back and forth with the flat of their blades. The farm itself was now swarming with legionaries, who had also pushed a few die-hard Senones down to the river bank. The Germans, true to form, were finishing off those who had run into the river. The poor bastards had thought to swim away and achieve safety from the horsemen, but the Germans feared nothing, from gods through wars to even fire from Hades itself. He'd once seen a group of Caesar's German cavalry leaping their horses over blazing kindling and beneath burning branches with very little clearance, just for sport.

The river certainly didn't faze them.

Some of the Germans were still mounted, mid-flow, their powerful home-bred horses swimming beneath them as they whooped and snarled, sticking their blades down again and again into the shapes swimming across the river. Other Germans had leapt from their horses and were swimming after their prey. Varus couldn't see in that kind of detail from this distance, but he'd be prepared to bet those men had their skinning knives between their teeth. He shuddered.

The most sensible of those Senones who had swum into the river had turned round away from the Germans and were even now once more climbing the near bank to surrender to the legion rather than face the brutal monsters in the water.

It was over. A resounding success with not a single enemy escaping the field.

And he had Drapes.

* * * * *

Varus stood at the westernmost of the three camps, atop the rampart, watching the oppidum of Uxellodunon, with Caninius beside him.

'Is all this strictly necessary?'

Caninius pursed his lips as he watched the two legions throwing up a turf rampart around the entire circuit, forming a ditch as they did so and replacing the earlier wicker fence atop the mound. It was starting to look like Caesar's circumvallation of Alesia last year, with towers being raised at the more vulnerable spots. He could just see a party of engineers draining that benighted marsh into the streams that ran through it with cunning and artifice and a lot of hard work. 'Perhaps not, but just because we have one of their leaders does not mean the fight is over. They've only lost half a thousand men, and I'm prepared for a fight. I'm not going to let something like that happen again.'

Varus nodded. They had managed to capture enough supplies to keep the legions fed for a week, maybe two if the food was stretched thinly enough. Drapes was in their custody and his identity had been confirmed. He was not being over-talkative, but torture for information would not be an option, at least until his dreadful head wound was healed. Indeed, it had been other prisoners who had confirmed his identity at first, since, when he had awoken, Drapes couldn't have told you what species he was let alone his name. His head must have felt like mush, given the fact that his skull had managed to hammer a deep dent in Varus' helmet.

The one nagging failure so far was the location of Lucterius. While Drapes was clearly the most senior man in their army here, Lucterius had been the instigator, and he had escaped. It would seem logical that he had retreated to the oppidum, but the problems he would have faced passing the Roman cordon and the wattle fence made that less likely. It was the considered opinion of the officers and scouts that Lucterius had fled the area in search of other allies.

278

And now, Caninius was settling in for a long siege.

'Sir?'

The two men turned, both assuming it was them being addressed. A legionary was standing at attention, panting, a little along the wall.

'What is it?'

The man, barely able to speak from running so hard, gestured to three riders cantering through the camp towards them. They were Roman officers, easily identifiable by their flowing red cloaks. Dismissing the man and letting him recover, Caninius straightened. Varus broke slowly into a smile as the three riders closed on them and he recognised the one at the centre.

'Fabius? Thank the gods.'

The newly-arrived legate returned his smile with one of his own. 'Seems as though you've got the rats pinned in their nest, yes?'

Caninius nodded. 'Lucterius has fled, we don't know where. We have the other leader Drapes in chains. And there are maybe ten thousand men trapped up there, well fed and apparently with a spring to supply them fresh water.'

Fabius laughed. 'Well perhaps we can do something about that now. I've brought the Eighth and Ninth with me. The Carnutes won't be troubling anyone for a while. I left their entire country pretty much a charred ruin.' He focused on Uxellodunon for a moment, deep in thought. 'This oppidum's long and pointed like Alesia, so it seems to me we could take a side each and concentrate our legions. You take southeast, since my men are coming from the north, and we'll settle on that side.'

Varus stretched. 'And my men and I will settle in for the wait and occasionally scout the area. Cavalry get bored in a siege, you know?'

Fabius chuckled again. 'The news that's flooding the north is that Caesar has finished putting down the tribes. He's headed back south and west and will be passing through Carnute lands soon. Gaul is finally beaten, apart from this one little fortress. We can afford to devote the whole summer to it if we want, so let's just keep them pinned and see what happens. Don't want to waste men on an assault if we don't have to.'

Varus nodded. One last stand. One last Alesia. And then Gaul was finally peaceful.

Chapter Sixteen

CAVARINOS replaced his mug on the rough-hewn table and smacked his lips with an unconvinced expression. 'Why is the average-priced stuff in a Greek city tavern better than the stuff I was sampling in your office this morning? You're supposed to be a quality wine merchant.'

Fronto snorted. 'You dipped into the office amphora? More fool you. That's not proper wine. That's *posca*.'

'Posca?'

With a grin, Fronto leaned back and sampled more of the wine on the table. 'Posca's what the legionaries drink.'

'Really? And they conquered a hundred nations on that? No wonder they're so implacable.'

The Roman chuckled. 'They drink proper wine, too, as often as they can, but they have to pay for *that* out of their wage, while the commanders give them an allowance of posca daily for free. The stingiest, and those who are saving for their retirement, live on posca and save money. A legionary's wage is good but wine, woman and dice takes a lot of financing.'

'Are you sure your army is doing it right? Perhaps it's really meant for cleaning armour, rather than drinking?'

'It's more or less vinegar and water with a few herbs, and made with the cheapest wine possible, too. We're experimenting with Gaulish wines at the moment. That stuff you tried was a mix of four parts water to one part Lingone wine, livened up a little with some of the cheaper spices that come in from Syracusae.'

'That stuff does not want livening up, Fronto. It wants putting down. But Lingone wine explains it all. After all, I've met Lingone *women*.'

Cavarinos grinned and Fronto took another swig of the house standard as he fixed Cavarinos with a steady gaze. 'I could use a man with knowledge of the tribes, you know?'

The Arverni simply shrugged off the comment as he had every time Fronto had tentatively tried to bring about such a subject. 'Do your men not want a drink?' he asked.

Fronto glanced up at Aurelius and Biorix, standing near the door like the Pillars of Hercules. Aurelius was far from small, his shoulders bull-like and his muscles impressive. His face was flat, framed with black hair that had grown longer than his usual cut and

280

taken on a slight curl that made him look more like a local. His hand rested on the knobbly end of a stick at his belt that looked a lot like a centurion's vine staff, and he leaned against the wall a little inside the bar. One of his seemingly endless list of superstitions apparently involved not standing on a threshold. Next to him, Biorix, the bulky Gallic engineer, stood in the doorway, his gaze wandering across the crowds in the street outside. Bigger than Aurelius – bigger than almost everyone in the bar – Biorix had taken advantage of his retirement from the legions and had grown out his blond hair once more, though he remained clean-shaven.

Neither of them wore armour or weapons other than Aurelius' stick, and both were dressed in nondescript local clothes.

Fronto shrugged. 'Normally neither of them would have an issue with throwing down a few jars. Even on duty. I know both of them can handle a few cups and remain sober enough to work. But since the news you brought, Masgava has all the lads on a strict no-booze-on-duty routine.'

'Good. Your men seem very loyal.'

'They've been through a lot with me. Up in the forest of Arduenna a couple of years ago...' he noted with a sly grin Aurelius ward himself against evil at the name of the Belgic goddess. 'And then of course in the war last year. We lost a lot of good men.' He noted a pained look cross Cavarinos' face. 'I know. You did too. Everyone did. But my little personal force was reduced to about a quarter over that time. Those who are left are closer than brothers.'

Cavarinos nodded. 'It is good for warriors to be like that. And it is good that they have experienced the horror and loss of war. Only warriors who remember what war is like should lead men. Those who do not know the consequences are too eager to bathe in blood regardless of the consequences.' The Arverni noble felt a flash of pain and guilt pass through him at the memory of his brother, dead at Alesia.

'Wise words,' Fronto agreed.

'Will you go back to your army?'

Fronto blinked. The question caught him totally off-guard, and when that happens, the first thought to flash into a man's mind is oft the unsought truth. The fact that as soon as Cavarinos had spoken, Fronto had pictured himself in armour with centurions and comrades at his side made him suddenly feel very uncomfortable. Not the least because most of those he'd instantly pictured around him had been dead for years. He bit down on that image and forced it back, suppressing it beneath common sense.

'I will never say "no" to that question. But I have no *plans* to do so. I'm far from a young man, these days, with a wife and children depending on me. No man can say I've not done my duty to Rome and her people now. Time for younger men to play the game.'

The Arvernian cocked an eyebrow. 'You sound like a man trying to convince himself. Good luck with that.'

'I miss the life,' admitted Fronto. 'But I don't miss the actual fighting. I saw things these past few years that most officers would never see. I have dreams…'

Cavarinos barked out a short, totally-humourless laugh. 'Let us not compare dreams. Mine would shock your hair white. If I were a man to believe in gods and superstitions I would think myself cursed.'

A short, slight whistle through teeth attracted their attention, and both men turned to see Biorix at the door step back into the shadow, nodding towards the street. With the hand of a practised deceiver, Cavarinos picked up the jar of wine and held it to the light, giving the impression from the doorway that both men were simply looking at the label on the jug, while enabling them both to clearly view the door.

Two figures appeared in the entrance and sauntered inside, one slapping the other on the back, laughing at some joke. Fronto peered at the men, wondering why Biorix had warned them, then recognised the pair a moment later. Glykon – Hierocles' man who had ruined Fronto's business from the inside for months unchecked, was chuckling at some jest of the man whose ribs Fronto had broken with a staff that night they had broken into his warehouse. Without intending to, Fronto shot up from his chair.

'Find another bar, shit weasel.'

The two men stopped, Glykon immediately recognising Fronto even as his friend tried to place the man. Glykon's gaze took in the hardened Gallic noble sitting opposite the Roman and also, as he spun with a sense of dread, the two former legionaries close to the door. In other circumstances, the man might have stood up for himself, even against Fronto. But with the odds so heavily stacked in the Roman's favour, he gave an obsequious smile and bowed from the waist.

'By all means. I find the company here unpalatable, anyway.'

282

The other man had now recognised Fronto, his hands shooting to newly-repaired ribs at the memory, and he began to pull at Glykon's shoulder, trying to turn him and eject him from the place. Two Greek sailors who had just entered behind them cursed the pair as they tried to get past to the bar, and Fronto's former enemies scurried out of the bar, almost knocking down another man as they went.

It took Fronto a moment to realise that he was growling, and he made himself stop. 'Bastards,' he grunted as he reached for the wine jug to pour another cup, but as his fingers closed on the pottery handle, Cavarinos' hand fell on his wrist and held it down.

'Don't look left,' the Arverni said, almost in a whisper. 'Laugh as though I told you a joke.'

Fronto panicked. Nothing in the world is more difficult than a convincing fake laugh at short notice. He chortled like an idiot at a freak show and felt thoroughly stupid, especially as Cavarinos gave him a look that conveyed just how moronic he'd sounded. 'Count to three,' the Arvernian went on in stilted Greek, 'then look to your right briefly.'

Fronto frowned, surprised to hear Greek from the Gaul, but not sure why. After all, the more southerly tribes had been trading with Romans and Greeks for centuries. It would be natural for them to speak the languages of trade. Then he realised he'd not been counting and, figuring it had probably been three already, he turned and scanned the bar interior to his right.

The only thing different from the last time he'd looked was the addition of the two Greek sailors and the local that had followed Glykon into the bar. Something about that latter figure nagged at him, though.

It was a warm spring day, and early evening. The sun had been high in the sky, searing the pavements and roofs of Massilia all day, and now the town was pleasantly warm even for Massilia as the sun began to sink and give way to the gold and indigo of evening. So why was the man so huddled up in an ankle length cloak of dark grey wool? And with a hood, too, though the latter was not pulled up.

He saw the new arrival start to turn and pulled back round to face Cavarinos sharply.

'You know him?'

The Arverni gave a slight nod, keeping his face lowered, his eyes on the cup before him.

'And he speaks no Greek?'

'I believe not, but keep your voice down just in case.'

'Who is he?'

Cavarinos scratched his neck, his arm covering most of his face. 'He is Aneunos, the son of Lucterius of the Cadurci.'

Fronto's eyes widened at the name. 'The Lucterius we fought at Gergovia? Who I understand was leading that relief force on the other hill?'

'The very one. Try not to say his name again. Your surprise is preventing you from speaking quietly, and he will doubtless recognise his own name and that of his father.'

'You think he is one of this group you were speaking of? The one I won't name, just in case?'

'It seems likely.' Cavarinos motioned him to stay silent and busily poured them both another drink, chatting inanely about the wine's quality for a few moments until he sat back and breathed easier. 'He's gone,' he announced, reverting to Latin.

'Gone? Where?'

'Upstairs. And he just spoke to the innkeeper, didn't get a key, so I presume he was already staying here.'

'Are you suggesting that this place is where they are all staying?'

'That would be my guess, yes.'

Fronto chewed on his lip. 'Anything else you can tell me? You said there were twelve of them identifying themselves with gods. The leader – this Molacos – was Taranis.'

'Yes. There is also a giant one – Mogons – and at least one woman – Catubodua. I saw that Aneunos' cloak bore a sun and a bow. That would suggest Maponos, which fits, given his youthfulness. I have vague recollections of young Aneunos winning a great archery contest a few years back, when he came of age. You would probably think of Maponos as Apollo.'

Fronto continued to chew on his lip. 'Definitely one resident. Possibly twelve. It's a bit of a gamble.'

Cavarinos straightened, his eyes dark. 'It is. But if you wish to discover more and perhaps damage them, this may be your only opportunity.'

Fronto gave him a meaningful look. 'This is not your fight, Cavarinos.'

'Oh it is.'

'You know what I mean. You shouldn't kill your own people.'

'You Romans seem to do it often enough. Civil war seems to be a Roman sport.'

'That was decades ago. Listen, are you sure you want to take part in this?'

Cavarinos placed both hands on the table. 'These are not good people, Fronto. These are maniacs, set on prolonging the agony for all the tribes. They have to be put down if my people are ever to flourish again in any form.'

Fronto nodded. 'Aurelius? Biorix?'

The two men strolled over, pausing at the table.

'The cloaked man that came in... he's one of them. Cavarinos saw him go upstairs.'

Aurelius slapped his head in irritation. 'I thought he looked odd in his cloak on such a hot day, but it slipped straight from my head with all that Glykon crap.'

'I think we need to go upstairs and have a little chat with the young fellow,' Fronto muttered. 'But we also need to be prepared to run like rats from an aqueduct if that door opens and we find all twelve of them in there. It's risky.'

Aurelius reached up and tugged at his protective, white and blue eye pendant, muttering his prayer, then set his face hard. 'Wish I had my sword,' he muttered, then patting his stick resignedly, he added 'let's go rip the runt a new bum hole.'

Fronto grinned and momentarily caressed his own Fortuna pendant before rising from the table and crossing the room, the other three at his back as he neared the bar. The innkeeper finished serving the two Greek sailors with an off-colour joke and then turned to them.

'I would like to know what room that fellow that just went upstairs is in.'

The innkeeper's expression darkened. 'I don't want no trouble in my place.'

'Then you're letting rooms to very much the wrong people. That's a known killer up there, as are his friends.'

'No trouble,' repeated the innkeeper, and Fronto rolled his eyes.

'Biorix, give this man five obols for the room number and another five for his conscience.'

As the big Gaul counted out the coins in a surprisingly threatening manner, the innkeeper's expression wavered. Fronto glared at him. 'Greed usually leads to trouble, and you said you didn't want that.'

The man sighed. 'Up the stairs and at the end of the corridor. Last door. It's my bunk room. Usually caters for the crews of small trade boats.'

'Thank you,' Fronto replied quietly. 'I would heartily recommend that you forget this conversation ever happened.'

'Gladly,' the innkeeper grumbled and scurried off to the other end of the bar.

Fronto turned to the others. 'Come on.' With Cavarinos, Biorix and Aurelius following close behind, he approached the stairs and began to climb them. The wood creaked alarmingly beneath his soft boots and he automatically shifted to the edge of the stairs as he climbed, reducing the noise as best he could.

A moment later he emerged in the corridor above, with two doors to each side and one at the end. Taking a deep breath, Fronto stalked along the passage, coming to a halt outside the bunk room. As the others stopped behind him, he pressed an ear to the door. He could hear movement inside but no conversation, which suggested low occupancy. With relief, he crouched and looked through the keyhole, which was large to accommodate the bulky iron key that would keep the room secured against intruders.

His relief increased as his view turned out to be unobstructed. No key in the lock likely meant that it remained unlocked. Moreover he could see the young Gaul, now de-cloaked, standing by a window and looking down at the street. The light was fading outside, and no lamps had been lit, so the room was dim and monochrome. Swivelling his eye to get the best view he could, despite the restrictions, Fronto picked out the edges of double-tier bunk beds to either side of that window. And, interestingly, two long Gallic swords resting against the end of one of them, their tips downward. Rising again, he turned and used his fingers to explain that he could see only one man and that there were at least two swords to the right as they entered.

The other three nodded and stepped lightly forward, crowding him as he reached for the ringed handle. Given the creak of the stairs and the poor condition of the door's ironwork, subtlety was no longer required. Even if the handle didn't creak loudly, the hinges would. Fronto gripped the handle and, nodding a count of three in his head, turned and pushed in one move. He felt panic rise for a heartbeat as the door didn't budge, but then it gave suddenly, the mechanism tight and badly-kept. As the portal swung inwards, he barrelled straight across the floor at the man in front of the window.

The young Maponos turned in surprise as Fronto burst into his room and powered towards him. The Roman officer sensed rather than saw Aurelius and Biorix split off to either side, making sure the rest of the room was empty and securing whatever blades they could find. Cavarinos was still following him and despite everything Fronto felt a tiny thrill of fear at the knowledge that the man right behind him had been every bit as much his enemy as the one in front only a year ago. What if Cavarinos had always harboured a flame of revenge?

But he had no time to ponder on his doubt, for the young Gaul before him had turned and, as Fronto hit him full on, thudded back against the windowsill with a gasp.

The Roman immediately reached up and grabbed the young Gaul by the throat, but was surprised as Maponos easily knocked his grasping hand aside and delivered a sharp punch to his ribs that almost felled him immediately.

Oddly, despite the danger and trouble of the sudden turnaround in the fight, what struck Fronto most of all was how embarrassed he was and how glad he was that Masgava wasn't here to see what a monumental cock-up he'd made of such a simple attack.

As he reeled, he backed into Cavarinos and the Arverni was forced to stagger back to keep his footing. The young rebel was quick to act, grabbing a ceramic jug from the table by the window and, as Fronto made another lunge for him, slamming the thing into the Roman's face. Fronto was blinded. Partially by the ceramic surface being squashed into his face and partially by the mix of sweat and blood trickling into his eyes from some cut the jug had delivered to his brow… but mostly by rage.

Ignoring the jug, the pain and the stinging blindness, he roared and grasped with both hands. He felt his left achieve a grip on a wide swathe of wavy hair. Satisfied with this, he yanked downwards and was rewarded with a yelp and a change of scenery as the jug vanished from in front of his eyes. Still gripping and pulling the hair, he used his other hand to wipe away the sweat and blood and focused on the Gaul.

His world exploded in pain again as Maponos stamped on his foot and then punched him in the gut. He reeled backwards again, halted by both the close presence of Cavarinos behind him and his grip on the Gaul's hair. Finally, the long locks gave way and tore free with an unpleasant sound, accompanied by another scream.

As Fronto cast aside the hair and straightened, trying to breathe through winded lungs and ignore the pain in his midriff, the Maponos figure lurched back against the windowsill. For just a moment he tottered, his point of balance dangerously close to the level of the window. Then Fronto's hand shot out and grabbed the man's neck again, tightening instantly, given what had happened with his first attempt.

'Oh no you don't,' he growled, squeezing until the young warrior gasped.

A sword hilt appeared next to him and he glanced aside to see Biorix proffering the blade to him. He took it with his free hand and stepped back, letting go of the man's neck just as he brought the point of the blade up to tickle the Gaul's throat apple. Maponos remained quite still, aware that even the tiniest move might well open his windpipe.

'You and I are going to have a little talk.'

Fronto could feel the others close behind him. 'You three could maybe have been a little more help.'

Cavarinos snorted. 'I couldn't get past you. You were too busy blocking the way getting beaten to a pulp.'

Fronto sighed, keeping his gaze locked on the young warrior in front of him. 'He was alone?'

'Yes,' Aurelius replied. 'But there's twelve kit bags here, so the rest will be back at some point.'

Fronto nodded. 'We might not want to be here when that happens. Four against eleven isn't good odds.' He turned back to the young warrior, applying just the slightest pressure to the sword in his hand. 'Now, I would like you to tell my friend here everything about the Sons of Taranis.'

'Fuck you, Roman.'

Fronto resisted the urge to just push the blade and counted to ten in his head.

'Fronto...' Cavarinos said quietly.

'Fronto?' snapped the young warrior at his sword's point. 'The commander of the Tenth?'

'The same,' grunted Fronto.

The warrior laughed, which caused several small lacerations at his neck. Blood trickled in three rivulets down into his tunic. 'The Roman hero of Alesia playing the Greek merchant and hiding from his enemies in Massilia. You fool, Roman. No one could save you and your putrid master from the vengeance of Taranis!'

Fronto tried to hold back a sneer that threatened to cover his face, with only moderate success. 'I have no fear of your god's vengeance, young Aneunos, son of Lucterius.' He was gratified by the widening of the young man's eyes. 'Yes, I know all about you. And your leader Molacos, too. So I know that it is not the vengeance of Taranis that I face, but the rather paltry retaliation of a failed warrior chief.'

'You have no idea...'

Fronto drew another bead of blood with the tip of the sword. 'Oh just stop babbling your threats. I don't fear you or your people. And we will not let you go to Rome and free your king. Even Vercingetorix knows your cause is over. Your people are beaten, Aneunos. Gaul is Caesar's now. And next year it will be Rome every bit as much as Narbo or Illyricum, with its own governor and tax system. And then it will get roads. And aqueducts, and temples and fora, and eventually maybe even citizenship. But it will never again be your tribes. And I can understand how that saddens you, but it's the truth and what you are trying to do is only going to kill thousands more of your people. Caesar will put down your new army, and I will stop your own little mission.'

'You will do nothing,' sneered the Gaul.

'Be quiet.'

'You will be too busy mourning.'

Fronto frowned and, distracted for just a heartbeat, he was unable to stop the young warrior as he lunged forward, driving his own throat onto Fronto's sword. The spray of crimson from the arteries washed across Fronto, as well as Cavarinos at his shoulder, and then soaked the windowsill and the table as he fell away, gurgling and shaking. Fronto leapt back, almost knocking Cavarinos to the floor again.

'The idiot.'

'He didn't want to tell you anything,' muttered Biorix, unhelpfully as he reached down to the table next to the window and brought up a Gallic ritual mask of terracotta, glazed with some darker tone and with a strangely expressionless straight mouth.

'I can see that. But…'

Fronto stopped. 'Mourning?'

'Oh shit,' said Aurelius quietly. 'One of them here. Eleven absent.'

'The villa!'

Seconds later, armed with blades from the room and two of them coated liberally with blood, the four men were pounding back along the corridor and down the stairs. As they burst into the bar, armed and bloodied, a clamour arose among the patrons, and the innkeeper, white-faced and apoplectic, screamed imprecations at them.

Then they were out in the street, turning uphill and racing for the villa outside the walls, high on the hills and overlooking the sea.

* * * * *

Fronto's heart was hammering fit to burst and his breath coming in sore, rasping gasps as the four men emerged at the crest of the hill on the villa's access road and raced towards the open gateway to the villa. The sun, threatened by an encroaching layer of cloud, had finally disappeared beneath the perfect horizon of the sea at the moment they had passed through the Eparchion Gate and the mile and a half from there had been a tiring slog in the gathering gloom, that cloud bank sliding over the world to lock in the heat and shut out the light.

The villa stood solid and stoic, issuing a welcoming golden glow from its windows and front doorway, and Fronto at first felt a massive wash of relief flood his senses as he'd half expected to arrive and find the house a burning mass. There were at least a dozen men at the villa, all trained and armed now, protecting the family. Masgava had chosen and trained the men well and his rota made sure that the villa was always protected since Cavarinos had brought his tidings of danger. And yet despite a parity of numbers against the eleven remaining enemies, Fronto had found himself reassessing as they ran.

The young Gaul they had fought had been *good*. He was maybe twenty summers at most, and that was being kind, and he had been lightly built and relatively inexperienced. Yet he had almost done for Fronto – a man more than two decades his senior and with a lifetime of combat experience – with sheer speed, strength and skill. And if he was the youngest and least trained of these 'Sons of Taranis', the gods only knew what the rest were like. Certainly they would be more than a match for the hired men of Masgava's force.

Still, the villa seemed quiet.

Too quiet?

His heart began to race again. Why were there no patrols or guards outside to challenge them? Why was the front door wide open and issuing that welcome glow when the place was supposedly sealed against intruders?

His mouth suddenly felt unpleasantly dry. He had spent the winter tired beyond belief, plagued by nightmares of those dying Gauls – especially the young lads. *The children.* And this afternoon another such soul had joined that nightmare throng to await him in his dreams. But suddenly all of that seemed trivial and immaterial, for in his imagined nightmares he now pictured himself holding the butchered remains of Lucilia and the boys.

Ice filled his veins.

The open door called to him desperately and yet he dreaded passing through it.

The four men reached the gate in the outer wall – also open – and ran inside, crossing the lawn rather than the gravel path that might attract too much attention. Fronto in the lead, they bore down on the glowing rectangle of his home's door and Fronto gripped the sword in his hand so tight that it almost shook.

His breath held, fingers tight and face white with fear, Fronto edged towards the door.

'What in the name of Baal Hamon's ballsack happened to you?'

Fronto's feet left the ground in panic at the soft spoken words close by, and if he'd thought his heart had already been pounding before, now was truly something else. His throat felt as though it were pulsing with each hammering, racing beat. A shadow detached itself from the darkness of the walls a few feet from the open door and Fronto felt a maelstrom of panic, anger and confusion as Masgava stepped into the light, his teeth and eyes shining bright in his dark features.

'For the love of life itself don't *do* that!' Fronto gasped.

Masgava was merely studying Fronto and his gaze led the Roman to look down. In the golden glow of the doorway the swathe of drying blood across his chiton was rather prominent, and the sword in his grip was still oily red with spots of coagulation. He must look a sight.

'I say again,' the big man said quietly, 'what happened to you?'

Fronto brushed the question aside. 'Is everyone alright?'

Without waiting, Fronto rushed into the doorway, Masgava turning to follow, the other three behind.

'Of course they are.'

'Why is the front door open?'

Masgava tutted. 'Fronto, it's exceedingly warm. You have a headstrong wife and two young children. A through draft was required.'

Fronto turned to see the three behind him: Cavarinos, Biorix and Aurelius. 'Shut that door. Aurelius, you stay and keep watch. Biorix, head round the villa and make sure every door and window is secured.

'You think they're coming?' Masgava murmured.

Fronto indicated the crimson spray on his chiton. 'Not all of them. We met one in the town. But that means there are eleven unaccounted for. I had assumed they were here. The one we met knew me by name and knew that I was a wine merchant, so we can assume they are well aware of the villa. Somewhere down in town they will have found directions for the villa. Get everyone on full alert and make sure all staff are accounted for.'

Masgava inclined his head.

'Who's at the back door?' Fronto added.

'Arcadios.'

The former legate felt his heart begin to slow as he made his way through the villa, tutting irritably at the open shutters he passed time and again. The rear door was as open as the front and lit by an oil lamp in the shape of a giant winged phallus. Like Masgava at the front, Arcadios was bright enough not to be standing presenting a tempting silhouette in the doorway. The Greek archer was seated on a marble bench to the left of the door, outside. True to professional form, his bow was strung and leaning against the wall a foot from his hand, and five arrows stood vertical from the raised flower bed into which he had pushed them for easy access. Unless they had very sharp eyes, anyone coming for the back of the villa would be pinned to the sheds before they even knew there was a man in the shadows there. Fronto nodded his satisfaction. For an archer, the glow of the door would provide a useful distraction to dazzle any on-comer. The back door was safer open than closed with Arcadios there.

As he turned and made his way back towards the atrium, Lucilia appeared from a side door.

'What is...'

She stopped mid-sentence as she took in the state of her husband. 'I assume none of that blood is yours, my love?'

Fronto smiled reassuringly. 'Not a drop. Well, the bit on my forehead, but that's just a scratch from a water jug.'

She looked him in the eye and reached out, rubbing his upper arms soothingly. 'This was no bar fight?'

'No. They're here and they know about me. The good news is that one of the twelve is already gone and won't be bothering us again.' He lifted the mask he had taken from Biorix, and Lucilia shuddered as she peered into the lifeless, humourless clay face. 'The bad news is that eleven more of them are still out there, and even the youngest one was a beast in a fight.'

Lucilia shivered. 'What do you want us to do?'

Fronto smiled warmly. Lucilia might oft-times treat him like a recalcitrant child and she would never tire of trying to change him, but the simple fact was that for all her wilfulness – inherited from her military sire – she was clever and understanding enough to know exactly when to defer to his experience. Fronto was now completely in control and she would not argue.

'Keep the children at your side at all times. Keep away from the windows and for preference somewhere unexpected. In fact, get the spare bedding and cushions and so on and set up a temporary home in the wine store. Most of the stock is down at the warehouse, so there's plenty of room. We can't ignore the possibility that they know the basic layout of a villa and their initial targets will be the places where they will think to find us. Keep the most trusted of the servants in there with you, and Pamphilus and Clearchus will stand by the door. They're impulsive and a little bit thick, but they're strong and loyal.'

His wife nodded.

'And what will you do, Marcus?'

'Fortify this place and wait. If they haven't already been here, then they must be coming. They know a former legate lives in a villa on this hill.'

Lucilia stopped dead in the process of turning to organise things.

'Two, you mean.'

Fronto frowned. 'What?'

'Two former legates live in villas on this hill. Don't forget my father.'

Fronto felt the colour drain from his face. Not only would Balbus be there, but his youngest daughter, Lucilia's sister too! Why had he not considered that straight away? There was every chance that the Sons of Taranis might get the wrong villa. In fact, Balbus' residence was actually closer to the city and would probably be the first they came across. Unless their information was incredibly thorough…

He turned, panic beginning to rise in him. Masgava had already heard the exchange and was bellowing the names of his men. As guards came rushing in, including Arcadios from the back door, the big Numidian reeled off a list of names and positions for them to take up. The four who were left joined he, Fronto and Cavarinos. 'Sorry, Fronto. Not enough men to protect this place and go to master Balbus' in force. If you take Aurelius and Biorix again, can you manage with eight of you?'

'I will.' He clasped Masgava's giant, lined hand tight. 'Thank you, my friend. Keep this place safe. We'll be back.'

Leaving the big Numidian to take control of the villa, Fronto gestured to the others to follow, picking up Biorix in the atrium and Aurelius at the door. Along with the three of them and Cavarinos, he had four of Masgava's recent recruits: Agesander the former boxer, a huge Greek marine called Procles and two mercenaries – Zeno and Evagoras. Good men all, from what Fronto had seen. Would they be a match for eleven trained murderers?

He would soon find out.

Opening the door, they forged out into the darkness. Behind them Masgava shut the door tight and it took a few moments for their eyes to adjust to the darkness. The night was becoming stifling, the day's heat trapped beneath that low, thin layer of cloud that held no rain but effectively cut out almost all moon and starlight.

By the time they were fully aware of their surroundings they had passed through the gate once more, making for the faint looming shape of his father-in-law's villa. Balbus' home was a copy of his own, having been the one from which the design for his was taken. It was sited just close enough to be visible from his own, but far enough away to provide a sense of separateness.

He could see pinpricks of gold around the villa, indicating that the lamps were lit. More importantly, there was no huge column of roiling black smoke above it, as he'd half expected. Their weariness all-but forgotten, the eight men ran at speed across the springy turf, avoiding the bare rocky patches that rose from the green here and there.

Balbus' villa was similarly surrounded by a low perimeter wall with a high gate in the front. The wooden portal stood open as they approached and Fronto noted with sinking spirits that his friend's front door was thrown back, issuing a golden glow from within. Not a good sign.

He turned as they ran, and gestured to Agesander and Procles to peel off and skirt the villa proper, securing the grounds and coming at the back door once they were content that they were not in further danger from outside. Fronto's eyes scoured every bush and hollow in the immaculately-tended garden as he and his small force ran for the door, the two assigned men veering off to their own tasks. He saw no signs of movement. The night was still, with not a breath of wind to move the layer of cloud that had set in, which at least meant that he was not jumping at the sound of leaves rustling in the wind.

What would he tell Lucilia if…?

His worst fears were confirmed as they reached the threshold and the first body. To the right of the door was one of Balbus' prized climbing rose beds, but the trellis was lying flat on the grass atop the broken and felled flowers. The body of a man in a Roman tunic lay in the mess. His head lay a short distance away, and three black-shafted arrows protruded from his back. Fronto prayed on his behalf that the arrows had been lethal before the blow that had taken off the head had landed.

He wouldn't be able to show her her father's body. Or her sister's.

He might not be able to look at them himself.

Balbus had been as close as a father to him even before he had met and been wooed by the man's daughter. He was as close a friend as Fronto had ever had – one of a very diminished circle, these days. And Balbina was so young – had witnessed so many horrors in her short life, yet had been starting to recover, they'd thought. Panic was starting to give way now to anger.

He pushed in through the door, knowing now what he was going to find and hoping against hope that he could catch a few of these bastards and gut them in the name of Nemesis – the lady of vengeance.

Two more bodies lay in the vestibule. One – a guard with a sword – had knocked over the shrine to the household gods as he had taken his fatal blow and fallen. The thoroughness of these Roman-haters was evident in that the attackers had wasted time pausing to grind the figures of the villa's spirit protectors into dust and broken shards under their heels. The other corpse was a young serving girl, the blow that had killed her smashing her spine in the lower back as she ran from the intruders. Fronto reached up to the twin figurines hanging at his neck.

Fortuna give me your blessing in my sword arm tonight. Nemesis, give me the bastards to use it on.

As he paused in the atrium, taking in the pile of bodies that had been dumped in a tangled pile in the central impluvium pool, Cavarinos appeared at his side. The Arvernian noble looked every bit as angry and vengeful as he and Fronto gave thanks to Fortuna for bringing him a Gaulish friend on whom he felt he could truly rely in his time of need.

'Not there?' Cavarinos murmured.

Fronto peered at the pile, the once-delicate square pool with its mosaic floor now filled with dark crimson liquid, obscuring the pattern beneath. There were seven of them, accompanied by the odd separated limb, but none of them wore the good clothes that would mark out Balbus, nor could he see the bald head, framed by faint wisps of grey hair. No children either, thank the gods.

'Doesn't look like it.' He tried not to think about what Cavarinos had told him – about how the killers tended to take Roman officers and torture them to death, displaying their broken bodies in an almost ritualistic fashion. Of course they wouldn't just heap *Balbus* – a former legate – in a pile with the servants.

He didn't even need to give the orders. Zeno and Evagoras disappeared through doors to the left, searching, while Aurelius and Biorix did the same to the right. Balbus was a semi-regular visitor to Fronto's villa, and all the staff and guards knew him well enough to recognise him.

'They've been and gone,' Fronto said through gritted teeth.

Cavarinos nodded. 'This is a tomb, not a fight.'

Fronto let out a low grunt. Nemesis was taunting him.

'Come on.'

Leaving the others to search, Fronto led Cavarinos off to the farther rooms. A quick glance found no Balbus in the old man's chamber, triclinium or office, though the latter held the villa's chief servant – the master's favoured man – draped over the table with his arms removed at the shoulders and a gladius driven down through his neck and the table top, emerging beneath, where the dripping into the dark lake had almost stopped. It had been some time since the attack, then.

'Unless he tried for the servants' quarters, he probably ran for the baths and he'll have had Balbina with him. She'd be his first concern.'

Leading the Arvernian through the side passage into the bath suite, he was surprised to find the place partially-filled with choking smoke. Baffled, he blinked away the grimy itchy soot, bending low to avoid the worst, which fugged the room from chest to ceiling height. Two rooms revealed nothing, but the third was fascinating. The warm room had been damaged. A wide heavy basalt labrum had stood on a pedestal, filled with cold water to complement the heated floor, but that labrum lay on its side, the bowl chipped and broken. For a moment Fronto simply believed that the water had evaporated from the floor with the warmth, but then he realised that the heat in the floor was mediocre at best. And one of the square stone slabs that formed the floor had clearly been moved. The surrounding stones were still a little wet, but this one was dry. His heart leaping with hope, Fronto pointed at it.

'Help me.'

Using his hard-won Gallic sword somewhat ignominiously, he used the tip to lever up the edge of the stone square until Cavarinos slid his fingers beneath and heaved, nodding. Fronto joined him, casting aside the sword and lifting the stone enough to drop it back.

A gleaming blade lanced out of the darkness and scored a narrow line across Fronto's forearm before he could leap back.

'Pax!' he shouted. 'It's me!'

As he edged towards the lip of the hole and peered down, his vision still poor with the smoke above, he spotted the most welcome sight of his day. Balbus sat, painful and blackened in the stunted space below floor, where the heat from the furnace circulated to warm the floor. The youngest daughter sat beside him, soot-black but wild-eyed. The old man's sword wavered for a moment.

'Marcus?'

Fronto cast a thousand simultaneous thanks to Fortuna, promising her an altar for this, and grinned down at his father-in-law. 'At least you had the sense to hide.'

'I saw what they did to my best men. I'm a soldier, not an idiot, Marcus.'

As the two men reached down and lifted the young girl to freedom, then helped the old man out of the cramped space, Balbus straightened with a hiss of pain, rubbing his sore back.

'That was a stroke of genius,' Fronto laughed. 'You used the labrum of water to extinguish the furnace?'

Balbus nodded, coughing in the thick atmosphere. 'I hadn't quite counted on the quantity of smoke. We almost expired from that alone.'

'Ha.' Fronto turned as Biorix appeared. 'They're safe. Round up the men and get ready to head back. We'll deal with all this mess in the daylight.'

As the big former legionary hurried off, Fronto looked his father-and sister-in-law up and down. 'Let's get a horse and get you over to my place. Then we can get you in the bath and cleaned up.'

Balbus gave him a sour look. 'If it's alright with you, I'll just dunk myself in the horse trough here before we leave. I've had quite enough of bath suites for one night.'

* * * * *

Fronto sat with Balbus, the old man busily cleaning out a sooty ear with a square of linen. Cavarinos and Masgava also occupied the room, every other available able-bodied man in an assigned position around the villa keeping watch while a few lucky ones caught up on sleep. In a couple of hours the sun would begin to make its presence felt, and in just under an hour the rota would change, different men going to rest and those relatively refreshed rising to take their place.

Lucilia had been ecstatic at her family's return and Fronto had found himself musing that if they all lived through the next day or so, his home life would be considerably more relaxed for a while. Indeed, despite his bloody exertions the previous afternoon and the soulless horror of what he'd seen in his father-in-law's house, he felt blessed and immensely relieved that everyone he really cared for in Massilia was now under one roof with a very watchful guard, Balbina safe with Fronto's own boys

Balbus had repeatedly refused Fronto's insistence that he bathe to remove the layer of grime and dirt that even a dip in a horse trough had done little to remove, but a brief sharp word from his daughter had put paid to that and the old man had emerged from the baths refreshed and clean, dressed in Fronto's clothes. Fronto and Cavarinos had also changed, their own bloodied apparel sitting in a washing pile. It had made Fronto chuckle to see the Arvernian in a Roman officer's spare tunic and belt, though Cavarinos had looked less than pleased with the change, and had insisted on retaining his trousers, despite their state.

'Will they really try again?' Balbus asked quietly, excavating his other ear. 'If their goal is to get to Rome urgently and they have a ship waiting, will they waste the time?'

Cavarinos shrugged and glanced across at Fronto. 'How long until your treasure fleet sails?'

Fronto pursed his lips. 'A day or two. No, definitely two. It won't be today.'

Cavarinos turned back to Balbus. 'They will want to be away from this place before the fleet, else they might fall foul of Roman marines at sea. But that still gives them today. I expect them to sail tonight, at the last real opportunity. They will stay as long as they can and try as hard as they can. They may have a goal to achieve, but these men are fanatics, legate Balbus. They are rabid haters of your officers. I have seen what they have done before now. And if they have been thwarted once tonight, they will try all the harder. Molacos will not want to lose face with his men.'

'I have to say, prince Cavarinos, that your arrival was gods-sent. Thank you. But for you, I would likely have died and so would Marcus here.'

Fronto saw Cavarinos wince at the use of a title. There was an unintentional bitterness in the Arvernian that coloured everything in his life now. It was why he could not wear his face and hair as a Gaul, yet would not dress himself as a Roman. It was why, despite clearly hating every morsel of his soul for doing it, he killed his own people in saving a nominal enemy. It was why he would never stay, no matter how persuasive Fronto thought he might be. It saddened him to see the Arvernian brought so low. A year ago, at a strange native sacred spring, he and Fronto had spoken privately and had discovered in each other a kindred spirit, abhorring the nature of the protracted war that was ruining Gaul and wishing there was any way to end the matter peacefully. And now Gaul was lost and Cavarinos was a ghost. A slight change in fortunes at Alesia and it might have been a whole different matter.

'I owe Fronto a debt. He released me from slavery in a Roman camp. My people consider such a debt paramount. It is a life debt in effect. When the Sons of Taranis no longer threaten him, that debt will be paid, and into the bargain there will be no new great rising. The people of our tribes will turn from war to the fields, nurturing crops and children, trying to rebuild within the arms of Rome.'

'Would that many Roman nobles could express so noble a sentiment,' admired Balbus. 'You would do well in our senate.'

Fronto smiled at the look of horrified fascination that crossed Cavarinos' face at the very thought.

'What was that?' interjected Masgava sharply.

'What?'

The four of them fell silent, and then they all heard the clanging of the bell at the front door. In two heartbeats the alarms were clanging all over the villa. 'Where?' Balbus asked.

'The first alarm was the front door,' Masgava replied, snatching his sword from close by and belting it as he made for the exit. Behind him Cavarinos was already moving. Balbus grabbed his own gladius, sheathless since he had taken it into his bath house. Fronto gripped his Gaulish sword with the slight kink near the tip where he'd levered up the slab. He'd had the chance to retrieve his own sword he supposed, but over the evening he'd grown comfortable carrying the big weapon. It gave him a surprising reach.

Through the villa the four men ran, joined by a sleepy looking Arcadios and Aurelius who had clearly just hauled themselves from their cots and grabbed a weapon without even taking the time to belt their tunics.

The front door was ajar, and Catháin was peering out into the darkness.

'What is it?' Fronto shouted.

'Archers, Fronto. At least three, from the regularity of the strikes. They're not particularly good – I've seen better – but they're getting close. Once they've found their range they'll be able to take anyone at a door or window at their leisure.'

'I'd not seen them as archers in my head,' mused Fronto.

'Remember young Aneunos?' replied Cavarinos. 'He was an archer, and a good one. There will be others. Molacos had been a hunter himself.'

The door to their left opened to reveal the brothers Pamphilus and Clearchus. Both had their blades drawn and a trickle of blood ran from the latter's scalp down into his eye, which blinked repeatedly.

'Bastards have found the range for the windows,' grunted Clearchus.

'Why did you open the shutters, then?' sighed Fronto, wondering at how two such numb brothers had survived the streets of Massilia for so long.

'Can't see the enemy through solid wood, sir.'

'I swear that if either of you had an original thought...'

His insult went unfinished as an arrow whispered through the open crack in the door, almost catching both Catháin and then Fronto, and clattered off along the floor into the atrium.

'Bastards, bastards, bastards!' roared Clearchus, wiping the blood from his eyes. 'C'mon.'

Pamphilus reached past them and yanked the front door wide open, almost pulling Catháin from his feet. Brandishing their blades, the brothers ran into the open door, straight towards the unseen archers. Neither made it across the threshold before Masgava's huge meaty hands slapped down on their shoulders and jerked them back inside. Two arrows filled the air, one tearing the shoulder fabric of Clearchus' tunic and drawing blood, the other missing Masgava's ear by a finger-width as it rattled off across the atrium.

Without waiting for the order, Catháin pushed the door to so that only a narrow sliver remained. Enough to see through, with very little danger to the observer.

'They are improving their aim rapidly,' Arcadios said quietly. 'Let me give them something to think about.'

Catháin nodded and stepped aside. As the others watched, the Greek archer withdrew three arrows from his quiver, nocking one, with the other two held by the point in the fingers that gripped the bow.

'When I say, open the door, count to six quickly and then close it.'

The northerner who managed Fronto's business nodded, turning a lopsided grin on his employer. 'While I like a punch-up as much as

301

the next man, proper battles are extra. I shall be expecting a raise tomorrow. Or at least a healthy bonus.'

He was still smiling wide as Arcadios breathed 'now!'

The door pulled inwards and in the most fluid movement Fronto had ever seen from an archer, Arcadios released the first missile out into the night, dropping the second to nock even as his shoulder rolled, bringing back the string and releasing, the third arrow following suit in perfect timing like some kind of machine.

As he stepped back and lowered the bow and Catháin muttered 'six' and closed the door to a sliver again, they all heard a yelp and shouts of alarm outside. For a long moment there were no further thuds of arrowheads hitting door and wall, and when it started up again, it was slower, more cautious.

'Nicely done,' Balbus complemented the archer.

Arcadios smiled shyly. 'It's an eastern technique. Hard to get right, and not easy to be accurate with. But when what you need is speed and surprise, it can be very effective.'

'It sounded pretty accurate to me,' Fronto whispered, impressed. 'Into the dark against hidden targets and it sounded to me like you hit one.'

'Luck,' muttered Arcadios, though Fronto suspected self-effacement rather than chance.

'Let's hope you got the son of a dog in the heart or the eye,' Catháin grinned.

'Why are they doing this?' Cavarinos mused.

'What?'

'Why the arrows?'

'They already tried a direct assault,' Fronto reminded him, 'and look how that one turned out. Their quarry managed to get into hiding in time. Maybe they're just trying to keep us contained until it's light so that they don't miss anyone this time?'

Cavarinos shook his head. 'No. They'd wait for daylight to begin if it was darkness that was hampering them. This is different. There are maybe three or four of them out there... so where are the rest?'

Fronto's eyes widened. 'A ruse? A decoy?'

Cavarinos nodded. 'How well protected is your rear?'

Fronto noted sourly the presence of Arcadios. Without the expert archer at the back door, the answer was: a lot less protected than he'd like. Arcadios had been called from his bed to the front door because of the archers.

'Who's looking after the rear door?'

Arcadios frowned. 'Zeno and Evagoras.'

Fronto gestured to Catháin and Arcadios. 'You stay here. Keep trying that little trick every now and then and keep them busy. You two,' he pointed at Pamphilus and Clearchus, 'stay with them. Let no one in.'

With a beckoning finger to Masgava, Aurelius, Cavarinos and Balbus, Fronto raced through the villa, heading for the rear door. As he rounded the final corner, his heart in his throat, he was dismayed, though far from surprised, to see the door wide open and the two Massiliot mercenaries sprawled across the threshold in a wide pool of their own blood.

'Shit!'

He looked at the four men with him.

'Masgava, you stay here. Don't let anyone in or out. You are my rock, alright?' The Numidian nodded, drawing his blade at last and standing, implacable like a colossus, at the door's side. Fronto turned to the others. 'Balbus, can you check the private suites. That's where they'll have made for straight away, but they've probably found them empty by now. Cavarinos, look after my father-in-law.'

Despite Balbus' sour look at the command, he nodded and Cavarinos gave Fronto a supportive squeeze of the shoulder before running off to check the family's rooms.

'Aurelius? You're with me. Let's hope the wine store's still secure.'

* * * * *

The wine store was a large, brick-vaulted room built into the substructures of the villa proper where the hill began to slope away with a view of the sea. It had two doors: one down a short flight of steps from a corridor in the rear of the house, and a second from the grassy slope outside. Yet despite it having an external door Fronto had deemed it a safe location, partially because the enemy would naturally seek them out in the living areas of the house, but also because that rear door was as secure as the villa's walls unless opened from the inside. The outer door was wide and high and formed from oak planks over a hand-width thick, reinforced with cross spars also of oak. For this door, when opened, came down rather than swinging out, forming a shallow ramp, up which to move heavy loads of amphorae. It was one of Catháin's modifications to the business and had sped up movement of the huge jars no end. But with the enemy inside the villa now, such external security measures were immaterial.

Fronto and Aurelius hurtled round the corner at a run and the former legate felt his heart leap as he saw the open door at the top of the stairs. For a heartbeat or two he found himself wondering in a panic where Pamphilus and Clearchus, who were supposed to be guarding the door, were and then he remembered them emerging from that room by the front door. The idiots! They had heard the troubles and run towards it, abandoning their position here. He made a mental note to beat them black and blue for that, once he had control of the villa again.

Furious, he turned into the doorway. He could hear swearing in Latin in an elegant female voice, which could only mean that Lucilia was still alive. His heart in his mouth, he took the steps three at a time, Aurelius right behind him.

His worst fears were realised as his gaze took in the room. Pamphilus and Clearchus had given that large external door a little extra security when they had moved his wife's living quarters down here, in that they had shifted all the racks of heavy amphorae and propped them against the door. Of course, in doing so they had also effectively cut off the only escape route from the room if it were breached from the inside...

The far side of the bare brick room held his wife's well-appointed bed and the smaller ones of the two boys, as well as temporary cots for the four women on the house's staff. A table and two chairs and a single chest completed the furnishings, the whole lit by three oil lamps in niches on the walls.

Close to the stairs entrance, Fronto could see four cloaked figures with their backs to him. There had clearly already been a brief altercation as two of the villa's slave women lay in the middle of the floor in a spreading pool of blood. Beyond that stood Lucilia and Andala, his wife holding his glorious orichalcum-hilted gladius defensively as she let forth a stream of curses and invective that would make a centurion blush, while the Bellovaci girl brandished his second best sword in a very purposeful manner. Behind the two women, the remaining two slave girls sat on the bed, holding back Balbina and little Lucius and Marcus and brandishing small eating knives desperately.

Rage threatened to take hold of Fronto. He'd felt it happen a couple of times before in his life – the ferocity that took him so thoroughly that he lost all sense of time, place and self, simply surrendering to the killing fury until there was no one left to fight. Britannia had been the worst. *Not here!* With immense difficulty, he forced it back down. This was no time for unchecked rage – he had to remain in control and make sure the women were safe.

As he stepped into the room, Aurelius coming up beside him, three of the four cloaked men turned their eerie, expressionless masks on him. For a moment, Fronto wondered why the four men had stopped in their attack in the first place. Even though Andala was whirling the sword as though born to it – and had clearly struck well with it, from the blood running down the tallest enemy's free arm – they could still have easily overwhelmed the remaining women if they'd so wished. He realised rather sourly that they had held off killing the women so that their screams – or curses in his wife's case – might draw their true prey to them. They might delight in killing Roman women and children, but it was Fronto they were here for.

Even as the three men facing him raised their weapons and stepped forward to strike, Fronto was bringing his own sword up. The centre one, tall and thin and willowy and with the wounded arm, stepped aside despite the press, twirling, and brought his wide blade across in a sweep that would have bitten deep into Fronto's side had Aurelius not been there instantly, smacking the blow away with his gladius before whipping it back in an attempt to skewer the attacker, but the short, bull-shouldered man to the side was there immediately, blocking that blow.

Fronto's sword lanced out forwards in a practised lunge, but the third, lithe, figure to the right simply turned sideways and the blade tore through his cloak alone. Not only was the man exceedingly fast, but Fronto was still largely unused to this long Gallic weapon and the weight and balance for such a thrust was all wrong.

Steel clashed and grated as he and Aurelius and the three men facing them danced their lethal jig, whirling, lunging, stabbing and swiping. Despite the two Romans' skill and experience, they were still doing little more than defend their selves, holding off the three men. The Gauls were good at what they did and they outnumbered Fronto and Aurelius. It couldn't go on like this. The Romans would tire first.

305

In brief snatches Fronto caught a glance of the room beyond their clash. Lucilia was still standing protectively in front of the children with the sword brandished, cursing the attackers like a foul-mouthed sailor, but Andala was weighing into the fray like a gladiator, her blade flashing and whirling as she parried and fought off the man facing her with far more style and skill than Fronto could have imagined her having.

As he repeatedly turned and parried blows from the front and the right, trying to hold off two men at once, in one of those clarity-in-battle moments, he instinctively felt rather than saw his opponent's mistake. The lithe one on the right suddenly over-extended, trying to bring his blade around to Fronto's unprotected side. Gritting his teeth, the Roman took advantage, bringing his own sword up and striking at that extended arm, driving the point into the muscle.

As the lithe one cried out, his sword falling from shaking fingers, Fronto almost died there and then. In attacking that man so, he'd opened himself up in exactly the same manner to the tall one in the middle, whose blade had been aimed unerringly for the point just below Fronto's collar bone until it was caught by the desperate upswing of Aurelius' blade and knocked aside.

There was no time to thank the man. Even as Aurelius, thrown off-balance in trying to protect Fronto, took the third warrior's blade in his left arm, the middle Gaul came in for a second strike with surprising speed. Fronto found himself back-stepping towards the stairs, the tall one lashing out again and again at lightning speed, like a snake's flicking tongue, forcing him on the defensive. The Gaul he'd wounded was recovering from the shock, using his good arm to draw a dagger from his belt, and would soon be in the fight once more, helping force Fronto back.

Aurelius clashed again and again with the man in front of him, and Fronto noted that even Andala was in trouble now, the fourth Gaul pressing her back towards the bed and his wife. As he swung and parried, desperately holding off their blades, Fronto saw brief flashes between the figures. He saw Lucilia motion for the slave women to keep the children back as she herself stepped forward. He felt his heart stop for a moment at the sight of his wife stepping into the fray, handling her blade inexpertly, but with a willpower he recognised as unstoppable.

Even as he fought, he reached up with his free hand and touched the Fortuna figurine at his neck. Across the room, Lucilia's initial blow was clumsy and easily turned. But Andala was proving to be smart. Despite the failure of his wife's attempt, the cloaked Gaul had been distracted by the attack, and gasped as Andala drove Fronto's second best blade deep into his neck, turning it as she did so, ruining windpipe, gullet and arteries all in one, mincing the man's throat before ripping the sword back out. She was of the Bellovaci, a tribe of the Belgae, and Fronto could remember their first campaigns up there six years ago. *Even the women were dangerous*, they'd said. Thank the gods, they had been right!

There was no shriek from her victim – he had no throat with which to do it – and as he staggered and dropped to his knees, Andala stepped forward like a victorious gladiator, ripping away the torn cloak and driving her blade down into his chest from above, executing him swiftly.

All this came to Fronto only in brief flashes, and his attention was pulled away as he felt a nick to his side, slicing through his chiton but leaving only a light flesh wound. Hissing, he dipped to the side, knocking the dagger from the third Gaul's hand with his sword's pommel and leaving that man unarmed once more.

Aurelius staggered as a heavy blow from the bull-necked one facing him slammed his blade back against his face and almost did for him.

And then Andala was there like one of the furies unleashed, stabbing Fronto's gladius into the back of Aurelius' opponent repeatedly and ripping it out – *stab, rip, stab, rip, stab, rip*.

The bull-necked one shrieked and stumbled forwards, but Aurelius just pushed him back and added his own blade to the flurry that was killing him so viciously, stabbing him in the chest even as his back continued to be ravaged. For a moment, Fronto wondered why Andala had concentrated on that one when Fronto was busily struggling to hold off *two* men, but the look in her eyes and that in Aurelius' when they met across their keening victim answered that question readily enough.

The one Fronto had disarmed had stepped back, seeking his fallen sword now, and Fronto took advantage of the situation, finally facing only one opponent. He met the tall one's blade with his and as the man tried to pull it back for another swift lunge, Fronto's free hand grabbed the man's wrist, yanking it to one side. He had the advantage now over a man with only one effective arm, the other being the bloodied result of Andala's first scuffle in this room. The

Gaul gasped. Even as Fronto's grip tightened, pulling his blade down, so his own sword came up from hip level, point first, driving into the man's flesh just above the bladder and shearing up through organs inside his rib cage until he felt the tip hit shoulder blade, arresting its gory progress.

The eyes behind that mask widened and the man shuddered as he dropped his sword, a huge wash of blood sheeting out from his belly and across Fronto's hand. He coughed, and spatters of the blood that he'd spat into the inside of his mask sprayed through the mouth slit and then dribbled down the ceramic chin.

Behind the dying Gaul, Aurelius crossed the room and swiftly dispatched the unarmed one with little difficulty.

Fronto stood in the doorway, chest heaving from the effort, surveying the scene before him.

Four of the Sons of Taranis lay on the floor of his wine cellar. Four! He could hardly believe his eyes. Moreover, apart from the regrettable demise of the two slave girls, only a few minor cuts and grazes remained on the surviving combatants to show for what they'd lived through.

He *owed* divine Fortuna. He owed her a great debt.

Reaching down, he lifted the golden figurine of his patron goddess and kissed her fondly.

He watched with a newfound respect as Andala went around the room, putting his second best gladius through the hearts of the four fallen Gauls, just to be sure, ripping away their cloaks as she did so. Lucilia ran across the room, hurdling the corpses, and flung herself into his arms, and Fronto had to lean slightly to prevent the waving blade in her hand catching his arm.

'I thought we were lost,' she breathed.

Fronto cradled her close, smiling his thanks to the others, and when she finally stepped back, he laughed. 'Lucky you had your favourite Amazon here!' Andala gave him a confused look and stepped forward, proffering the sword to him, hilt first. He shook his head as he plucked his best sword from his wife's hand. 'Keep it, Andala. It's yours.' And to Lucilia: 'you'll have to see to her manumission, you know?'

'So, seven left then?' Aurelius murmured as he crouched over the butchered one and peeled the mask from his moustachioed, ruddy and flat face, rising with the cloak in his other hand.

'I guess so. Lucilia? You and Andala stay here with the boys and Balbina until we're sure the house is clear.' As his wife and the Bellovaci girl backed over to the bed area again, Fronto gathered up the rest of the masks and cloaks. By the time he and Aurelius were carrying them up the stairs, Balbus, Cavarinos and Masgava had arrived in the corridor.

'Everyone alright?' the old man asked and his eyes widened as he saw the masks his son in law carried. 'Lucilia and the children are fine,' Fronto replied reassuringly. 'Luckily it seems that our new Belgae girl is rather handy with a blade. She held them off until we arrived and dispatched one of them herself.' He threw the cloaks across to Cavarinos. 'Anything here you recognise?'

The Arvernian noble turned them over and around one by one until he could find the lines of symbols stitched into them.

'A hammer and a bowl. Most likely that's Sucellos "the striker". Not sure what you Romans would call him.'

'Yes, well, he got *struck* about forty times, between Andala and Aurelius here.'

Cavarinos peered at the other cloaks. 'Stone and a severed head – that would have to be Rudianos. And there's Toutatis here, and Dis, too if I am not mistaken.'

'Good. The names are all I need. Masgava, could you make sure the rear of the villa is secured again and that the rest of the house is clear. Cavarinos? Come with me.'

A few moments later, with Cavarinos and Balbus in tow, Fronto arrived at the front door. Arcadios and Catháin were still there, and Pamphilus and Clearchus continued to hover, looking irritated and twitchy. Fronto stopped in the vestibule, reassuring his men that yes, everything was fine, but turned and pointed an angry finger at the two brothers. 'No thanks to you two. You were supposed to be guarding the women's door.'

Clearchus frowned in consternation. 'The mistress said they would be fine, sir. She urged us to come and help.'

Continuing to wag his finger, he glared at them. 'The mistress of the house she may be, but you work for *me*. When I set you a task, you do that task, even if Jupiter himself pokes his face through the clouds and tells you otherwise. Do you understand me?'

The two men, chastened, nodded sullenly and Fronto let his angry gaze linger for a while before gesturing to the door. 'Open it, Catháin.'

As the northerner did so, Fronto stepped into the doorway, repeating four names under his breath so as not to forget them. An arrow thrummed out of the darkness and clattered into the wall close by, but Fronto ignored it, standing proud in the doorway and holding up one of the expressionless cult masks, letting the light catch it from many angles as he turned it this way and that.

'Dis!' he bellowed into the night, and then cast the mask out onto the gravel drive where it landed with a crunch. He took a second and raised it in the same fashion.

'Sucellos!'

Crash.

'Rudianos!'

Crash.

'Toutatis!'

Crash.

'And before you flee to your bolt-hole, just for good measure: Maponos!'

With a last crunch, the mask he had taken from the young man in the inn hit the gravel. No further arrows were forthcoming, and Fronto took a step out into the garden, his hands on his hips like an indignant landowner bellowing at interlopers.

'Five gone. All for some pointless petty revenge. Listen to me, Molacos of the Cadurci: Take your last six men and go home. Raise ugly children, drink putrid beer and just be damned grateful that you lived through the war. Because – and mark my words – I will *not* let you free your king or kill any more officers. Your mission is over.'

Turning his back, and casting up only the tiniest prayer that he not get struck in the back with an arrow, Fronto stepped back inside and let his employee close the door.

'That'll have shaken the buggers,' he said flatly. 'Their numbers almost halved in one day and with no appreciable gain.'

'And the fact that you called Molacos by his name, too,' added Cavarinos.

'Exactly. Is there any chance that they will actually stop, in the face of this setback?'

The Arvernian shook his head. 'No. They'll not stop. In fact, the problem with men like Molacos is that failure just fires their blood. Now he'll be more determined than ever.'

'Then I suppose we had best go back down to the inn and see if we can finish this?'

'I think that's the sensible decision,' Cavarinos agreed grimly.

'Catháin, you are in charge of the place. I'll leave half the men with you to make sure the villa's secure, while we go to deal with the rest of these Sons of Whores.'

* * * * *

Fronto nodded to Masgava.

'That's the one – the Chimaera's End.'

The inn, with its gaudily painted sign of an overly-muscular Bellerophon riding a winged horse that looked a little too fat to fly, was still open for business, despite the fact that it was too late for all but the exhausted drunks and the night workers. That, of course, was why it had become one of Fronto's occasional haunts – it was a quick stroll from his warehouse and catered for those carters and labourers at the various warehouses who wanted a nightcap or twelve when their work ended. How those who stayed there managed to sleep was beyond him, though these were not rowdy customers, but quiet ones.

He was grateful. To have to wake the innkeeper would be to risk alerting the Sons of Taranis to their approach, and the only other way would be to climb the outer wall to the room's high window, which would be near impossible with any level of safety and stealth.

Fronto and his small force of men approached the open doorway, from which issued a warm glow and the muted murmur of conversation. As they reached the building, Masgava clapped his hand on Fronto's shoulder and gently manoeuvred him into the middle of the group rather than the front.

Arcadios came up to join the big Numidian, Biorix and Cavarinos staying close to Fronto protectively. Aurelius they had left with the other group up at the villa, well aware of the prevalence of bats in the streets of Massilia at night and Aurelius' inability to handle those flying rodents without shrieking.

They stepped into the bar and the murmur stopped immediately – ten armed men will have that effect on a quiet inn.

Each man brandished his weapon of choice, many of them old service gladii, others the fairly common Greek *kopis* sword. None of the inn's occupants made to move against these armed arrivals, though. Most of them were wary and tired, a few too inebriated to stand, let alone fight. The innkeeper suddenly burst forth from the end of the bar, waving his hands and shouting 'no, no, no, no, no…'

Masgava's free hand snapped out and grabbed the chubby man by the chin, his large, powerful fingers and thumb sinking into the wobbly flesh of the man's jowls as he forced his jaw shut. Fronto watched, impressed, as the innkeeper fell silent, intimidated beyond words by Masgava's expression alone. It was only when he was lowered back to the floor that Fronto realised the big Numidian had actually lifted him off the floor by his chin. As the man alighted again and let out a nervous fart, Masgava put a shushing finger to his lips, tapped his temple with a finger and walked on towards the stairs. As Fronto passed the innkeeper, the man was shaking like a leaf. Not one pair of eyes in the room was looking directly at any of them.

It paid to have good men with you, Fronto smiled.

The party took the stairs one at a time, slowly and keeping to the side again to prevent creaks. The corridor above was dark – no oil lamps lit at this time of night. The ten of them moved stealthily down the corridor until they reached the door at the end. Again, Masgava motioned for silence and put his ear to the door. He shook his head, indicating silence within, and then crouched to the keyhole. Rising, he shrugged his uncertainty. He looked back at Fronto and indicated his shoulder questioningly. In reply, Fronto mimed opening the door by the handle.

Quietly the Numidian grasped the ring and turned. Next to him, Arcadios hefted his gladius and prepared. Stealth now abandoned in favour of surprise, Masgava threw the door back and he and Arcadios swept in like a river in flood, Biorix and Cavarinos behind him, Fronto and the rest following on.

The room was pitch black, the window shuttered tight, and Fronto panicked as he entered, suddenly well aware that the enemy were at a serious advantage in pitch black in a room they had occupied for days. His fears were realised as he heard first a strangled grunt from Masgava ahead in the dark, and a cry of pain from Arcadios. His own sword slashed out, blind, into the darkness at the side, where an enemy might lurk, but certainly no ally.

Nothing. His eyes were adjusting slightly, but not enough to pick out anything but the vaguest of shapes. His sword lanced, slashed and swiped in the darkness and he felt a triumphant surge as it connected with something, only to realise it was a bed post.

Someone threw open the shutters and the room burst into clarity in the low light from the street outside and from the moon, which had made a brief but most welcome appearance in a gap in the clouds.

The room was empty.

Well, not *entirely* empty. The thin cord that had been stretched across at neck height might well have crushed the windpipe of a running man, but Masgava had caught it first and, at his height, it had hit him below the collar bones. Arcadios was leaning on a bed, swearing and, as the room came into view, yelled '*tribuli!*'

Fronto looked down. The floor was scattered sparsely with pointed iron caltrops, one of which Arcadios was busy removing from his foot, accompanied by some choice curses and the patter of blood droplets.

'Some leaving gift,' Biorix grunted, kicking one of the tribuli carefully aside. Apart from the painful traps, the room was empty. No Sons of Taranis. No kit bags, weapons, cloaks or masks.

Fronto sheathed his sword. 'They must have come back here after the villa, so they can't be far ahead of us.'

'Unless they cleared out first and took everything with them to the villa?' Arcadios mused.

Cavarinos shook his head. 'They cannot have believed they would fail a second time. They have just left.'

'No use asking the barman,' Fronto sighed. 'They wouldn't have told him anything, even if he'd asked, which he wouldn't. But we know they're somewhere in the city and now there are only seven of them. Will they try again?'

Cavarinos pursed his lips. 'If they are true to their mission, no. They couldn't risk any more losses if they hope to free the king. You can never be truly sure, though, with a man like Molacos. Fanatics are bad enough normally, but when you thwart them like you have, it can push them over the edge of the madness cliff. If Molacos still has a grain of sense, he had his ship ready to sail before they came for you. I would place money on them already being at sea.'

Fronto straightened and crossed to the window, stepping around the caltrops. He stood for a moment, leaning on the window and looking out across the city, and came to a decision. Turning, determination filling his expression, he folded his arms.

'It's time to take the fight to them, then. I did this with Hierocles and his Greek thugs for months, trying to stay peaceful and on the

313

right side of law. And at every opportunity the slimy bastard ruined me and hurt my people and my business. And in the end I had to show my teeth to stop him. Now these rebel killers are doing the same. They keep us penned in the villa, defensive and panicked, waiting for the next attack. It's time to show our teeth again.'

'But how will we find them?' murmured Biorix.

'We know where they are going: to the carcer in Rome. That is where we'll find them.'

'And your family?' Cavarinos prompted. 'You can't leave them here for fear of reprisals, and it would be too dangerous to take them with you.'

Fronto nodded. 'Catháin has been badgering me to let him go to Campania and secure better sources of wine. He and a few of the men can accompany Balbus, Lucilia and the children to Puteoli. They'll be safe at my mother's villa there, especially with Andala with them. And Galronus is in Puteoli, too, so he'll look after them. That means that once we pass Ostia we can concentrate on the remaining seven rebels.'

Masgava sheathed his sword. 'It's a good plan.' He glanced at Cavarinos. 'Will you be leaving us here?'

Fronto felt a strange lurch inside. He hadn't thought of that. Would Cavarinos willingly walk into the Roman eagle's own nest? Would he really want to see the jail that held his king; his *kinsman* in fact. Would he be able to face that and not feel the need to free the man himself? Cavarinos may *seem* one of them, but when faced with his own people languishing in the carcer…?

The Arvernian's face betrayed his indecision, but resolution came down fast and complete. 'I will see this through to the end. The Sons of Taranis must be stopped.'

'Can we stop them sailing?' Arcadios asked quietly. 'I know we're talking as though they've already left, but we can't be sure.'

'We know the enemy have a friendly ship,' Biorix replied, 'but it's probably already left, and even if it hasn't, with no name and the number of Gallic traders in port, tracking them will be like trying to find a particular turd in the latrines.'

'You are full of delightful images,' snorted Fronto. 'But you're right. They may well already have sailed. It's not common to sail at night, but the port's open and there's nothing to stop them. Best we get ahead to Rome and see if we can find them there, like I said. Brutus' orders do not cater for passengers in his fleet, but I will secure a place for all of us and he will not argue with me. The family and most of the staff and guard will come too. And at Ostia we'll transfer the family onto a ship bound for Puteoli before we continue upriver.'

Cavarinos picked up one of the pointed tribuli from the floor and turned it round and round in his fingers. 'Roman. Imagine that. Despite their aversion to Rome, they're not above using your own weapons.' He sighed and cast the caltrop aside. 'To Rome, then.'

'To Rome.'

Chapter Seventeen

MARCUS Antonius leaned close to Caesar, trying not to catch the eye of Calenus on the general's far side. 'You think Gaius is safe among the Bellovaci?'

The general turned his aquiline features on his friend, confidante, distant cousin and senior officer. 'You think he is not?'

'Gaius is a good man, I know. But he's little experience of command yet. A legion and a half to keep the Belgae in place. Have we done enough to pacify them?'

A knowing smile played on the general's lips. 'This is anxiety over our strategy, then? Not simply fraternal concern?'

'I would hardly... it's not my place...'

'Ha.' Caesar chuckled. 'Worry not, Marcus. Your little brother is quite safe. He has some of my best tribunes and centurions with him, and the Belgae are beaten for good. They could barely raise a cheer, let alone an army. Besides, your mother would tear me to pieces if I placed Gaius in real danger.'

Antonius laughed. 'I suppose you're right. I've never seen a quieter people than the Bellovaci now.'

A roar brought their attention back to the open square before them. Cenabum was not what it had once been. The Carnutes had damaged the important river port in their original attack that had ignited the flames of that great revolt which had died at Alesia. In response, the legions had all-but razed it. Now a new village was rising amid the ashes of the old port. One day there would be aqueducts here, and paved roads and a forum, temples to the Capitoline triad. Now there were huts among the ruins. The smell of charred wood lingered even after so many months – years now, in fact. The place smelled like a pyre, and it would take a generation for that to fade. But they were not in Cenabum for the facilities, nor for the air. They were in Cenabum to make a statement.

Two legionaries emerged from one side of the square, amongst the throng. Each held a long, leather cord, and a moment later the man at the other end appeared. The Gaul was one of the Carnutes – the tribe that had founded this very settlement, had colonized the land around it, had fostered rebellion here, murdered Romans here. He was a noble and, according to rumour, a druid – the very druid who had raised up Vercingetorix to be king among the Gauls. He did not look quite so noble now.

'Why Fabius didn't do away with the man while he was here, I cannot fathom,' murmured Calenus.

'Fabius had enough on his platter,' Antonius replied quietly, 'as we now know. In fact, I cannot understand why we are here ourselves, Caesar, and not marching south to help the legions at Uxellodunon?'

The general leaned back, folding his arms. 'Sometimes, gentlemen, something symbolic and powerful needs to be done to drive home the nails of suppression. Caninius, Fabius and Varus are more than capable of containing an oppidum until we arrive, and this is important. The central tribes are quiet. The Belgae are now settled. Caninius and the others are dealing with the south, but this region is a hotbed of trouble and has been since first we came. The Carnutes are every bit as guilty of protracted murder and rebellion as the Arverni.'

The defiant Gaul had to scurry forward to avoid falling and being dragged. He, Guturvatus by name, had taken two weeks to track down. And that following a week of investigation as to his identity. The druid-chieftain was stripped to the waist, his grey wool braccae soaked with sweat, his feet bare and bloodied from the painful journey across the ruined city.

'But if he is, as they say, the man behind all the risings, would it not be better to have the Carnutes here in their thousands to witness it?'

Caesar turned to Calenus and gestured to the far side of the square where perhaps a dozen Gallic nobles stood with sour faces and slumped shoulders. 'They are the leaders of what is left of the Carnutes – Fabius was thorough in the short time he was here – and what transpires this morning will filter through the entire region in a matter of days. You have spent plenty of time in Rome, Calenus, surely you are familiar with the astonishing speed of gossip?'

Calenus smiled, though he still looked faintly unhappy. Caesar could understand the man's reluctance, of course. He was not a man used to the brutality of war, despite having led legions in Gaul now. And what was about to happen was... well, Caesar had foregone breaking his fast, despite a persistent rumbling in the belly.

'Besides, half of this is for the benefit of our men, not theirs. This is one of the architects of the risings that have kept them marching and camping in Gallic winters these past three years. He is responsible for countless legionaries being heaped into the burial pits

317

or onto pyres. Once in a while it does the legions good to see the filth that has so ruined them face justice. The value of watching their revenge being carried out is incalculable in terms of morale. Guturvatus' death will buy more goodwill with the men than a thousand loot and slave payouts.'

The Carnute leader, who had been betrayed by his own frightened tribe as the Romans hunted him, was now being dragged towards two thick posts driven deep into the ground some eight feet apart. The officers couldn't quite see the man's face, but they could picture the wild, terrified eyes. The prisoner started to fight the inexorable momentum towards the posts, struggling with the cords, trying to free himself. Despite his ravaged feet, he dug in his heels and almost succeeded in pulling down one of the legionaries dragging him. The centurion who even now stood to one side of the posts had chosen his detail well, though. The two legionaries at the cords were oxen in human form – massive, with necks like oak trunks and muscles like burial mounds. With little difficulty they regained their control and yanked hard enough for the man to fall face first into the dirt. When he struggled upright again, coughing and spitting out dust, his nose was flat and bloodied and his face was torn in several places.

'Bet you wish that was the traitor Commius there,' muttered Antonius with a vicious smile. 'I wonder where *he* is.'

'Somewhere among the Germans, I suspect. There will be time to find him later, when I am back in Rome if not before. My reach is long, even from the city. Commius is too important and loves power too much. He cannot hide forever.'

A nod from Antonius. 'Commius on the run. Vercingetorix in the carcer. Ambiorix and Indutiomarus dead. Now Guturvatus dragged here in chains. Only Lucterius in the south to go, I think?'

Caesar nodded. 'The heads of the hydra become fewer with every strike. With Fortuna's aid, Lucterius will be the last and the beast will lie still.'

Still struggling to the last, the prisoner was being tied in place, the leather cords now fastened tight to the wooden posts at just an acute enough angle that his shoulders would already be feeling the pain. The centurion looked up at Caesar, awaiting the command, and the general gave a slight nod of the head. Stepping around in front of the prisoner but slightly to one side so as not to obscure the officers' view, the centurion, whose voice had been honed on a hundred parade grounds and battlefields to carry clear even in the most hectic din, cleared his throat.

'Guturvatus, son of Lemisunius, you have been accused and convicted of conspiring to bring war against Rome in defiance of the Pax Romana to which your tribe have pledged. Your crimes have infected your neighbouring tribes, spreading discontent and further endangering the stability of the region. Your rebellions have both directly and indirectly cost the lives of many thousands of Romans and many more Gauls who, were it not for your influence, would have remained allied with Rome and at peace. Thus, given the gravity of your crimes, the Proconsul of Gaul has sentenced you to death by the scourge.

An auxiliary of the Remi tribe in gleaming mail and a white cloak stood close by, repeating the centurion's pronouncements in a language the prisoner and the watching Carnutes would be able to understand. As his more guttural words ended, a discordant echo of the centurion, Guturvatus began to struggle again. His futile attempts achieved little more than to make the leather straps bite deep into his wrists, and he began to curse and shout and spit. Two legionaries in the crowd burst out laughing at some private joke and the optio just along the line roared as he clouted them in the shins with his staff.

Having fallen silent once more, the centurion looked again at Caesar, who repeated his nod. 'Proceed.'

At the officer's command, a muscular soldier with arms like tree boles and a chest around which Antonius reckoned his arms would barely reach stepped forward. In his hand he held the coiled scourge and as he walked towards the prisoner and the other Romans backed away to leave the two men alone in the square, he shook out the weapon. Three long tails of leather hung from the heavy handle, weighted down with spiked wheels of carved bone that had been attached at set lengths along each strand.

Standing silent and taking three slow breaths, preparing for strenuous activity, the legionary pulled back his arm and swung.

From even thirty paces away the officers heard the tearing sound and the unpleasant, unmistakeable sound of bone on bone. Guturvatus screamed. Calenus wiped his forehead and lowered his face.

'This damned heat.'

Caesar turned a fierce gaze on him. 'Straighten up, man. You're an officer.'

He could only imagine what Calenus would be doing if he had the view most of the legionaries had, where the actual damage was happening. All the officers could see was the intense agony on the man's face. Again, the soldier swung the scourge and this time a spray of blood to the side was joined by small scraps of flesh.

The third strike connected while Guturvatus was still screaming from the second, and consequently the Gaul bit off the end of his own tongue in the process, his mouth filling with blood. Caesar made an irritated motion to the centurion, who waved at the executioner. 'Slow down.'

The legionary nodded and began to count to twelve between strokes.

The ground was becoming sodden with red in wide sprays from each blow, and Antonius glanced across at Calenus, who had gone pale, his face taking on a very waxy sheen. This was why you didn't employ lawyers to command legions, no matter their position on the cursus honorum or the influence of their family. You ended up with men like this. Calenus needed toughening up if he was going to stay in service for a while. Mind, when Caesar returned to Rome shortly, the man would probably end up as a provincial governor.

Still…

Antonius smiled wickedly. 'His back must be all ribs and organs by now, Caesar. Time for a change?'

The general gave him a questioning look, and Antonius nodded at Calenus, who was repeating 'So hot… so damned hot…' his eyes revolving to look anywhere but at the victim. Caesar gave a curt nod and waved to the legionary with the scourge. 'Front, now.'

Calenus stared at Caesar, who cleared his throat quietly and leaned close. 'You will watch like a stoic officer, Quintus Fufius Calenus, and if you should even think about vomiting in front of the legions, so help me I will have you strapped there in the victim's place. Have some backbone, man.'

The executioner moved around the figure, taking up a new position at the front. Guturvatus was barely conscious now, every scream feeble and half drowned by the blood that filled his mouth. Another twenty lashes would be the end of him. At a nod from the centurion, he began again.

By the third blow, the man's chest was open, bone visible and blood everywhere. On the fourth, one of the spiked wheels caught on a rib and the legionary had to scurry over and extricate it which, from the screaming, seemingly hurt even more than the scourging. At the eighth blow, the screams had stopped and even whimpering seemed too much effort. The man was almost dead, his breathing shallow and ragged.

'Enough,' commanded Caesar. 'Take the head.'

Another legionary stepped out from the lines, wielding one of the long, heavy blades favoured by the Gaulish tribes. Unsheathing it, he nodded to the scourge man, who folded his nightmare coils and stepped out of the square. The swordsman took his place, pulling back the huge blade and pausing for just a moment.

His swing was perfectly positioned. The blade slammed into the prisoner's neck from behind. Though it failed to sever, it crunched through the spine, killing him with the first strike. The second blow finished the job. The swordsman bent and picked up the head, approaching Caesar and holding it high. The two officers glanced sidelong at Calenus, who still looked extremely unwell, though he'd held himself together throughout the proceedings.

'Have it spiked and raised above Cenabum's main gate.' The general focused on the distressed Carnute leaders opposite. 'There will be no more revolts. No more risings or troubles. The Carnutes are now once more bound by the Pax Romana. If there is even the slightest unrest here again, what happened to Guturvatus today will become the fate of each and every last member of the tribe. Am I understood?'

There was an uncomfortable shuffling of feet among the Carnutes and he straightened in his chair as he gestured to the centurion. 'Get them out of my sight.'

The Carnutes were herded from the square and the general stood, stiffly. 'The legions are hereby granted one full day's furlough, following which we will be moving south at speed to bring the final few rebels in Gaul under control. Uxellodunon is our goal, men of Rome, and with its fall, we can tell the senate unequivocally that Gaul is ours.'

* * * * *

Varus swatted at an insistent bug that flitted around his chin and neck, watching the cavalry elements of the Tenth and Eleventh legions moving across the wide grassy valley of the tributary river which encircled Uxellodunon's northern slopes, hooves pounding the earth. Perhaps eight hundred horsemen all told, their standards having been reported by the pickets.

The officers were out ahead, riding in a small knot with a guard of Aulus Ingenuus' Praetorian cavalry and a few native scouts, and that vanguard even now climbed the lower slopes to Fabius' camp, where he, Varus and Caninius waited. A thin grey blanket of cloud was rolling in from the south as if to meet the new arrivals, blotting out the blistering sun, but replacing it with an oppressive muggy heat that brought incessant clouds of insects from the low-lying land.

'The rest will be following on, I presume. Two more legions, then,' Fabius murmured. 'Six might even be adequate to crush this place.' He sounded unconvinced, and with good reason, Varus mused, given their attempts so far at an action against the fortified town. 'I presume the others have been distributed in garrison,' the legate went on.

'Perhaps the general lacked confidence in our ability to put an end to this,' Caninius sighed.

'He's right to do so,' Fabius replied. 'We are no closer to a conclusion now than we were two weeks ago.'

The three men stood silent for a moment, contemplating the truth of that. Though Fabius' arrival had doubled the Roman numbers, the few minor forays they had attempted at the vertiginous slopes of Uxellodunon had been costly and abortive. Even with information beaten out of the captives, none of the intelligence had proved useful. Uxellodunon was sealed tighter than a Vestal's underwear.

'Quiet now,' Varus hissed as the newly-arrived officers closed on them, reining in atop the slope, their horses sweating and whickering, tired from the long journey. Caesar sat astride his white mare, calm and collected as usual, lacking his ubiquitous red cloak and foregoing a cuirass in deference to the stifling heat, yet still resplendent in a linen arming jacket with white and gold pteruges. His aquiline face, however, looked slightly more drawn than usual, and his hair thinner and greyer – to Varus' eye, anyway.

'Gentlemen,' the Proconsul of Gaul inclined his head as he came to a halt and the waiting legates and cavalry officer saluted in response. 'You have found me another Alesia, it seems. This land appears to be full of them. And is this Lucterius a facsimile of Vercingetorix, too?'

The two legates exchanged a look and Caninius cleared his throat. 'It would appear not, general. He and his fellow chieftain

Drapes made a lunatic attempt to deprive us of a grain store and in the process both men were defeated. Drapes sits in chains in my camp and Lucterius took to his heels during the fight and fled, we know not where.'

The general frowned. 'Into the oppidum, perhaps?'

'We think not, Caesar,' Varus replied. 'It would have been exceedingly difficult for him to do so, and since that scuffle we've observed none of the posturing or cunning we had seen in our earlier days here. It seems that the tribes up there are somewhat directionless, sitting tight in their stronghold and holding us off, but nothing more, as though they are awaiting a command to do something.'

'Good. Then we will take advantage of the situation. Wherever Lucterius has run, he cannot hide for long. Just as Commius' days are numbered, so are *this* rebel chief's. Particularly without his army. Walk me through the situation,' he commanded, dismounting and squinting at the 'upturned boat' shape of Uxellodunon.

Fabius scratched his chin. 'According to the prisoners, interrogated separately and therefore with no reason for doubt, the oppidum has adequate grain, veg and livestock to see them through until next spring, even with an army that size encamped there. It would seem that Lucterius had been intending to use Uxellodunon as some sort of gathering point or staging post. Starving them out will not be as easy as it would have been at Alesia.'

Caninius nodded. 'The slopes are treacherous and well defended. There are strong walls even atop the cliff stretches, and the flatter slope to the northeast, which is the natural assault point for infantry, is extremely well protected by a high wall pocked with towers that create an impressive arrow-reach from the parapet. We've probed the defences from every angle, and there is no guaranteed method. Indeed, I see *any* approach as being extremely costly and with remarkably little chance of actual success.'

Caesar nodded, tapping his chin as he strolled back and forth, looking over their objective. 'The water supply? If assault and starvation are unfeasible, that is the only remaining option.'

Varus pointed down into the valley. 'Apart from a narrow stretch to the northwest, the entire oppidum is surrounded by two of the tributaries of the Duranius River. Interrogation has also revealed the location of a fresh-water spring that grants them a permanent supply. The spring is close to the walls on that north-eastern slope, too close to assault without coming under concentrated attack from the walls. We looked at cutting the water supply, but it's just as unfeasible.'

Caninius gestured around them. 'And without the potential for assault or starvation, we have settled in for a long siege. Since Fabius arrived we have had adequate manpower to carry out siege works and, as you can see, have achieved a circumvallation almost comparable to your Alesia example, general.'

Caesar nodded absently, still squinting down into the valley beyond the Roman lines. 'A cursory glance at the terrain tells me you did the right thing. Pointless wasting men on fruitless assaults, and we cannot overwhelm them by force. Only poor morale or starvation will win this for us. Could we get a traitor into the walls to burn their granaries? Are the artillery capable of launching fire missiles that far?'

'Neither, I'm afraid, Caesar,' replied Caninius. 'Since the debacle that lost them both leaders, nothing has passed that wall in or out and it is carefully guarded. They withdrew any pickets on the slopes at that time and sealed themselves in. And it's too far for the artillery.'

The general blinked a couple of times and peered off into the distance, towards the confluence where the fight in the marsh had taken place.

'Can we divert the rivers?'

Varus frowned. 'The engineers had a dreadful time just draining the marsh area. Apparently the tributaries are both fed by hundreds of tiny streams coming down from the mountains themselves. It is an immense job. I asked about it before we heard of the spring, and the senior engineer just looked at me as though I'd asked him to lower the sky a little.'

Caesar gave a low chuckle. 'Engineers are the same the world over.'

'Besides, the rivers are inconsequential while the enemy control the spring,' Fabius noted.

Caesar's nod was noncommittal. 'Alright. You have auxiliary archers and slingers, and I have more following on with the Tenth and Eleventh. Arrange all your missile troops and artillery to cover the approaches to the rivers. Concentrate on any position where a natural descent from the oppidum might bring a man with a bucket to the water.'

The three defenders were frowning in bewilderment.

'General,' Caninius said quietly, 'the rivers are immaterial while they can draw from the spring.'

'They are indeed. That is why we must remove the spring from the equation. The spring is the clear target. But once we have done so, they will use the river instead, unless any Gaul who comes within twenty paces of it is pinned by arrows.'

Varus coughed and swatted away the fly again. 'Caesar, we cannot even get to that spring without opening ourselves up to their archers, slingers and rocks. We could conceivably reach it with a testudo without losing too many men, but the terrain is terrible and they have such an advantage. Fabius sent a half century close to the spring a week ago, to test the waters as it were, and the enemy sallied from the walls just far enough to destroy the advance. With the angle of the slope, the height of their walls and the range of their archers it was a slaughter. Of forty men, a dozen returned. They were unable to maintain a testudo in the presence of the enemy infantry, and as soon as they lowered shields to take on the warriors the archers put down more of them. There is the possibility that if we flood that slope with men, we might be able to take the spring, but we'd never hold it, and the loss of life would be crippling.'

Fabius nodded. 'He's right general. It's unfeasible. There simply isn't a way.'

Caesar gave the three men an infuriating, knowing smile. 'I think there might be, gentlemen. I think there might.'

* * * * *

Atenos, primus pilus of the Tenth Legion, swung with his vine cane, connecting with the reinforced mail shoulder of the legionary, who jumped in shock and then stepped back, clutching the painful joint.

'Get that helmet back on, soldier.'

'Sir, the engineers are…'

'The engineers are a law unto themselves, Procutus, and I am inclined to leave them to the business they know well. *You* are *not* an engineer, Procutus. You are a *legionary*, and a particularly dim-witted one at that. The ramp may be done but it could do with a bit more packing down and flattening yet. Now put your helmet back on and take those rocks to the slope, and if I see you doing anything other than hard work, or with one piece of kit out of place, I will be sending you up to the oppidum's gate to ask them for a cup of wine. Do you understand me?'

The legionary saluted and scurried off, collecting his basket of rocks. Atenos watched his men work. There had been endless complaints – and not just from the legionaries, but from veteran centurions too – at having force-marched from Cenabum with just hard-tack rations only to arrive at Uxellodunon and be launched straight into hard labour.

But the general had waited impatiently six days for their arrival and was not going to put off his scheme for one morning longer. It was, perhaps, a little lacking in compassion to put the bulk of the newly-arrived Tenth and Eleventh to work on the ramp, but the Ninth and Fifth had joined them. The Fifteenth had been assigned to the engineers and had been churning out vineae, as well as a giant, ten storey siege tower, even before the new legions had arrived. The Eighth had been given the completed vineae and had created a series of safe, covered accesses to the higher slopes all around that more accessible north-eastern approach. The surroundings of Uxellodunon had been a hive of activity before the Tenth and Eleventh had arrived, but now it had intensified.

Cries up ahead confirmed that Atenos' men were taking the latest in a long catalogue of batterings from the walls. An entire century of the Fifth had been given the huge, thick wicker shields and had formed a defence against the archers, but they were clearly proving inadequate. Every now and again, though the Gauls kept their arrow storm slow and careful to preserve ammunition, they would suddenly launch into a flurry and a dozen legionaries would be escorted back down the ramp either dead, with shafts jutting from crucial places, or gritting their teeth and hissing in pain, arrows wedged in limbs or shoulders, helmets wedged onto their heads with horrific dents from the thrown boulders.

Atenos peered up the ramp. The wicker shields moved and parted and then solidified once more. He could just make out the tall stone that marked the position of the enemy spring. This had better work. This morning alone, the Tenth had lost just shy of a hundred men, with twice that number injured. It was like target practice for the Cadurci up there. And the Tenth had got off lightly. Last night – the general had them working through the night too – the Ninth had lost one hundred and sixty two men, with more than three hundred injured. It was fast crippling the legions.

Still, they were nearly there, though what use the ramp and mound would be was beyond Atenos. Taking the spring was going to be costly and hard, even with the tower, but holding it against the enemy for any length of time, let along long enough to starve them out was just unfeasible. Last night the enemy had forayed and managed to take in three barrels of water while the Ninth were reeling from the assault.

'What do you suppose they're doing?' murmured Decumius, his third centurion, pointing at the line of vineae off to their right. Several dozen legionaries were gathering beneath the shelter, not far from the works at the spring.

'A gold coin to the man who can reveal the mind of Caesar,' grunted Atenos.

'Uh oh. Look out, sir. Senior officer approaching.'

Atenos turned back down the slope to see a tribune approaching, wearing a worried expression, probably due to his proximity to the enemy archers' range markers. The two men saluted.

'Centurions. Which of you is Atenos?'

The big Gaulish officer, senior centurion of the Tenth, took a pace forward. 'That would be me, sir.'

'Compliments of the general. He is pleased with your speed and asks whether the ramp is complete enough to take the tower? The *sacerdos* has read signs all morning and informs us that there will be a downpour this afternoon, so the general is of a mind to begin the action with all haste.'

Atenos sighed and nodded. 'Apart from some dressing, it can be done, sir. There will be a couple of places near the top that might not be adequately compacted yet, but the engineers tell me that such things can be circumvented with the use of heavy planks. With enough manpower we'll do it, sir.'

'Good.' The tribune peered up at the slope's crest, where the arrows were now coming more sporadically once again. Legionaries were hobbling back down the slope and a few were being dragged on makeshift pallets. According to the engineers' odd design, the ramp smoothed the more vertiginous sections of the slope, providing a steady ascent for the tower, but where it approached the spring, the ramp had been continued in the form of a wide mound in an arc around the spring, hiding it from the oppidum. The tribune smiled a condescending smile. 'Well done, centurion. Just a little more now, eh, and we'll have the damnable rebels on crosses, eh?'

Atenos nodded politely, catching Decumius rolling his eyes behind the tribune and biting down on a chuckle.

'Good, good.' Repeated the officer, one of the Fifth's junior tribunes, he thought. A man who had been in Gaul for all of four months and already thought he knew everything. A politician. The word made Atenos want to spit. 'Very well. Have your men take the wicker shields and form up defensively at the spring while those from the Fifth lay the planks you need on the ramp. The tower and the army will be along shortly to relieve you.'

Again Atenos saluted and waited for a count of ten until the officer was jogging back down the slope out of earshot.

'Boys in men's jobs.'

The other centurion laughed. 'I'll give you ten sesterces if we see him again until it's all over and the arrows have stopped flying.'

'Be kind, Decumius. He's probably still adjusting to wearing a man's toga.'

Another chuckle.

'It's all very clever,' Decumius sighed, 'and we'll stop the bastards getting to the spring for a while, but every man in the army – barring chinless down there, anyway – knows we can't hold it for more than a couple of days at most. Hours, probably.'

Atenos nodded. The losses they were seeing now were small, for they were only a small building crew and had not yet really tried to deny the enemy access to the water. The death toll once they brought a sizeable force up here and cut the supply would be appalling. For then the defenders would stop half-heartedly sending flurries of arrows down at them and would push back for real. The enemy would be able to stretch their water supplies over many more days than the legions could afford to throw men into the grinder up there.

'It's a testament to the general, for certain.'

'Sir?' Decumius frowned.

'Whole armies have revolted against their commanders for such things – being thrown away pointlessly, I mean. Yet the men trust Caesar. They know he always has a plan, always finds a way. And he does. Even when we're up to our knees in the shit, the general never fails to produce a way out. This all looks untenable, Decumius, but you've only been in Gaul a year and a half. Mark my words: the general has a reason for this.'

'I hope you're right sir,' the centurion replied, 'else we're going to lose a *lot* of men up there.'

328

Atenos gestured to the nearest legionary.

'Sir?'

'Get up the slope. Tell them to stop packing it now. Have them lay every board we have at the weaker spots and then form up along with those lads from the Fifth. Share the wicker shields but get in the lea of the mound, out of sight of their archers until they're needed. Any moment now the tower will be moving. As soon as it comes anywhere near arrow range I want you all back out protecting it until it's in place.'

The legionary saluted and ran off up the ramp. Atenos turned with his fellow centurion and peered down the slope. The tower was moving out of the defences now, still horizontal. At a surprising speed it was trundled across the flat ground to the point where the purpose made ramp began. The tower had not been given wheels and was instead being propelled forward by means of placing carefully adzed timber boles beneath it, removing those from the rear it had already crossed and placing them at the front in preparation. As the two men watched, six centuries of men moved around the front with long ropes and began to haul the monstrosity upright.

It was powerfully tall and heavily constructed, covered with hides soaked in water, with timber walls beneath. In fact, it was as good a siege tower as Atenos had ever seen, and taller than any he'd witnessed, too. The beast slammed down, its base impacting upon the log rollers with a noise that echoed like the back-handed slap of a god even this far up the slope.

'Glad I'm not on one of those ropes,' noted Decumius with feeling.

'Quite.'

Slowly, inexorably, the tower moved onto the ramp and Atenos watched it begin the slow, painstaking ascent. Now eight centuries of men were moving it up the slope, engineers running ahead and arranging pulleys on the posts driven hard into the ground at the sides of the ramp, threading the next ropes through them. It was an old method, yet to be bettered. The ropes led from the tower up the slope perhaps fifty paces, where they passed through the pulleys and back down beside the tower to where the soldiers hauled in relative safety, protected from attack by the tower itself. The ones in the most danger were the engineers rushing out ahead to thread the next set of pulleys. But then, they weren't pulling something that weighed the same as a trireme up a slope.

An hour crawled by as the two officers watched the monstrous tower crawling up the ramp towards them, Decumius producing a small flask of Fundanian wine and sharing it with his commander as they waited. Atenos had chuckled to see that the flask had a stamp on the neck that labelled it MFM. The temptation to see that as 'Marcus Falerius, Massilia' was overwhelming. Any other year, Fronto would have been standing on this slope with him, watching the tower and drinking the wine rather than supplying it. Perhaps, then, he was here in spirit. The tower was closing now, almost two thirds of the way up the slope and, ready for action, the unassigned men of the six legions were falling in behind it, bringing the remaining vineae with them in readiness for missile attack, shuffling slowly in ordered lines.

Atenos, feeling something in the air, prickling the back of his neck, turned to look back up at the oppidum. The high walls of Uxellodunon were gradually filling with more and more of the enemy, flooding the defences ready to repel the Roman invaders. If each of those men carried a bow or a sling or a free hand for rock throwing, this would be a slaughter. The veteran centurion felt a shudder run through him.

'You alright sir?'

'Yes,' he smiled grimly. 'Just thinking about what's coming.'

He was gratified to note a similar shudder run through Decumius as the other centurion peered up at the defenders and pictured the coming fight.

And still the tower rumbled on. Time passed nervously and Atenos heard something ping from his helmet. Looking up he noticed for the first time the bulky, boiling dark grey cloud rolling across the sky above them like the prow of Jupiter's own ship.

'The sacerdos was right, it seems. There's a monster of a storm coming.'

Almost as if sensing the approach of the inclement weather, the tower lurched forwards with a new turn of speed. Two or three more spots of rain hit Atenos as he watched the tower reach a point just twenty paces from him and pause while the engineers changed the pulleys and ropes again. While they worked, a small force of auxiliaries scurried forward with buckets, climbing to the top of the tower and tipping water in torrents down the outer faces, continually dampening the hides against fire arrows. As soon as they had finished, the tower jerked and began its ascent once more.

The centurions came to an attentive stance as Commander Varus hurried past the structure to where they stood. 'Atenos,' he nodded. The primus pilus saluted in return. 'Caesar's instructions, since you are in charge of the installation: using the tower and the mound, hold the spring as long as possible. Prevent access for the defenders. They will throw everything they have at you so it'll be a tough job, but you must hold for as long as possible. You will have two cohorts of the Tenth, one of the Fifth and two units of Cretan archers. I know that sounds a lot, and on parchment it is. But in truth that's about twelve hundred men in all. There will be a reserve, but the more men we put up here the easier it will be for their archers to kill us. Use the vineae, the tower and the mound as defensively as you can and make the most of the archers to keep them at bay. And this from me: don't get yourself killed, Atenos. The Tenth can't afford to lose any more good officers. You're at a premium now.'

The primus pilus smiled and nodded. 'Will do, sir. And you should know by now that there's nothing made by man that can get through *my* thick hide.'

Varus snorted with laughter. 'Especially advice. Do your best. Pull out only if there is no other option. Mars and Minerva go with you, centurion.'

'Thank you, sir.'

As Varus jogged off back down the slope, skirting the approaching tower, Decumius sighed. 'Lucky cavalry, eh, sir? They can't do much today, so they sit and drink wine while we hold the spring.'

Atenos nodded absently. 'They earn it. I know they're not popular with you Roman legion men. But a man of the tribes can see their advantage and for five years before you joined us I've watched that man muck in with the best of us, up to his armpits in blood and bone. He's a proper soldier, not just an officer.'

Decumius simply nodded and at a motion from his superior stepped off the ramp to allow the great tower to pass by. Once more, the engineers rethreaded the ropes. A few more sporadic raindrops clanged off Atenos' helmet and he threw up a quick prayer to Jupiter Pluvius – and to his native Taranis, just in case – that the storm hold off until the worst of the fighting was done. Sometimes truly bad weather halted battle, but that seemed unlikely today, and the idea of fighting for the spring in a deluge was not attractive.

The tower rumbled on and arrows began to lance out from the ramparts. At first they fell far short of the approaching monstrosity but as the tower approached the painted stone that marked the Romans' estimate of arrow range, those men at the top of the ramp moved into position, the huge wicker shields raised to block as many arrows as possible.

Arrow range was confirmed as a shaft thudded into the tower and the one strike sparked a mass of activity. In a dozen places along the wall, braziers were brought up and fire arrows were launched. As yet most still fell short, one or two hitting the wicker shields, where the legionaries hurriedly pushed the points back out with boots or wrapped fists to prevent the shields igniting. Then the range closed. The tower reached the top of the ramp and was turned, trundling parallel to the wall and into position atop that huge earth mound that arced around the spring. Fire arrows were now thudding into the hides covering the tower with every heartbeat, and men at the wicker screen were falling with almost mechanical timing. At the last moment, two centuries of men hauled on new ropes attached to the back of the tower, preventing it tipping as it reached the end of the log rollers and thudded into the earth and stone base. For a moment it teetered and Atenos waited, his heart skipping a beat, for the huge edifice to simply topple over into the spring. But after a few tense heartbeats it steadied and a cheer went up. The tower was in position, flat to the top of the big mound. It was still some twenty feet below the level of Uxellodunon's walls, but a good archer atop it might pick off the defenders on the walls.

The advance force with the wicker shields was down to about twenty men now and they were rapidly diminishing. An enterprising centurion from the Fifth sent his men across to bolster the screen, which, along with the vineae being brought up, sheltered the arriving legionaries from the worst of the arrow storm.

There was a distant rumble of thunder and Atenos looked up in time to be struck in the eye by a fat droplet of water. A horn blast from a discordant carnyx atop the oppidum's wall announced the general attack and what had been a fairly disorganised shower of missiles suddenly bloomed into a hail of death showering down from Uxellodunon onto the Roman attackers. Even with the tower, the mound, the vineae and the wicker shields, everywhere Atenos looked men were falling to the ground, screaming.

It had begun.

Taking a deep breath, the primus pilus turned to Decumius. 'Shall we make their acquaintance?'

* * * * *

Atenos ducked into the tower and looked up the interior stairs. The various platforms were filled with men sheltering from the incessant arrow storm and he could not see, but could clearly hear, the Cretan archers at the top bellowing imprecations in both Greek and Latin and calling on the gods of both peoples as they released their deadly missiles at the wall. They were good. Atenos had to admit that they were among the best archers he'd seen. Yet still only one arrow in four struck home, between the difficult angle of attack and the height difference, the solid parapet behind which the enemy were well protected and the continual oncoming missiles.

As he watched with satisfaction, he spotted the men he'd detailed hoisting buckets of water up from the spring and using it to douse the seemingly endless fire arrows the enemy loosed into the tower. There were so many wet, half-charred arrows jutting from the timbers and hides now that an enterprising man could fairly easily climb the outside of the tower.

There was a sudden scream that cut through the general din and a blur flashed past, quickly followed by a wet crunch as the man who had fallen from the top struck the ground outside. Though the fire was doing little to dent the Roman's position, the arrows were. A single glance at the piles of bodies pulled back from the action or the continual line of men being carried or dragged back out of arrow range for the capsarii to treat told a horrible tale of declining numbers.

Decumius appeared next to him.

'It's my heartfelt advice that you send for the reserves, sir.'

Atenos shook his head. 'Not until things are desperate.'

Decumius blinked. 'This isn't desperate?'

'You were at Alesia, right?'

'Ah. Got you, sir. When I can't move for bodies and Hades' horse is nibbling on my gonads. That kind of desperate.'

Atenos laughed at the wild grin on his fellow centurion's face. He'd ordered Decumius back down the slope three times now, the first when the centurion had been hit in the shoulder with a sling bullet that had put his left arm out of action, the second time when an arrow had carved a neat furrow in his hair – his helmet long gone, misshapen from a thrown rock – and the third time when another arrow had taken a chunk out of his calf. Still the man stayed, limping, bleeding, complaining, but waving his vine staff and bellowing his men into place.

'I'm actually *wishing* for the rain now,' Decumius grunted.

'What? Why?'

'Dampen their bow strings. Give us a bit of respite.'

Atenos shook his head. 'No good. They'd still have slings and rocks, and if we didn't have our archers in commission, this whole place would be flooded with enemy warriors in the time it would take you to fart.'

Decumius snorted as he left the tower and Atenos took a deep breath, making the most of a last moment of shelter before diving back out into the rain. One of the optios was scurrying towards him as stones and bullets clattered and zinged around him, one hand holding a dented helmet down on his head.

'What is it?'

The man thrust a hand out. In it were a pile of purple flowers. Atenos frowned. 'Explain.'

'Dunno what their called, primus pilus, but one of my lads who's a farmer says they're about as poisonous as anything he's found. Kills goats in hours, he says, and there's blankets of the things in the woods just down the hill. We could poison the spring and then abandon this, sir.'

Atenos raised an eyebrow. 'Poison a free-flowing spring?'

'Yes sir.'

'Can you see any hole in your logic, man?'

The optio frowned in confusion. 'Not really, sir.'

'Then I suggest you head back down to the camps and pour a little dye into the river and see how long it sticks around.'

As the man scratched his temple in incomprehension an arrow came out of nowhere and pinned his foot to the floor with a meaty crunch. The optio looked down in surprise and the lack of a reaction suggested to Atenos that the man did truly have the brains of an ox. What was a man like that doing in a position of command? The big Gaul crouched and none-too-gently snapped the arrow just above the flesh, causing the man to whimper in pain. 'Get to the capsarius and have that seen to.'

Gratefully, and still clutching his poisonous burden, the optio hobbled and hopped off down the slope. A shout of triumph drew his attention and he turned back to the walls as a sling bullet whipped through the air close enough to ruffle his eyelashes.

Atop the ramparts the defenders were raising what looked like small kegs. As Atenos watched, men lit the kegs, which must be filled with something incendiary, using tapers from the wall-top braziers. A lucky shot from one of the Cretan archers struck a man with a lit keg and he crumbled beneath it. There was a muffled bang behind the parapet and three men were suddenly aflame and screaming.

The scene was one bonus in a diorama of nightmare, though. Another half dozen kegs were ignited and cast from the walls, carefully aimed. Two of them hit badly and broke open upon impact, spreading out across the damp grass in a flaming mass. The others hit the slope well and bounced on, careening down the hill at the Romans. One struck the mound just below the tower, doing little but burn the turf black. Another was knocked askance and disappeared off down the hillside into the woods, and ultimately the river. The other two hit the line of men with wicker shields who helped protect the approach up the ramp. A double boom cracked the murky sky as a score of men exploded into blazing fire that ate up the wicker screens in moments and began to scorch the vineae that gave them shelter.

Tallow or pitch, or some such, it had to be. The fire clung like a lover to the wood of the vinea which had been regularly doused with water against fire arrows. The fire was too much even for damp wood, and the structure was quickly ablaze. The approach from below was no longer protected. The men could still come up through the woods but it would be hard going. Two small detachments of men arrived from somewhere with scorpion bolt throwers and cases of ammunition, hurrying to position themselves on the mound, but before they could even crank back the weapons, several of them had been taken out of the fight with arrows. A half century of men formed a mini-testudo and hurried over, providing shelter while the remaining artillerists began to load and release the weapons.

Atenos looked back and forth across the chaos. Despite what he'd said to Decumius, the situation was rapidly becoming untenable and he would need the reserves very soon. The vinea was now an inferno and the two resourceful men who'd come with buckets of water to try and douse it were even now jerking and dancing as arrows and stones thudded into them. The legionaries who had manned the wicker screen were almost gone, just a pile of charring bodies in a golden pyre, odd ones still thrashing around and croaking.

The general had better make this worth it.

He grabbed a running soldier. 'Find some friends and move that second vinea out of line before the whole lot catch fire.'

The legionary, his face betraying fear bordering on panic, saluted desperately and turned back.

Another series of booms drew his startled gaze and he realised they were in real trouble now. A second wave of burning barrels had been cast down with better precision this time, all centred on the tower. While most simply exploded on the mound's slope, one lucky barrel had rolled on with impressive momentum up the mound and burst against the base of the tower.

'Shit. Shit, shit, shit.'

He turned to order men with water to the tower. *Thank the gods for a handy spring, eh?* He laughed bitterly. Legionaries were already at the task, throwing buckets of water on the flames. Another battle now raged against the fire itself, and it was a hard fought one, at that.

There was an ominous wooden thud and, already knowing what had made the noise, he rose to peer over the chaos. Sure enough, the oppidum's nearest gate was open and warriors were flooding out of it like a swarm of locusts.

'Here they come.'

Decumius was there again, suddenly. 'We've got trouble. The burning kegs have made part of the mound unstable. A few more exploding there and the whole tower might go over.'

'Shitting, shitting shit!' Atenos barked with deep feeling. 'If it goes it will be over towards the oppidum itself. Have four of the ropes completely drenched and then use them to anchor the tower from behind. Then find a contubernium of fearless lads and get them round the front of the tower with planks, wedging the bottom as best they can.'

Decumius saluted and ran off, and Atenos cleared his throat.

'All unoccupied men of the Tenth and Fifth to position. Shield wall with second and third row testudo cover, marking off from the optio to the right. Prepare to receive the enemy.'

The various centurions and optios under his command gathered their men and moved into position, weathering the arrow storm as well as they could, men falling with every third step into place. Another set of barrels came down and burst against the mound and the base of the tower, igniting the boards used to shore it up as well as the men busy putting them into place. One misthrown barrel hurtled past the wreckage of the burning vinea and the pile of carbonised legionaries and bounced on intact down the ramp with unerring accuracy. Atenos watched it go in surprise and felt a slight burst of relief as he saw the reserves hurrying up the slope, running out wide to avoid the rolling fiery barrel, which hit a random rock two hundred paces down the hill and coated the slope in sticky fire.

'Reserves are coming, lads. Hold the enemy.'

They couldn't hold. No strategist in the world would find a way to hold this. Caesar had been warned by them all, he knew, but had gone ahead anyway. *If there is a trick in your pouch, general, now is the time*, he grumbled under his breath.

The hastily assembled shield wall, with a sloping roof of shields on the second and third rank protecting as best they could from arrows, quavered for just a moment as the howling, screaming horde of Cadurci and their allies crested the ramp's edge and charged the line.

Atenos had a horribly clear view from his position. The shield wall almost folded under the pressure of the attack, buckling in several places. And wherever the shields parted, arrows and stones and bullets penetrated, killing and wounding men by the dozen. It was little more than a slaughter.

A quick glance over his shoulder. A cohort or more of men were running up to join the fray. They would buy half an hour extra at most in this meat grinder. And the tower was ablaze now with no real chance of its being extinguished. At what point did he call the situation untenable and back off?

With a preparatory breath he rushed over to the embattled legionaries and attracted the attention of an optio at the rear as he crouched and grasped a discarded shield. 'I'm going in. If the enemy break through to the rear, the tower goes, or you can readily count the number of men left by sight alone, sound the rally and get back down the hill.'

'But sir…'

Atenos ignored the man's imploring tone and shoved through the press of men, making for a small gap where missiles and battle-maddened warriors had caused a breach. Howling Cadurci were smashing down with swords and axes and jabbing with spears, and no sooner had Atenos plugged the gap than a gleaming spearhead glanced off his cheek plate and tore through the leather strap at his shoulder that held his medal harness. There was a snap and the whole thing slumped to one side, one of his hard-won phalerae falling away to the ground below. Atenos bellowed in fury and his first blow entered the spear-man responsible at the cheek, almost cutting his head in half horizontally.

'Bastard. Those medals are *mine*!'

Fury, tempered with experience and discipline, took over. His second blow all-but severed the sword arm of the man to his right. His third took an axe man in the throat. Stab, hack, slice, stab. Shield up. Shield locked. Smash with the boss and back into position. Stab and thrust. Stab and thrust.

The press was too much. He knew it. The shield wall was doomed even as those reserves arrived and began to fall into position. A stray axe blow took the corner off his shield and carried on into the sword arm of the legionary to his left who shrieked and fell back to be replaced a heartbeat later by a man from the second line, his teeth gritted.

'Juno's tits!' someone shouted away to the left. Atenos was too experienced to allow himself to be distracted by conversation. He concentrated on the axe man before him as he asked what was going on without turning his head to look. His sword caught the man's axe arm in the pit, sinking in with satisfying ease – one of the killing blows any sword trainer in the army will teach early on. Along the line, that same voice called out.

'More cohorts. It's a general advance. They're storming the place from all sides!'

No. Atenos felt the anger rising. After all this mess buying time, the general cannot have been so unprepared and stupid as to throw away six legions in such a foolish manner. But the centurion could hear the buccinae of the other legions in their advance up the slope. What was Caesar doing? He *must* not have wasted this opportunity!

Above, the heavens opened with a boom, and torrents of water battered the fighters on both sides. Bowstrings would be unusable in a few heartbeats' time, when they had been stretched beyond drawing. The fires might even be extinguished. It was a small blessing now in the grand scheme, but a truly unpleasant one for the men locked in mortal combat with the enemy.

A sword came out of nowhere and slammed into his forehead. He heard the projecting brow of his helmet give and split with a metallic crack, felt the lip of the helm bite into the flesh of his forehead, felt the sharp, hot pain as the blade's edge struck skin.

* * * * *

Marcus Antonius turned to Caesar, his expression pained and impatient. 'The spring is about to fall back into their hands, and we'll have lost four cohorts of men there alone, forgetting the rest of this insane assault. It's perhaps half an hour past the point where we should have sounded the general order to fall back. We've lost.'

Caesar turned a sly smile on his friend.

'Have you so little faith in me?'

Antonius narrowed his eyes angrily. 'If you have some ridiculous plan then put it into action while we still have an army.'

'It is all a matter of timing, Marcus.'

'Don't be so bloody infuriating, Gaius. One day you'll keep your plans too close to your chest and one of your fits will take you off to Elysium without the rest of us knowing what to do!' The general's sharp glance did nothing to shut him up. 'Yes I know about your *episodes*. Atia told me all about it. She worries about you. But that's not the issue now. Fuck the timing, Gaius. Legionaries are dying by the century out there.'

'Then I think you will be pleased by that sound.'

Antonius frowned and cocked an ear. Over the hiss of the falling rain – warm rain, even the downpour wouldn't make the sticky heat any more bearable – he could hear rumbling. Not the first peal of thunder he'd heard while he watched the legions falling like reaped wheat on the slopes of Uxellodunon. They should have ridden out the siege, even if it took a year.

'Thunder. Very helpful. Their archers will be less trouble. And I can see some of the fires going out. It's not going to help. You've committed the legions to their death for what? To buy time?'

'Precisely,' Caesar smiled. 'And the moment is upon us.

'Thunder is…'

'Not thunder, Marcus.'

339

Antonius blinked and his gaze rose to the spring along with Caesar's pointing finger.

'Sacred Venus, mother of man, what in Hades is that?'

* * * * *

Atenos blinked. His world was a red blanket. Reaching up in automatic panic, he balled his fists and rubbed his eyes, squeezing the sheet of blood from them. Again and again he blinked. His hand went up to his forehead. His helmet was gone and someone had thoughtfully tied a wrapping around his wounded head, but the blood was free-flowing and that wrapping was now crimson and saturated. Beneath the wrapping he could feel a lump the size of a hen's egg.

He deflated. In the press of men, he'd been certain that that was his death blow. He'd been waiting for one for over a year now. The centurionate had a ridiculously high mortality rate and though he continually claimed invulnerability on account of his Gallic bones, there was a saying among Caesar's legions since Alesia. *Lead the Tenth to glory, but put a coin in your mouth first.* Priscus, former primus pilus of the Tenth, had fallen at Alesia. Carbo, latest in that role, had fallen in the disastrous retreat at Gergovia. How long until the latest incumbent fell? He was sure the other centurions in the Tenth were running a lottery on when it would happen, though he'd never caught them at it yet. But it seemed that the spring at Uxellodunon would not be his time. He had a thundering headache and had seemingly lost quite a lot of blood, but he was able to think and move. He was, to all intents and purposes, intact.

He sighed as another rivulet of blood blinded his left eye. Unseen hands suddenly loosened the wrapping and the blood came again. Then there was the feel of something slimy being slapped on the wound. Honey. Dear goddess Minerva let it be honey and not one of the dung-based poultices used by some hopeless medics. He felt some relief as a fresh dressing was tied in place, and a damp sponge – not a shit-sponge, please – wiped away the blood from his face.

A concerned, young face appeared in front of him.

'What is your name, centurion?'

'Atenos, primus pilus of the...'

'How many fingers am I holding up?'

'Four, if you count the thumb as a finger.'

'You're fine,' the capsarius pronounced. 'Took a bit of a knock there, centurion. You might want to stay seated for a while until your brain stops rattling around in your skull.'

Atenos wanted to berate the young medic for any implication that he had a small, wizened brain, but as he turned sharply, he felt suddenly very sick and had to concede that perhaps the man had a point.'

'How's it going?' he asked, wincing.

The medic shrugged. 'Into Hades by the moment. 'Scuse me, but my talents are required.'

Atenos nodded at him, and the man was gone.

He took a moment to look around himself. Whoever had pulled him out of the fighting line had not only got him back to safety and a capsarius, he had thoughtfully kept him in the vicinity of the fight. He sat with his back to the earth mound, the creaking, smouldering tower looming above him, the ropes maintaining its stability passing above him, anchored there at the other side of the spring.

He was next to the spring.

Finally he registered the fact that it was raining very heavily. The angle of the rain was such that the tower was keeping it from him and he sat in its lea, a small, dry island in a land of downpour. The surface of the spring's pool seethed. Last time he had seen it, it gurgled with small ripples as the flow poured from the rock, and the excess flowed out over a lip into a channel that distributed it into the earth down towards the woods, where it became one of the numerous tiny streams that fed the river below. Now, however, the surface of the water churned and stippled as a million raindrops pounded it.

Somewhere across the mountainside, he could hear the general order to fall back being called.

At last the general had seen sense.

But could he not have done so without such dreadful loss of life?

He glanced back down at the surface of the water. Above him the sky clashed with the sound of Vulcan's hammer striking. The storm was in full flow and would not be abating any time soon. He sighed and tipped his head rather painfully back – his neck had apparently taken a jolt from the blow. The rain battered his face and he was rather grateful for the experience.

At least he wasn't dead.

Now, the Tenth and Fifth were sounding their recall. All around him the men were moving. He could hear them even if he couldn't see them, preparing to abandon the hard-won ground and retreat down to the camps. Presumably someone would come and help him down. He wasn't at all sure he could stand unaided without throwing up.

Another rumble of thunder.

And another.

His brow furrowed in concentration, and that hurt more than he could possibly have imagined. The previous peals of thunder had been perhaps a count of twenty apart. Those last two had been so close together there was hardly time to count at all.

Another rumble.

What in the name of divine Taranis was going on?

His eyes widened in disbelief and alarm as the ground gave a shudder and suddenly all the water drained from the spring as though someone had removed a plug at the bottom. Despite his pain and discomfort he leaned forward, peering into the depths. Amid the dark rock, the slimy green weed and the coins thrown in as offerings, Atenos could see a number of wide fissures that had opened in the rock.

What in Hades?

And now the mouth of the spring itself was sputtering, odd gouts of brown water leaping from it into the empty pool. And then nothing. The spring was gone.

There was another rumble and the ground bucked like an unbroken horse.

Hands were suddenly beneath his arms, helping raise him to his feet. 'Time you were away from here, centurion,' announced the unseen helper. Atenos could not agree more, baffled as he was. As he struggled upright, the ground gave another ominous creak and groan and in a moment that almost stopped his heart, a swathe of woodland vanished into the earth in a long avenue down the hill.

As he boggled at the sight, the capsarius at his side helping him down the slope, he spotted the water seeping and saturating the ground down at the end of that flattened avenue. With a slightly painful grin, he spotted the figures there and finally understood.

Engineers, one officer, and perhaps two centuries of legionaries, all covered in earth and muck. Sappers.

All the time the tower at the top, the desperate fight of Atenos' men and even the general advance had been keeping the defenders busy, the general had been undermining the hill. And finally, all at once, the tunnels had broken through to the spring's underground source and diverted it way down the hill. And then the tunnels had been collapsed as the miners left them.

The only readily accessible source of water for the oppidum had been denied them. Where the water now came up from various places it would be undrinkable for some time, but would regardless be too close to the Roman lines for safe use and too far from the walls of Uxellodunon for the locals to defend.

The old goat had done it.

Atenos was grinning from ear to ear all the way down the slope and the appearance of the limping Decumius carrying his fallen phalera only made it all the wider.

* * * * *

Antonius glared at Caesar.

'Isn't it bad enough that you keep your surprises even from your senior officers without being unbearably smug about it as well?'

The figure of Aulus Hirtius was busy striding up the hill towards them, his lean, gaunt figure gangly and ungainly, as though he had too many knees for one human being. The pinched face had an odd expression that might be a mix of satisfaction and abhorrence. He'd somehow managed to get himself drenched, and the sopping white tunic and cloak clung to his frame making him look all the more like a crane fly.

'All goes well, then, Hirtius?'

The man stopped and saluted. While Antonius and Caesar stood in the shelter of the porch of the general's forward observation tent, Hirtius remained in the torrential downpour, sheltering his forehead as though that made the slightest difference in his soaked state.

'The engineers and men of the Fifteenth acquitted themselves well, Caesar. The nearest accessible flow to the walls now is around a third of the way up the slope,' he turned and pointed. 'Somewhere near that large elm. We can cover the site with both artillery and archers with little difficulty from our lines. The enemy will not be able to get within fifty paces of water.'

'Excellent.' The general turned to Antonius. 'Might I be allowed just the slightest hint of smug, now?' he winked.

Antonius rolled his eyes. 'If Fronto were here he would be standing a foot from your face, bellowing by now.'

'If Fronto were here, Antonius, he would have been the one at the mines.'

Caesar peered up through the torrent and spotted Varus wending his way down the hill towards them. Turning, he spotted an older soldier, unarmoured and with a voluminous, hooded oiled-skin cloak wrapped tight around him against the rain. His favoured sacerdos. The priest of the Tenth, with the knowledge of ritual and some skill at divination. With a crooked finger, he beckoned.

'Sir?'

'Can you tell me what Jupiter Pluvius has in store for us?'

'Of course, General. Despite the current downpour, I expect the sky to clear before sunset and lead to several days of dry heat. The *ass' manger* last night was bright and unobstructed, and that speaks of good weather. Also a crow gave three distinct calls above the camp at dawn, which I thought to be at odds with the coming deluge, but now I see presaged a good period to follow. In the...'

'A simple 'good weather' would have done, man. Thank you.'

The old soldier nodded and retreated five steps and into his hood once more.

'We have to assume that they have good residual water supplies in the oppidum, and every cistern and reservoir they have will be uncovered to catch the storm rain. Still, they have many thousands of warriors up there in addition to the general population and the large number of animals to provide sustenance. They cannot have been expecting to lose their water supply, and this will be a very final blow to them. Their water will soon run dry in fine weather.'

Varus approached and saluted rather soggily, his face tired but satisfied.

'What's the lie of the land, Quintus,' asked Antonius.

The cavalry commander stretched and rolled his shoulders. 'We took serious losses near the spring. It was a good call assigning the Tenth under Atenos. That man would hold the gates of Hades itself against Cerberus if you asked. I hear he took a place in the front line and suffered a head wound, but is in no danger. The general estimate is somewhere around eight hundred dead. Wounded are few. Nearly anyone who engaged the enemy is gone, rather than injured. As soon as the spring disappeared, the enemy lost heart and pulled back. The other varied assaults suffered minor casualties, but never really got the chance to involve themselves before the mines did their job.'

344

He gestured over his shoulder with a thumb. 'The enemy are already starting to come down the slopes in twos and threes, testing our resolve and trying to get close to either the new spring spouts or the tributary rivers. They'll get a nasty surprise. I watched one of the scorpions finding their range and the artillerist put three bolts into the same tree way beyond the water, so unless our men fall asleep there will be no water for Uxellodunon.'

'Shame we can't get anyone inside to ruin the water supplies,' Antonius mused, and Varus nodded his agreement.

'No matter, gentlemen,' Caesar smiled. 'In my experience, Gauls are impetuous, and only a strong leader can impose any true order, in the Roman sense, over their forces – they are too individual in their ways. They have no leaders, for Lucterius is fled and Drapes is ours. The Gauls will drink their water in desperation, without thought for a long-term plan. Where their supplies might be made to last weeks, in current conditions I would expect it to manage only days.'

Somewhere behind Varus, in the trees at the lowest slopes of the oppidum, the distinctive sound of artillery at work cracked and thumped and echoed, their victims adding counterpoint with screams and cries of alarm. The Cadurci were learning a hard lesson, it seemed.

'There will be a night and a day of such attempts, I think,' Caesar mused. 'They will want to try the cover of darkness, and will hope that we become complacent the next day. We must continually rotate the units of archers and artillerists on watch and make sure we plug any gaps, and then the day will be ours, gentlemen.'

'Will they not make an attempt to break out?'' Antonius mused.

'No. Not without their leaders to drive them. They are surrounded by our defences and outnumbered, with six legions here. And their life expectancy in the oppidum has just been reduced to almost naught in a matter of hours. Tonight there will be desperate last attempts, and throughout the morning, especially if it remains misty in the valleys as seems the norm. If we continue to deny them water, I will expect their first emissaries after noon tomorrow. By the kalends of the month, we will be dividing the spoils and the slaves, reducing the oppidum and assigning winter quarters.'

'I somehow expected a fight,' Antonius frowned.

Varus cocked an eyebrow. 'I wouldn't voice that sentiment near Atenos and the men of the Tenth and Fifth if I were you.'

'You know what I mean,' grumbled Antonius.

Caesar smiled and slapped his friend on the back, raising a shower of rain droplets. Above, the rumble of thunder had moved off, southeast. 'Not every season need end with an earth-shaking contest of arms, Marcus. Be grateful that we have thwarted their army here and now. Gaul, my friends, is pacified. We will be forced to make an example, of course, to prevent further risings, but I do believe that this winter we can begin the grand task of turning this place into a province.'

Varus nodded wearily. By autumn, there was every chance that many of the legions would be disbanded and settled strategically in colonies among the Gauls. And where would that leave the officers? Where would that leave him? Back to Rome to climb another rung of the Cursus Honorum, chasing on the heels of his little brother Publius, who had flouted the family's ties to Caesar and thrown in his lot with Pompey? To be rewarded for his long service to this army with a comfortable provincial governorship, where he could grow fat and slow as slaves fed him peeled grapes and rich, red Rhodian? After eight years of cavalry service in Caesar's army, it would take a decade to remove the constant smell of horse-sweat and oiled leather from his nostrils.

He laughed at the thought of Varus the Senator.

'Something amuses you?' mumbled Antonius.

'Oh nothing really. Just pondering on the vagaries of the future, picturing myself joining the ranks of men like Fronto the wine merchant and living the peaceful life.'

The three men smiled at the thought.

Chapter Eighteen

OSTIA steamed in the early summer heat. Despite its coastal location, no matter how much Rome seemed to drown under spring and autumn rains, Ostia had seemed universally parched and warm whenever Fronto passed through. The trierarch of the *Black Eagle*, which had brought them from Massilia as part of the military escort, was bellowing commands to his crew as the vessels prepared to unload Caesar's huge convoy. Ten huge, wide, shallow-bottomed barges waited to take the precious cargo on upriver to Rome, where the larger military triremes would have difficulties navigating. The *Black Eagle* was an escort – a trireme with little space for cargo – and thus had only a tiny fragment of the entire convoy to unload. The great trader vessels that formed the bulk of the flotilla carried the lion's share of the loot and slaves. Three sailors carried the small party's gear down the boarding ramp and deposited it close by. There was little of the usual array of bags and boxes that followed Lucilia whenever she left home. They travelled light.

'I do not like this,' Masgava said for the fifth time that morning.

'I'll be fine,' Fronto sighed. 'There are ten of us and we are all good men, Masgava. You trained most of us, after all. Seven of them in an unfamiliar and hostile city. Ten of us, a number of who know every guardhouse, courthouse, storehouse and whorehouse in Rome.'

He caught a look from Lucilia and grinned weakly. 'Or some of those, anyway.'

Masgava continued to look unconvinced.

'Lucilia's safety is more important than my own, and so is that of the boys. You and Arcadios have a responsibility to them. With half a dozen of the lads I expect you to take good care of them.'

'Andala is competent with a blade, also,' his wife added with a warm smile, 'and Galronus will be there.'

Fronto felt a sad little tug for a moment that he was continuing on into peril in the heart of the republic, and not with this small group who would soon be reunited with his old friend the Remi prince, as well as his mother and sister. 'We'll come to Puteoli as soon as we're finished in Rome. Perhaps we'll even stay for the autumn and winter. It's been some time since I enjoyed a Campanian break.'

Across the dock, Catháin came scurrying lop-sidedly, still unable to shake off the rolling gait of the practised sailor. He clapped his hands together and rubbed them, grinning, and Fronto couldn't help but smile. For days now the strange northerner had been almost vibrating with excitement at the chance to reorganise the very root of Fronto's business at the wine production centres of Campania. Catháin coughed. 'The captain of the *Cassiopeia* will take us for a very good low fee. He is stopping at Antium to unload a cargo, but otherwise is straight to Puteoli and then Neapolis and Pompeii.'

Fronto nodded his satisfaction. Nowhere would be safer for the others than the family villa.

'Sure I can't persuade you to join them?' he murmured, glancing across at Balbus, who was busy settling his heavy, bulky toga in place.

'Hardly. A threat to Rome is a threat to all Romans. And I owe these animals for what they did at my villa.' The old man cupped Lucilia's chin in his large hand. 'Be safe, daughter. We will join you soon.' Stooping, he reached out and hugged Balbina who remained silent as usual, though the pain in her eyes at his departure was almost tangible. 'Look after your sister and your nephews. Don't let that reprobate Galronus have you drinking his nasty Gaulish drinks.'

Straightening, he nodded to Masgava, who reached out to Fronto and clasped his hand. 'Be careful. These are not Hierocles' muscle. They're dangerous and, to have got to Rome intact, they must be clever and careful. Don't underestimate them, and remember: you may not be able to carry a sword in the city, but to a gladiator anything can be a weapon in the right circumstances.'

Fronto smiled and let go as Catháin waved the small party on towards a Greek merchant ship that wallowed at one of the jetties, loading cargo as efficiently as possible in a harbour filled to the gills with Caesar's fleet, another twenty ships still waiting out at sea for their turn. Fronto watched his wife and children and their eminently capable guards make their way across the wide dockside, ready for the next leg of their journey south to safety, three of the hired hands from Fronto's small but trustworthy force carrying the bags on their backs and shoulders.

'They will be safe,' Cavarinos said, as if reading his innermost thoughts. 'Greek sailors know the Middle Sea like no others, and each man with them – and the women, in fact – are strong and trustworthy.'

'I know.'

'Then stop looking at them with such sad eyes, as though they were leaving you forever. They have a Bellovaci woman with them sworn to your wife's protection and a warrior prince of the Remi awaiting them. Oh, and some Romans, too.'

Fronto turned a scathing look on the Arvernian, who flashed him a tight smile. 'You need to focus on the task at hand.'

He nodded and, as the men from the ship unloaded the last of their kit, looked around at the men who had come with him – some through loyalty, some for pay, others for vengeance or some indefinable Gallic motivation Fronto couldn't quite follow.

Balbus. His father-in-law, old friend and former peer in the legions. Despite the heart trouble that had seen him leave the Eighth half a decade ago, Fronto would say that the old man looked fitter and leaner than he had for years and was, of course, every bit as wise and clever as he had always been.

Cavarinos. To all intents and purposes, the man was one of the enemy, or at least had been so quite recently. But the Arvernian was an enigma. Concerned with the survival of his people more than their ascendance, he had quickly become as close to Fronto as any Roman he could name. The former legate would have no qualms over having Cavarinos at his back. Would that be the same, he wondered, when the men they faced were the Gaul's countrymen?

Biorix. The hulking Gaulish legionary and engineer who had come to his attention half a decade since and had endured and triumphed through every strand of adversity that Fronto and his bodyguard had encountered these past three years.

Pamphilus and Clearchus. None too bright, it had to be said, but as loyal as the day was long, and with strong arms and stout hearts. And the other three men who had served at the villa were all tried and tested, having fought off the enemy during that heart-stopping night attack – Dyrakhes the slinger, Agesander the boxer and Procles the giant Greek former mercenary.

And the last of the ten-man army was now hurrying back across to them, his eyes rolled upward, watching the gulls that filled the sky with their cries and swooping, aware of the potential for aerial deposits and veering close if he thought they might occur. After all, a gull dropping its business on you was among the luckiest of signs. Aurelius. If Masgava was the head of Fronto's guard, Aurelius was its heart and soul. The former legionary stopped in front of them, heaving in breaths from his run, though with a curious smile and a splash of white across the shoulder of his tunic.

'Port officials say they've had at least a dozen Gallic ships in over the past day and they don't keep records down to tribal levels so they can't confirm if any of them are Ruteni. All Gallic vessels marked down are registered at Narbo, Massilia, Agathe or Heraclea, but that doesn't help as any of them could belong to the Ruteni and could have been at Massilia. The last was logged a little over two hours ago, so even if the bastards we're after were on that ship, so long as they were sharp they could be in Rome even now, either by road if they bought horses or by swift passenger ferry upriver. Little chance of us catching them in Ostia.'

Fronto nodded. He'd not expected to contain them here, but had held onto a small thread of hope that it might happen nonetheless. 'To Rome, then. We know where they're going.' He turned at the sound of his name and saw Brutus walking across the dock towards him, a legionary leading the officer's horse behind him.

'Decimus. Are you bound for Rome, now?'

Brutus shook his head. 'Soon. Can't let this convoy out of my sight, else Caesar will have me strung up. A lot of his consulship and political future rides on these barge-loads. I'll wait until the last of it is loaded and bound for the city and then follow along, to be safe. I was going to say that I'm bound for the house of Casca, but as soon as I'm done with the duty, I'll head home and stay there unless Casca requires me. You know our family's houses in Rome, yes?'

'I do. Which one?'

'I'll be on the Palatine – the villa overlooking the Vestals' compound.'

Fronto chuckled and Brutus flashed an embarrassed grin. 'A foible of my grandfather. I think he narrowly avoided prosecution by sealing up two of the more overhanging windows. Anyway, you know where to find me if you need me. And you?'

Fronto shrugged. 'Home, on the Aventine. The place is back to functioning normally these days, though it's been unoccupied by anyone but a caretaker for a while.'

'Right. Good luck, my friend.'

Fronto eyed a wagon-load of booty being manhandled with difficulty across a ramp and into a wide barge. 'You too.'

Turning away from the dock, he threw a heavy pouch to Aurelius. 'Take Dyrakhes and Biorix and buy ten horses. They don't have to be race winners, but I'd prefer it if their legs didn't fall off as soon as we leave Ostia. The rest of us will gather a few supplies and meet you at the Rome Gate in an hour.'

* * * * *

Fronto sipped his wine – lightly watered to preserve the rich flavour, though taken in a small quantity. A clear head was required now. The others sat on the same folding stools as he, standard fare for military campaigns, without the comfort of a civilian couch but with ease of transport and storage. The townhouse of the Falerii had been completely restored after the fire that had torn through it, but there was yet little in the way of furnishing or comfort, having not been fully occupied for some time. Indeed Glyptus, the sour-faced but excruciatingly efficient freedman Faleria had retained to maintain the house, was even now out in the city with a purse of coins, purchasing bedding for ten and a few home comforts. It was late in the evening to shop, really, but in *this* city – the greatest in the world – there was no time of day or night that goods could not be purchased if one knew where to look.

Outside the squeak of bats flitting about in the dark added a harmonious line above the distant surge and murmur of the late night horse race in the circus for the Apolline Games. Each squeak was accompanied by a twitch in Aurelius' eye and in order to try and concentrate the man's thoughts on the task at hand, Fronto had been forced to close all the windows despite the growing stuffy heat.

The party of ten had arrived in the city not long after noon, all weapons and equipment safely stowed in their packs in line with Roman law. They had made their way up to the house to a gruff greeting from Glyptus, who had set about lighting the furnace, but they had declined his grudging offer of a meal, instead strolling down to a tavern Balbus knew well on the Gemonian Way, rather aptly named the 'Huntsman's head'. The food had been standard fare at slightly inflated prices and the wine an extortionate cost for a poor vintage, but Balbus had been quite right about its unparalleled view of the carcer. They had spent an hour there having a midday meal, and then another slowly supping wine while they observed, filling the void with harmless small talk.

Not one of them had been concentrating on the food or the drink or the gossip, for all their harmless, mundane appearance to passersby. In fact, their attention had been fully locked on the state prison opposite, its surroundings and the local populace. While it seemed highly unlikely that they might spot a cloaked and cowled figure in a mask strolling through the forum in daylight, they could not preclude the possibility that the Gauls had shed their disguises and were now trying to blend in. There were a few foreigners here, of course. Greeks, Egyptians, Spaniards, Africans, Levantines, Thracians and so on. Not many of the fair haired northerners, of course, but a few. Enough that a subtle Gaul could walk through the streets without raising too much comment.

And then, finally, they had made their way to the public baths to scrape away the dirt of travel and refresh themselves, all the while listening to the conversation and gossip of the men sharing the great complex with them. Anything might be of use after so long away from the city, after all. Fronto had been fascinated watching Cavarinos as he experienced a true Roman bath complex for the first time. The Arvernian had used Fronto's baths at the villa, of course, and had learned, with some surprise and perhaps a little scorn, how such things as strigils and spongia worked. But having fully depilated naked slaves tending to his personal hygiene seemed to cause something between fascination and horror for the Gaul.

A little walk around, introducing those who had not visited the city before to its ways and districts, and finally they had returned to the house of the Falerii in time for an evening meal as the sun descended behind the Aventine's slopes. Glyptus was either a far better cook than Fronto had taken him for or, as Fronto suspected, one of the local and better *cauponae* owners was grinning at a small pile of coins and an empty ingredients larder. Now, as evening rolled on, in private and with the day's research to work through, the ten of them sat around a model of the forum's western end and the slopes of the Capitoline constructed out of boxes, bowls, pots, pans, wax tablets and anything else Fronto could find to add to the growing plan in his tablinum.

'So how is this carcer run?' asked Cavarinos, peering at the small ceramic honey pot that represented Rome's infamous prison.

Fronto nodded to Balbus. 'You're more informed on city matters than me these days, Quintus?'

The old man leaned back and coughed. 'Well, now. For a start there is no permanent guard staff on the place. What you need to remember is that the carcer is only a temporary measure. It is a place where important criminals or captured enemies are kept until their fate is decided, not a punishment in itself. As such there are occasions when the place is completely empty for protracted periods, though in times of war and civil strife it can be quite busy. As such it becomes the responsibility of the consuls in office at the time. Often control of the carcer is delegated by those consuls to one of their clients. When Pompey was in office, his man Afranius was responsible and the place was full of Pompey's enemies, so Afranius brought a sizeable force of loyal men to run the place.'

'And now?' prompted Aurelius.

'The current consuls are Claudius Marcellus the younger and Sulpicius Rufus. If Pompey still had control of the carcer, there would be little chance of our gaining access to it after Fronto's disagreement with the man. But even Pompey might have been easier than these two. Marcellus is an outspoken enemy of Caesar, a true hater of the proconsul, and he is the man with current control. It might be possible to circumvent him by going to Rufus, but although Rufus has never officially stood against Caesar, he has often spoken out against him and I think would be no friend to us. Besides, playing off one consul against another usually has bad repercussions. Anyway, Marcellus was a tribune in Pompey's army early in his career and he's put one of his former officers in charge of the carcer along with, I understand, five former legionaries. I think we can assume they are experienced veterans and incorruptible. Marcellus ran his campaign for consul on the ticket of stamping out corruption, so he would have to be careful about his employees.'

'If they are so incorruptible, can we not just go to this Marcellus or his officer and tell them about the Sons of Taranis?' mused Cavarinos. 'Surely they would put the security of Rome's most important prisoner above petty rivalries?'

Fronto snorted. 'If you think your tribes are prone to infighting, you've a thing to learn yet about Rome. Most of the powerful men in the city hate most of the other powerful men, and no small amount of them would burn down half the city to embarrass their opposite numbers. We used to have a bit of balance when Crassus was still in the picture, as there were three camps and something of a stalemate. But now it's polarised and everyone is either for Pompey or for Caesar. You say the wrong name to the wrong people and you'll be wandering the street looking for your teeth.'

Balbus sighed and turned to Cavarinos. 'What our friend is trying so eloquently to say is that divisions run so deep in Roman politics these days that Marcellus might well free Vercingetorix himself just to embarrass Caesar if he thought he could get away with it. He certainly wouldn't listen to us and take action to stop the Sons of Taranis. In fact, he'd probably welcome their intervention. If Gauls from a land that Caesar claims to have conquered manage to free their king and get him out of Rome, Caesar would suddenly find himself extremely unpopular in all circles.'

Cavarinos shook his head. 'How your people ever conquer lands is beyond me.'

'So,' Fronto murmured, tapping the honey pot with a finger, 'six men inside who will have nothing to do with us, and no way to readily gain access. That puts us more or less on the same footing as the enemy. The difference is that they have to find a way in. We just have to stop them doing so. That's our main advantage.'

'Wish we knew where they were,' muttered Biorix. 'That would make things a great deal easier.'

'True, but we don't. And barring the disfigured Molacos, who will have to be extremely cautious and is probably not going outside at all, we have no idea what they look like. We will have to be truly alert and perceptive. No one is to get too drunk while we're in the city, and everyone is expected to get a good night's sleep every night. If the worst comes to the worst, there are people we can call on in the city: Caesar's niece and family, Brutus, old friends from the army. But we can't drag them into this unless we need them. The more people involved the more likely something will go wrong.'

'The Sons of Taranis will have to examine the carcer and learn what they can,' Cavarinos said. 'They do not have the advantage of being able to pass for city folk like you. Most of them might not speak Latin or at least will speak it with a thick accent, so they will be limited in terms of who can do their research. Moreover, they will not have the level of knowledge of Balbus here. There is every chance that we are already way ahead of them in finding out everything we need to know. That means that they will likely still be watching the carcer.'

'Good point,' Fronto nodded. 'And if they are, *we* may be able to spot *them*. So our first goal is to put a watch on the carcer ourselves. We'll have pairs of men watching the place from the Huntsman's Head. Most of you are more than capable of blending in at a city tavern. Stay on the alert side, but try to look like you're relaxing on your day off. While two men observe there, the rest can stay here out of sight and rest. We'll rotate the duties so that a pair is never repeated. Sadly myself, Balbus and Cavarinos are off the list. We are far too well known to the enemy, though we might stay nearby to be on-hand at times. With Fortuna's grace, the Gauls will slip up and we'll catch them watching the place. If we can get a lead on them before they make any real move, then we're in with a chance. We might be able to mob them early.'

'What if we get involved in a fight?' Dyrakhes mused. 'You say we're not allowed weapons in the city and I understand you not wanting to break the law, but you can bet that these Gauls aren't bothered. If they've come this far they won't baulk at concealed weapons. I fought in the pits in Tergeste, but I don't relish the idea of facing well-armed men with only my fists if I can avoid it.'

The others nodded and Fronto sighed. 'It's not simply a matter of not wanting to break the rules, Dyrakhes. It's a sacred law as old as the city. When you cross the pomerium – the sacred boundary of the original city – there are rules as old as the gods. Carrying a weapon of war in public is a terrible violation. It doesn't apply in your own homes, of course, and it doesn't apply to tools and eating knives and all that. And there's some bending of the boundaries, to be honest. When I was young, before Sulla extended it thirty years ago, the pomerium barely covered the centre and stopped just this side of the circus. My great grandfather built this house before the Aventine became the domain of the plebs largely because this hill was outside the pomerium then and he felt safe from flouting sacred law. Caesar officially broke the law by crossing it and coming to this house a few years ago, since he should have laid down his governorship to do so, but no one would dare cross the general at the time, and many would argue that the recent extension to the pomerium wasn't legal anyway and that Caesar hadn't crossed the true one. Even some magistrates probably only consider the original ancient pomerium a proper legal boundary.' He frowned as he realised that he'd drifted off into an almost tutorial explanation, and smiled at himself. Age, perhaps? His grandfather had done that a lot.

Balbus gave him an odd look. 'The long and the short of it is that a man can be fined, beaten, exiled or even executed for carrying a weapon within the pomerium, depending on his status, so we do not do it even if it puts us at a disadvantage. But,' he smiled, 'there are no rules against carrying a good eating or whittling knife, or a cleaver, or even a good stout staff. Just weapons.'

Fronto nodded. 'And that is what we'll do. Permissible arms only. We'll start in the morning.'

Aurelius shook his head. 'Respectfully, sir, the Sons of Whores or whatever they're called won't be sleeping on it. They might even be there right now, trying something. If we're settled on the plan – that for now we observe and try to spot the enemy – we should start right away.'

'Everyone is exhausted after the journey, Aurelius.'

'Not really, sir. I understand the taverns on the Argiletum and the Clivus Argentarius stay open ridiculously late if not all night, so the Huntsman's Head will probably be the same. I've pulled all night watches many times in the legion and I'll feel better in a lively place than here with your unusually loud and large collection of bats. I'll take on the first watch.'

'I will too,' murmured Biorix. 'I know the look of a tribesman as well as Cavarinos there. And who better to look like a couple of retired veterans enjoying a cup of wine than a couple of retired veterans?'

Fronto sat thoughtful and silent for a moment. 'Alright. Pamphilus and Procles will relieve you in the third watch of the night. That should give them ample time to rest first. Once you're relieved, you two, get straight back here and to sleep. I need everyone on their toes.'

Aurelius and Biorix said their farewells and left the room, and Fronto peered at his large model. 'I suppose there's not much else we can do until we know more. I'll leave this here for further use, but I guess we would all be best served now by getting some sleep. In the morning I'm going to the city tabularium to see what I can find out that might be of use.'

* * * * *

Fronto unrolled the next scroll and ran his finger down it until he found the name he was looking for. Lucius Curtius Crispinus. There he was in ink: Marcellus' carcer man. A former senior centurion out east who'd received his retirement early while Marcellus was the legion's senior tribune. Seems the two had been linked even then. When Marcellus came back to Rome so did Crispinus, ignoring the nice parcel of Illyrian land he'd been granted as his honesta missio. The scroll told a story of an exemplary officer. Decorated numerous times on campaign, winner of the *corona aurea*. Fronto's kind of officer, in fact. He reached up for the other ledgers he'd brought from the shelves. After some furious rifling through, he stabbed a finger down on the centurion's name again. Interesting. Crispinus owned that estate in Illyricum but also occupied one of Marcellus' town houses rent free. He was clearly indispensable to the consul to be kept in such a manner, but what was *truly* interesting was that Crispinus also had his name on the deeds of another property on the Viminal. A property that had previously been registered to Pompey himself until he had moved his family to the grand new house by his great theatre. Did Marcellus know that his client centurion was bypassing him and taking handouts directly from Pompey?

It made little difference to the matter in hand. Crispinus might be a true veteran centurion with an excellent record – he might be incorruptible and the paragon of Roman *virtus* – but either way, whether he was Marcellus' man or Pompey's, it put him a long way from Fronto's reach. Marcellus was an enemy of Caesar, and Pompey... well, everyone knew where *that* was going. And Fronto was well known for his connection to Caesar. A dead end there.

With the deep sigh of the thwarted, Fronto returned the documents to their assigned places and left the building, the clerk by the exit giving him a cursory look-over to make sure he had removed no files from the place. Despite the danger of recognition by the Sons of Taranis, he took a quick dip across the long sloping road to the open front of the Huntsman's Head with its excellent view of the carcer. Pamphilus sat, looking somewhat irritable, toying with his bread and cheese. Across the table from him sat the hulking shape of the Greek marine, Procles. Fronto had expected a certain amount of irritability from Pamphilus, having been split from his brother Clearchus, but really between them they barely produced enough brightness to illuminate a barrel. Splitting them up and pairing them with more inventive thinkers had been a natural decision and Procles, for all his size and shape, was a surprisingly quick-witted man.

'Morning, lads.'

'Marcus,' nodded Procles, talking over the top of Pamphilus who'd started to call him sir. Anonymity was important at times like this.

'What news?'

'Oh this morning's fascinating,' grinned Procles, patting a spare seat. Fronto sank into it and poured himself a cup of their wine. 'Do tell.'

'Well, Procles smiled,' glancing around to make sure no one was listening too closely. 'There might only be six men inside, but they change regularly. They do shifts with three changes a day, if I've worked out my timings properly from what Aurelius told me. And the latest shift arrived not long ago, but only five of them arrived. Six men left and five entered. Since then we've heard a lot of raised voices from inside, but you can't quite hear what they're saying from here.'

Fronto frowned and opened his mouth to answer but at that moment the carcer door opened with a bang and two men appeared, one angry and one clearly anxious.

'To the barracks, Corvus, and fetch another man.' Crispinus. It had to be. Fronto had spent most of his adult life around centurions and he knew the tone. The way that voice carried across the open space it was clearly used to filling a parade ground. The man being lashed by the former centurion's tongue quailed nervously. 'Statius is never late for work. Something's happened to him, sir.'

Crispinus waved a dismissive hand. 'He spends too much time in the drinking pits of the Subura. Probably got himself knifed, but I'll look into it later. Can't be below compliment with *these* guests, now get going.'

Fronto watched for a while as the nervous man ran off, presumably back to Marcellus' compound to gather a replacement, and the centurion retreated into the carcer, slamming the door shut angrily.

'I presume I'm not alone in imagining the worst for this Statius fellow?'

Procles nodded. 'Suspicious timing for an accident or a random knifing.'

'And who do they have in there that requires a full complement, I wonder,' Fronto murmured. 'Five men should be adequate to watch over locked cells unless somehow they are already expecting danger?'

'Surely he meant Vercingetorix?'

Fronto shook his head. 'Plural. He said *these guests*, so who else high profile is in there?'

'I will keep an ear open,' Procles said as he took a sip of his drink.

'Let me know anything else you find out as soon as possible,' Fronto muttered, and then slipped from the tavern and crossed the road once more, stealing along the path between the tabularium and the temple of Saturn, making for the Aventine hill without passing through the crowded forum. Throughout the journey back from the forum, past the curved end of the circus and up the slope of the Aventine, he continued to think about the carcer from all angles. There was no way to get inside, which of course was the same for the Sons, but it limited their abilities. Something would happen soon. Fortuna, let us be prepared.

* * * * *

'An interesting afternoon,' said Procles as he closed the door behind him. Pamphilus nodded his agreement as he went straight to a couch and sank onto it with a groan. Dyrakhes and Clearchus had taken over at the tavern, and Agesander was prowling the forum, listening to gossip and keeping eyes open for anything potentially pertinent.

Fronto glanced at the others in the room and then back at the new arrival. 'Well, go on, then?'

'I found out who your extra prisoner is,' the big Greek said and took a seat opposite Fronto. 'His name is Arrius Ferreolus. He's a city decurion from a place called Comum. I'd never heard of it, but there were a couple of nicely wine-stooped and talkative fellows came into the tavern and they were already chatting about it. Didn't take much leverage to open them up. This Comum is one of Caesar's pet towns up in the Alpes. It's a Gaulish place that's been right behind the proconsul from the start. Seems that last year he granted the whole of Comum citizenship.'

'I remember that,' Balbus rumbled. 'Some big show of largesse. He had the swamp there drained and helped rebuild the place in Roman style. Half the streets are named after him now and there's balding statues all over the place.'

'Yes,' muttered Procles, 'well it's not *all* come up sweet and flowery. Seems Caesar granted citizenship to Comum, then went through the formality of requesting it from the senate.'

359

'Standard practice,' replied Fronto. They all do that. No one checks with the senate first.'

'Well it seems Marcellus has declared Caesar's grant illegal. He claims the general is flaunting his powers and assuming more authority than he should, even over the senate. Sounds like he's got half the senators riled up and ready to lynch the proconsul when he comes home.'

'It's a dubious claim,' Balbus mused. 'Laughable even, really. But there are plenty of senators with no love of Caesar, and Pompey's camp is powerful. The proconsul's reputation will take a serious knock from this. I wouldn't be surprised if Caesar gets dragged through the courts for it.'

'Impossible,' snorted Fronto. 'They can't level their charges while he's governing Gaul, and as soon as he gets back to Rome he'll get his consulship and be immune from prosecution for the year. With the money he's sent back with Brutus, he can buy most of Rome's votes in that time.'

'Don't underestimate his enemies,' Balbus warned. 'Caesar may think he's safe, but the cess-pool of Roman politics rarely delivers what you expect.'

Cavarinos frowned. 'However did you manage to suppress my people when you cannot even govern a city without arguing among yourselves? You are more like the tribes than you'd like to think, you know?' He rubbed his neck. 'So what is to happen to this decurion from Comum?'

Procles shrugged. 'That I couldn't find out. Seems he had come to the city at the head of some sort of delegation, bringing the thanks of his town, but as soon as Marcellus heard about them, the decurion was grabbed and thrown in the carcer. His retinue and companions were ejected from the city unceremoniously.'

'The courts will have to rule on the validity of Caesar's grant before anything happens to the decurion,' Balbus shrugged. 'But it's going to be high profile, this. And that means there'll be a focus on the carcer by both officials and the public. That will be why Crispinus was so adamant he wanted a full complement, Fronto. Marcellus' case against Caesar will ride partially on the man in that prison, so Crispinus will be very careful to be secure and legal and perfectly organised at all times.'

That presents us with both a positive and a negative,' sighed Fronto. 'The added political kerfuffle will mean potential opportunities for trouble, maybe even an *in* for the Sons of Taranis. Routine will go out of the window, and will only get worse if Caesar's grant and the decurion are ruled against. That means we'll need to step up the manpower near the carcer. Anything might happen now, so we need to keep plenty of hands to the reins. On the other hand, it also means that Crispinus and his men are going to be a lot more alert, which will make the Sons' task more difficult.'

'I wonder what happened to the missing guard, then,' Cavarinos mused. 'In the circumstances, it seems unlikely that any of those on duty will be putting themselves in danger or getting drunk in the slums.'

Fronto nodded. 'We have to assume that somehow the Sons of Taranis got to this guard. And that means they probably know everything we do, and a lot more besides. I'd be tempted to send one of you to get drunk with another of the guards and ply him for information, but I don't think they'll be readily accessible now. Crispinus will have them all on their guard.' He narrowed his eyes at the Arverni warrior. 'You know these people and their type better than any of us, Cavarinos. The hour is coming when they're going to have to make a move. If they want to get Vercingetorix back to Gaul before the campaigning season ends, they're running out of time. Will they move at day or night, you think?'

Cavarinos gave a sour look and shrugged. 'I am no more familiar with most of them than you are. But Molacos? He's a fanatic. If he was given this task by his master Lucterius, he'll do it or he'll die trying, and you can put walls and barred gates and legions of men in the way, but you'll have to put him down to stop him. That sort of man can be unpredictable. They do not conform to any kind of common sense. If it was *me* in charge of this – gods, but think about that: it almost *could* have been – then I would move at night, towards the last watch, when the guard shift are tired and at their lowest ebb. That would allow the Sons to move through the streets easier, especially with Molacos there. And, of course, if they succeed they will need to get the king out of the city before anyone even knows they've gone. Night-time is the clear and obvious option. Yet, given Molacos' fanatic nature, the shortness of time and the brazen nature of the swathe they cut through your Roman installations in our lands, we simply cannot rule out a daytime assault.'

'Very helpful,' grunted Fronto.

'They are just too much of an unknown quantity, Fronto. We will have to watch the place and be ready to move at all times. I would say their prime times to move are just before and just after a shift change and towards the end of the night. If we are all available at those times, and we send men back to sleep in shifts in between, that is the best we can do to be ready, I'd say.'

Aurelius cleared his throat. 'If it's any help, I've been chatting to one of the girls in the tavern and she's got quite… friendly.'

'I'm not sure how much help that can be,' grinned Clearchus.

'Not the girl. But she showed me around. There's an outbuilding behind the tavern that isn't used. They just store old rubbish in there, but it's quickly accessible from the street as well as the tavern. We can store staffs and sticks and knives and anything we want in there for quick retrieval.'

'Good man,' smiled Fronto. 'Get all the stuff we might need and move it there ready.' He took a breath. 'Alright, Cavarinos said it. All hands to the steering oars now. I want every pair of eyes in the vicinity of the carcer and on the alert. The moment one of their faces shows I want a boot on their neck and half a dozen of you holding him down.'

* * * * *

'Heads up,' hissed Aurelius, as he jogged into the tavern where, despite his original convictions to remain hidden, Fronto now sat with several of the others. At least he had kept himself in the shadowy interior rather than sitting at the open frontage, where Aurelius and Agesander watched the prison across the road.

'What's happening.'

'Someone important's coming,' the former legionary announced, breathless. 'Whoever it is is surrounded by tough looking men, toga-clad sycophants and *lictors* with their stick-bundles. And he's headed this way from the Argiletum.'

Fronto felt the hairs on the back of his neck prickle. Something was about to happen, he could feel it crackling like lightning in the very air. 'How many lictors?'

'Lots.'

'More than six?'

'Lots,' repeated Aurelius meaningfully.

'That's a consul, then. Anyone fancy wagering it's Sulpicius Rufus?'

The table remained silent. 'No, me neither. Shall we go see what Marcellus is here for then?'

There would be no issue with being seen out in the open now for, as they stood and moved towards the entrance of the tavern, Fronto could see the citizens and the poor of Rome gathering like moths to a lamp, filling the sides of the street in response to the arrival of one of Rome's two most powerful officials. The consuls, two elected each year, held unparalleled power in the republic and, consequently, drew a crowd whenever they moved in the city.

Pushing his way in among the eager watchers, Fronto caught sight of the approaching group. Aurelius had been quite right. Twelve lictors – the official guards of the city's magistrates – moved ahead in six pairs, bearing their bundles of sticks tied with linen. Behind them he could just see a tall man with reddish blond hair and a face like a constipated frog. Based on appearance alone he took an instant dislike to the man.

The sky was dull with light grey overcast cloud that locked in the muggy warmth of a Roman summer, and Fronto was thoroughly thankful that he'd foregone the expected toga as too restrictive if it came to a fight. He could see the beads of sweat on the consul's wide, waxy forehead. Marcellus was suffering in the heat.

'Procles and Agesander, stay here and keep an eye on things. Everyone else get down the road into the forum. Spread out there.'

'The forum?' muttered Balbus. 'Why?'

'Because if Marcellus is here, it's for something big and public, almost certainly involving the captive decurion, and he'll do it in the forum. If the Sons of Taranis are here, they might go for the carcer, but they'll certainly want to know what the consul is doing, especially since Comum is basically Gaulish and half the crowd are muttering about captive Gauls. Keep your eyes open everyone. Find me one of these bastards and I'll give you his head-weight in denarii.'

Without waiting, Fronto shoved his way through the press, drawing argument, barks of annoyance and the odd sharp elbow. A moment later he was passing the Basilica Opimia and the Temple of Concord on the wide road that led down from the top of the Capitoline hill to the forum below. Already the crowd was gathering in force as rumour spread and Fronto repeatedly heard the consul's name whispered, along with the words *decurion, Comum, Gaul* and *Caesar*, none of which came as any surprise. Looking around hurriedly, he settled on the temple of Saturn as the best place of observation. Scurrying up the steps to the colonnaded front, he leaned against one of the tall columns and took in the scene.

The crowd was continuing to gather, filling the wide public space, but the people of Rome knew their spectacles well, and the path down the road was left clear, as was a large area by the rostrum where public speeches were made. His eyes roved around. He could make out the squat entrance to the carcer up the slope and though he couldn't quite make out Procles and Agesander, he could see that Marcellus had entered the prison complex, his entourage gathered outside.

Aurelius was close to the rostrum at the heart of things. Fronto picked out Pamphilus on the lower steps of the temple of Concord and therefore the unimaginative Clearchus who had remained close to his brother as always. Both were wearing hoodless cloaks despite the muggy heat and once more, Fronto wondered about what went on inside their heads other than a light breeze and occasional echoing birdsong.

Balbus was in the doorway of one of the new shops fronting the Basilica Fulvia. Biorix was just visible not far away. Dyrakhes and Cavarinos he couldn't quite see. Good, though. The lads had spread out well. Now all they needed was for this sudden activity to bring out the Sons of Taranis and all would be excellent. He was still watching the crowd as a commotion arose up the steps and drew his attention back to the carcer. Marcellus had emerged and his lictors were crowded around him as three men herded a man to the road and shoved him none-too-gently forward. The man, clearly from his appearance the Comum decurion who had been incarcerated for days, staggered forward and managed to keep his footing only through blind luck. Stained and covered in his own filth, the poor man who had been raised to citizenship by Caesar and had come to Rome an important official only to be imprisoned, was herded to the open space before the rostrum.

Fronto watched the parade arrive and his eyes widened in shock as he spotted the man following the prisoner. The two who were jostling him to the centre of the wide circle were obviously men from the carcer. The third was Lucius Curtius Crispinus, Marcellus' centurion, who commanded at the prison. And in his hand was a *scourge*!

'No,' Fronto whispered under his breath. 'Surely not?'

The same reaction struck throughout the crowd and there was an audible hiss of mass-indrawn breath. Beyond the scene unfolding, Marcellus climbed the steps, his lictors spreading out, keeping the circle at the centre of the forum free of observers, guarding the rostrum and its occupant. The man from Comum had turned and seen what the guard commander carried and now he cried out – his accent as Gallic as it was Roman – and struggled against the two guards. There were no punishment posts here such as a legion might erect and despite the man's feeble protests and struggles, the two guards slipped leather leashes over his hands, yanking them so tight they bit into his flesh and drew blood. As he cried again and ran out of fight, turning into a blubbering mess, the two guards walked apart, wrapping the other end of the leashes around their own forearms and pulling them so tight that the decurion was jerked straight, his arms pulled taut, so much so in fact that his shoulders almost separated. While the guards held him in position and their commander unfurled the scourge, Marcellus cleared his voice.

Fronto missed the opening of his address. In his head he was revisiting every scourging he had watched in his time with the army, and there had been a few. One or two to the death, many others in multiples of three or five. Few went above twelve, for that was almost certainly a death sentence anyway. And Crispinus was a centurion with no small amount of muscle and will. He would not stint on punishment, Fronto knew, and what he held was a proper military scourge with bone wheels on it. He swallowed. Not only did he feel for the poor bastard down there who had done absolutely nothing to deserve this but to have been connected to the wrong man, but what he was witnessing here went way beyond law and punishment.

This was a statement.

This was, in fact, a declaration of war.

The public might not see it yet, but this was a direct challenge to Caesar by one of the duly elected consuls of Rome, a man with ties to Pompey. Even if they could not bring a prosecution against the general while he remained Proconsul of Gaul or when he took up his consulship, his enemies were today making their statement clear. Fronto could picture Caesar's face when he heard about this. In a mad, fleeting moment, he pictured Caesar, incensed beyond all reason, finishing mopping up the last of the rebel spirit in Gaul and then sweeping down against Rome with twelve legions. It was a mind-blowing thought. And not impossible. Sulla had done just that, after all.

What were these mad men doing? What was *Marcellus* doing? Trying to start a war with Caesar?

'...and so with the support of the Senate of Rome, I sentence this Gaul to six lashes with the scourge for the crime of impersonating a citizen of the republic. He will then be returned to the carcer until he is well enough to travel, following which he will be returned to Comum there to show his scars to a proconsul who thinks he can ride roughshod over the senate.'

'Shit,' Fronto said to himself, drawing some murmurs of agreement from the few crowd members around him, though his comment was not directed at the scene in the forum, where Crispinus was shaking out the scourge. In fact, he had been cursing himself for getting caught up in the action and forgetting to keep his eyes on what he was actually here for. He glanced around the forum again, failing to spot anyone but Aurelius by the rostrum and the brothers on the steps of Concord's temple. His gaze rose once more to the slope, where the crowd had melted away, following the action down to the forum. He could see two figures that had to be Procles and Agesander from their size and shape, standing by the side of the road up there. At least nothing had happened there so far. That was a relief. It was only now striking him that the carcer was currently manned by half its staff right now, while most of Fronto's men were in the forum. Damn it. He threw a prayer up to Fortuna that the carcer stay secure for now and returned his attention to the crowd.

He almost missed it. In fact, he did the first time.

His gaze had passed across the dark figure and fell upon Aurelius and it had been that hackle-raising sixth sense that had made him double-take and look back across the curia behind the scene. The scourge blows were being delivered now, and the Comum man was screaming and shrieking fit to shake the gods. The crowd were in that curious mix of disgust and fascination, Pompey's partisans cheering it on, Caesar's supporters – notably fewer – yelling their disapproval. But past that scene and past the rostrum with its unpleasant consul and his lictors, a figure moved. Almost hidden by the shadows of the arcade that was all that remained of the *senaculum*, the figure was well hidden.

Fronto held his breath at the sight of the hooded cloak and waited. Sure enough, the figure turned and he caught a momentary glimpse of light shining on a glazed surface within. *The bastards were here. In broad daylight and in their cloaks!*

His desperate gaze picked out Aurelius nearby and he realised that the former legionary was intent on the scourging and had not noticed the figure so close to him. Fronto started to move. It would be a struggle to get through the crowd.

As if that same sixth sense that had so alerted Fronto was at work for the enemy too, the cloaked figure turned for a moment and looked straight at him. Then the Gaul was moving, running past the entire complex towards the Subura where he could easily lose pursuit in the maze of streets and alleys. Fronto cursed. He would never get there in time to stop the bastard.

Damn, damn, damn, damn. He pushed against the crowd but someone pushed him back and he thumped painfully against the column.

'Aurelius!' he bellowed. Such was the volume desperation lent his voice that many of the crowd turned towards him, despite the graphic scene playing out before them as the fifth of six blows was delivered to the shuddering, weeping man standing at the centre of a spray and pool of his own blood and flesh, a puddle of vomit by his foot.

'For the love of Venus look at me, Aurelius,' he yelled again. After a few tense heartbeats in which he watched the cloaked figure retreating from the scene, finally Aurelius caught sight of him and waved an acknowledgement.

'Get him!' Aware that his words would not carry that far, Fronto climbed onto the decorative lip of the column base. It wasn't much, but it pushed him another half-foot above the crowd. Clinging to the column with one hand he gestured desperately with the other, pointing at the near-invisible figure, motioning for Aurelius to turn round. As the legionary dithered, apparently unsure what the gestures meant, Fronto felt his frustration rising.

His eyes darted to the side and he spotted Pamphilus and Clearchus moving. Even the dimwits had understood.

Finally, Aurelius turned, scratching his head. For a moment, Fronto thought he'd lost the man, for the cloaked figure had dipped

367

out of sight. Then, in a stroke of luck, the clouds parted for just a heartbeat and a rare gleam of sunlight picked out the cloaked shape moving to the next building. Aurelius was running immediately.

'Thank you, Fortuna.'

Cavarinos, Dyrakhes, Balbus and Biorix were moving now, having spotted him, everyone converging on the edge of the forum where the road ran up past the carcer and other ways led into the Subura. Aurelius was out of sight in moments and Fronto could do little but offer up another prayer to Fortuna and trust to Aurelius' abilities. But if *one* had been here, perhaps there were others…

Casting his gaze around the forum even as the execution ended and Marcellus harangued the crowd with anti-Caesarian politics, Fronto could spot no others. Cavarinos and Balbus were now at the place from where Aurelius had been watching. Fronto fought through the crowd and as he converged on the group, he spotted Pamphilus and Clearchus emerging from the press on the left. His eyes widened in disbelief.

Pamphilus' hand emerged from his voluminous cloak, and gripped tight in the fist was a gladius, unsheathed.

'No!'

The fool. What was he doing?

As he turned to try and stop the idiot, a murmur of anger rippled through the throng. Fronto struggled, trying to push between two of the crowd to get to them, but a man in a dark blue tunic with the muscles of a blacksmith and a lantern jaw beat him to it. The man yelled something at Pamphilus and the Massilian idiot reacted instinctively, lancing out with the sword. He managed to cut a deep line along the big Roman's arm and the man roared and threw himself at the Massilian.

Pamphilus dodged the big man and started to run the other way. Fronto burst from the crowd, but was clearly too late to prevent chaos erupting. His spirits sinking even further, he watched Clearchus also draw a sword from his cloak and run to the defence of his brother. The last he saw of either of them was both brothers disappearing with a shout and a flurry of tunics amid the press of angry citizens who piled onto them, kicking and punching. Fronto turned to see Balbus shaking his head in disbelief and jogged over towards them.

'Idiots,' the old man said, rather unnecessarily. Fronto nodded. 'In a way I hope the poor bastards get kicked to death down there. If they make it through, that scourge will come out again for the backs of two Massilians.'

'And they work for you,' added Cavarinos.

'Gods, yes. I can't wait for the backlash from this to land at my front door. Our one consolation from all this is that Aurelius left the forum on the trail of one of the Sons. With luck we'll have a lead on their location shortly, so long as Aurelius is careful and doesn't get himself killed. Come on. Let's go speak to the others up at the carcer.'

'What about them?' Cavarinos gestured to the brawl with a thumb.

'Nothing we can do for them. If it was an ordinary fight I'd weigh in, but they've broken both the city's sacred laws and their vows to me. They've brought this on themselves and they're beyond help now.'

As they moved up the hill to meet up once more with Procles and Agesander, Fronto found himself praying as hard as he ever had that Aurelius be careful.

* * * * *

Fronto had been pacing back and forth across the tablinum, nervous and impatient, almost since they had returned to the house. He'd half expected some heavy handed mob of angry citizens to turn up at his door baying for blood from the man whose hirelings had broken the most sacred laws of Rome. Or a deputation from the consul inviting him to a lengthy and dangerous court appearance for the same. But aside from the things he worried over, the thing he'd really *waited* for was his missing man, and so when he heard the front door opened and closed by Glyptus with muttered conversation and then the striking of hobnails on the marble floor, he almost collapsed with relief.

Aurelius appeared in the doorway of the office where the other five men waited – Dyrakhes and Biorix were on watch at the tavern – and there was a collective catching of breath. What had happened with the brothers in the forum suddenly paled into unimportance. Aurelius was limping, gripping the doorframe to remain upright. His left leg was soaked through with dark, sticky crimson and a rent in his tunic at the upper thigh told why. From the amount of blood, he was clearly lucky to be using the leg at all and not lying in a ditch somewhere. His face, correspondingly, was so pale as to be almost translucent. Blood dripped in a slow but regular patter from his right hand which hung loose at his side, and there was an area of his scalp that was matted and torn, the flesh cut and blood snagging his hair together.

As Fronto's eyes flitted hither and thither over his friend, assessing the damage, they widened.

Aurelius' right hand dripped blood, but his left was intact and clutched in the whitened, tightened fist were two cult masks, one with a piece missing from the mouth slit down, both spattered with blood.

'Hope you don't mind,' Aurelius murmured with a smile, 'but I started the party without you.'

Balbus was there as Aurelius collapsed, grabbing his arm to stop him falling and lifting him, supporting him by the shoulders. Cavarinos was there a moment later at the other shoulder and the two men gently helped the former legionary across to the nearest couch and lowered him to it.

Fronto looked up to see the concerned face of Glyptus in the doorway.

'You know of any local medicus?' he asked the caretaker.

'There's a Greek down near the Porta Lavernalis who people say is good but extortionate, and there's a Jew near the circus who sorted my gammy leg out and is a bit easier on the purse.'

Fronto didn't even need to think or look at Aurelius. 'Go get the Greek. If he's busy, tell him I'll pay double, but get him here as soon as you can.'

Balbus was looking Aurelius over. 'I wish my medicus was here,' his face darkened at the memory of the servant's body lying with the pile in the atrium of his villa. 'I owe these scum for that among many other things.' He gently probed and moved Aurelius' right arm, causing gasps and whimpers. 'Grip my finger.' Aurelius did so, a weak grin spreading across his face. 'If you tell me to pull it, I might have to punch you, sir.'

'What with?'

Aurelius' fingers wrapped feebly around the old man's finger.

'Nothing permanent, by the looks of it, and the wounds have all begun to clot. You'll be alright until the medicus gets here. Unless there's something I'm not seeing, you should be fine in time.'

The former legionary snorted and threw the two masks across the floor, where the broken one hit the leg of the table that held the model and shattered. 'I'll be fine. Them, less so.'

Fronto leaned close to him. 'What happened?'

'Let him rest, Marcus,' murmured Balbus, but Aurelius shook his head.

'I'm alright. The man in the cloak spotted me following him at the forum. I saw him slip into the metalworker's market in the Subura. I guess he thought all the noise and clutter would save him. Problem is, my dad used to sell pots and pans there and I know the place well.' He paused, wincing, as the effort of talking took its toll, and finally breathed slowly three times and despite Balbus' protestations continued. 'There are three other entrances to the place, but one comes out near where he went in and one is usually closed because the horse traders are across the road and the smell is appalling. So I just went round the outside to the Vicus Longus entrance and waited there until he emerged, thinking he'd lost me.'

'Good man,' Fronto nodded. 'So what happened?'

'There's a house in the shadow of the temple of Salus on the Quirinal where they're staying. The one I followed went in and I slipped into a doorway opposite. I saw another one appear at a window. It was a woman, without a mask on, and she closed the shutters as soon as they went in. I asked one of the locals about the house, wondering who rented it to the Gauls, but apparently the owner died a month back with a missing will and his twin sons are in litigation over the house's ownership, so it's been empty for weeks. Perfect hiding place for the Gauls.'

Fronto nodded. 'No one up in that area is going to ask too many questions either. Proper gang territory round there.'

'Precisely,' Aurelius nodded. 'Anyway, I was just moving around the other side of the house, trying to listen in at a window when the shutters opened and this young lad with blond hair saw me and yelled. Next thing I know I'm belting through streets and alleys on the Quirinal with three of the bastards chasing me. I lost one of them soon enough, and the other two caught me in the knife-workers' street. Good luck for me, 'cause as soon as I was armed, I stopped running. I had to empty my purse to a bunch of street kids to dispose of the bodies for me, so I might need a bonus this month, boss. That head's weight in denarii you offered, maybe?'

371

Fronto snorted. 'You took two of them down on your own? Impressive.'

Aurelius shrugged modestly then groaned with pain at the movement. 'The tall one I took by surprise as he rounded the corner. I left him with a fork sticking out of his eye, so he didn't get much chance to do anything, let alone unshoulder his bow. Imagine that! The pisspot had a bow and a sheaf of arrows within the pomerium, the brazen tossbag. Anyway, the other one was a bit tougher – the blond lad. He gave me a real run for my money. Took some putting down, I can tell you.'

He frowned and then smiled as he recalled something and fished in the pouch at his belt. With an exhale of breath, he slumped and held out a hand. Cavarinos took the scraps of wool from it.

'From their cloaks,' Aurelius muttered.

'A tree beneath a haloed sun,' Cavarinos noted, examining the designs marked into the wool. 'That's probably Abellio. And the other sun alone will be Belenos.' He frowned as though hunting something among his memories. Slowly something surfaced as he tapped his lip. 'Trying to remember who you've removed so far.'

Fronto crossed the room to his still mostly-packed kit bag and dug around in it until he removed a fabric pouch, which he tossed to the Arvernian. Cavarinos fished out the collected and saved scraps of material, laying them out on the couch. His brow furrowed as he worked, changing the order they were in again and again until he was satisfied. 'Toutatis, Belenos, Maponos, Dis, Sucellos, Rudianos and Abellio. I thought it looked familiar. There was a nemeton at Gergovia where the first pact was made between my king and the druids. I remember it well. It was one of the most sacred sites outside Carnute lands, until after the war. The Romans in charge of resettlement pulled it down and used the stones in rebuilds. There were twelve menhir dedicated to the gods who had been heard to speak there. I'm trying to remember which five are missing.'

Balbus shook his head. 'It's very colourful and religiously significant I suppose, but does it have a bearing on the matter?'

'I think so. Those we've killed correspond with their god. Toutatis, Rudianos and Dis were the ones you fought in the villa. There was one who looked thin and death-like, who would be Dis. One was a big, bull-necked man, who would be Rudianos the war god and taker of heads. Not sure about Toutatis. I wasn't there for the fight, but I'd be willing to wager there *is* a connection. Abellio is a hunter and forest god, and Aurelius said the man had a bow. Belenos is the shining one. Blond. Young. You see what I mean? Perhaps knowing who the others are will give us an advantage?'

Fronto nodded. 'Go on, then.'

'Well we can assume that Molacos is Taranis, *the Thunderer*, who you'd call Jupiter I guess.' He paused, pinching the bridge of his nose with his eyes shut and mouth working as he turned slowly in a circle, pointing at stones he could only see in his mind's eye. 'Belisama. Bright huntress, sister of Belenos.'

'She'll be spitting teeth now then, after Aurelius butchered her brother. Might be easy to bait into doing something stupid.'

'That's a fair assumption,' Procles murmured. 'When my brother died, I tore half a ship apart in revenge.'

'Cernunnos,' the Arvernian went on. 'The forest lord. Beloved of the druids.'

'Could he *be* a druid?'

'Very possibly. They are not averse to taking action. They don't usually get involved in battles, but they have no qualms about killing, and plenty of them are still around, bitter at having raised a rebellion that failed. Next would be... Mogont.' He nodded. 'I remember *him*. I saw him before I came to Massilia. Big man. Huge. Like an ox in a man suit.'

'Wonderful. At least he should be easy to spot.'

'And the last one is... Catubodua. The battle crow. She'll be vile and tough to handle.'

Fronto nodded as his friend straightened and opened his eyes. 'Molacos, a druid, a vengeful sister, a giant and a vile woman. Lovely. The Cadurci breed them odd, don't they?'

'They won't all be Cadurci,' Cavarinos replied. 'There'll be Arverni in there, no doubt, and maybe Carnutes. All those mad and disaffected left over from Alesia have a stake in this.'

'I remember you telling me you hated druids and didn't believe in the gods and all that,' Fronto mused. 'You were quite scathing about the whole thing, if I recall. How come you know so much about them?'

Cavarinos shrugged. 'My brother was an obsessive on the subject, as well as a moron. I grew up around it. I'll bet you know all about how your engineers build aqueducts even though you've never done it.'

373

Fronto shook his head. '*No one* knows the mind of an engineer. Peculiar bunch.' He straightened. 'Alright, lads. Grab a staff and a knife and let's go clear the rats out of this nest.' Aurelius made to rise and Fronto placed a hand on his shoulder, gently pushing him back down. 'Not you. You wait for Glyptus and the medic.'

* * * * *

Fronto kicked the sleeping mat irritably, watching it skitter across the floor and the cockroaches scatter from beneath it.

'Should have guessed they'd have run for it as soon as they were located.' He reached down to the wooden bowl filled with some miscellaneous stewed meat. 'Still warm, so they'd only just gone when we got here. And now we're back to square one.'

'Not quite,' Procles muttered. 'Now there are seven of us and only five of them. The odds have changed.'

'Not for the better, though,' added Balbus, who had been excavating a pile of refuse in the corner and now rose with something in his hand, holding it out for Fronto, who took it. Dirty and scratched as it was, the inscribed bark chitty was clear enough.

'It's from the graecostadium,' he sighed, rubbing his hair and sucking his teeth irritably.

'The what?' Procles asked.

'The slave market behind the forum. Someone in this house bought fourteen Gauls yesterday for a bargain price. Paid in Massiliot drachma, too.'

'So now instead of ten against seven, we're seven against nineteen? Shit.'

'The only bonus is that the slaves will have come in recently from Massilia, probably in the same bloody fleet we joined. They were probably being unloaded as we disembarked. You remember those slaves – they weren't in top condition. They'd walked from Belgae lands to Massilia, then were loaded into ships for a shaky voyage. They'll be wasted and weak for a long while yet.'

'They'll have fire in their hearts, though,' Cavarinos noted.

'True. Well here's the situation as I see it. We don't know where they are again. We're outnumbered and they know we're onto them, so there's no chance of us making an attack on them or springing any kind of surprise anymore.'

'So,' Agasander asked, frowning, 'if they aren't here now, where are they?'

'No idea. Lurking in an alley somewhere?'

'Nineteen Gauls, some cloaked and masked, some clearly slaves with brands, all armed and one with a ruined face. There's no alley in Rome dark enough to hide that lot at this time of day,' Balbus said.

'Might they have a second safe house?'

'If they did, why keep this one?' Fronto felt a cold stone settle in his belly. 'They're *not* hiding, are they?'

Cavarinos caught his look and chewed his lip. 'No. They're making they're move. We're busy dithering here and they're on their way to free the king. *We've* triggered it, too. Aurelius killed two of them, and they know their time's up. They had to go now or they'd miss their chance altogether.'

'They're probably already at the carcer,' Fronto breathed. 'Shit.'

A heartbeat later, the seven men were out of the house and running. 'They can't be far ahead of us,' Procles huffed as he ran. 'Quarter of an hour? Half at most.'

'That's long enough,' Fronto said, breathing heavily and, as they turned into the Vicus Longus a few streets later, he turned to Cavarinos, running alongside him. 'Are you comfortable with this?'

The Arvernian turned a surprised look on him. 'Comfortable? Of course not.'

'Want to go home and stay out of it? Last chance.'

Cavarinos simply shook his head and ran a little faster.

Chapter Nineteen

MOLACOS of the Cadurci stepped out of the side alley, his breath fogging his eyes, funnelled by the sweaty inside of the ceramic mask and kept locked in by the thick woollen hood of the cloak.

'What in Hades are *you* supposed to be?' the salesman snorted. 'Something for the festival?'

The tip of Molacos' long, Gallic sword appeared between the folds of his cloak.

'Listen,' the man said, nerves now inflecting his voice, 'tell Rubio that I know I'm late with the money, but I'll have it by the kalends. Don't do anything...'

His words trailed off into a soft exhalation as the blade slammed home into his throat just above the notch where his collar bones met. Molacos instinctively stepped aside, maintaining his grip as the jet of crimson splashed through where he'd been standing. Blood on the cloak would attract far too much attention. Quickly he wrenched the blade out, unable to twist it from this angle, and so fighting the suction of the ravaged flesh. As the man fell away, shaking and gurgling, blood bubbling and spurting, surrounding him with a red lake, Molacos stepped back, wiped his blade on a rag and tossed the scrap onto the shaking body.

'Who buys shit like this,' big Mogont murmured, stepping out of the shadows and picking up a lamp in the shape of a phallus from the laden cart.

'The Romans think they're lucky,' Molacos growled from within his mask.

'*He* doesn't think so,' murmured Mogont, looking down at the body. The big man seemed to be far more relaxed and cheerful than Molacos, but then he always did when he didn't have to wear the mask and cloak. In fact, he looked the most comfortable of all of them, since he had proved far too big to disguise. None of the endless clothes they had stolen from washing lines fitted the giant, and so Molacos had grudgingly let him stay in his Cadurci garb, grasping a baton and playing the part of a bodyguard. No one would glance twice at him in that respect, despite his size.

The others looked less comfortable as they emerged into the small deserted space where three alleys met. Cernunnos was still smarting from shaving off his beard and moustaches and hacking his hair short. In his stolen tunic and belt with the light leather sandals it both impressed and disgusted Molacos how much his druid friend looked just like one of the hated Romans now. No one, even in the forum, would bat an eyelid at him. Better still the learned man, despite his convictions, spoke Latin like a native. He might just as well be a Roman now. The curl of his lip and hardness of his eyes alone gave away how much he truly hated every moment of this.

Belisama had refused to dye her hair and still stood out among the crowd with her almost white-blonde hair down to her waist. However, she had taken little persuading to rub dirt and grease into it and, with the clearly peasant garb they had stolen, she looked like a street worker or a slave, unless one looked directly into her eye, where the fires of fury and vengeance burned, consuming her soul.

But Catubodua was the least comfortable of all.

Dressed respectably, like a Roman merchant's wife, she was the picture of everyday plebeian womanhood. Apart from the sword scar that ran from her left eye across beneath her nose and down to the opposite side of her chin. And the raven feather in her hair, which she had flatly refused to remove. And, Taranis protect them, the arm-ring of a warrior that was only poorly hid by the *palla* draped over her shoulders. The arm-ring had belonged to her husband, Sedullos, king of the Lemovices, slain on the fields before Alesia. It had been passed to her as the only reminder of her husband who lay mouldering in a Roman-dug grave, though she had earned the warrior's prize many times over since then. Still, the disguises did not have to be perfect. They just had to get them to the carcer.

Mogont returned to the alley and collected their weapons, each one an offence against Rome's laws. One by one, he slid them under the top of the cart full of lamps, bowls and trinkets. Mogont's blade was too long by a hand, but Molacos simply draped the cloth that covered the stock on the lower shelf over the end, hiding it from view.

'We should have held the swords tight in our hands and marched on the carcer,' the widow snarled, fretting at her Roman clothes.

'We would have got nowhere near the place.'

'Rome has no guards or army here,' Belisama put in. 'There is no one to stop us doing so.'

'You say that,' Molacos replied with strained patience, 'because you did not see what happened in the forum earlier. Two of the legate's men armed with swords were mobbed by ordinary people. They take this law seriously. Nothing must be left to chance.'

'And yet you cost us precious time in finding such a disguise. What if the soldier and his men manage to warn the carcer of our plans?'

'What of it? Are you afeared of Fronto and his pets?' He gestured to the alley behind him, where more than a dozen slaves who had once been free men of the Carnutes and Senones waited in Roman peasant clothes, sticks and knives in their belts. They would merge into the crowd, splitting up and following the small party with the cart. Individually they were sick, weak and broken. But their spirit was strong, and their desire for vengeance on Rome even stronger. They might be of no use in taking the carcer and freeing the king, but they could at least hold off any pursuit and buy the Sons time to get Vercingetorix away from this place, down to the river and freedom.

Cernunnos took his place beside the cart, his spiteful 'wife' beside him and their dirt-stained 'daughter' behind. The Gaulish bodyguard took position nearby and Molacos, cloaked still, bent over the cart and lifted its rear legs, beginning to push.

This was it: a moment they had dreamed of for half a year now. It would have been nicer to be more prepared and under less pressure, of course. Molacos had planned to strike after the Comum man had been taken from the carcer in a few days – when the soldiers there would let their guard down slightly with the reduced importance of the inmates – but the arrival of Fronto on the scene and the deaths of poor Belenos and Abellio had forced his hand.

Nothing would stop them.

For back to the north and west, far from this nest of vipers, his chieftain Lucterius and the army of the tribes waited on the border of Rome to sweep south and crush Narbo.

Chapter Twenty

DYRAKHES and Biorix lounged at a table in the open front of the Huntsman's Head, their conversation ribald and varied, their drinks well-watered, their attention constantly on the carcer and its surroundings. Fronto ran up from the Argiletum, panting and sweating, the others behind him, and the two men watching from the tavern rose in surprise.

'Sir?'

'No sign of them?' Fronto panted.

'Them? The Gauls? No.'

The former legate turned his eyes to the sky and blew a kiss. 'Thank you, Great Lady. I won't forget this.' He looked back at the pair in the tavern. 'Go to the shed at the back and arm yourselves, and bring a few extra staves and knives out with you too.'

Biorix's frown was a question in itself and Fronto nodded. 'They're coming. Now.'

'You're sure, sir?'

'As we can be. Time to try and secure this place.'

As Biorix and Dyrakhes disappeared behind the tavern to retrieve the better makeshift weapons, Fronto peered across at the heavy door of the carcer. Behind him Cavarinos, Balbus, Agesander and Procles stood tense and ready.

'How do we do this, then, Marcus?' Balbus asked. 'You're the strategist.'

'Perhaps if we secure all the approaches...?'

'Do it fast, then,' Biorix hissed, reappearing around the corner of the tavern and pointing down the street. This time in the early evening there were not so many people around as there had been at the height of the day, and towards the Porta Fontinalis a strange tableau was approaching. A Roman merchant and his family were moving along the street, drawing interested looks but little more. Fronto's eyes were, however, first drawn to the hulking Gaulish giant accompanying them, then to the cloaked figure pushing their cart. His keen gaze quickly picked out a variety of what could only be gaunt and dirty Gallic slaves weaving their way through the crowd. Suddenly he was unsure about this. The numbers were extremely uneven.

'We don't want a war in the street,' Balbus muttered.

379

'And it would go badly for us,' Cavarinos added. 'We are outnumbered almost three men to one.'

Fronto nodded absently. They couldn't hold the street against that lot, and even if they did, civilian casualties would be unacceptable. They were out of time and out of options. Taking a deep breath and squaring his shoulders, he ran across to the carcer door and hammered on it. The other six crowded behind him and as he hammered again, and then a third time, Fronto's eyes kept being drawn to the approaching cart and its panoply of oddly-garbed Gauls. For a heartbeat he wondered at their dress, then the reason dawned on him and he peered at the cart, knowing what it contained even if he couldn't see the iron itself. The 'merchant' was bellowing his offers and wares, and it would sound perfectly normal to anyone who hadn't spent the last eight years in Gaul and couldn't spot a Gallic accent even when faint.

Finally, the door of the carcer creaked and opened inwards, emitting a waft of stale, fetid air. The face that appeared in the narrow gap was broken-nosed, lined with three distinct scars and bore the short hair that was the norm for a legionary.

'Yes?'

'No time to explain,' Fronto barked. 'You need to let us in.'

'Piss off.'

The door started to close and Fronto stepped forward, jamming his foot in it as he spoke. 'Listen, you... ow!' The muscular legionary had pushed the door with every nuance of strength in his large arms and though Fronto's foot had definitely stopped it closing, there was a crunch and a flash of blinding pain shot up his leg as foot bones broke. The legionary frowned in surprise as the door failed to close and tried again with the same force. This time, Fronto's foot was further in and he felt the heavy timber close on his ankle, scraping the flesh from it and almost breaking the vital joint.

'Listen,' he hissed through teeth gritted against the pain, 'there are some well-armed and very determined men coming here to free one of your prisoners and they outnumber you three to one. Let us in.'

'Only my centurion...'

Fronto shoved hard and the door slammed inwards, smashing into the surprised legionary's face and sending him reeling back. In a heartbeat, Fronto threw the door open and ushered the others in, taking a swift look back out along the street. Perhaps fifty paces away a bunch of street urchins had arrested the cart's progress, ribbing the *merchant* and making lewd suggestions, comparing the phallic lamps to their owner.

Thank you lady Fortuna, he smiled again, and turned to see a tense stand-off in the guard room. The last time he had been in this chamber he had been in the company of Pompey and it had been *his* men staffing the place. Pompey had ruled the carcer a 'non-public' place, and had allowed his men blades. It seemed Marcellus was sticking rigidly to his law-abiding persona beyond reason. Even the carcer's guards now carried only wooden batons. All six of the place's staff were here in this room, their bowls of food and game of dice forgotten in the face of this intrusion. With the discipline of legionaries – a level of which Fronto heartily approved – the half dozen men had armed themselves and stood even before all the arrivals were inside. Three of them had moved to block access to the heavy armoured door that led through to the cells.

As Fronto's men gathered in a small knot and moved into the place, Fronto dropped back the latch and peered at the keyhole. No key. Stepping away from the door, he approached the three most threatening men, the ones guarding the way to the cells. In the absence of the centurion, he didn't know who might be in charge, and the leader was far from evident.

'Listen, you lot. There are near a score of Gauls coming to free your prisoner and they're all armed with swords...'

Before he could get another word out, one of the guards had lunged at him, almost knocking the short staff from his hands. Fronto jabbed back in automatic response and as if that exchange were a trigger the room erupted into chaos, the guards and Fronto's companions alike jabbing and blocking with their batons and staves.

In the chaos, he heard a voice shout 'Go tell Crispinus!'

He turned, his broken foot agonising, but the man who was intent on stopping him smacked him painfully in the knee with his club. Fronto wheeled and shoved the man, sending him lurching back. Again, he turned to the entrance to see the man with the broken nose who he'd hurt on entry unlatching the door.

'No!'

But his attention was drawn again to the man facing him who'd recovered and was swiping again with the short length of ash.

'For the love of Bacchus, will you lot *stop this*?'

381

Again he shoved his attacker out of the way and glanced over his shoulder. The door stood open, the doorman gone, running to find the centurion. Even as he turned to run and close the door again, a knife thudded into the oak frame, thrown from somewhere in the street.

'Shit!' yelled the guard who'd sent his friend running – the man in charge now, Fronto presumed. The man leapt over to the door and peered out. Pressed in the struggle, Fronto couldn't get a reasonable view outside, but he saw the guard's eyes widen and could picture the scene in the street. 'Shut the bloody door!' he yelled.

Nodding in shock, the guard did so, dropping the latch.

'Carcer!' the senior guard yelled above the din, 'Ad Signum!'

The call cut through the chaos and the effect was instant. Whatever trouble the guards were causing for them, Fronto found himself impressed with the way, even after years of retirement, the call to standard pulled the men immediately from what they were doing. A moment later all five were lined up to one side. Fronto's men, panting, huddled together again. Miraculously everyone was upright and there appeared to be no broken bones or major wounds – just a few bruises and contusions.

'Who are you?' the speaker asked, addressing Fronto.

'Marcus Falerius Fronto, legate of Caesar's Tenth Equestris, retired.'

The five men saluted automatically and Fronto had to brush aside the etiquette.

'Who are *they*, then, sir?' the man asked.

'A bunch of Gaulish warriors and slaves. The five with the cart are all very dangerous. They're coming to try and free Vercingetorix, and they won't stop 'til they're all dead. Find the keys. Lock that door.'

The legionary's face folded into an expression of contrite embarrassment. 'Afraid Paulinus had the door keys, sir.'

'Let me guess: Paulinus is the one who just left to warn your centurion?'

A nod.

'Turds! The latch won't hold them for long. Still, your commander might bring help. Where is he?'

'He'll be at barracks, sir, up on the Viminal, top end, near the walls.'

Fronto made a quick mental calculation, assuming the barracks to be that house he'd found the records of which had formerly belonged to Pompey. A little over a mile from here to there, he reckoned, and all uphill. Paulinus was clearly fit – all these former soldiers were still in good shape – but still that would be more than a quarter of an hour. Plus the same back, or slightly less allowing for the downhill. Plus any time taken by Crispinus to gather and arm men in between.

'No help coming for three quarters of an hour or more, then, so it's down to us. There are twelve of us, and nineteen of them altogether. We can manage that, I figure. Most of them are half-starved slaves.'

The door suddenly erupted in a din of thuds, thumps and bangs as the Gauls outside began to hammer at it. The latch immediately groaned and strained, and Cavarinos gestured to Procles. The two men grabbed the heavy table with the meal accoutrements on it and tipped it sideways, jamming it up against the exterior door.

'Hang on, sir,' the senior guard said, and ran over to the corner where two cupboards stood. Shoving one aside roughly, he scrabbled around in the grime behind and withdrew something, turning in a cloud of dust and holding something out. Fronto stared at the two gladii in the man's hands. Both were very standard military issue and clearly unused for some time, from the thick coat of muck.

'Left over by the previous occupants, sir,' the man said. 'We meant to get rid of them, but you know how it is.'

Fronto grinned and grabbed one of the blades, tearing it from its scabbard. It was pitted with rust from lack of care, but well-edged and still eminently usable. He hefted it comfortably as the guard pulled the other and did the same.

'When they get in, don't mistake my men in the press for theirs, will you.'

The guards nodded, peering intently at Fronto's companions and committing their faces, shapes and clothes to memory.

A thought struck Fronto. 'How many prisoners do you have?'

The guard frowned. 'Just the two, sir.'

'Vercingetorix and the Comum decurion?'

'Yessir.'

'Do you still have keys for the cells?'

'Yes.'

'Then get in there, let the decurion out and give him a club.'

383

'I can't do that, sir.'

'You damn well can and you damn well will. We need all the help we can get and Marcellus notwithstanding, the decurion is a Roman. Get him out and arm him.'

'But sir, he's still badly torn and in agony, and all wrapped up in dressings.'

'And yet he could still hold a club. Get him out.'

Reluctantly and with a shaking of the head, the guard scurried off, opening the door to the cells and disappearing within. Fronto turned to the rest. 'Everyone prepared? Whatever we do, none of the attackers get to the cells and none of them get out alive. Even if we all have to die to stop it.'

Nods all round.

Across the room, the latch gave an ear-splitting shriek and then tore in two with a crack. The door jerked in a foot or so and the table butted up against it crept backwards.

'This is it. Be prepared. No quarter.'

With a noise like a siege tower collapsing the door burst inwards, the table clattering across the floor. Fronto could hear the sound of keys and muffled conversation in the cell chamber, and the eleven men in this room levelled their weapons and planted firm feet. Fronto winced at the pain in his foot as he did so and gritted his teeth, bracing for the enemy.

A man two heads taller than him and twice as wide at the shoulder barrelled through the doorway. The big man hefted the longest, heaviest sword Fronto had ever seen, one that made the grand long Gallic blades he'd seen look like fruit knives. The Gaul's face was oddly happy, a mix of release and exultation, as he leapt forwards, his first side-swipe taking one of the guards in the left arm, ripping it in two and slamming home deep into the man's torso. He screamed and fell away, tripping one of his fellows and taking him down in the flurry. Procles was there in an instant, a decade's experience fighting off pirates and raiders aboard triremes and merchant vessels lending him useful skills in dealing with restricted space. The big Greek former marine hammered down with his club at the giant's hand, trying to disarm him of that great sword. His blow struck but glanced off the sword hilt, bruising the big man's hand at best. As the marine reeled back, lifting his club for the next strike, his eyes widened in surprise. He'd not seen the huge Gaul's other hand whip a knife from his belt. The force of the blow from that ham-sized hand was such that Procles felt his ribs and sternum crack and splinter, the knife driving the bone apart as though it were butter in its search for the heart.

Fronto saw the guards fall, saw Procles jerk back with a cry, dropping his club and clutching at his chest, but he had his own problems. The older woman had let her palla fall away now and had torn away the skirts of her stola to allow freedom of movement, and she advanced across the room with the grace of a dancer and the determination of a gladiator, a blade in each hand, whirling and stabbing. Her first blow had caught Cavarinos on the left arm and the Arvernian had cried out but found himself locked in a dance of death with the fake merchant. The woman, one hundred and twenty pounds of snarling, hate-filled death, was on Fronto like a whirlwind, slashing and hacking as she spat curses in her native tongue. Despite his general aversion to fighting women – even after that German cow had wounded his ankle so long ago – Fronto found himself fighting for his life with no qualms. This wasn't a woman. This was one of the Furies given form. Swords slamming into one another, grating, sparking, they fought again and again, Fronto's braced foot aching and throbbing with at least two broken bones. Others were having less luck. They may have closed the gap in numbers, but the Romans were mostly armed with sticks and a few eating knives while the Gauls, by way of their cart, had brought ample good blades with them. Even some of the slaves – sad, filthy, gaunt creatures – were armed with swords, slavering with hate as they leapt upon the Romans, who fought them off as best they could with clubs and knives.

He saw two of the Gallic slaves go down, Agesander managing to get inside the range of their weapons and smack their heads together with his big boxer's hands. But at the same time, he saw Dyrakhes disappear, gurgling, blood bubbling up through both the mouth in his face and the second one in his neck. Chaos reigned as weapons struck and swung, the air filled with grunts, screams, cries and curses in two languages, all in a fairly dim constricted room, lit by two oil lamps and the open, splintered door.

The Gallic witch snarled.

One of Fronto's desperate blows had taken a chunk out of the harridan's shoulder, and a desperate punch had smashed her nose and front teeth, yet she fought on like some kind of Hades-born harpy and Fronto had felt the fiery pain of two hits from her blades, one on his forearm and one his leg, neither of which was deep enough to take his mind off the ongoing pain in his foot. Years of warfare had trained him to detach his mind from concerns over non-incapacitating wounds, leaving them to nag in the background, allowing him to concentrate on not dying.

He hadn't even realised his mistake before it was too late. He'd overreached like a novice – like a young *tiro* in his first week with the legion – and as he tried in vain to recover, the woman was on him, the tip of her left blade slashing through the air at the side of his head even as the right blocked the club in his other hand.

In a blink of the eye he prepared to meet the final boatman, without even the time to apologise to Lucilia for leaving her so abruptly. A sword whispered through the air a hair's breadth from his ear, blocking the witch's blow, which should by rights have killed him. Instead, the force of the woman's swing knocked the life-saving sword into his temple so that his mind spun unpleasantly. That same blade continued on into the face of the dreadful woman, smashing in through her cheek, into her brain and cracking the back of her skull from the inside, though Fronto only vaguely witnessed it in his fugged confusion.

As he attempted to recover his wits, Fronto blinked to see that the head guard had returned from the cells with the staggering, pained Comum noble swathed in bandages, and only his timely intervention had saved Fronto's life. As the senior guard with the sword took his place, Fronto tried to stop his mind from lurching in his head in a vomit-inducing manner.

Things were going poorly. Half a dozen of the Gallic slaves lay dead, as well as the horrendous witch warrior, but Procles was gone, as were Dyrakhes and three of the six guards. Balbus was on the back-foot, fighting for his life against Molacos, whose cloak and mask seemed to hamper his fighting ability not at all. Biorix was struggling with the blond woman, and Agesander had, thankfully, managed to collect a fallen sword and was using it desperately to parry the massive hammer blows of the Gaulish giant again and again. Even as he watched, he saw another slave fall, and another of the carcer's guards.

Agesander found a momentary opening and lunged out. Fronto felt a moment of elation as he saw the former boxer's purloined blade sink deep into the giant's belly, angled upwards, ramming up inside the ribcage, severing organs, but his relief was short-lived.

Even in death the giant was dangerous and unstoppable. The knife in his offhand found the side of Agesander's neck, ripping a great gouge in it. The two men collapsed together, the giant's innards slithering out atop them both as the spray from Agesander's neck drowned all nearby in crimson, his lifeblood leaving him so fast that he was greying with every heartbeat.

Fronto's practised commander's mind, clearing now of his thumping fuddlement, performed the calculation automatically. Seven slaves, Molacos, the blonde and the druid totalled ten of the enemy still fighting. Against eight of us...

Another of the guards collapsed screaming, clutching a stump.

Seven, then.

Balbus fell with a yelp and Molacos issued a cry of triumph even as he turned on Fronto.

The Roman's heart hollowed. His *father-in-law!* Fury filled him even as the leader of the Sons of Taranis fell upon him like a war god. Fronto lashed out with his blade, a blow the Cadurci hunter easily turned, but Fronto's rage was threatening to take control, and his fist smashed into Molacos' masked face. He felt a finger break, but also felt the mask crack. As the strange, impassive visage fell away leaving Fronto staring into the ruin of that awful face, the final barrier snapped in Fronto's mind and for the first time in years he let battle claim him utterly, surrendering to the bloodthirsty beast that lived suppressed within all born warriors.

Molacos was good, and perhaps given over to the same fury as he. Even in the mindless rage that had claimed Fronto, he registered the quality of his enemy as the two men battered at one another madly, each blow driven by blind fury and battle lust. The sword edges clashed and clanged and both men took cut after cut after cut, heedless of the blood and fiery pain in their wrath. And suddenly Fronto was moving. He had his free arm around another man's throat and was squeezing with the sound of the more delicate bones in the neck snapping. Unaware of who it was, his blade was still slashing out at Molacos, but they were moving as they fought. Unnoticed, they had backed through the doorway towards the cells.

There was no time now to pay attention to anyone else's fight. He and Molacos were locked in a dance of death. He felt the agony as something penetrated his side, but the recognition of a real wound did nothing to stop him fighting. He heard a scream outside in the main room and recognised it vaguely for that of Biorix.

'Legate!'

Fronto's head cleared. Somehow, in the same way as the *ad signum* command had brought the former legionaries instinctively to attention, so the use of his old title cut through the noise and the mess, the pain and the fury, and drew Fronto back from the abyss.

Molacos was still fighting him, but Fronto had wounded the Sons' leader in three or four places in his unrestrained anger. Warm, sticky liquid ran down Fronto's side and leg and he knew that the wound in his side was serious from the quantity of blood alone.

He blinked, his sword still desperately turning Molacos' blade, and looked to both sides to determine the source of the call.

The leader of the guards was in this room now, too, and in dire trouble. The druid, his face coated with a swathe of blood from some head wound, had pressed the guard back and back until the poor fellow had found himself pressed up against the bars of a cell, where its inmate had taken grisly advantage.

It had been a year since Fronto had set eyes upon Vercingetorix of the Arverni, king of Gaul and rebel commander. The months had not been kind. The once tall, powerfully-built man with the dazzling eyes, proud face and flowing hair was now a stooped, thin, matted creature, coated in filth and with a beard to his midriff. But whatever strength he had left in his arms was now locked around the guard's neck.

Even as the man fought off the druid desperately, the imprisoned king heaved, strangling the life from him. As the guard's last breaths came in gasps and wheezes, someone was there beside Fronto, flicking a sword defiantly at the druid, taking the dying Roman's place.

Cavarinos.

Fronto twisted out of the way of another of Molacos' blows and staggered, his broken foot giving way at the most inopportune time. A strange silence fell in the cells, filled only by the muted groans and flailing of the wounded and dying out in the main room, along with the occasional clang and crunch of a fight still going on somewhere.

The druid backed away and Cavarinos was suddenly standing in the centre of the room, just out of reach of the cells, a space around him. Even Molacos, while still fending off Fronto's occasional blows and launching the odd half-hearted one of his own, was paying more attention to the eerie tableau than his own fight.

There are moments when the great games of the gods are poised on a knife-point and the outcome could go either way. At such times, the world holds its breath and even death seems inconsequential next to the enormity of the moment. The gods' dice teeter on their points, waiting for gravity to pull them down and declare a winner.

Once again, Fronto felt the hair rise on the back of his neck as he stepped back towards the bars of the empty cell behind him, disengaging from Molacos.

'What are you doing, brother?' Vercingetorix whispered in a hoarse rattle from the cell.

'This has to stop,' said Cavarinos, and Fronto's heart lurched at the hint of pleading in the tone.

'All can be as we designed,' the king hissed. 'There is one Roman left. Kill him, Cavarinos, blood of my blood, and we will be away from here.'

The Arverni noble in the room's centre lowered his blade and Fronto felt a rush of cold panic as he saw Cavarinos' sword swing down until the point rested on the floor.

'I cannot kill him, my king, any more than I could kill you.'

'Then you are my companion and countryman no longer. You are not Arverni...'

'Those words cannot cut me now, my king. I've known that truth for a year and more.'

The druid took a step forward, raising his blade, but the king waved a hand at him and he stopped in his tracks.

'We have won, Cavarinos. Molacos, the most favoured hunter of our age stands proud before us, and Luguros, our own druid of Gergovia, the man who presented you and your brother to the gods at your first naming day, will free me. We have won here, and when we return to our native lands, the Romans will rue the day they let me live and curse the name of Alesia.'

Cavarinos had not yet turned from the druid to face his king, and as he did so, Fronto was filled with unexpected sympathy for his friend. The fight in the carcer was a paltry thing compared to the war going on behind the Arvernian noble's eyes. The struggle there was overwhelming him. Fronto felt his pulse quicken and he cleared his throat. 'Cavarinos...'

The Arvernian glanced at him, and the trouble in that glance was palpable. Then he turned back to the king in his cell. 'I hate this, my king, truly I do. But if Molacos wins, you will drag on a futile war we cannot win and a million more men, women and children of the tribes will die. As it is, it will take generations for our lands to recover.' He turned to the druid – Luguros. 'When you were in Gergovia in all your glory and we children listened to your words as though they spilled from the mouths of the gods, you used to teach that sacrifices were made for the good of all the people. Well now the good of the people means peace, at any cost. *Any* cost. Don't you see that?' He turned back to the king. 'And that sacrifice today is twofold. Your head, and my soul.'

The druid stepped forward again, and his sword tip came up to dance near Cavarinos' throat threateningly. 'If we cannot persuade you, then you will have to die along with your Roman friends. We win, with or without you.'

Fronto made to move but he was too slow, between his broken finger, broken foot and the strength-sapping blood loss from his side. Molacos was quicker, his own blade lancing out and blocking Fronto's movement, knocking his sword away before coming to rest on his chest. One hard push on that sword and Fronto's heart would be pierced. And yet still Molacos stood riveted to the scene before him. Fronto realised what the hideously disfigured hunter was waiting for – what the druid and the king were waiting for. Fronto was helpless now. So was the Arvernian. Cavarinos would either kill Fronto, or he himself would die on the druid's blade.

Cavarinos turned to him, a horrible, riven, pleading look in his eyes. Fronto could almost read the words. *Kill me*, the look said. *Put an end to this*. The Arvernian's blade came up, quivering towards Fronto's face, the druid's sword tip still held threateningly close to his neck. Cavarinos took a step. Then two more. His sword tip approached Fronto even as the druid followed him, keeping his blade close.

'Don't do this, Cavarinos. You're stronger than this.'

The gleaming point of the Arvernian's sword came to rest just under Fronto's chin. The man swallowed. Fronto daren't do the same despite the dryness in his mouth.

He felt the nick as Cavarinos' blade cut through the flesh and for just a moment wondered what dying would feel like. But that was all it was: just a nick. For the Arvernian noble was swinging around now with remarkable speed. In that curious slow-motion in which a heartbeat can take a year, Fronto realised what his friend was doing and, his own life hanging by a thread, fell heavily backwards to the ground.

Cavarinos spun with the blade still at neck height. Luguros, druid of the Arverni and tutor to the great rebel king tried to cut out with his own sword to stop it, but he was far too slow, taken completely by surprise. Cavarinos' blade bit into his neck on the right side and only stopped when it wedged between the joints in the spine. The druid's nerves pulsed and the sword fell from his twitching fingers. His head lolling unpleasantly to one side, Luguros, who had for a year borne the cloak of Cernunnos the forest lord, turned in jerky motions to stare in horror at his killer. Cavarinos let go of the sword, which remained wedged in the neck even as he tried to talk and instead folded up to land in a heap on the floor.

Fronto, only peripherally aware of this, hit the floor hard, the pain of the wound in his side almost overwhelming. And yet his senses were still active. As he hit, his arm was already sweeping out. The gladius may be lightly pitted with rust for lack of cleaning, but its previous owner had been diligent at the time, and the edge was as keen as any Fronto had seen. The blade cut deep into Molacos' leg just above the ankle and snapped the bone with the blow. The Cadurci hunter screamed as his leg separated above the joint, only a narrow strip of flesh and muscle connecting them. He spun and fell, shrieking.

As he hit the ground Fronto was already lunging across the floor, his gladius jabbing into any flesh he could find, striking foot, then ankle, then shin, thigh, groin. The blade slid home there until only the hilt protruded next to Molacos' manhood and blood from the severed artery flooded the man's tunic, forming a huge lake that flowed to meet that of the fallen druid nearby.

Molacos coughed once, tried to say something, and then jerked and fell still.

Fronto hauled himself round in the crimson pool and slowly pushed himself up to his knees. Cavarinos was standing over the fallen druid, but his eyes were on Fronto.

'For a moment,' the former legate breathed, 'I thought you were going to do it.'

'For a moment, I was,' Cavarinos answered flatly, and there was no hint or trace of humour or wit in his tone. 'Today I have finally cast out the last of what I was and left myself hollow.' He turned to look at his king and Vercingetorix backed away across his cell, sickened.

'Well however hollow you may feel, my intact gut and soul thank you,' Fronto muttered, hauling himself painfully to his feet, his hand still gripping the crimson, sticky hilt of the old gladius.

'It is over,' Cavarinos said quietly.

'Probably,' Fronto corrected. 'There might be survivors out there.'

'Not that. Not the fight. My *world*. My world is over, Fronto. The tribes are doomed. This is the death rattle of the land you call Gaul, here in this room. The world will never be the same. *I* will never be the same.'

'You did what you had to. What you knew to be right. There are those of us, even those who fought your people again and again, who can see a value to a future together. Gaul and Roman, building something that is better than both. Labienus suggested such a thing years ago when we were facing the Belgae, and at the time we thought he was dreaming, but in retrospect, I suspect he was ahead of his time there.'

The room fell silent, just the groans and thuds of the wounded outside insisting on their thoughts.

'I have to go.'

Fronto blinked. 'Now? Where?'

'Anywhere. Galatia, probably. As soon as the tide will take me.'

'Then you will have time for a last meal with us.' Fronto crossed the room and clapped his hand on Cavarinos' shoulder, wincing at the pain in his side as he did so. 'For now, let's go see if anyone else is alive...'

* * * * *

Biorix was on his knees at the outer room's edge, clutching his side, from which leaked torrents of blood. A few paces away, the blonde woman lay on the floor, propped up with one arm. Occasionally the pair would swipe at one another with their blades, though both were clearly exhausted and half dead from wounds and blood loss.

Other than them the room was a house of the dead, bodies strewn in a carpet, some still shuddering or moving, groaning in their final moments. Almost casually, contemptuously, Fronto stepped between the corpses and slammed his gladius home between the blonde's shoulder blades. The woman gasped, croaked out a man's name almost too quiet to hear, and slumped to the ground.

'Fronto!'

He turned to see Cavarinos waving him over, and stepped between the bodies, nodding respectfully at Biorix as he did so.

His heart jumped, then thundered.

Cavarinos was helping one of the wounded up.

Balbus coughed and winced.

'Fortuna, you beautiful bugger,' Fronto grinned, hurrying over.

His father-in-law was pale as death, a lump the size of a hen's egg on his forehead, coloured black and purple. His sword arm was crimson and soaked, but the old man was a veteran of many wars and knew precisely what to do. Before the severed artery had bled him dry, he'd whipped off his scarf and tied it so tight around the top of his arm that the blood flow had been staunched. Fronto knew that if he washed that arm it would be a pale purple-blue from lack of blood. He also knew that the arm was almost certainly lost, but the sacrifice of the limb might well have saved the old man's life.

'I think we'll need both those doctors Glyptus knew,' he murmured.

'For you, as well,' Cavarinos replied, pointing at Fronto's side. 'You're as pale as an Arvernian winter. Anyone else alive?'

Fronto nodded to Balbus, who clearly still felt too weak to reply, and rose, prowling around the room, pausing occasionally to administer the mercy blow to the few Gallic slaves or guards who were fighting against the pull of Hades. Procles and Agesander were still and silent. Dyrakhes was gone.

He stopped, startled, as the decurion from Comum groaned. Crouching, he helped pull the man to his knees. He did not seem to be exhibiting any wounds from the fight, though the general coating of blood from his scourge injuries that had leaked into the wrappings made it rather hard to tell.

'Jove and Minerva!'

He turned at the shout from the doorway to see a guard – the one who'd run before the fight – standing in the square of light, a truncheon in hand and a look of disbelief on his face. Even as Fronto rose and held up conciliatory hands, the figure of Curtius Crispinus, head of the carcer guard, appeared next to him. The shapes of numerous other guards were visible behind them in the street. The centurion's face worked repeatedly between fury and incredulity.

Fronto coughed nervously and looked around. The room was a palace of the dead and wounded, blood coating most of the surfaces, organs and bone in ample evidence.

'I can see how this might look…'

'You would free the decurion?' Crispinus demanded angrily. 'I was told to watch out for Caesar's men as they're duplicitous and dangerous. It would seem Pompey has you figured.'

Fronto realised that he still had one hand on the Comum man, who was barely conscious and half dead, as well as a bloodied sword in his other hand. Promptly, he dropped the sword and snatched his hand away from the decurion as though the touch burned.

'You would even bring a sword into the sacred bounds of the city?' Crispinus snapped. 'Have you no shame, man? Have you no respect for the laws of men and gods?'

Fronto sighed. Somehow he couldn't see an argument that the blade had already been here but hidden behind a cupboard going down very well with the centurion. Slowly, painfully, he rose. 'I would explain, but I fear your conclusions are already drawn, Curtius Crispinus. Just bear in mind that had we not been here, your carcer would now be empty of Gaulish kings. Keep the decurion. Get him well and send him home.'

As he spoke, he rose and crossed the room, helping Cavarinos with Balbus and Biorix. Once upright, the four men, supporting each other, limped painfully towards the door, their weapons discarded in the mess.

'If you think you're leaving this room…'

'Get out of my way,' Fronto snapped. 'The old man and I are citizens of Rome, veteran officers, and nobles of the city. We've been convicted of nothing. Now, move!'

Crispinus failed to do so, but Biorix growled as the four approached and the centurion reeled back as if struck. Fronto and his friends stalked past without even glancing at the man's face, which was cycling through a dozen emotions, uncertain where to stop.

'This matter will be brought to the attention of the Consul Claudius Marcellus, mark my words. Don't think you'll get away with this. We'll find out who you are,' the man shouted as they stumbled away along the street.

'Marcus Falerius Fronto,' the former legate shouted back. 'Sorry about the mess.'

Chapter Twenty One

LUCTERIUS of the Cadurci straightened himself and brushed down his stained, torn and generally ruined clothes. He did his level best to trim his straggly facial hair with the dagger from his belt and retied the braids in his hair. He was a chieftain – a man of property and authority. He might *look* like a vagabond...

The ramparts were still high and despite all that had happened in recent months, there were curled plumes of smoke rising from houses. Of course, the Romans had never had cause to come here with their legions and machines of war, so the township had continued on with their lives as though the war had not happened, despite the loss of many of their folk of fighting age in that last great battle.

Nemossos was no Gergovia. It had neither the size nor the prestige of that great place where they had almost defeated Rome. But it had two benefits. Firstly, it was home to the highest ranking surviving Arvernian noble. Secondly, because it had been untouched, there was no Roman resettlement officer here. This was a town of the Arverni with no outside influence. And the Arverni were the last people – the only people – who could still hope to raise and field an army against Rome. Caesar had exempted the Aedui and the Arverni from his rulings after Alesia, and so those two tribes alone in the land could still claim a sizeable population. And the Aedui, the duplicitous and treacherous Aedui, would never lead a revolt against their Roman masters. But the Arverni were still true to their past and if they could be persuaded to rise once more, which might be possible if they knew their king was on his way back to them, then perhaps the treacherous Aedui might join, and the tribes of Aquitania might throw in their lot.

With a long, slow breath, he began to stride up the slope towards the gate. Two Arverni warriors stood there, looking bored. With distaste, he noted that the two men wore very Roman style belts to hold their knives, possibly even Roman-manufactured and purchased from a Roman trader.

'What is your business,' asked one of them harshly as he approached.

Despite the state of his clothes and appearance, Lucterius still had the torc of leadership around his neck and the arm-rings of a warrior on his biceps. The sword he bore was a good quality one. He tried to exude authority.

'I am Lucterius of the Cadurci.'

'And I am Julius Caesar,' the guard sneered. 'Piss off.'

Lucterius drew himself to his full height, pushing out his chest, his lip twitching in irritation.

'I *am* Lucterius, chieftain of the Cadurci, as the torc should confirm. My appearance is so poor as I came here from a fight with the proconsul's men.'

'So you won then,' grinned the guard, and his companion sniggered.

'I have no time to argue with idiots who stand silent while good men of the tribes die on Roman spears. Your magistrate Epasnactos knows me from the councils of Gergovia and Bibracte. He will confirm who I am.'

The two guards shared a look and shrugged. 'If the chief doesn't know you, then I'll be taking those stolen arm-rings and torc and the rest while you get whipped through the streets. Still want an audience?'

Lucterius clenched his teeth angrily. When he was back in command with Epasnactos at his side these two men would be buried up to their neck and left for the scavengers. 'Take me to Epasnactos,' he snapped.

Nemossos was quiet and peaceful as they moved through the streets to the headman's house. Lucterius had to stifle a sneer at every turn, noting with disgust how many Roman belts, pots, cloaks and the like were in evidence. The Arverni had once been Rome's greatest trading partner among the tribes until Caesar came and it seemed that since discarding their arms, they had returned to their old ways. That would have to stop. The Roman merchants could be the first casualty of the new revolt – a fire arrow in the sky to begin the conflagration, as Cenabum had been in its time.

He strengthened his resolve to execute these mindless brutes as they none-too-gently guided him around the corners with the butts of their spears. Hissing his anger, he otherwise restrained himself. Now was not the time to cause trouble. Finally, the great long house came into view.

The last time he had been here had been with Vercingetorix. Then, of course, it had been Critognatos and Cavarinos who had held the true power in this place behind their ailing uncle, and Epasnactos, their younger cousin, had been little more than an observer. Since Critognatos' death at Alesia and Cavarinos' subsequent disappearance, Epasnactos, who had taken part in all the rebel councils, and yet had been too young to be granted a command of men, had taken his rightful place as head of Nemossos and a chieftain of power among the Arverni.

The world missed men like Critognatos and Cavarinos, true warriors of the tribes and leaders of men who had led the fight against Caesar. Still, Epasnactos had been in awe of his cousins. He was still young and impressionable. He could be moulded into a new rebel prince under the wing of the great king.

There was some sort of court session being held in the house and as they entered and stood to one side, an argument over land boundaries was settled by the young man on the carved wooden dais-chair. Lucterius examined the boy as he waited, only half listening to a judgement that seemed wise enough and fair enough to prove the new magistrate had a mind at least, if not the muscles to lift a sword.

Epasnactos looked a lot like his cousins. Like Cavarinos, anyway, lacking the bulk of Critognatos. His facial hair was still rather fuzzy and youthful, but would soon bloom into a full beard. His hair was neatly braided. He wore a torc and arm-rings, even though he could not ever have had cause to draw a sword. Lucterius would let that one pass – the boy was almost a king, after all. The young man's face was serious and his eyes clear, even inflected with a sparkle of wit and wisdom. One day, Lucterius decided, Epasnactos might make a fine king. Now he must make a great decision.

The plaintiffs over the border dispute backed out of the room and in the gap before another case was brought, one of the older warriors at Lucterius' side escorted him to the centre of the hall. Around the edge stood the magistrate's own warriors, members of his veteran bodyguard. Their age, clear experience, and fine armament confirmed his thoughts that the Arverni could still raise a strong army.

'Epasnactos,' one of the two guards said with a bowed head.

'Evicaos?'

'This man approached the west gate, claiming to be Lucterius, the chieftain of the Cadurci and demanding to speak with you.'

The young leader leaned forward in his seat, squinting in the gloom. 'Bring him closer.'

Lucterius strode across, not giving his escort the satisfaction of driving him forward with their spears.

'Magistrate, I know you will be able to vouch for me, despite my appearance. You have seen me many times, and heard my voice in councils along with your cousins and our king.'

Epasnactos leaned back in his seat, drumming his fingers on the chair arm. 'I know you, Lucterius. What brings so honoured a Cadurci chief here in such a condition?'

'I come from the siege of my home at Uxellodunon.'

'I hear tell of this. Caesar has six legions there, does he not, along with sundry auxiliary forces?'

'He does.'

'You were fortunate to evade them, clearly.'

Lucterius frowned. This was not how he had imagined this going. 'My army in Uxellodunon matches Caesar's and can hold out for a year if they have to. But even now agents of our two tribes free the great king from Rome to return to our shores and command a new revolt that will sweep Rome into the sea. I bring you an opportunity, Epasnactos of the Arverni. Raise your tribe to our banners and help break the siege of Uxellodunon. Our combined forces will be able to raze Caesar's army from the land. And when my tribe are relieved, we will move south and free Narbo and the southern tribes from Rome's fetters – a gift to Vercingetorix when he returns.'

'You bring this opportunity to me alone, Lucterius?'

The Cadurci's frown deepened. 'Yes.'

'In other seasons I might be tempted to grasp your proffered opportunity, but sadly I must decline on this occasion. You see, I simply cannot raise enough men to be of use to you.'

Lucterius shook his head in confusion. 'You have the manpower. Of all the tribes, you and the Aedui still have the manpower. Caesar left you your warriors.'

Epasnactos nodded as he leaned forward in his seat again. 'He did. And I have to say we were more embarrassed than grateful at the time, for our standing with the other tribes suffered dreadfully. But since I took this throne and watched the whole land suffer, farms going untended, fields dying with mouldy crops for want of men to harvest them, I have come to see our embarrassment as more of a boon. Alone among the tribes, the Aedui and the Arverni will not starve this winter.'

Lucterius stared in disbelief.

'And *this* is why you cannot spare the men to finally defeat Rome? Because they tend your farms?'

Epasnactos sighed. 'Not so much. I mean, they do, but at the moment most of my warriors are absent on campaign.'

Lucterius stared in bafflement. 'What?'

'They are to the west, forming an auxiliary force in Caesar's siege of the last rebel stronghold.'

As Lucterius goggled in shock, his mouth flapping open and closed, Epasnactos gestured to the warriors in the room. 'Seize the traitor chief.'

Lucterius started to move, but the two warrior escorts were there instantly, grabbing his arms, relieving him of his sword and pushing him down to his knees.

'No! This is not *right*. I am the last chance for freedom. I bring you an opportunity! I carry the hopes of our future...'

Epasnactos shook his head sadly. 'Like my cousins and father before me, I must look to the future and the good of the Arverni before some crazed doomed hunt for glory with a man who doesn't know when his world has ended. We are part of the Pax Romana, Lucterius. So are you, if you would just sit down and accept it. Rome is the future, man.'

Fury pounded through Lucterius and suddenly he jerked free of the warriors' grip, bursting forth and running at the young magistrate. His ire drove him on, but as he closed on the young man, Epasnactos rose from his seat and drew a heavy sword from the side of the dais, levelling it in a surprisingly steady hand. Lucterius skidded to a halt, the blade's tip levelled at his face from the raised dais. His hand dropped to the dagger at his belt, which had not been confiscated.

'I would strongly recommend you leave that where it is, Lucterius of the Cadurci,' sighed the young leader. 'I am quite familiar with a sword's use.' He tapped an arm-ring with his free hand. 'They don't give these to people for making decisions, you know?'

Slowly, Lucterius raised his arms from the knife, backing away. The warriors were on him again in a trice, this time a dozen of them. He felt several kicks and punches as he was dragged down. Submitting to pain and captivity reluctantly, he heard the young magistrate addressing his men.

'Careful not to kill him. Bind and secure him and deliver him to the proconsul with my compliments. And make sure he gets there intact. If he slips past you the way he did past the legions, I'll have a new set of spiked heads decorating Nemossos' gates.

As blackness claimed him, Lucterius felt the future melting like wax on a hot day, dripping through his fingers and disappearing forever in the dust.

He had failed.

Epilogue

THE prisoner was roused from what might, after a year, have only generously been termed sleep, by a murmur of activity outside the gate. He turned to look at his fellow prisoners. Gattus had been broken for weeks now. He'd stopped talking a month ago and now just sat hugging his knees, rocking back and forth in complete silence. Almost a week had now passed since he had eaten anything and his body was on the brink of collapse, his rocking slowed to a jerky shudder. Ovidius was mad. Of course, he'd seemed mad when he was brought in almost a year ago. He'd actually torn the ear off a guard with his teeth as he was manhandled into the stockade. But he'd started... well there was no other way of saying it... eating himself. He'd taken bites out of his limbs and the damn Gauls, even if they had cared, had no brilliant Greek medics to deal with such things. Their healers were the druids, who seemed not to really care too much about the health of their Roman captives. Ovidius' wounds were festering and while he seemed to be whole, if mad, he would not survive long with the rot set into his body. The only strong one remaining was Duorix, a Remi cavalryman who seemed to take every day with such a stoic calmness that it was only his example that had kept the prisoner going.

There had been more than thirty of them when they were first herded together. Now there were four. The prisoner had forgotten his name half a year ago – no one in here had known it anyway.

But the noise was interesting. There was a tone to it that the prisoner recognised from other fights. The sound of abject hopelessness – the sound of a loser. Somehow, given that they were his jailors he found that tone at once incongruous and utterly hilarious. He started to laugh.

Ovidius started to laugh with him, but that was hardly a surprise. Ovidius laughed at everything, even when he shat himself – *especially* when he shat himself. But Duorix seemed to have picked up on the same thing completely independently, and he was chuckling away to himself.

There was a groaning, scraping sound and the gate of the timber compound swung open. The prisoner tried to look through the mist of stink and the flies that had gathered around the rotted food – not everything they gave you was still fresh enough to eat, the human waste – no latrine or bucket, the latrine was the same place as the floor and the bed, and the bodies – the dead were only removed once a week or so, and there were still two festering legionaries in here.

The Gauls were shouting now. What were they saying? The prisoner had learned some of the Gallic language in his time here, though it had become rusty over time in seclusion and he had no idea what they said, but they sounded angry and desperate. One of them pointed at the survivors and made a walking gesture with two fingers, then pointed out of the gate.

Were they to be executed?

The tame Cadurci druid did that...

The prisoner had spoken to one or two of the less rabid druids belonging to the Aedui and the Remi years back and they had been clever, spiritual, well-spoken men. But when they considered you the enemy everything was different. They turned from erudite shepherds of the people into vengeful, irate maniacs with a thirst for torture. He could remember still when they had taken Manlius. The captives had been able to smell him cooking even as he still screamed. The prisoner shuddered.

But he moved on cue. Any progress, even to Elysium, was welcome now. For soon there would only be he and Duorix, and he knew damn well he would break first. Better to be dead than be found wanting in the last count. Ovidius tried to savage the Gauls as he passed them, but spear butts kept him painfully in place.

The four of them were urged out into the street and more care was seemingly being taken with their current movement than had been in their capture and imprisonment and the shifting from oppidum to oppidum in between.

Finally, one of them, who was clearly in charge, started shouting out orders to his men and the prisoner realised their tongue was coming back to him. He started to listen again. They were to line the prisoners up.

'Gattus – legionary Roman,' rasped one of them. Gattus, without a word and barely able to stand, shuffled forwards. 'He might be dead before we reach the bottom,' the Gaul said to his friend. Well, the prisoner could unpick perhaps every fourth word, but he could fill in the blank for the gist.

'If he falls, you'll have to carry him,' the leader barked with no humour.

'Ovidius – legionary Roman.'

'That's me. Marcus Ovidius, master on the field or in the sack. Or at least that's what your whore of a mother told me!' Ovidius exploded in laughter until *guard one* hit him in the stomach with a spear butt, folding him over.

'Stop that,' said his friend. 'Don't damage important commodities.'

'Duorix – Remi traitor.' Duorix barely acknowledged the man, chin up, head high as he fell into line.

The prisoner waited with bated breath.

'Is this one alright?' his jailor said. 'He's a funny colour.'

'It's permanent. He was like that when he was brought in.'

The first man shrugged,

'Carbo – centurion Roman.'

Ah yes... *that* was his name.

* * * * *

'I don't know whether to salute you, support you or punch out your bloody teeth for leaving us all that time thinking you were dead,' Atenos snorted as Carbo gulped down very watered wine as though it were the last flask in the world.

'*You* spend a year with the Cadurci and let's see how *you* feel, you big Gaulish ass.'

Atenos laughed out loud. 'It's my profound regret that Fronto is not here to see you. I'll send him a message, even though I'm still waiting for a reply to my last. This will make his year. Mine too, 'cause now I can get back to being an ordinary centurion. Primus Pilus is a pain in the arse. Too much writing and administration for my liking.'

'Don't get too ready to drop back down the ranks,' Carbo coughed, and the effects kept him busy for some time. He was still idiotically weak. Eventually, when the fit subsided, he grinned. 'I might be out of the business for a while. I might never be up to it again, in fact. A year of this ruins all your muscle tone. I might look at something cushy like camp prefect, or chief quartermaster if the general can be persuaded. You can keep your special tunic for now.'

A scream across the slope ripped through the still evening, and Carbo frowned. Ten heartbeats later there was another scream. Another. Another. When it had been going on long enough that

Carbo had stopped counting, he gestured to Atenos. 'What *is* that? Executions?'

'That, sir, is the dulcet tone of Caesar's leniency.'

'What?'

'Every scream is a Cadurci sword-hand being removed at the wrist.'

Carbo's brow rose. 'How many?'

'All of them. Everyone who rose against us – every male of fighting age that was in Uxellodunon. They're all to live, mind you. The louder shrieks you can hear aren't the hands being removed. That's the capsarii using burning pitch to cauterise the stumps. Caesar doesn't want *any* of them to die. He wants them all to go home and spread the word, tell everyone what happens when you raise the standard of revolt.'

Carbo nodded slowly. 'A grand show was ever Caesar's way.'

Thudding footsteps stopped their conversation and both men turned to see Varus, the horse commander, jogging towards them.

'It's true,' the man said with a grin. 'I would not have believed it if I'd not seen it with my own eyes. You must have the constitution of Cerberus, man.'

Carbo gave a weak salute.

'It is truly good to see you again, centurion. Good to see something pleasant come out of this evening.' He winced at the sound of another dismemberment and turned to Atenos. 'Caesar wants the Tenth's First century to take control of a very special prisoner.'

Atenos frowned a question and the horse commander chuckled.

'Our Arvernian friends have just ridden in with a rather disconsolate looking Lucterius strapped to a horse. Caesar probably has something special planned for this particular thorn in his side, but he doesn't want the slippery little maggot to get away again. Your own century – the best of the veterans – are on that one man.'

The big Gallic centurion's expression became serious. 'He'll not get past us. I heard that the couriers arrived this afternoon, sir. Anything from Fronto if I might ask?'

'Nothing,' muttered Varus, looking uncomfortable. He'd sent a messenger to Massilia some weeks back with the news of the campaign, and nothing had come back. 'But other news has come in, and it's good. Labienus has apparently utterly crushed the Treveri. According to the tribune who wrote the missive it sounds like a traditional Labienus victory. He took very few casualties, actually killed remarkably few of the enemy, yet still managed to douse their rebellious spirit totally. That man would make a good consul, though we'd miss him out here.'

'Is that it, then?' Carbo muttered. 'Gaul is peaceful?'

'It would seem so,' Varus replied. 'Caesar believes so anyway. There are no further sparks of rebellion we're aware of and each region has a Roman presence. Caesar is talking about rewarding our Gallic allies, too, especially the Remi. Grants of citizenship have even been rumoured. Imagine the Remi as citizens of Rome. Anyway, the general's already talking about winter quarters but, with it still only being late summer, he's planning to take a small force down into Aquitania before the campaigning season ends. There might be no trouble down there, but he wants to be certain before he sends to the senate. Plus, it seems that when young Crassus was down there a few years back, he thought it might be a rich and abundant country, and it's been poorly investigated thus far.'

Atenos sighed. 'I hope the legions will still be needed next year. I'm not ready to run an inn at Agedincum or a farm near Bibracte yet. Still, when the time comes for Caesar to go back to Rome and take up his consulship, no one will be able to deny him now. He's made a *province*. The lands of the tribes have somehow become Gaul, and Gaul has somehow become part of the republic. When he settles the veterans of twelve legions the place will be civilised at last, and with that kind of success under his belt Rome will fall all over him.'

'Especially since he'll have bought most of it,' noted Varus with a sigh. 'Rome is rapidly turning from an ideal into a commodity.'

* * * * *

Lucterius almost fell as he was pushed into the Roman stockade, though he kept his feet and held his head high. His legs were still stiff and ungainly from spending so long strapped across the back of a horse, as well as the residual bruising from the Arverni traitors' cowardly attack at Nemossos. Behind him the gate slammed shut. Perhaps three dozen men were incarcerated here, presumably for being the more avidly anti-Roman, noble, and dangerous of Caesar's captives. That might yet serve him well. He'd heard tales as he was manhandled through the camp – the proconsul had had the weapon hand struck from his entire army. Yet here there was no such dismemberment in evidence. Burning, hate-filled eyes turned to the new arrival. Here were warriors and nobles, still wearing their arm-rings, though disarmed and without their mail. And the fire in their eyes might be useful. He would still free himself, with the aid of these men. But first he had to get one difficult confrontation out of the way.

'Where is Drapes,' he demanded of the other prisoners.

Two or three hands pointed and Lucterius' gaze followed the fingers to see a heap of ragged flesh and bone in the corner. The man was clearly dead, though Lucterius couldn't decide whether that was a good thing or a bad one. 'What happened?'

'Starved himself,' grunted one of the men.

Lucterius straightened. 'Then he had less backbone than I thought. But we are different. We are Cadurci, and Arverni, and Carnutes and other great names. Men of tribes with a thousand year heritage of battle and honour. We will never bend our knees or our necks to Rome. Come, brothers, and we will plan our escape and to where we will run and regroup.' He hadn't expected a rousing cheer, but *something* positive would have been nice. Instead, he was greeted by a stony silence and glowering eyes.

'Have heart, brothers,' he cajoled. 'Vercingetorix is being freed from the Roman prison as we speak, and this is far from over. I am Lucterius of the Cadurci, who led the...'

'We know who you are,' snarled one of the warriors.

'Then we...'

'You are the bastard who persuaded us that we could still win and then abandoned us to our fate. You are the bastard who led us to our defeat and death yet again. You are the man who has condemned the Cadurci to the fires of the underworld. This is all your doing, Lucterius. All your fault.'

Lucterius frowned as he recoiled at the words. 'Now, listen...'

But the three dozen men were rising now, like the shambling dead from the graves of Alesia, fists balled and eyes afire. And they were closing on him.

'Everything I have done, I did for the good of the people of all our tribes,' he stuttered defensively.

'Tell that to the king of the dead when you meet him,' snapped the first person to reach him, and swung a fist like a sack full of sharp stones, sending him reeling and to one knee. He had no time to recover, though, as someone behind him stamped down and shattered his leg. Lucterius fell prone to the ground with a scream as the flurry of fists and feet began to rain down. From somewhere a secreted makeshift wooden knife appeared in the flurry. It pierced several organs a dozen times before it found his heart and finally ended Lucterius, architect of rebellion, and his dream of a free world.

* * * * *

The triclinium of the Puteoli villa was as full as it had been in years. Fronto, still breathing carefully due to the slowly-healing wound at his side, sat close to his recent companions: Aurelius, who had his arm strapped up to his chest and hissed when he moved; Balbus, with the bindings around his scalp that he prodded and scratted at constantly with his good arm, the future of the other still uncertain; Biorix, with wrappings on each limb and often prone to fits of memory loss; and Cavarinos, marked with a few scars but largely intact, at least physically. The Arvernian had agreed to travel south to Puteoli with the others, despite the fact that since the carcer his conversation had largely revolved around his intense desire to find a new world where nothing was familiar. He had passage to Galatia booked with a merchant from Neapolis, who would sail on the Ides of the month, and Fronto was taking daily opportunities to try and argue him out of it, as yet with no luck.

Across from the survivors of Rome, Lucilia cradled the boys as both Falerias – elder and younger – cooed over them. Galronus sat close by, his face uncharacteristically grave. Fronto had never seen his old Remi friend looking more Roman, from the clothes to the stance to the hair, to the gravitas. Throw a toga over him and he could walk into the senate's curia without drawing much of a glance. Masgava and Arcadios were here too, seated close together with Catháin, who had spent the past few weeks completely reorganising Fronto's business and rarely sported anything other than a satisfied grin.

It was a busy place. The villa was full of life and laughter. Reunions had been warm and happy, and even news of the dreadful events that had taken place in Rome had done little to mar the last few nights of festivities as family and friends reunited, some after more than a year.

Then, this morning, everything had changed.

There had been a knock at the door and as the visitor was escorted in while his entourage were settled in the guest quarters, Fronto had felt his heart lurch at the sight. Decimus Junius Brutus would always be welcome in his house as an old friend and fellow officer, but anything that might bring him this far from Rome at a time when his duties there would be all consuming could hardly be good. Finally, the tired-looking Brutus was ushered in by one of the servants and took a seat gratefully, the proffered glass of wine even more so.

'It's good to see you all,' Brutus sighed after his first sip.

'I'd like to say the same,' Fronto replied with a sad smile, 'but I suspect this is no social visit? Caesar and Casca's business I fear will keep you in Rome for months yet?'

Brutus nodded unhappily. 'The matter is resolved and I am but a courier, for all my station. Your name has been dragged through the mud in the senate and the courts, even through the streets, just as we expected. I do wish you'd stayed in the city to help defend yourself. Coming south just made you look all the more guilty. There's only so much even a great advocate like Galba can do to defend someone in absentia, even with the funds Casca spared for the matter.'

'The senate will decide what the senate will decide, and my presence would have made little difference. If Galba's oratory and Caesar's money couldn't swing it, then there was nothing I could have done to change things. Marcellus was targeting me from the beginning since it's well known I'm Caesar's man. The whole matter was simple lies drawn from circumstantial evidence, anyway. I told you what really happened.'

'And I believe you, of course. After all, I'd seen these 'Sons' at Massilia. Yet the word across Rome remains that you drew a gladius within the pomerium, killed citizens in the carcer, and tried to free a political prisoner against the consuls' explicit will. Marcellus hardly had to do anything to ruin you. You'd all-but ruined yourself, and running away just compounded it. Galba fought tooth and nail in that courtroom, and while Caesar's money helped turn a few purses your way, Marcellus was Croesian in his generosity to those who might be bought. Pompey might not have been involved in the case, but you can bet his money changed hands in its regard. Galba fought your corner valiantly, but his best hope was damage limitation. The only thing that really worked in your favour was that Pompey deliberately distanced himself from the whole Comum affair, and that meant he had to stay completely out of the case against you and leave it to Marcellus. He couldn't be seen to be butting heads with Caesar, you see. In fact, I hear that Pompey is furious with Marcellus over the Comum thing.'

'Come to the point, Brutus. We're all tired. What actually happened in the end?'

'Marcellus tried to bring a verdict of treason against the state. After all, though the evidence was entirely circumstantial, it was pretty compelling nonetheless. You've got to try and see it from an objective point of view. You were found over the bodies of both Romans and Gauls with a sword in your hand – within the pomerium, in a building that theoretically contains no blades. The presence of the Gauls and their blades wasn't likely to do much to change the verdict. Fortunately, Galba managed to turn that blow well enough. Even the serpents in the senate baulk when asked to bring a capital verdict against a patrician with a history of valiant military service.'

Fronto let out a relieved sigh. 'Good. I'm sick of putting the good of Rome above self and family and with no consideration in return. I've spent seven years helping conquer Gaul for the republic, but it's starting to strike me that I've done the world irreparable harm there. It's becoming unpleasantly clear to me that the Gauls have an innate sense of justice and loyalty that is sadly lacking in Rome. Just look at the men in this room alone. Biorix, Galronus and Cavarinos. Each one a Gaul of some tribe who has put their life and freedom on the line time and again to help a republic that couldn't care less about them.'

'There *are* still good men in the republic, Fronto,' said Brutus defensively. 'Look at Galba, for instance. Without him you'd be facing a death sentence.'

Fronto huffed. 'A few years ago I pulled away from Caesar. I saw trouble in him. I saw him treading a dangerous path of power and becoming a new Sulla, commanding Rome alone and with an iron fist, disposing of his enemies and directing policy – a king in all but name. Seeing how much worse Pompey was drove me back, but I still think that's the general's end goal. The odd thing is: the more time I spend in this pit of serpents, the more I think that a new dictator might be just what this sickly, diseased republic needs.'

He had expected some rebuttal from Brutus, but his friend's expression was bleak.

'I *didn't* get off free, did I?'

'No. I am the bearer of awful tidings, in fact.' He passed over a sealed document with a troubled expression. Fronto looked down, wiping a faint sheen of sweat from his forehead, cracked the seal, unfurled the document and read down it, his face darkening as he did so.

'What is it, Marcus?' Lucilia murmured nervously.

Fronto took a deep breath, his face stony. 'It is the judgement of the senate that the evidence of my motive is far too circumstantial to support any accusation of treason, or even of murder, despite the bodies at the scene. However, since there is clear record that I was bearing a military blade whose source could not be adequately determined as coming from anywhere other than my own person, I have been tried and convicted of breaking the sacred laws of the pomerium.'

'And?'

'And for a period of ten years, I am banished. I am to remove myself from Rome and all Italian soil for the duration of that sentence. Additionally, all my property is forfeit and has been claimed by the state.'

Lucilia's hand flew to her mouth in shock. 'This cannot be, Marcus?'

Fronto shook his head slightly as he looked around the assembled faces. Many dark or disapproving, some shocked or even horrified. Only his mother seemed to be oddly unaffected. 'It is,' he replied. 'Our holdings in Rome will go. The Campanian vineyards and the house at Paestum. This villa, too, since I am official paterfamilias of the family. All of it.'

His mother nodded. 'In these vicious days of politics, such a sentence is commonplace. Many of your contemporaries have suffered exile in their time, and usually for standing up for what is good against tyrants. It speaks well of you, my son, that you are so righteous that the snakes of the senate need to banish you to feel safe.'

Fronto gave his mother a sad smile. His strength – his moral character had all come from her blood.

'Your senate exiles you, but only for a time?' Cavarinos frowned.

Balbus nodded. 'Ten years is long enough, but the property confiscation is usually worse. It's basically a sentence of destitution

411

or even death for most. Luckily, I have plenty of funds, so you'll not find yourself lacking, Marcus. Where will you go?'

'To Massilia, of course.'

'But our property…?' his sister murmured, still in shock.

'Massilia is not inside the republic and, as the city's boule have been so fond of reminding me this year, the land on which our villas are built is contested ground. If Rome tries to confiscate a villa on land that Massilia considers theirs there will be a great deal of trouble. I think the senate and even Marcellus will leave us that land rather than risk opening a war against free Massilia.'

'Besides,' Balbus added, 'the deeds to the place are actually still in my name. I keep meaning to lodge the records with your name instead, but I've not got to Rome yet to do it. Officially you own nothing at Massilia, and the senate's decree will not stretch to my property.'

Brutus nodded. 'And thanks to Galba's expert defence, it's only a lesser banishment, not *Aquae et Ignis Interdictio*. At least you get to keep your citizenship and leave with your head held high, so in ten years' time you can take up where you left off, and so long as you can maintain funds, your boys' future won't suffer.'

Fronto nodded. 'All is not lost. This stinking pit of corruption and failure might take against us, but we have somewhere to run and a name to hold on to. There are still men in the republic who will see me in the same light as always.'

Lucilia frowned suspiciously. 'You're going back to Caesar, aren't you?'

'No,' Fronto shook his head. 'Just Massilia. Somewhere safe.'

But he couldn't meet the gaze that burned into him from beneath her furrowed brows.

The world was closing in now, and the republic was polarising. With Marcellus in Pompey's purse and the consuls of Rome actively defying Caesar, two sides were emerging from the chaos of the past few years as he'd been fearing for so long, and Fronto couldn't help but feel that the lines were already being drawn.

When it came down to the bones of the matter, Fronto knew where *his* lines were.

And Massilia would be close…

THE END

Author's note

THE final year of Caesar's Gallic wars presents an author with several difficulties. The main first-hand account was not written by Caesar himself, as the previous seven had been, but by one of his senior officers – Aulus Hirtius. The style is noticeably different, and we are led to question whether such an account might be more objective, or perhaps less. Moreover, the events described in the book cover the period of 51-50BC, rather than a single campaigning season, which drags out into political meanderings. Since I was concerned here with only the first year, I have had to take only part of Hirtius' story – no bad thing in my opinion. And while there is one great event in this year, much of it merges into a banal blur of siege and suppression so repetitive and unimportant that even Hirtius cannot be bothered to go into detail, such as describing the sieges or even naming the towns. Thus I was faced with trying to make the Gallic campaign side of the book interesting without Fronto's involvement or too many really bloody battles.

I chose to use Varus as the main military protagonist in this novel as he and his cavalry could appear in almost every place of interest in the campaign, allowing us to see it largely from a single viewpoint. Plus, of course, Varus is an old hand. This is his eighth outing and everyone knows him. Much of the year in Hirtius' writing, then, is fairly tepid, then suddenly the second greatest siege of the war appears in the summer, following which things peter out and Caesar goes off on a jolly, exploring the hills and valleys of Southwest France. So the story needed to end at Uxellodunum, as far as I was concerned.

A quick note on Uxellodunum: some of this is largely conjectural. Since the exact location of the Cadurci oppidum is still highly contested, there is no ground evidence to back up Hirtius' writing. The oft-accepted site is near the town of Vayrac in the Dordogne, though there are many strong voices also placing it at Capdenac on the Lot. Neither fits exactly with Hirtius' description, but both are close enough to stake a good claim and, after all, if we accept Alise Saint Reine as the site of Alesia, then Caesar's description doesn't quite match up either. Leeway simply has to be given. Thus my description of Uxellodunum is a mix of Hirtius' description and the physical landscape of the Vayrac site.

What did Lucterius hope to do with this last year of revolt? This question was what led me to build the plot of book 8. For the simple fact was that the tribes were beaten and having fought at Alesia, Lucterius has to have known how utterly useless a new revolt would be with only his new small confederation of tribes. Thus I have tried to build on the idea that he had a grander plan – that there was still some hope that he could rebuild what had been destroyed the previous year. I gave Lucterius a great scheme to drive out Rome, raise the southern tribes and retrieve their captive king.

Fanciful, perhaps. But this is fiction, after all.

Equally fictional is Caesar's great loot convoy. You can, of course, be absolutely certain that Caesar *did* send vast amounts of loot and slaves back to Rome. We know for a fact that he brought back so many slaves that he flooded the market and most of Rome's rich complained that their expensive slaves had become basically worthless due to the collapse in the market. We also know that Caesar, once he got to Rome, spent money like water.

My description of Massilia (which was probably still named the Greek Massalia at this point by the locals) is based on fact, though the knowledge is fairly scant, given the successive centuries of rebuilding. Massilia must have been a fascinating place in 50BC. It was one of the greatest ports in the west, an independent Greek city-state surrounded by Rome and despite Caesar's new trade route over the Alps, it must have remained a very important place for the transport of men and supplies.

I enjoyed Fronto's move into the wine trade, and I hope you did too. Roman wine is already a complicated subject. But Greek wine was also famous and very varied and a whole complex thing of itself. And then there is the fact that although French wine as it is began with the agricultural policies of the emperor Probus, the Gallic tribes even before Rome came were making wine, though of a much different sort. I'm sure there will be those of you out there who are unhappy with the move away from Fronto's military career. Rest assured, that career is far from over. But between 52 and 49BC there is a tense time of political posturing and threat where very little actually happens for the legions. I decided long in advance of writing this that Fronto would need to take a hiatus during that time, as I simply could not write books about the military with Fronto in command where they sat in camps and rolled dice. Plus, we all, I think, know what's coming. When the next giant turd hits the giant fan, Fronto needs to be motivated enough to pick a side. And with his history there has been a little uncertainty at times what side he would pick. I think book 8 has probably settled that issue.

I have over the last two years had a number of mails suggesting long-gone characters that might be able to come back. Some were clearly mad, and others not interesting enough. But I had already decided about three books back to return Andala to the plot when the opportunity arose. I don't like wasted loose ends. Carbo, though, was a suggestion of a friend. And at the end of the book I have finally returned Galronus to the fold. Things are starting to come together and the cast is being assembled for the second phase of the series – Caesar's Civil Wars.

Cavarinos has been one of my favourite characters to write in the entire series, and even though he's only featured in two volumes, he has become a popular one, apparently. It is sad, then, that we are to see him flutter off to eastern climes. Simply, keeping him here would stretch the bounds of probability to breaking point, though he might pop up in the next book for a bit, and who knows what the future may hold.

The laws of Rome and in particular the bearing of arms inside the pomerium of the city is central to the last part of this book. What strikes me as odd is that the pomerium was a sacred boundary supposedly defined when Romulus ploughed a line around the city, and yet the dictator Sulla some two decades earlier had extended the pomerium to a new area. The Romans might have been a practical people, but they were also a religious one. How would the more pious population take the extension of a sacred boundary by a blood-soaked dictator? And so I have had the people of the city in my story a little dubious about the new boundary. And Claudius later extended it as well. In fact, it is said that one of the reasons the senate met at this time in Pompey's theatre complex was that it was outside the pomerium and therefore senators who were forbidden by their position to cross the pomerium could attend. And yet at the time of Caesar, the Sullan extension put Pompey's theatre inside the new line. A complex subject that I have chosen to make rather fluid for the sake of ease.

And while anyone who has visited the Tullianum prison (the carcer) in Rome's forum might think I have been rather fanciful with my depiction of the place, there is some evidence and a lot of discussion over its earlier form. After all, that entire end of the forum has changed completely since those days – even the rocky landscape itself due to the massive quarrying for Trajan's forum.

Things are closing up in Rome. Caesar's enemies are beginning to make their moves.

The general himself is hoping to return soon and take up a consulship during which he will continue to be immune from prosecution. Anyone care to guess what his future holds? Already his gaze must be drifting to that oh so important boundary line at the Rubicon River.

50 BC will be a year of great change, following which Rome's future will be decided in dreadful civil conflict. And everyone's favourite legate will be there to help, of course.

Thank you for reading and see you in Massilia soon.

Simon Turney, August 2015

If you liked this book, why not try other titles by S.J.A. Turney

Interregnum (Tales of the Empire 1)

For twenty years civil war has torn the Empire apart; the Imperial line extinguished as the mad Emperor Quintus burned in his palace, betrayed by his greatest general. Against a background of war, decay, poverty and violence, men who once served in the proud Imperial army now fight as mercenaries, hiring themselves to the greediest lords. On a hopeless battlefield that same general, now a mercenary captain tortured by the events of his past, stumbles across hope in the form of a young man begging for help. Kiva is forced to face more than his dark past as he struggles to put his life and the very Empire back together. The last scion of the Imperial line will change Kiva forever.

The Thief's Tale by S.J.A. Turney

Istanbul, 1481. The once great city of Constantine that now forms the heart of the Ottoman empire is a strange mix of Christian, Turk and Jew. Despite the benevolent reign of the Sultan Bayezid II, the conquest is still a recent memory, and emotions run high among the inhabitants, with danger never far beneath the surface. Skiouros and Lykaion, the sons of a Greek country farmer, are conscripted into the ranks of the famous Janissary guards and taken to Istanbul where they will play a pivotal, if unsung, role in the history of the new regime. As Skiouros escapes into the Greek quarter and vanishes among its streets to survive on his wits alone, Lykaion remains with the slave chain to fulfill his destiny and become an Islamic convert and a guard of the Imperial palace. Brothers they remain, though standing to either side of an unimaginable divide. On a fateful day in late autumn 1490, Skiouros picks the wrong pocket and begins to unravel a plot that reaches to the very highest peaks of Imperial power. He and his brother are about to be left with the most difficult decision faced by a conquered Greek: whether the rule of the Ottoman Sultan is worth saving.

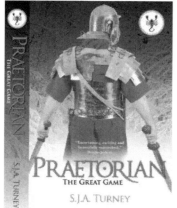

Praetorian: The Great Game

Promoted to the elite Praetorian Guard in the thick of battle, a young legionary is thrust into a seedy world of imperial politics and corruption. Tasked with uncovering a plot against the newly-crowned emperor Commodus, his mission takes him from the cold Danubian border all the way to the heart of Rome, the villa of the emperor's scheming sister, and the great Colosseum.

What seems a straightforward, if terrifying, assignment soon descends into Machiavellian treachery and peril as everything in which young Rufinus trusts and believes is called into question and he faces warring commanders, Sarmatian cannibals, vicious dogs, mercenary killers and even a clandestine Imperial agent. In a race against time to save the Emperor, Rufinus will be introduced, willing or not, to the great game.

"Entertaining, exciting and beautifully researched" - Douglas Jackson

Printed in Great Britain
by Amazon

57034800R00255